DISTILLING
LIES

DISTILLING LIES

A NOVEL

CAROLYN
DENNIS-WILLINGHAM

RIVER GROVE
BOOKS

Published by River Grove Books
Austin, TX
www.rivergrovebooks.com

Distributed by River Grove Books

For ordering information or special discounts for bulk purchases, please contact Greenleaf Book Group at PO Box 91869, Austin, TX 78709, 512.891.6100.

Design and composition by Greenleaf Book Group
Cover design by Greenleaf Book Group and Damon Freeman
Cover image used under licence from Laura Ranftler / Arcangel

Publisher's Cataloging-in-Publication data is available.

Print ISBN: 978-1-63299-667-1

eBook ISBN: 978-1-63299-668-8

First Edition

To the women who roared in the 1920s and to the women who, 100 years later, are doing it again.

And in memory of Buffy, my childhood dog, who taught me about the three-legged variety.

And Cole, my four-legged best friend, who showed me how to persevere against the odds until time reminded him it was okay to rest.

I can't go back to yesterday
because I was a different person then.

—Alice, in Lewis Carroll's *Alice's Adventures in Wonderland*

EMMA JUNE

10 WEEKS AFTER THE CARNIVAL

Daddy stood next to Miss Helen and strained to smile. This day, like so many others recently, wouldn't be easy for him. But it was his idea, not mine.

Choppers barked, then whined. I turned away from the window and distracted him with a quick belly rub so he wouldn't notice me tossing my cloche hat into the suitcase. He knew I was leaving. Perhaps he thought of me as one more missing part.

I would get on that train if, for no other reason, than to pacify Daddy. Eighteen years old and I had never traveled without a parent.

If I was being honest, part of me wanted to see for myself if the hubbub I'd read about in magazine articles was true. The endless dances, the sporting events, the student agitation to stop Prohibition. All those books to devour.

But my heart would remain here in Holly Gap, waiting.

I lay back on my bed and closed my eyes. I needed a moment.

In my daydream, I pictured Mama barging through the front door yelling, "Doll baby!" I would inhale her lavender scent as she squeezed me and said, "Stop apologizing, baby. You have absolutely nothing to be sorry for."

If only.

Nothing stayed the same. Life fluctuated like the flow of the Brazos River depending on the rainfall, or like the direction the steam drifted from Miss Helen's distillery depending on the wind.

Before the spring carnival the worst thing that had happened to my family was the amputation of Choppers's leg five years before. After that, drastic change returned to the easy kind. Like cutting my hair into a fashionable bob and wearing shorter dresses. Or Miss Helen coming up with another name for her moonshine and having to glue new labels on all the Mason jars.

Anticipated changes, like spring turning into summer, were as commonplace as a morning yawn. So when the 1928 March page was forever ripped off our Coca-Cola wall calendar, the rhythm of the upcoming months was supposed to be familiar. I thought I knew what to expect and ignorantly planned accordingly.

I pictured Betty, Mama's best friend, showing me how to bloom wild and carefree like the Texas bluebonnets and Indian blankets. And, like the wildflowers, Betty would provide our Cross Timbers and prairie land with much-needed color. She would continue to add pizzazz to our small town and laugh at the rolling eyes of gossipers.

I remained blind, ignorantly thinking catastrophe could never find my small town, or me, for that matter. I believed Mama would drive us to Mineral Wells to see picture shows, and Charlene and me to church picnics. While among the not-so-holy-rollers, we would place bets on which Methodist would be the first to get ossified on Miss Helen's moonshine. Then we'd up the ante and guess which upstanding churchgoer would be first to holler at Sheriff Gunny Gibbons to "keep up the good work"—which really meant "thanks for ignoring Prohibition."

Summer would turn into a heat that bore into our Texas bones like a drill pumping for oil. Except for keeping an eye out for rattlers, the heat wouldn't stop us. The Brazos River was at the ready for splashing and squealing with my girlfriends long enough to bring our dreams of being citified, and our boy talk, to a brief halt. And on those warm summer evenings, the fireflies would almost provide us enough light for reading. These were my expectations of coming days when a calamity meant the latest Sears and Roebuck catalog was overdue on its delivery.

I counted on the everyday rhythm of these sounds that were so deeply rooted in my marrow they had synced with my heartbeat. Miss Helen's moonshine distillery thumping and hissing next door. Her son, Scooter, calling out to me, "It's gonna *grow*, Emma June," after he buried one of her kitchen utensils or some other whatnot in their yard. Jazz music radiating from our Victor Victrola when Mama played her favorite records. The steady ticking of our grandfather clock. Cricket music soothing me to sleep. And before the first rooster crowed, the hazy rumbling away of Ol' Bess, Daddy's work truck, as he left each morning for the dairy.

But as I wore naïveté like the latest fashion, all normalcy came to a grinding halt. My fear became so loud I could scarcely hear the familiar, comforting sounds of a cricket's chirp or the rustling of oak leaves when the wind blew. Because the snakes didn't wait for summer to coil at our feet. They came on carnival night, flicked their lying tongues, and took Mama with them.

And then I met Frank.

FRANK

TWO WEEKS BEFORE CARNIVAL NIGHT

Frank held on to the little strut he had left and headed for his flop-house. Another long day at the shipyard loading and unloading crates left him bone-weary and stinking of everything from bananas to fish.

But the music would revive him. Always did. Jazz and blues. Who needed anything more at twenty-one years old?

He had just enough time to make it back to his dump, rinse away his stench, and put on his glad rags and finer flat cap. He'd stick his blues harp in his pocket then stroll to the Upper French Quarter to hit a few clubs.

Although the days kept their order—crates, music, booze, and bed—sometimes the in-between differed. Last week the new employee at the shipyard had tried to steal his work order. The scuffle started with yelling and Frank getting punched in the face. It ended with Frank dislocating the sap's shoulder.

The night before, he'd gotten drunk enough to work up the courage to pull out his harmonica at the Dog House and strutted his pride when invited on stage to play with the band. It made for a perfect ending on a day that started like all the others.

Ready for a quick change, he turned down the alley toward his pitiful abode. He spotted Irene standing by his door. Another in-between surprise.

Last year when she visited, dressed to the nines, munitions heavily applied to her face, she had actually swung the pearls around her neck in a cheesy greeting.

This time was different. Her usual perfectly toned skin looked pasty as old newspaper and the bags under her eyes seemed to carry a load of trouble. No cloche hat covered her dark, disheveled hair. And from the looks of the large stain, her plain dress had finished off most of her coffee or Coca-Cola.

"Ma? What are you doing here?"

"Frank. Thank God."

"For what?" He pushed past and opened his door.

"I need your help."

"Landlord kick you out for having too many martini parties?"

"Can I please come in?"

Frank walked in ahead of his mother. If she wanted to sit, she'd have to shove his music books off his one chair. The bed was off-limits. The scraps of paper weren't haphazardly strewn across the mattress like she probably thought. The notes and lyrics to his original songs needed to stay in order.

Irene remained in the doorway, a forlorn look on her face as if she'd been the one left behind. It wasn't true. Soon after his father lammed off, his mother had left Frank with Aunt Patsy and hit the road before his second birthday. But passing him off to her sister turned out to be a good thing. Aunt Patsy wrote the book on good mothering. Irene was clueless.

Ma hadn't completely disappeared. Once or twice a year she'd peel herself away from the glitz of New York City and pop in for visits. The last time was nine months ago when she came to Aunt Patsy's funeral. Unlike Pete Sanders, his deadbeat father, Irene visited on occasion. Maybe he should be grateful for those morsels of attention.

"What do you want?" he asked.

"Like I said. I need your help."

Frank turned his back, changed into a new shirt, and slicked back his hair.

"It's important, Frank. I wouldn't ask if it wasn't." She swayed on her feet. Not from booze this time. Her head seemed clear enough.

He moved the books and pointed to the chair. "To do what?"

"To come with me. We'll catch the train back to the Mineral Wells station. Drive the rest of the way to Holly Gap."

"Where the hell is Holly Gap?"

"A small town in north Texas where I've been living for six months. And don't look so disgusted."

"Are you nuts?" No way he was going to Texas. Ever since Aunt Patsy died, he'd become used to not counting on anyone. And no one counting on him. It freed him up to focus on music.

"Only for a short time. I'm being blackmailed, Frank."

It didn't surprise him. To Irene Sanders, a clean life meant her martini glass was smudge-free. "Your last letter said you were scraping pennies at some diner," Frank said.

"The blackmail is why I'm broke. The man knows me from a long time ago and remembers . . . something about me. I've been paying him to keep a secret so . . . so a good friend won't think less of me." She stared down at her scuffed low-heeled pumps. The Irene he knew was never ashamed of her actions. "Now the money's run out."

He knew better than to lend her dough. He'd done that once, and it set him back six months. "What did you do a long time ago? Rob a bank or something?"

Irene ignored his cheeky comment. "Bernice and I are friends. I don't want to let her down."

Frank felt the heat in his face. *He* was the one she'd left high and dry. "Whatever it is, just tell her," he said, his jaw clenching. "I don't have dough to give you."

"I don't need money. I want you to keep an eye on my blackmailer. Cover my back. In two weeks. Bernice and I are taking her daughter and friend to the Mineral Wells carnival. I'll tell her then."

Frank shook his head. "You want me to be your muscle." At five feet eleven, he was barely a brute. But he did have a fine right hook.

She lit a cigarette with a shaky hand. "I need to tell her, Frank. I need to right a wrong."

One wrong? Irene Sanders clearly couldn't count.

She looked down, then rubbed a shoulder with her free hand. "Bernice doesn't know I'm Irene Sanders. In Holly Gap, I go by Betty Bedford. It's . . . complicated."

It sounded to Frank like his mother had to cover her tracks. Not hard to believe, since *complicated* seemed to be her middle name. "And what exactly is in this for me?"

"For you? If all goes according to plan, Frank, your life will change for the better, like it's meant to be."

Now she was talking. To Irene Sanders, or whatever she called herself, *better* meant money. With enough dough Frank could open his own club in New Orleans, dress in fine suits, move out of the dump he lived in.

Leaving with his mother, the woman he barely knew, was a crap-shoot. But then everything in life was a gamble.

Like Aunt Patsy used to tell him, the biggest risk was not to take one.

Next stop, Hicksville, Texas.

....

CHAPTER 1

EMMA JUNE

Spring carnival night started with sweet anticipation.

I planned on starring in my own picture show. Opening scene: Wade sitting next to me on a well-chosen bench, the carnival lights catching the shine of silk on my legs as I slide my dress up to a knee.

Mama's best friend had told me time and again that nobody would follow along to our parade if we didn't strut with pomp and circumstance. Except Betty didn't just strut her parade. She shimmied. When she swanked her style down Main Street, puffing a cigarette from its holder and taking snorts from her fancy flask, I could almost hear a jazz band strike up and march behind her. It's one of the reasons I liked her. And another reason Daddy didn't.

I slipped on my galoshes but kept the buckles stylishly unfastened.

"And if you don't win, it means those judges are a bunch of lily-livered saps." Daddy's voice traveled from the kitchen to my bedroom.

"Oh, Theo, now you're just thinking one-sided," Mama said.

"Problem is, I can't decide which side I like better," Daddy chuckled.

Our house was sturdier than most in Holly Gap, but the thin walls meant secret-telling was outdoor business. When Charlene came over, we spent a lot of time sitting under the post oaks at the twenty-five-yard line between my house and the Munsons'.

"You watch out for our girl," Daddy continued. "No telling what kind of riffraff will be there."

"Okay, gloomy Gus. I'll make sure everything is peachy."

"You know what I mean, Bernice."

More finger waves would have looked better, but there was no time to gel and set my hair again. I shook the bottle of nail tint but, for the same reason, changed my mind about a third coat.

I slid the stockings up to my thighs, rolled down the tops, and gave thanks to the Sears and Roebuck Gods for the timely delivery.

A quick knock and Mama entered my bedroom holding a rose-colored dropped-waist dress and matching headband. "I don't know what you planned on wearing, Emma June. But you can have this. I'm too fat to wear it anyway."

Mama was beautiful and miles from being fat. Her burgundy hair, smooth skin, and high cheekbones made her look barely over thirty instead of thirty-eight. From a distance, Mama and Betty looked like they could have been sisters. Although Betty had brown hair, they both had stunning big eyes and hourglass figures.

"And, doll baby," she whispered. "Wear pink lipstick, not red. Your father's too young to have a heart attack." She tossed me a wink and closed the door behind her.

Daddy thought all young women who wore bright red lipstick would end up in the back seat of a roofed motorcar followed by a polliwog growing in their bellies.

While the world rotated toward change, Daddy wouldn't budge. He thought the loosening of morals would be the downfall of humanity and worried the invention of new machines would take jobs away from workers. The telephone, he said, was the lazy man's way of checking on neighbors—which was why we didn't have one.

Yet he had no problem walking the fifty yards to use the Munsons' candlestick telly.

I pushed the side lever upward on the tube and pressed color to my lips. Overshooting the critical bow shape, I wiped the corner of my mouth and started over.

Betty applied her cosmetics with perfection. Coal smudged eyelids, lipstick never missing its mark. And her clothes. The fit of her flapper dresses could knock the sour out of a lemon.

The main reason I liked Betty had to do with the light that turned on inside Mama. The moment Mama met Betty, she tugged off her corset skin, breathed easier, and had more fun. Daddy had smiled at her new zeal for life until he learned her enthusiasm came from a "questionable source."

Choppers whined, his pitiful Labrador eyes melding into his German shepherd face.

"I know," I told him. "It's only a carnival. But if I want something good to happen, I have to dress the part." Another quote from Betty's book of wisdom.

I slipped Mama's chiffon dress over my chemise. The shoulders drooped because dressmakers thought all girls had bubs bigger than teacups. Not that it mattered. Dresses were supposed to make us look pancake-chested.

My rhinestone dangles, the final touch. I twisted the back of the earrings, screwing them tightly in place.

"She's not going to be there, is she?" Daddy's voice.

"Honey, I do wish you would stop this old-fashioned nonsense."

"It isn't nonsense, Bernice. That woman moved here and brought those big city morals along with her. You've changed, you know, in the six months you've known her."

"I drank before, Theo. Hard not to when you live next door to a lady-legger."

"Never will understand Helen making moonshine under the same roof she raises young Scooter. And Leonard goes along with it."

As if Leonard had a choice. The string Miss Helen tied around her husband had little to no stretch.

"Theo, we're emancipated women now. We can vote, smoke, dance, even drink if we want to."

"Betty gave you a flask, for Christ's sake. What kind of person gives a flask to a respectable wife with a young daughter?"

A fun one, I thought.

"Theo, I gave that away, for pity's sake."

The Mama and Daddy Bickering About Betty Hour played louder than Will Rogers on the radio. Louder than Jelly Roll Morton's jazz on the Victrola. Daddy seemed to think the only reason Betty came to town six months before was to initiate Mama into the "immoral" flapper scene of New York City.

Betty said she moved from the excitement of speakeasies and skyscrapers to ho-hum Holly Gap in order to recoup her losses. It didn't work out as planned. The cousins she had intended to stay with had moved the year before.

"Ready, Emma June?" Mama called. "And grab the pecan pie from the kitchen, will you, doll baby? Hold it by the brass carrier handles."

"I got it, I got it," Daddy mumbled, his broad shoulders nearly bumping the top of my head as I darted past him.

Mama, already in the revved-up roofless breezer, *tap, tap, tapped* the steering wheel with an impatient index finger.

Daddy opened the passenger door and handed me the pie. "Madam," he said, with an up swipe of his palm.

"Thanks, Pop."

"Pop?" He frowned. "What happened to Daddy?"

I patted his hand. "He's here somewhere. If you see him, don't tell him I have red lipstick in my purse. He'd have a conniption." I batted my eyelashes and blew him a kiss. "Okay, Mama. Let's blouse."

As Mama drove toward the end of our long weed-trodden drive-way, I looked back. Choppers was running to the side of the house like a dog with four legs instead of three. And Daddy, tall and fit, stood on the front porch with his thumbs tucked in his breeches and a scowl on his shadowed face. His early work hours at the dairy meant he couldn't come along. Without his watchful eye, I'd have more freedom at the carnival. I threw a wave out the roofless motor-car and said another prayer of thanks to Klinger's Dairy.

"Scooter's waving to us, Emma June," Mama said.

Across the scraggly grasses, soon to become sticker burs with the hotter weather, Scooter hopped up and down on his front porch, his arms flapping in our direction. "We'll be back, Scooter," I yelled, on the off chance he could hear me over the distance and the breezer's rumble.

Three years younger than me, Scooter Munson was the clos-est thing I had to a brother. Folks in town called him dim-witted, maybe because when he spoke, he accented random words. But folks in town didn't know a piss from a pot. Scooter was kind, funny, and generous to a fault.

"Still feel bad about not bringing him?" Mama said.

I answered with a shrug, yet still felt guilty. I knew how Scooter's eyes would have lit up seeing all the rides, all the people, all the food. I also knew that if he came, I'd have to spend every second coaxing him along. Scooter could use up an hour just watching an earthworm wiggle. The night belonged to Wade and me. And, well, to me and Charlene. I'd make it up to Scooter later.

"Mama, you feel bad about Daddy not coming?"

"It's good for him to have some peace and quiet. But he—"

"Is too old-fashioned. It's 1928, for crying out loud."

"I was going to say your daddy could worry warts off a frog. But he's a good man and a fine husband."

"I didn't say he wasn't. It's just that . . ." I waited for Mama to count down from three.

"Well, go on. It's just that what?" she said, giving in to the silence.

"You can't even bring your best friend to the house. He doesn't like Betty and hasn't even met her."

Mama slammed on the brakes and threw my wits in the back seat. "Poor fella."

She pointed to the armadillo moseying to the side of the road. "Watch out, mister," Mama said, lowering her voice. "No telling what kind of riffraff is in those woods."

I chuckled at her imitation of Daddy.

Before Betty came into our lives, Daddy laughed more. A few weeks before, when Daddy drove us past old Mr. Porter's farm, Mama lifted herself off the seat, put a hand to the side of her face, and yelled to his cow, "Make them ask before they touch your udders." Mr. Porter, the same man who cursed motorcars when he rode his mule into town, happened to be watching. Daddy grimaced and muttered something about bad influences.

"Now," Mama said, finally picking up speed. "Don't blame Daddy. I think Betty's afraid to meet him."

"Pshaw." Betty wasn't afraid of anything. Not skinny dipping in the Brazos. Not calling out the old bench sitter, Mr. Finch, for pinching her behind on Main Street as she walked past him.

"It's true. I made the mistake of telling her your daddy was stuck in his ways. She laughed and said, 'I best stay clear of him then. He wouldn't like me.'"

"She can't help being widowed young and needing income. And she's not a taxi dancer anymore. Even if she was, you told me it was honest work." Roseland's, New York City's largest dance hall, paid good money for women to dance with lonely men, many of them immigrants. The women were not allowed to drink or do anything with the men other than dance.

"It was respectable work," she said. "But small towns spread gossip."

I wanted to scream. Betty had witnessed firsthand the real world of speakeasies, flapper lingo, fashion, and music. If it weren't for her, the only taste I'd have of the outside world would come from *Vogue* or *Photo Play*. And if it weren't for Miss Helen taking her regular trips into Mineral Wells, I wouldn't have those either.

Mama reached over and squeezed my hand. "Holly Gap's not such a bad place."

"Yeah, if you don't mind settling for church picnics as your main form of entertainment."

"We have dances at the Methodist church." Mama glanced at my lap. "And don't let the glass lid slip off the pie. I worked too hard on that pinched crust."

"You call waltzing a dance? You barely touch, for Christ's sake."

"Oh, doll baby." Mama tsk-tsked and laughed. "Do we need to have another chat about the birds and the bees?"

"I know about pollination, Mama."

"Yeah, well, keep your pollen to yourself. You're not an adult yet."

Maybe not. But I was getting close. I could almost taste the sweetness of eighteen, could almost touch the endless possibilities of what I might do. Anything would be more exciting than skimming rocks on the Brazos River or having to hear Miss Helen rant on about the art of moonshine-making.

Mama lifted a hand from the steering wheel and reapplied her lipstick. "Speaking of Betty." She smacked her lips together. "After we pick up Charlene at Johnson's Variety, we need to swing by The Diner. We're giving Betty a ride to the carnival."

....

CHAPTER 2

FRANK

Frank hadn't seen his mother since she unloaded him in the dump of a house. Apparently, she'd rented the place just before showing up at his doorstep in New Orleans. His mother, quite the glamorous planner.

Unless you counted flat land with weeds, brush, and mesquite trees as company, the desolation made a nuthouse seem like a step up. On the other hand, maybe he could take advantage of this inconvenience and write a few songs. That is, if he could find any inspiration from the nothingness.

Sitting far off from the road, the peeling blue paint and warped boards of the clapboard house weren't noticeable. Close up, the place looked like you could push it over with a stick of chewing gum. The inside was worse. The sitting room, bedroom, and kitchen combined were maybe a hair bigger than his place in New Orleans.

After he had rid the place of cobwebs and dust, and the front porch of wasp nests, he took advantage of Irene being gone. He slept on the old mattress on the bedroom floor. When she returned, he'd have to get used to sleeping on a dusty pallet in the sitting room.

Not unusual for her to pop in, then take off. He'd become

used to that. But he wasn't used to living in a crappy town. No music. Anywhere. The nearest form of entertainment consisted of a shoddy hash house where the flies and cockroaches strutted across plates like elected officials. The Diner, on the outskirts of town, was the only place she thought safe for him to go until he heard from her again.

Her list of conditions was firm and final:

> *Do not tell anyone we're related. If anyone finds out, we'll both be in danger.*
>
> *Do not let anyone know you live here or that I rented this place for you.*
>
> *The blackmailer, Earl Foley, lives nearby. Find a way to keep track of him and his son, Wade.*
>
> *Remember, in Holly Gap, I go by Betty Bedford. You don't know her either.*
>
> *No one is allowed in this house except you and me.*

What had he gotten himself into?

He wouldn't have to endure the place much longer. Tonight was carnival night and Irene would spill whatever beans she carried in her pot of secrets. Then, somehow, his life would improve.

Frank hadn't met Earl Foley, but if he was anything like his son, Wade, they had both attended the same club for dimwits.

He had run across the eighteen-year-old dunce at the Dogcrap Diner a few nights before. Irene had given a decent description of both Foleys and Frank spotted Wade right away: reddish hair that appeared darker with its layer of grease, small scar over an eyebrow, about Frank's height. A country bumpkin.

The wannabe tough boy had sat at a table with a man a handful of years older. Wade called him Moody, and the name fit. Black hair and muscled, his mouth held a permanent scowl on a face pocked with acne scars.

Frank had sat at the counter drinking joe, his ears perked to their conversation.

"What're we supposed to do again?" Bumpkin asked.

"Whatever he tells us is what."

Frank assumed "he" meant Earl, Wade's father, the bleeder of Irene's funds.

"Well, there ain't nothing tonight," Wade continued. "Let's stroll into town. Peek in some windows or somethin'. Bring along some shine."

Frank had seized the moment. He swiveled his body around the stool and faced them. "I hear you say shine? Didn't mean to eavesdrop, but I'm new here and could sure use a belt or two."

Moody ignored him.

"Where you come from?" Bumpkin asked.

"New Orleans. Home of the blues. Feeling that way now, not knowing anyone."

"Then why'd you come here, dumbnuts?"

Frank ignored the insult. "Let's just say the city and I didn't get along. I got escorted out."

"That yeller eye have something to do with it?"

Frank had forgotten about the punch to his face three weeks ago. His eye, once black, had faded to yellow. It came in handy now.

Frank shrugged his indifference. "Bygones."

Wade, looking down like a boy asking his daddy's permission, asked Moody if he could step outside and share some hooch with Frank.

"Stay close," Moody said.

Frank offered Wade a smoke and, in return, got a few swigs of god-awful coffin varnish.

Frank tried not to grimace through the swallow. "Any way to make a buck around here?"

"Ain't much. Mostly odd jobs here and there."

"What about for fun?"

"Ain't much to choose from when it comes to broads. I've tried most of 'em. But the Mineral Wells carnival's coming up. Lots to pick from there, I reckon."

Frank ignored the boneheaded comment and thought about the carnival. Irene had made it plain it was off limits. "So, you're going?" he asked.

"Damn straight. Come hell or high water."

"Wade?" Moody stood by the door. "Time to get."

Wade had hopped up like a doughboy answering to his colonel.

Now, as Frank sat on the sorry excuse of a front porch, he thought about this evening. While Wade scouted the carnival for some poor gal to slobber, Irene would reveal some secret to her best friend. Tomorrow, if his mother was right about things looking up, a new cornet might relieve that itch in his palm.

He stared at the night sky. Stars. No city lights to absorb them. The first checkmark in the positive column for living in the middle of nowhere. He pulled out his blues harp and played for the twinkling crowd.

....

CHAPTER 3

EMMA JUNE

Mama and I drove toward Main Street. With Betty along, I'd get free pointers on how to finesse my way into a romantic evening with Wade.

"Don't worry, baby doll. I didn't lie to your daddy. I just left out a little sugar in the husband-wife recipe. And Emma June, I'm not going to tell you what to say or what not to. But if your father finds out about us driving Betty—"

"Tell him? And watch Daddy flex his righteous jaw muscles? I'd rather listen to the needle skip on the Victrola."

Mama giggled and backhanded my shoulder. Matter settled.

I also didn't want to add to Daddy's aggravation. Since Betty's arrival, he'd taken to tossing motorcar and gardening tools a little harder and further than necessary. His agitation was uncharacteristic of the father I'd grown up with. It troubled me. But I also knew he was no Mr. Kennedy, the previous owner of the hardware store, who walked out on his family and never returned. Mama, Daddy, and I were like Choppers's legs—a sturdy threesome.

Mama turned onto Main Street. Motorcars were rapidly replacing horses, the real world finally creeping into Holly Gap. The best thing about the town center was Rosie's Café, where I earned enough dough to feed a few habits.

The rest of town offered old-fashioned country businesses. Jasper & Brothers Feed Store, Mercer's Bank, Grace's Lace dress shop, Dixie's Drug Store, Hank's Food Market. Most smelled of old musty wood.

Johnson's Variety sat smack dab in the center of Main Street. Owned by Charlene's father, Mr. Johnson had plenty of money. But unless his precious daughter demanded a new dress, Charlene's father stretched his dollars tighter than a clothesline.

Charlene barreled out of the store with only a few inches of blonde bob showing beneath her pink beret. So different without her long, bouncy curls from the month before.

"Finally," Charlene said, sweeping the back of her hand across her forehead like the dramatic Clara Bow in her silent pictures. "I'm free of the drudgery."

I waited for her to get settled in the back seat and told her the good news.

"Betty's coming? Berries!" she said, using her favorite expression. She adjusted her pink beret, then leaned forward. "I need to tell you something about Wade."

I was about to tell her to clam up when her mother called out and scampered toward us.

"Hold up a minute, Mrs. Crawford."

"Rats." Charlene sighed. "Here comes pry baby."

Mama peered over my head. "Yes, Edith?"

Mrs. Johnson didn't acknowledge me. Ever since the dowdy woman learned of Mama's friendship with Betty, she barely tolerated my friendship with her daughter.

She poked her uppity nose in the air. "Bernice, what time can we expect Charlene home? Before ten, I hope."

Only the old folks went home by ten.

Mama pointed to the pie on my lap. "Depends on what time they judge the pie contest. You know how slow those judges can be. Half of them push wheelbarrows with rope handles."

"Well, the sooner, the better. We have church in the morning. Don't want to keep the good Lord waiting for Charlene to peel her eyes open."

Charlene's folks, card-carrying Holy Baptists, couldn't seem to unhitch their Victorian shackles. Like Daddy, only worse.

Most of Holly Gap's citizens had a real fondness for Mama, and for good reason. Mama went with the grain of their varied personalities and left the townsfolk feeling a little better about themselves. Charlene's mother was the exception. Both Edith Johnson and Mama had a hard time hiding their dislike for one another.

"I'll do the best I can, Edith. If I could control those judges, I'd win for sure." Mama threw her head back and let out a fake laugh.

Mrs. Johnson remained somber-faced and glanced at the empty spot next to Charlene. "And it's just the three of you, right? No one else tagging along?"

While the men in town thought Betty was the cat's meow, the women wanted to give her a one-way train ticket and a kick in the behind.

"Scooter's staying home," I said before Mama had to either lie or tell the truth. "We worried that if he came—"

"Don't worry, Edith. I'll take good care of Charlene," Mama said, like giving an imaginary pat to Mrs. Johnson's hand.

As Mama drove away, intentional or not, the breezer blasted a circular puff of smoke in Mrs. Johnson's face.

"Ugh," Charlene said. "When we get to Mineral Wells, remind me to buy her a big jug of Crazy Water."

Crazy Water. Legend had it that in 1881 a demented old woman sat by the town's well every day drinking that awful tasting stuff. When her mind returned, the Mineral Wells community became believers in its benefit and marketed the water. The city became more than a dust spot in the road. And whenever they opened the fourteen-story Baker Hotel, it would become a big red dot on the Texas map.

"Now, Charlene. Your mother loves you, and don't forget that," Mama said.

"Tell it to Sweeney," Charlene mumbled.

Barely two miles east, dust sprouted wings and swirled through the motorcar. Cactus, Texas thistle, and mesquite trees replaced the cattle ranches and farmland that thrived on our side of town.

The Diner divided Shanty Town, the side where the penniless white folk lived, from its neighbors where, penniless or not, all the darker-skinned folk lived, including my boss, Miss Atta. Neither side had room to turn sideways in their lean-to homes but had ample amount for hard times to blow through their front door. This commonality didn't stop the two communities from being separated just because of differing skin colors.

Mama had told me life was less discriminatory in New York City. She said that the same fair-minded thinking would make its way to Holly Gap like fashion trends. Ha, some reassurance. We still had to order our shorter dresses from the Sears and Roebuck catalog.

We pulled up to The Diner. Betty stood outside holding her long cigarette holder with enough sophistication to put Coco Chanel to shame. But instead of chandeliers and martini glasses as her back-drop, buckled and peeling gray wood siding stood behind her. It was a lousy place to make a living, and I counted my blessings that I worked at Rosie's. Unlike Betty's boss, Miss Atta didn't forgo repairs and drink up the profits.

Betty waggled her hips, accentuating the big hip bow on her flap-per dress. "Darlings!"

I hopped out of the motorcar. Betty grabbed my shoulders before I could climb in the back with Charlene. "Well now, don't you look swanky?" The faint smell of gin wafted from her lips. "Those boys will see you coming a mile away."

"Don't encourage her, Betty," Mama hollered. "I need to get her home in the same condition I brought her."

She meant untainted.

Betty drifted her fingers across my cheek. "She's a good girl, Bernice. Aren't you, Emma June?"

Betty usually looked as if she'd walked off the cover of *Vogue*. Not then. She had bags beneath her eyes and a redness within them. Instead of her customary spirit of gaiety, her vim and vigor had evaporated.

"Betty, everything Jake?" I whispered.

Betty pivoted in her heeled Mary Janes and hopped in the front seat. She pulled the fancy scrolled flask from her garter, a gift she'd received from some friend with the initials I. S. engraved at the bottom. "Let's show those carnival saps a thing or two about how to party." She downed a healthy gulp, then ran her fingers over the flask's surface as if attempting to etch the scrolling of vines anew.

"Wish I could have some of that," Charlene said as I settled next to her.

Mama wagged a finger. "Not on my watch. Your mother would never—"

"I know, I know. Never let you take me anywhere ever again," Charlene huffed.

"So, Zelda Fitzgerald," Mama said to Betty. "Give us the skinny. How was your getaway with the ex-beau?"

Betty had recently returned from a ten-day road trip to see if anything worth keeping remained of their relationship. Although we had never met him, I pictured him looking like Rudolph Valentino.

"Oh, that. Let's just say I got away from the getaway as fast as possible." Betty held up a lipstick tube and turned sideways. "Blood red, anyone?" Her eyebrows moved up and down with enough piz-zazz to entice a town of do-gooders to rouge their knees.

Mama shook her head and focused on driving. She had yet to take a good look at her best friend.

"I'll take some." I grabbed the tube.

"Not too much, doll baby," Mama said. "Or I'll have to hold your hand at the carnival."

Betty shrunk in her seat. "I'd give anything to be their age again."

I nudged Charlene, pointed to my eyes, and then to Betty.

"Hey, Betty," Charlene said. "That bandeau you're wearing? Is it new?"

Betty straightened and turned to Charlene. "Like it?"

"You *have* been crying," Charlene blurted. "Are you unzipped things didn't work out with your old beau?"

Subtle Charlene.

"Betty?" Mama said. "Something wrong?"

"I'll tell you what's wrong. I'm in a motorcar with three killjoys." She rose from her seat and shouted, "Time to paint the town ruby red!"

But she slunk down into the seat, the corners of her mouth turning downward again.

Mama changed the subject and told us the gossip she'd heard about Sheriff Gunny Gibbons. Gunny, a funny name for a sheriff who rarely carried a weapon. Last time he toted his pistol, he was on a stakeout for the coyote preying on Mr. Peterson's chickens.

"Gunny was mad, all right," Mama continued. "Fired his new deputy for making the mistake of invading bingo night at the Methodist church."

"Why would Gunny hire a deputy anyway?" Charlene said. "Everyone knows he prefers to work alone."

"True," Mama said. "He probably fired him for just that reason." Mama sighed. "I feel kinda sorry for that young deputy. How was he supposed to know that gambling and bingo go hand in hand at Holly Gap Methodist?"

Betty turned sideways and stared at the passing countryside. "Lots of things we're supposed to know but don't."

Charlene scooted closer. "Emma June, you still plan on seeing Wade at the carnival?" she whispered a bit too loud.

"Shush. Keep your voice down." Meeting up with Wade was one secret I couldn't share with Mama. Although Daddy never said he hated the Foleys, he made it clear by adamantly telling me and Mama to stay away from them.

"Well, are you?"

Charlene wouldn't let it go. Two bad things about sitting in the back seat of the breezer were swatting bugs from your face, and having to endure Charlene's nagging. "What if I am?"

"Loretta came to the store today. She had bruises on her arms."

"What does that have to do with Wade?"

"She says he gets mean sometimes. That's what I'm saying. Her brother's starting to act like their vile father."

The only bad thing about Wade was how he made me swoon. I counted down the minutes to arrival.

"Betty?" I said, ignoring Charlene. "When the Baker Hotel opens for business, let's be their first customers."

The upcoming Baker Hotel and all its extravagance were all she had talked about for months. But Betty said nothing, only gave an almost imperceivable nod, then took another snort from her flask.

"Which will you do first, doll baby?" Mama asked. "Swim in the mineral-water pool or get your hair done at the beauty shop?"

I didn't answer. I was too busy wondering if Betty's current slump was a sign that for the first time, she'd rather be anywhere than with us.

CHAPTER 4

EMMA JUNE

Traffic in Holly Gap meant having to maneuver around old Mr. Canter's truck when he parked in the middle of the street to load his feed. Not in Mineral Wells. With a population of over six thousand, every motorcar invented seemed to be in our way. So many Model Ts backfiring, it sounded as if the Great War had resumed. Mama navigated her way through town with a constant pitch and yaw of the breezer. I thought I'd throw up.

Past the crowded train station, Mama made it to a parking area the size of our entire town. She screeched to a halt with a "thank God."

We joined the throngs of people filing toward the entry gates. Mama, an arm looped through Betty's, held on to her pecan pie with both hands and strutted tall and proud.

Bodies of all shapes and sizes swarmed in a hive of electrifying joy. The closer we got to the ticket booth, the louder the chatter and laughter. Carnival lights, spotlighting a rotating carousel, had turned the blackness of night into the light of day.

Mama stood in the ticket line and held up a "wait" finger.

Charlene leaned up against a post and pointed. "Look at Betty. Swaying like a clock pendulum. Miss Bernice looks none too happy."

Charlene might have been wrong about Wade, but she was right about Mama. She threw words in Betty's face like the day she confronted the mayor after Miss Atta had been turned away at the voting poll because her skin wasn't the color of Gold Medal flour.

By the time we reached Mama, she was picking up shattered pieces of her pie plate.

"Oh, Mama. Your pie!"

"It was an accident, right, Bernice?" Betty said, her arms criss-crossed her chest, hands clutched to her shoulders as if expecting a blessing.

"Here, Emma June." Mama handed me the tickets, then pointed through the entry gate. "See those flying chair swings? Meet me there in an hour for a check-in."

"Mama, we'll be swell. An hour is too—"

"One hour."

Mama's don't-cross-my-line voice meant no room for persuasion.

Charlene tugged me away, but I turned back. While Betty waffled between scanning the crowd and staring down at her shoes, Mama chucked glass into a nearby trash can.

"Come on, Emmy, they'll work it out. Let's breeze and have fun."

Right. They'd work it out. After all, Mama and Betty were best friends. And nothing was going to stop me from a romantic rendez-vous with Wade.

We navigated our way through the crowd inhaling the passing scents of popcorn, cotton candy, and women's perfume.

I turned to a man's voice. "Pinwheels. Colorful, twirling pin-wheels. Only five cents." The straps around the vendor's shoulders were attached to a box with holes. A pinwheel stuck out of each one. I thought about the sparkle in Scooter's eyes and placed a nickel in the man's dirty palm.

"For Scooter?" Charlene said.

"He'll have something else to bury besides forks and Tinker Toys."

"He ever dig up those marbles?"

"Nope. Still waiting for them to sprout."

The pinwheel's stick fit inside my purse, but its curls of blue paper twirled free, propelling me forward to my destination.

We passed the Helter Skelter slide, bumper cars, a long row of games of chance, all promises of fun. Charlene followed, unaware as to where I was heading.

A mob of people circled the wooden boxing platform, eager to see a local win five clams for beating the carnival champ. Chants of "lay him out flat!" and "get away from the ropes!" grew louder.

We weaved between the masses until we found space to breathe. "Butt me, will you, Charlene?"

She pulled a Marlboro from her pack and handed it to me.

I lit up and blew the smoke upward toward the sign. *Get Your Healing Water Here.* "Wade is here somewhere."

"Are you off your trolley?" she said, grabbing my arm. "After what I told you, you still want to meet up with him? You've never even had a real conversation with him."

"So? That's what tonight is for."

Over the years, I had kept Wade in my peripheral vision. His sister, Loretta, shy and thinner than a lamppost, was the same age as Charlene and me. Wade was a year older. When I still attended school, I'd see him stop by the schoolyard to give Loretta messages from home.

Sometimes, I spotted him at the river skimming rocks with his pals and, more recently, the Friday before at Rosie's. After I had taken his order, he asked if I wanted to meet him at the carnival. "Why not?" I told him, yearning to sweep a stray strand of his red hair away from his eyes.

"Coming or not?" I said to Charlene, not really caring one way or the other. I edged closer to the sign.

MADAM ZOLA'S EXPERT FORTUNE TELLER

PAST, PRESENT, FUTURE

CRYSTAL BALL GAZING, PALM READING

TAROT CARDS

"Hey, sexy Sheba."

I turned toward the deep voice and kept myself from squealing.

"I'm telling you," Charlene whispered, "even if he wasn't a mesquite chopper's son, he's still a wrong number."

"I'm dialing anyway." I stepped closer. "Hi, Wade."

"Time for some hooch. Found a spot behind that voodoo trap," he said, referring to the fortune teller's tent.

I pulled Charlene along before she refused and followed Wade and Louis, his beanpole best friend, past the line of hand-twisting people waiting to hear about their future. We crept through a narrow path until we entered a small area littered with boxes, barrels, and discarded wood scraps. The next tent over, a man screamed, "Knock down the milk bottles for a mere dime." Games of chance and grifters everywhere.

I felt overdressed. Wade wore a faded blue collared shirt. His trousers had oil stains that dotted down to his scuffed work boots.

Wade pulled down a box crate from its stack and took a seat, then patted the small space next to him. My heart clenched tighter than Charlene's fist. I'd never been so close to him.

Louis copied Wade and grabbed another empty crate. "I'll have my own, thank you very much," Charlene said, turning up her button nose.

Wade reached behind an empty pickle barrel and produced a brown hooch jug. "Just where I left it." He smoothed back his hair, revealing the small scar over his right eyebrow, then lifted the jug to his lips. His Adam's apple bobbed through each swallow. After wiping his mouth with a sleeve, he thrust the jug on my lap.

The booze burned down my throat and roiled in my stomach. Possum piss. Nothing like Miss Helen's five-star moonshine. I tried not to grimace and passed it to Charlene.

"Gals, y'all seen the fat lady tent yet?" Wade laughed. "Wish her rolls'a dough was real cash. Right, Louis?"

"Reckon," he mumbled, scraping the heel of his boot back and forth in the dirt.

"Good Lord," Charlene said. "This shit is terrible."

Wade belted out another laugh. "Only the first few sips. Then you don't notice and don't care."

The jug passed around again. Charlene refused.

Louis took a small sip and squeezed his eyes shut. "Thought yer daddy's new guy could get better."

"Shut up, Louis," Wade said, eyeing his surroundings.

I steeled myself and gulped more.

Louis spat off to the side, then turned back. "Flea circus. Them fleas can pull a tiny carousel two thousand times their weight," he said, in what was probably the longest and smartest sentence he'd ever strung together.

Charlene scratched one arm, then the other.

Wade slapped a thigh and chuckled. "Shoulda seen them Rock of Ages bims in the walzin' tent. No husband to dance with so they had to hoof it together."

As far as I was concerned, dancing didn't have an age limit. Betty told me dancing took away your worries. "Pivot your knees, Emma June," her ruby-red lips had smacked out between cigarette puffs. "And for Pete's sake, move your arms and kick your legs higher!"

Wade put a hand on my knee. "And damn if we didn't see that monkey pee on the organ grinder."

Charlene rolled her eyes. "Emma June, let's go ride the Tilt-a-Whirl."

Already lightheaded, the thought of twirling made me nauseous.

"You go with her, Louis," Wade said. "I'll watch over this bear cat next to me."

Louis hoisted himself off the crate with the speed of a sloth. Charlene rose from her wooden throne and gave me a "you're gonna pay for this" look.

Just the two of us, alone in probably the least romantic place on earth, Wade draped his arm around my shoulder. It felt awkward, stiff, almost creepy. Not at all what I thought his first touch would feel like.

He held the jug to my lips and poured. Then, in one quick movement, his hand plunged down my dress. He clamped down on my breast as if squeezing the bulb of a motorcar horn, then, before I could knock the smugness off his face, he leaned in.

....

CHAPTER 5

EMMA JUNE

leaned away from the grimy feel of his hands. "I need food. I'm going for popcorn."

Wade shrugged. "Suit yourself, Emma Jane."

Emma Jane. He didn't even know my name. Didn't offer to escort me. He merely threw me a mischievous grin and said, "Just come back so we can finish what we started."

Finish what we started? Starting meant honeyed words followed by sweet nothings whispered in my ear. Clearly, I was not in a romantic picture show. Instead of a rendezvous with Rudy Valentino, I got the Laurel and Hardy combo.

I had always prided myself on judging character. Whether a person showed more kindness than rudeness, more honesty than deception. How had I missed the mark so completely?

Before Mama met Daddy, she told me she dated a boy who seemed nice at first. But after a month, he showed his true character. He embarrassed her in front of a group of friends by saying she couldn't tell a fry pan from a piss pot. Mama told me, "If that ever happens to you, Emma June, fluff your hair, buff your nails, and sashay far in the other direction."

Although difficult to fluff a bob, I got the meaning. I pushed my way through the crowd of boxing spectators and ended up near a baritone voice yelling, "Snake oil, the cure-all! Only fifty cents a bottle!"

Rotgut snaked back up my throat. I would have given up a whole dollar if the slimy oil cured nausea. Two if it cured stupidity.

I stumbled past the vendors pleading for customers. Past the caged gorilla whose eyes seemed to beg me to free him. A juggler pedaled a one-wheeled bike, weaving between children screaming with excitement. Music blared from every direction. People melded into each other in a fuzzy swirl of motion. Through the untrusting blur in my eyes, a woman who looked like Betty ran through the crowd. I focused ahead, trying to find a quiet hole to bury myself in. Anywhere away from the masses and blaring lights.

My face hit the ground with a thump. My right palm stung through a layer of wet grime.

"Are you okay?" A male voice.

My nose at ground level, all I saw were the two-toned oxfords.

"Can I help you up?"

"What? I . . ."

"I saw you take a tumble. Easy to do with so many people milling around."

Strong hands guided me to my feet.

He was older than me. Maybe a tad older than Wade. Even in my drunken haze, I could make out his strong jawline, blue eyes, and what looked to be light brown hair beneath his tweed Ivy cap.

"I must look . . ." In complete shambles. Not him, though. He was a real knee-buckler. His unbuttoned blue-gray suit jacket revealed a pressed white shirt tucked into tan trousers.

"Oh, and I found this." He reached in his back pocket and pulled out my pinwheel. "I believe you dropped it."

I nodded, praying the violent movement wouldn't make me vomit.

"You look a bit . . . My uncle's here somewhere. He's a doctor. I can find him for you and—"

"No. No. Thanks. I'm . . . swell." I heard the slur in my words.

"Let me find you some water. Wait here."

As if I had a choice.

Oxford Two-Tone didn't live in Holly Gap. If he had, I never would have mooned over the likes of Wade Foley.

Legs of rubber, my head a constant spin, I tried to hold it back but couldn't. The contents of my stomach unloaded. No more fragrant scents of popcorn and candy. Only horse manure and my own vomit.

I moved away from my mess, sat on a piece of strewn plywood, and tried to ignore the splinters poking my butt. I had made a complete fool of myself.

I never asked his name. Never checked in with Mama. I couldn't stand, and my gut wasn't done with me. I remained there, alone with my stupidity.

"Emma June, thank God!"

I squinted and looked up, relieved to hear the familiar voice. "Charlene?"

"Wade told me you came this direction. It's bad, Emmy. Really bad."

"You too?" I said, clenching my stomach.

"What? No. I mean things between Betty and your mother. I saw Betty sobbing. And your mother is heated up like a firecracker. Emma June? Did you hear what I said?"

....

Our grandfather clock chimed ten. Ten. I never slept that late.

Choppers's face-licking turned my head toward the window. A

fierce sunray hit between my eyes like a dagger to my brain. Sweat had soaked through my cami bloomers and onto my bedsheet.

I didn't remember coming home. The last thing I remembered was Charlene screaming at me.

"Emma June?" Helen Munson had walked the avenue, our term for the ribbon of trodden wild grasses that connected our houses. Fifty yards, yet a thousand miles of visits from both directions.

"I'm coming in," her voice boomed through my open window. Mama was right. Miss Helen learned to whisper in a sawmill.

Calling for me instead of Mama meant she needed help with Scooter. I waited for Mama to cover for me, head her off, protect me from Miss Helen's endless chatter and requests.

The screen door squeaked open but thankfully, didn't slam shut. As usual, Miss Helen had used her round rump as a buffer to keep it from bouncing off the doorframe. "I'm coming in," she repeated and stomped into my bedroom carrying a small plate. If it held Bayer Aspirin, I'd forgive the intrusion.

The orange of her ugly smock-top plaid pajamas came close to matching her hair color. Regardless of what she said, her hair was not red. But no one dared correct a woman who drove a brand-new silver 1928 roadster all the way to Mineral Wells for a dye job. Or a woman who had built her own distillery and had half the town licking her heels, and their lips, for a jar of her moonshine.

Miss Helen puffed air from her cheeks like a leaky tire and sat on my bed. "Your mama told me you'd be needing it this morning." She set the plate beside me.

My stomach heaved at the smell and sight of burnt toast. I would have thrown it to Choppers had my body not begged for stillness. "Where is she?"

"That's what I need to talk to you about."

I hated the hand she set on my knee and the worry lines around her eyes.

"Only one way to tell you and that's straight out. Your mama didn't come home last night."

And I hated her awful truth.

CHAPTER 6

....

FRANK

The sun barely up, Irene fell through the door and slid down the wall to the floor, her dress covered in dirt. Skin, pale as a bone. Kohl eye shadow smudged down her face.

"It was awful," she whispered.

Frank got the feeling his fortune hadn't changed. "Ma?"

"Can you get me some water?"

In the small kitchen, he waited for the faucet to *drip drip drip* long enough to fill a glass halfway.

She guzzled the water and closed her eyes. "My things are in the jalopy. Bring them in for me, will you?"

After retrieving two bags, Frank found her in the bedroom, head in her hands. She looked up. "They're looking for me, Frank. Earl spotted Bernice and me talking. Well, I was talking. She was yelling. Earl knows I let the cat out of the bag."

"Good. It's over. Now I can go back home." *Freedom at last.*

"No, no, no. You don't understand," she said, taking in a sharp breath. "Now Earl knows he has no leverage to keep me quiet. I've become a liability."

"Hold on a minute. Keep quiet about what? And who's 'they'?"

Irene let out a shaky sigh and paused. "Earl and some thug. I overheard them planning something. But that's all I'm willing to tell you. It's too dangerous and I don't want you involved. They can't know I'm here. No one can."

"Okay," he said, drawing out the word. "You pulled me here, Ma. I never wanted to be involved in the first place."

Before he could walk away, Irene kept talking. "After I became friends with Bernice, Earl remembered me from years before. Not at first. He had come to The Diner a couple of times and never recognized me. I didn't recognize him either. Almost bald, missing teeth, fatter. Then I learned his name and put two and two together. Still, I avoided him best I could. Then one day, he heard me carry on a conversation with a customer. I guess something I said triggered his memory because he confronted me, pulled me aside. That's when the blackmail started. He knows who I really am."

Even a rat knew his mother better than Frank did.

But if Earl knew Irene's true character, then Bernice probably didn't like hearing that her Betty was a lying, self-absorbed floozy who probably broke the law in her younger days. No wonder she changed her name.

"I just wanted a friend," she said, a single tear sliding down her cheek. "And Bernice is the best I've ever had."

"So Bernice didn't like hearing about the real you."

"No, she didn't." She blotted her wet face with a palm. "I was also going to admit my real name but I saw Earl coming toward me with that evil look. I ran. The point is, Earl saw the fight between me and Bernice. He knows I told her the truth and he's pissed I no longer have to pay him. I'm afraid of what he'll do next."

Irene told him how she'd stayed hidden at the carnival until late, then finally found a ride into Holly Gap. From there, she skirted her way back toward The Diner, flinging herself to the ground each time she saw headlights or heard the rumble of a motorcar. By that time, it was early morning. She collected her belongings from The Diner and drove back to the shack. As far as she could tell, no one followed her.

She swiped her fingertips across her wet cheeks. "I need to talk to Bernice. But how can I with Earl trying to hunt me down?"

How could he answer that? She'd put herself in this situation. He had no interest in hearing anything else she had to say. Her shady past wasn't his problem. He just wanted his dough so he could go back to New Orleans.

"Emma June works in town at Rosie's Café," she said. "Drop by, get a cup of coffee. No need to introduce yourself. Just see if you can find out if Bernice is okay."

Her idea had its advantages. "So I have permission to leave the premises?"

Irene ignored the sarcasm and nodded. "Looks like I'm the one in hiding now. But the rules still apply. You don't know me."

She was right about that.

Frank changed into his white shirt and jacket and tugged on his flat cap.

"And Frank? We need food. Stop by the grocer's and pick up what you can for this." She reached across the mattress and pulled a clam from her purse. "It needs to last a while."

"How much money do you have, Ma?"

"Not nearly enough." She lay back on the mattress. "And buy some aspirin. It won't cure anything, but it'll help."

A thought occurred to him. "Ma, does anyone in town know about me?"

"What do you mean?" She looked away.

Of course she didn't tell anyone she had a son. As far as Irene was concerned, he didn't exist. That is, until she needed his help.

"I'm not ashamed of you, Frank. I'm proud of the man you've become. I know I had nothing to do with that. Patsy deserves the credit you give her."

No argument there.

Irene turned on her side and looked at Frank, her eyes sorrowful. "You know, something really bad happened to me when I was thirteen. Patsy was there for me."

"What—"

"Patsy was the only one I could trust. The only person I could talk to. She held me, comforted me when I told her about the rape."

Frank bit the inside of his cheek, hoping the offensive image would disappear. "Aunt Patsy never told me."

"She kept her word. Now, besides the bastard who did it, you are the only living person who knows."

"You didn't even tell Bernice?"

Irene shook her head. "Not even my best friend. Too much shame in it, I guess." She turned on her side, away from Frank. "Like leaving you."

He took a step back and squinted. His mother had regrets? Was this just more lip service or did Irene really feel remorse for abandoning him?

"Sometimes," she whispered, "I think God wants to keep me alive just so I can feel every morsel of the guilt."

Raped at thirteen, Frank's father lammed off, leaving her with a young child. Then she had gone from living the high life in New York City to living in a dump in the middle of nowhere. Although some things weren't her fault, she had plenty of sins to make up for.

Still, when he walked out into the morning air, he shook his head, puzzled at the foreign emotion—a tug of compassion for the woman lying on a bruise-colored mattress.

....

CHAPTER 7

EMMA JUNE

My feet hit the floor. "What do you mean she didn't come home? Where is she?"

Miss Helen shrugged a shoulder. "No idea. She woke me last night madder than a hornet. Told me she had to leave and to bring you toast this morning. Said you'd be needing it."

Even if Mama were mad at me for getting so drunk, she never would have told Miss Helen to bring me a charred piece of toast. "Had to leave? And why was she mad?"

"Honey, I know this makes no sense whatsoever," she said, talking to my back as I slipped on an old housedress. "Bernice Crawford might be ten years younger than me, but I know her like she was my own daughter. She's just out cooling her heels somewhere."

Miss Helen didn't know Mama at all. Running off was not how Mama cooled her heels. And the only time Mama spent the night somewhere without me was when she attended her aunt's funeral in Lubbock.

I ran to the bathroom and made it in time to heave over the toilet.

"You okay, sugar?" Miss Helen asked from behind the closed door. "What kind of hooch did you drink, for Christ's sake?"

I stayed on the floor and leaned my back against the toilet.

"Wade Foley's."

Miss Helen let herself in. She shook her head and grimaced. "Jesus Christ, girl. No telling where he got that crap from. He didn't get it from my stash, because I won't sell to his father. That man's crooked as the Brazos."

I forced myself up, splashed water on my face with hands too shaky to be my own. The face in the mirror didn't belong to me either. Red eyes. Puffy bags. I looked like Betty had the night before. "What exactly did Mama tell you?"

"Not much. Took off like a cat on fire."

"Where's Daddy?"

"I assume at work. As usual, I heard Ol' Bess rumble off before sunlight."

"No. I bet he went to meet up with her. Wherever she is."

"Thing is, I doubt he knows she's gone. After she had a fight with your daddy, Bernice told him she was coming to my house. Theo probably thought she spent the night."

I knew Mama had some sort of falling out with Betty. But Daddy? I'd only seen Mama and Daddy squabble a couple of times. Each time, Daddy was quick to calm Mama's tail feathers. "What fight? About what?"

Miss Helen shrugged. "Wouldn't give me details."

Leaving your family was what fathers did if they had to go to war. Or what Mrs. Butler did after her husband busted her up for the last time. But Mama blousing off?

Miss Helen looked down and shook her head.

"What?"

"Bless her heart. She looked a mess. Face smudged with dirt and tears."

That was another thing. I had never seen Mama so upset that she wouldn't fix her face before going anywhere.

"Come on, Emma June. Come eat your toast."

Miss Helen took a seat on the sitting room's sofa, then patted the space beside her hard enough to free the dust mites. "Sit here. I'll hold the furniture steady."

She wrapped an arm around my shoulder. I stared down at the rug, its green and yellow threads dissolving into a bottomless pit.

"Did Mama pack a bag?"

"Pack a bag? Can't say one way or the other. But if she did, it's an awful light one. I'm sure she'll be home before the day's out."

"What did Mama say? Ex-act-ly. Did the fight have something to do with Betty?"

Her eyes widened. "Why would you say that?"

"Stop dawdling and spill it for Christ's sake."

Miss Helen smoothed her pajama pants, then looked away. "Your mama was in such a tizzy she didn't make a lot of sense. Said she even threw her pie on the ground at the carnival last night."

Mama threw that pie. Not Betty. Mama never threw anything in anger. Except maybe a dishrag in the sink. "Go on."

"Said she didn't know who she trusted less, Betty or your daddy. Said something like, 'I need to finish this conversation.' Then she stormed out."

The sound of tires crunched up the distance between the road and my house. "Mama. Thank God."

Miss Helen started to stand but sat back down. "Thank God is right. Now I don't have to worry about your father falling in a gopher hole of despair. Let's stay put. Give her time to come in and settle herself."

Agreed. Jumping up meant throwing up.

My belly settled for the first time. I thought things would get back to normal, and we could start the day with music again. But with the volume low.

The rumbling stopped. A door slammed shut. Then, another. "Mama's not alone?"

Miss Helen headed to the door.

Leaning forward was the best I could do. "Who's with her?"

"It's not your mama," she said, her face drooping. She pushed open the screen door and thrust a hand to her hip. "Doc? What in tarnation are you doing here? Everything okay?"

Doc Ferguson. Handsome in a middle-aged kind of way, he had kind eyes and a forehead permanently creased from concern and fatigue. He nodded a smile toward me.

"Morning Helen. This is my nephew, Samuel." The door opened wider.

That's when I saw him. Not only did Oxford Two-Tone have a name, but he was inside my house. I felt the blush in my cheeks, remembering how he'd been there when I made a fool of myself. I glanced at him long enough to be polite.

Doc removed his Gambler hat. "Emma June, I understand you've met Samuel. He said you were feeling poorly last night."

Samuel took off his tweed cap and offered his hand in greeting. I stayed glued to the sofa.

"Good to see you again, Emma June."

I remembered that grip. Firm, kind. "How did you . . ." I couldn't finish. Through my drunken eyes the night before, Oxford Two-Tone was handsome. But Samuel was stunning. His hair was a sun-kissed blond, not light brown like I had thought. Unlike Wade's hair parted in the center and flattened with cheap Vaseline, Samuel's was combed back and pomaded to a healthy shine.

"Samuel's studying medicine at Baylor University," Doc said. "Hope it's okay but he's here doing rounds with me while on spring break." Doc glanced around the house. "Where's Miss Bernice?"

"Out," Miss Helen huffed. "Since you made the trip, go ahead and give Emma June a look-over."

Samuel leaned a shoulder against our grandfather clock and stared in another direction. Gentlemanly of him considering Doc was poking around on my belly while I lay on the sofa.

"Some fools don't know how to keep out the impurities," Miss Helen said. "Methanol poisoning's my guess."

Doc nodded. "Probably. But not enough to cause blindness. She'll be fine as long as she doesn't drink any more of that rotgut."

Miss Helen's back shifted to ramrod straight. "And this is why I'm the best in town."

I caught the grin on Samuel's face.

"Those jackass shiners," she continued. "All two crackers shy of the box. They cut corners any way they can. Kinda like Jasper at the feed store. He stiffs me an ounce of chicken feed every time. I don't snooker my customers. No sirree Bob. My customers get their honest money's worth." She took a breath and grinned at Doc Ferguson. "Speaking of money's worth, Doc. You want your payment in shine?" Miss Helen's illegal tender may have appeased many of our towns-folk vendors, but not the teetotaling doctor.

"Now, Miss Helen," he tsk-tsked. "Besides, no charge. Just doing Samuel here a favor."

"Then walk me over to the house so I can at least get you a break-fast roll."

"Now, that I'll take you up on."

"Plus," she added, "I've got something to tell you."

About Mama, no doubt.

Doc followed Miss Helen out the door, then turned back. "Emma June, might help to eat small portions of eggs or oatmeal. Feel better, now."

Doc and Miss Helen gone, Samuel lingered by the door, tweed cap in his hand.

"Take care of yourself, Emma June," he said. "And only drink the good stuff."

His wink stopped my breath. "Right," was the only word I could spit out. He headed down the porch steps.

The sweat that formed under my armpits had nothing to do with the hangover. I was gobsmacked.

Standing up took forever, but I made it to the front porch before he reached the end of the house. "Hey, Samuel? Wait up a sec."

He pivoted and strode toward me.

"I have a few questions," I said, trying to gather my composure.

"Okay. And just so you know, I don't blame you if you don't remember last night."

I was mortified. The things I could have done and forgotten were endless.

"I've heard about the Foleys' moonshine," he said, shaking his head. "No wonder you feel so sick."

If I had done something unthinkable, he was too polite to mention it. "How did you know where I lived? Did I even tell you my name last night?"

There it was again. The smile that curled my toes.

"When I came back with your water, your friend, Sharla—"

"Charlene."

"Charlene was there. We got you up, and I carried you to your mother, then to her motorcar."

He carried me, a vomit-smelling mess. I turned my head away, hoping to hide my embarrassment. "You met Mama then. How was she?"

"Kind. Introduced herself and told me she was grateful. She looked upset, though. Fidgety. Why? Is she okay?"

"Do you remember anything else? Anything she said?"

"Nothing. Sorry. After getting you in the back seat, the three of y'all took off."

Three people, not four. "Another woman wasn't with us? A couple of years older than my mother?"

"No. Just you three."

Betty. If Mama no longer trusted her, I needed to know why. I didn't know where Betty lived, but I sure did know where she worked.

....

CHAPTER 8

EMMA JUNE

Roadrunner, the name Miss Helen gave her roadster, sparkled in the distance and gave me a wink.

"I need to find my mother," I told Samuel. "She didn't come home last night."

I felt sure that if Mama needed comfort, she was safe in Miss Atta's small home across town. Miss Atta, or as Daddy called her, Atta Girl, wasn't just my boss but a family friend.

"I don't understand," he said.

"The woman who was supposed to ride home with us from the carnival. She needs to tell me what happened between her and my mother." I turned to go inside, then stopped. "And, well, thanks for helping me last night. Sorry if I was . . ." I stopped, not wanting to remind either of us of that horrid vision of myself. "I need to change clothes. See you around maybe?"

"Need some company?"

"Company?"

"A tagalong, to go with you to talk to that woman."

I couldn't imagine why he would want to come. Me, a bumbling fool who had disgraced myself in front of him. My eyes were still blurry from the rotgut, and the inside of my head had assembled a riotous gang of tuba players. "Oh, that's okay. I couldn't possibly ask you—"

"You didn't. I offered."

I hurried inside, changed into a simple shift dress, and added color to my lips and pale cheeks. I grabbed the object from my dresser and headed outside.

I found Samuel sitting on the front porch getting his face lathered by Choppers's tongue.

"Pinwheel," he said, staring at my hand and smiling.

I had a vague memory of him handing it to me at the carnival. "It's for Miss Helen's son."

Cool spring day or not, my legs wobbled toward Miss Helen's. I kept my head down and focused on lifting one foot in front of the other. Something as small as an armadillo divot could have thrown me face first.

"Scooter. Have you met him?" I asked Samuel.

"Last week. Mrs. Munson brought him into the office for . . . well, never mind. I'm not supposed to say."

"It doesn't matter. If Scooter has a finger scratch, Miss Helen rushes him to your uncle because, 'you know, it could turn to gang-green.'"

Miss Helen charged hell with a bucket of ice to protect her family. After Scooter was born, some folks in Holly Gap, even a preacher, tried to force Miss Helen to ship Scooter off to a loony bin. "And cut off my arm?" she had told them. "I am blessed with this child and this child only. He's mine for the duration. And if I ever hear anyone mention sending him away again, they'll be contending with more than just being on top of my hit list." She hadn't stepped foot in a church since.

Choppers darted ahead, grinning through his pant.

"Doesn't seem possible," Samuel said. "Running that fast on three legs."

"Yeah." I left it at that.

"Emmy, Emmy, Emmy!" Scooter leaped off his front porch and wrapped his arms around my waist. Strong for a thirteen-year-old, and thank God, he didn't pick me up and give me the usual bounce.

"Hey, Scoot Bucket." When he finally released me, I held out the pinwheel with a "ta-da" and received his eye twinkle.

"A twirly *bird*!"

"Yes, for you."

"Emmy *is* best." He faced Samuel and stuck out his hand. "Howdy-do, Samuel."

"Hi, Scooter. You remembered my name."

Scooter patted his slight belly pooch as if he'd just eaten a large portion of satisfaction. "Scooter *remembers*."

An understatement. Scooter still remembered the name of a traveling salesman who'd knocked on his door the year before.

I rubbed my hand across his burr haircut, his blond bristles a tad darker than Samuel's. "Scoot, where's your mama?"

"Moonshine *thicket*."

Samuel followed me to the cluster of post oaks that served as a canopy for Miss Helen's still. The scent of bubbling prunes and yeast thickened the air. And the back of my throat.

"Good Lord," Samuel said. "What a contraption."

Whereas most folks had next-door neighbors who grew rosebushes or vegetable gardens, mine fermented mash and turned it into alcohol. Eight years of gurgles and thumps from a still that produced a ghostly steam loop between the oak branches. Prohibition was Miss Helen's bread and butter, and she aimed to keep brewing her way to the top of the food chain with one-eighty proof.

Miss Helen sealed the cap on a Mason jar and looked up. "Ain't she a beaut, Samuel?"

Beauty wasn't a snake-looking tube that sat atop a barrel attached to a copper boiler pot. Beauty was Mama's burgundy hair curling around a smile that lifted you off the ground.

I shook away my thoughts of Mama.

"Miss Helen's been doing this since Prohibition started," I told Samuel.

Miss Helen wiped her hands on the gaudy green and yellow apron she'd thrown over her pajamas. "Emma June?"

"Miss Helen?"

"You want something, spit it out. I'm busier than a dog in flea season."

"I need to borrow Roadrunner. It won't take long, I promise."

"Where?"

"To get answers."

"Emma June—"

"You expect me to do nothing?"

"You can barely drive, young lady. Theo's given you what? Two lessons?"

True. After hitting our mailbox the first go-round, it took some convincing for Daddy to take me out for a second run.

Samuel stepped forward. "Mrs. Munson, I've been driving since I was twelve, seven years now. I'd be glad to drive Emma June."

"I'm *driving* the twirly bird," Scooter said as he ran in circles with the pinwheel held high. He came to a screeching halt and pulled out his prized pocketknife. "Now, I must *plant* it."

"Nice of you to get that pinwheel for him, Emma June." Miss Helen flicked her eyes between me and Samuel, then cracked a grin. "Don't be long. And Samuel, I'll tell your uncle not to wait for you.

He's inside with Leonard who's trying to talk him into buying one of his side tables."

Which would take a while. Leonard's words weren't exactly quick out of the chute, which made it easy for Miss Helen to talk over him.

"And no matter what, Emma June, you *will* walk Scooter to school tomorrow." It wasn't a question.

I told her I would, knowing I'd have to endure Miss Primrose's eye roll. She was still upset I had passed my exit exam and graduated in December instead of May. Younger than Mama, the school-marm acted as though her one trip to Chicago added extra snap to her garters.

After a wave to Scooter, Samuel and I started down the drive in a motorcar that smelled of White Rose Toilet Water, Miss Helen's wretched perfume.

Samuel looked in the back seat and whistled. "There's enough room in here to house a family of four."

I felt the smoothness of the seat's brown houndstooth fabric and hoped Mama had slept on something just as soft. Surely, she missed not sleeping next to her husband in the comfort of her own bed. But knowing Miss Atta, Mama was safe and sound.

"Where can I take you?"

As much as I wanted to talk to Betty, Charlene was on the way. "Johnson's Variety."

He gave me a dimpled grin. "Need a tight kerchief to wrap around your skull?"

"Yeah, if it's the kind that squeezes out answers."

....

CHAPTER 9

EMMA JUNE

Like the other stores in Holly Gap, a bell announced our arrival at Johnson's Variety. Except, at that moment, the soft ding sounded more like the gong at the start of a boxing match.

Mr. Johnson, Charlene's father, glanced away from the customer standing at the counter. "Morning, Emma June. I'll be right with you."

The customer, a young man I'd never seen before, looked a bit older than Samuel. Tanned face, strong jawline. A rough kind of handsome. He gave me a quick once-over and tipped his cap.

Mr. Johnson turned back to him. "Head down to Dixie's Drugstore. Block down on your right. They carry aspirin."

Aspirin. Judging from the stranger's cocksure appearance, his headache didn't reach my level of bad. He strutted out, the bell chiming his exit.

"Well, Emma June," Mr. Johnson said, "God created another beautiful day, now, didn't He?"

Not really. "Yes, sir. I need to speak with Charlene. This is my . . . this is Samuel."

"She's in the storage room. Go on back." Mr. Johnson gave Samuel the stink eye. "Son, you best stay here and let them gals do their gossipin'."

I found Charlene leaning over a small crate unloading small green and blue boxes of Star Harps, toy ducks printed on each one. I cleared my throat and got her attention.

"Geez Louise, Emma June. You look terrible."

"Yeah. I feel like I'm on a hill trying to balance my butt on a log."

"Told you he was no good. You never listen. Was it worth the bags under your eyes?"

Compared to Charlene with her narrow waist, full hips and breasts, her flawless milk-white skin, I looked like the grim reaper.

"What happened with Mama and Betty last night? Why didn't Betty drive home with us?"

"That's all you care about? What should have been a fun night ended up being a flop. And we had to leave before the evening even got started."

"Because I got ossified," I said, acknowledging my stupidity.

"Probably," she muttered. "After I shrugged Louis's cooties off my arm, I went looking for you and saw Bernice and Betty's war squabble. God, how people stared. Anyway, I found you sitting on the dirt. Then, after you were carried . . . After I got you back to your mother, Betty was gone."

"What were they yelling about? What did they say?"

"Why don't you ask your mother? She tells you everything," she spat. Charlene had always resented my relationship with Mama. While my mother listened and gave me honest advice, Mrs. Johnson nagged and judged everything Charlene said or did.

If I told her the truth, that Mama didn't come home, the whole town would know within fifteen minutes. "Mama didn't say anything about last night."

Charlene shrugged. "They stopped talking when I walked up. But right before, I heard Miss Bernice yelling something like, 'Why didn't you tell me?' When it was just the two of us in the car, and I don't count you because you were out cold, she wouldn't answer my questions. Just asked how you got to be so drunk. Most the way home, she stayed quiet."

"So what happened to Betty?"

"I asked if Betty met someone. She said, 'Oh, she did, all right. She's finding her own way home.'"

"I gotta go." I turned my back to Charlene and stopped. "Hey, you want to meet the boy who carried me to the car last night?"

"What? How—"

"Long story."

Charlene peered through the supply room door and gasped. "He's talking to my father. He better not say anything about Betty being with us last night."

I thought about Samuel's doctor oath, about him not revealing why Scooter had gone to the doctor. "He won't talk. Come say hello."

Charlene flicked dust off her work apron and tugged down one side of her bangs. "What? You carrying a torch for him now?"

"Are you coming or not?"

Charlene backed away. "No. Not with Daddy around."

"Suit yourself. And Charlene? About last night. I didn't mean . . . well, you were right. Wade is a creep."

"Yeah? And that boy out there? He might be one, too."

I left her alone with her crates and jealousy. Charlene and I had been friends for fourteen years. Hundreds of happy times spent together. Yet too many days had been ruined by her pettiness.

After passing through the aisles of sewing supplies, dishrags, cleaning supplies, and toy trinkets, I made it to the front where Samuel and Mr. Johnson stood chuckling.

"That beauty shop's called the Chicken Coop," Mr. Johnson said. "Can you imagine driving all the way to Mineral Wells just to get your hair dyed orange?"

"Well," Samuel said, "if I had that new roadster, I'd drive it to get my hair dyed green."

I cleared my throat. "Interrupting something?"

"Emma June?" Mr. Johnson said. "This young fella was just telling me how Helen Munson let him use her motorcar. Now, if that don't beat all."

"Beats all," I muttered and turned to Samuel. "Ready?"

A block down, we entered through another door where the entry bells were a soft reminder of comfort and kindness.

Adelaide Jackson, conveniently nicknamed Miss Atta for those who could never remember or pronounce her name, stood leaning over her least favorite wooden booth, the one by the window. Although Miss Atta never said so, I believed the booth's peeling seat was due to our heavy-weight mayor's overuse.

The loose skin on her arms swayed as she swept away crumbs while humming Bessie Smith's "Easy Come, Easy Go Blues." In a way, she looked like Bessie Smith. Big brown eyes and a smile you could crawl inside of to brighten your spirits. But unlike the singer's smooth skin, Miss Atta's face was lined with crevices made from suffering rains. Not only had her husband died early on, her only son, Toby, had been lynched seven years before just because of his skin color.

According to Mama, the whole town loved Toby. Everything he did, he did with kindness and a sense of humor, earning him the nickname "Brown Sugar." When news spread of his death, townsfolk sniffled and spoke in soft, somber tones. The louder voices grew a hunger to find the murderer and make him pay. But they never found him. Whoever it was deserved to burn in hell.

After the atrocity, Daddy and Gunny had pulled Miss Atta up for enough air to help her move forward. And she did. Ever since, Gunny by her side, both carrying a secret rapport for one another.

Miss Atta looked up and gave me a broad, white smile. "Why, Emma June. It's your day off. What are you doing here?"

The same newcomer I had seen at Johnson's Variety sat at the counter drinking coffee. I walked past him and into the comfort of Miss Atta's eyes. "Mama?"

Her face revealed no hint of concern, no sign that she knew anything about Mama's whereabouts. That's when the fear busted in.

"What's wrong? She doing all right?"

"I don't know, Miss Atta. I mean . . ."

She handed me a handkerchief and wrapped her arms around me. "Shortcake, don't carry your burdens alone. True friends hold you with both hands. And mine are right here."

I told her the little I knew.

CHAPTER 10

....

EMMA JUNE

amuel stayed quiet on the short drive to The Diner, giving me time to collect my wits.

Mama and I had never been to Betty's place. She'd told us it was nearby but too small for entertaining properly. I kept thinking that Mama had found out where she lived, went there to seek an apology, and ended up staying due to the late hour. As Charlene said, they were best friends, and best friends worked things out.

Samuel parked in front of The Diner and stared ahead. Almost every window was cracked, all so filthy you couldn't see inside. He ran around to my side of the motorcar and opened the passenger door. "Doesn't look like a very nice place to work."

An understatement. But it was the first job available when Betty moved here. "Wait till you see the inside."

We entered through The Diner's torn screen door. No jingling bells. No smiling face to greet us.

Crumbs and grease stains dotted the floor. Wooden tables, strewn haphazardly around the room, were carved up by bored customers hankering to practice their knife skills. Nothing like Rosie's clean and welcoming interior.

"I wouldn't eat a peanut from here," Samuel whispered.

And for good reason. The food tasted like the inside of a fertilizer bag. Mama and I only came when we wanted to visit Betty.

Bald and missing a front tooth, Betty's boss, Percy Yates, sat in a corner, his chair leaning on two legs against the wall. "If yer eatin' here, take a seat," he said, ogling me. He wiped his hands on a brown-stained apron and headed back to the kitchen.

"Betty working today?" I called after him. No response.

"Emma June? That you?" Miss Mabel's head appeared over the counter, the rest of her struggled to stand. She placed the remnants of broken glass in a trash bin and turned to me.

Slump-shouldered, Miss Mabel wore the same dingy pink dress and matching waitress cap she'd worn since the place opened twenty years before. Cloudy-eyed and sagged with age, her wrinkled lips only uttered unkind words to hostile customers.

"Good morning, Miss Mabel. This is my friend Samuel. I wanted to introduce him to Betty. Is she here?"

"Packed up and high-tailed it early this mornin'. Didn't say where. Maybe back to the big city. She talked about them skyscrapers almost as much as she talked about you and Miss Bernice. Surprised she didn't tell you."

I was more shocked than surprised. Betty told us everything.

Percy stuck his head through the kitchen window. "Good riddance, I say. Didn't give notice. Now I gotta wait tables when Mabel ain't here. Damn pisser's what it is."

Miss Mabel shooed an invisible fly from her face and ignored him. "How is Miss Bernice? Ain't seen her in a while."

"Neither of you saw Mama last night? Sometime after ten or so?"

"No women last night," Percy said.

Miss Mabel rolled her eyes. "Unfortunately. Nothing but a few mug-faced old-timers belching their sorrows. Nothin' like that handsome friend'a yours." She winked at Samuel.

Samuel blushed, a quality I secretly thought of as endearing.

Burning questions. Miss Helen had said Mama left to finish a conversation. If not with Betty, then who did Mama go to see? And where was Betty?

"Do you know where Betty lives?" I asked.

"Course I do." Miss Mabel pointed behind her. "In the back room. Least she did."

"The storage room?"

"The door next to it. She never invite you in?"

All that time and Betty never told us she lived down the short hall. "Can I see it?"

"Not much to see but go 'head back."

Samuel followed behind me. I opened the door, unprepared for what I saw.

The woman who took pride in her appearance and experienced the glamour and glitz of New York City lived in a room the size of my kitchen. A small shadeless lamp sat on a crate used as a nightstand. A weathered blanket and a hand mirror on top of a floor mattress. A few photographs of motion picture stars torn from *Photoplay* hung loosely on the wall. No clothes, no suitcase, no cosmetics. Only the faint scent of Betty's perfume.

"Emma June?"

Samuel stood over a trashcan holding a crinkled paper. "I found something."

He handed me the note.

Last chance. Bring the dough tomorrow or cat's outta the bag.

So Betty had more than one secret.

"I don't think we should tell anyone about this note," I told Samuel. "At least, not until I talk to Mama." Miss Mabel didn't concern me. Percy, I didn't trust.

Back in the grimy dining area, a few disheveled customers had straggled in for lunch—a man with paint-covered overalls, a middle-aged woman who looked vaguely familiar.

I waited while Miss Mabel finished taking an order, then asked who had picked up Betty and given her a ride.

"A ride? She drove her own self."

"How? She doesn't own a motorcar."

"Sure she does. That old jalopy she kept in back is gone. Surprised it started."

Yeah. Surprises all around.

Samuel and I sat in Roadrunner, its engine shut down like my ideas of where to find Mama. My body felt limp, unsupported by bones that had turned to jelly.

"I'm sorry, Emma June."

I didn't want Samuel to notice my shame and embarrassment. I didn't want him to think I came from a family whose ties were so fragile a little tiff would send one of us out the door. The Crawfords stuck together, plain and simple.

"She'll be back, you know," I said, mustering up confidence. "By the end of the day."

"Sure she will. It's good to get away, to be alone for a bit. Sometimes, in Waco, I go to a place called Lover's Leap. Legend has it that a couple of lovers from opposing tribes weren't accepted by the Apaches. It's called Lover's Leap because the couple jumped off the cliff into the Brazos River so they could die together."

"Well, that's sad."

"But the place isn't. You can sit high on the cliff and see for miles. And you know why I'm usually alone up there? It's hard to get to. The incline of the road is so steep, Model Ts have to drive up in reverse," he said, chuckling. "But I enjoy a good hike."

"You go there alone?" The thought of going someplace with a ghostly history, not to mention a difficult escape route, gave me the creeps.

"Alone is best for mulling things over," Samuel said.

It wasn't so bad being alone with a good book. Or taking Choppers for a walk while listening to nature. Abandonment was something else altogether.

"My house sits on a bluff above the Brazos," I said. "And it's easy to get to. Leaping's not allowed, though."

"You know," he said, smiling, "Waco and Holly Gap are over a hundred miles apart, yet we share the same river."

"As do a lot of other towns. The Brazos is over a thousand miles long."

"Yeah," he said, trying to hide an abashed grin. "My lame attempt at making a connection." He looked up, finding my eyes again. "Think you could show me your side of the river sometime?"

"How long are you staying in Holly Gap?"

"Till Wednesday."

Three days and *poof*, like he never existed. Barely enough time to bake a stupid pie.

"But I'll be back for the summer," he added.

As if that made a difference. Once again, he was Oxford Two-Tone, the boy in the fleeting shoes.

"You better take me home now," I said. "I'm not feeling so well."

We returned to Miss Helen's, where I said a brief goodbye to Samuel before Leonard drove him back to Doc Ferguson's office. I should have shown my appreciation, thanked him for trying to help. I didn't.

Across the avenue, the breezer's usual parking space remained empty like my house.

Scooter poked my back. "Emmy?"

"Hey, Scoot Bucket."

"Come *see*." He grabbed my hand and led me to the towering post oak rooted between our houses. He pointed to the ground. "*Twirly bird's* here."

The pinwheel. "You buried it."

Scooter nodded. "*Can't* see it. But it's *still* here."

Like Mama. She wouldn't be home when I entered, but everything about her was still inside.

"Thanks, Scooter." I kissed the top of his head and trudged forward.

In the sitting room, our grandfather clock had stopped ticking. I skirted my way around it without rewinding. I didn't need a reminder of more passing time.

I collapsed on my bed and curled up beside my three-legged dog.

Five years before, we had taken Choppers with us to town. I was supposed to be watching him, but a new dress in the window of Grace's Lace caught my eye. I turned back in time to spot Choppers running across Main Street. The feed truck driver didn't see him.

But I saw. I witnessed the terrifying *before* when I was unable to stop it. The *during* of the horrible tumble and yelp beneath the wheels. And the *after* when my confused, pain-stricken dog tried to run off with a mangled mess of a leg. I thought for sure he would die.

Daddy rushed him to the vet where the doctor amputated his leg. A few weeks after, Choppers forgot it was even missing.

But I remembered that awful day all too clearly. I had paid more attention to a stupid dress than to Choppers.

And on carnival night, I had been so obsessed with Wade and his moonshine, I wasn't there for Mama when she needed me. Not before, during, or after.

....

CHAPTER 11

EMMA JUNE

"Bernice?" Daddy's voice. "Sweetheart?"

Rising from a dead sleep, I imagined Mama standing in the kitchen making chicken fried steak wearing a flour-covered apron, Daddy sneaking up behind her for a hug. The vision didn't last.

I found Daddy staring out the front window rubbing a hand through his thick dark hair.

"Daddy?"

After a flinch of his shoulder, he turned. "Honey? Where's your mother? Not like her not to be here at suppertime." He took another glance out the window.

"I don't know where she is. Tell me what happened last night."

Daddy squinted. "What happened?"

"I know you fought with Mama."

"How . . . Your mother told you then. Well, maybe she told you more than me because I had no idea what she was talking about. Didn't help that I was half asleep."

"No, Mama didn't tell me. She hasn't come home since last night." Before my legs failed to hold me up, I sat on Granny's rocker and tried to breathe.

"Emma June? Honey? What's going on? You look—"

"I'm worried, Daddy."

He squatted before me, his hands on my knees. He stared into my eyes. "What's happened?"

I told him how Mama went to Miss Helen's and then left. That no one had heard from her since.

Daddy slumped onto the sofa. "It doesn't make sense. Your mother was upset, all right. Said I'd lied to her about Betty. I've never even met that woman."

I didn't want to tell him about Betty going with us to the carnival or finding Betty's threatening note and her taking off. I didn't want to talk about Betty at all.

Gunny, round as a wagon wheel, hobbled up our porch steps. Once inside, he refused Daddy's offer for evening coffee, saying, "Got enough trouble sleeping. Stove up with the gout, ya know."

I tried picturing Gunny chasing an outlaw. Him waddling, his gunless belt jiggling as his puffy red cheeks huffed, "Come back here so I can slap on your handcuffs." Then I pictured him scouring through his Packard trying to find a pair.

His questions were repeats of what we had already told him. "Didn't say where she was headed? Didn't pack a bag? A husband-wife spat, you say?"

He looked up from the foot he tried to reach. "What about family members?"

Daddy stopped pacing. "No, Gunny. No relatives for her to stay with. Bernice is an only child and lost her parents way back. My brother lives in Oklahoma, but Bernice doesn't get on with his wife."

Mama and I referred to religious Aunt Josephine as Hippo-Critter. Mama would rather hand-feed hyenas than be anywhere near that woman. Not only that, like me, Mama couldn't understand why any decent person would live in Tulsa, a city where bigoted whites had massacred hundreds of people seven years before.

"Theo, Bernice ain't the kind of woman to take off."

"We know that, Gunny. That's why you're here."

"I'll ask around. See if anyone knows something."

Ol' Bess was gone when I woke the next morning. Daddy told me the night before that working was better than fretting—which is what he'd done in the wee hours of the night tromping back and forth on our wooden floors.

I went through the motions of beginning a day, but without Mama putting a record on the phonograph to "get our blood flowing." I walked Choppers, ate Cream of Wheat, and dressed for work—which didn't require wearing a stupid pink uniform like poor Miss Mabel at The Diner.

The Diner. Where Betty had lived in that dreadful room next to a storage closet. Where she stowed secrets.

Midway to the Munsons' house, where Scooter had planted the pinwheel, Samuel unhitched his shoulder from the scaly ridge of a tree trunk.

"I'm sorry, Emma June. I didn't mean to scare you."

"What—"

"I remembered you were walking Scooter to school today. Mind if I tag along?"

"Sure. Okay," I said without thinking. I told myself not to be wooed by his charm. He was leaving in a few days and an attachment would only lead to disappointment. I didn't need another bitter pill to swallow.

"So you're finished with school then?" he said, matching my footsteps toward Scooter's house.

"Finished in December. Mama made the teacher give me an exit exam. Told her if I passed, I was out."

"Guess you passed," he said with a fleeting touch to my elbow.

Daddy, an avid reader, taught me more than Miss Primrose ever had.

Almost to Scooter's, he put a hand on my shoulder and stared into my eyes. "You look quite fetching today, Emma June."

I glanced down at the purple suspender dress Mama bought me the month before. At first, I balked at its simplicity, its inability to make a fashion statement. But it was both comfortable and practical for working at Rosie's.

"Thank you. Mama bought me this . . . Oh, did you mean I finally look presentable?" Unlike carnival night and hangover day.

Samuel grinned. "I meant what I said. You look charming."

Charming. He didn't say I looked like a sexy Sheba or a dish to be eaten and spat back out. If he was telling the truth, that he thought I was charming, he'd positioned his broom for sweeping me off my feet. I had to stay on level ground.

"Did you tell the sheriff about the note?" he asked.

"Not in front of my father." I told Samuel how Daddy disliked Betty and her citified ways even though he'd never met her. "Why? Do you think I should?"

"Might help Betty if she's in trouble."

"What . . ."

He leaned forward, finding the fear in my eyes. "Emma June? What is it?"

"What if Mama's in danger? Got tangled up in Betty's mess?"

Samuel glanced briefly at his feet, then back to me. "Listen, not knowing is the worst. But do you think maybe, well, you might be jumping to conclusions?"

A nice way of saying I was being dramatic. That was Charlene's nature, not mine.

"Give your mother a chance to come back," he said.

I let out a deep breath. Samuel was right. Any moment Mama

would drive up to the house, assure us everything was fine, then apologize for scaring us.

I led Samuel inside the Munsons' house. Lucky for us, we didn't have time to sit down. New purchases covered the sofa—shoes still in boxes, an electric toaster, magazines, including *Good Housekeeping*, one Miss Helen subscribed to but obviously never read.

In the middle of the floor, Scooter sat atop a pile of bedding, his daddy buried beneath it.

"Okay, Scoot. Let your daddy breathe now," Leonard said.

Scooter patted the quilts. "Grow, *grow*."

Bit by bit, Leonard stirred from under the bedding until his prayer-clasped hands emerged. As his fingers spread apart, his sinewy arms and scarecrow body broke through the soil of blankets until he reached his six-foot-two height. Scooter's hands clapped as fast as hummingbird wings.

"Emmy, *Emmy*." Scooter gave me a squeeze. "Sam-u-*el*."

"Hey, Scooter. Mr. Munson." Samuel stuck out his hand for a shake.

"Emma June?" Miss Helen appeared from the kitchen wearing an awful green and yellow apron. "What's the scuttlebutt?" she asked.

"The Yankees won?"

She rolled her eyes. "They didn't play this week. Now next week will be a humdinger. They're playing the Red Sox. And since that's clarified, Miss Wit, tell me. Any news?"

"Nothing yet."

"Well . . ." The woman who could talk the legs off a chair had run out of words. She retreated to the kitchen and returned with Scooter's lunch bag and a sack of linden sticks. "Emma June, you tell Miss Primrose to let me know when he runs low so Leonard can get more." She stuck her hands to her hips. "Leonard, you fix the handle on the hooch house yet? Can't have it open as an invitation to enter and steal."

"Uh . . ."

"And don't forget to knock down that hornet's nest while you're at it." She turned to Samuel. "Tell Doc that the spot on Scooter's hand went away. Thank God. I couldn't imagine his hand covered in ringworms like Faye Porter's at the bakery." She kissed the top of Scooter's head. "Now stop dillydallying and go on before you're late for school."

Another typical morning at the Munsons'.

"Linwood?" Samuel said as we made our way toward Holly Gap School.

"For whittling. Last Christmas, Scooter's daddy bought him a pocketknife. Miss Primrose lets Scooter whittle beside her desk. The only ducky thing about her."

Samuel grinned.

"What?"

"Hard to picture Miss Helen allowing him to have a sharp knife."

"Yeah, Leonard spent the whole winter break teaching him everything there was to know about knife danger. Miss Helen spent the whole break wringing her hands and mopping her forehead."

"Share everything *except* pocketknife," Scooter said, then skipped ahead.

"The promise his daddy makes him keep," I said.

I recalled Scooter and me strolling in town on a cold January afternoon. We passed a bench sitter who muttered, "That boy carries his brains in his pocket." Scooter smiled and said, "No, that's where I keep my *pocket*knife."

"Hey, Scooter," Samuel called out. "What do you make when you whittle?"

"Toothpicks!" he shouted back.

Samuel and I shared a laugh and, for a brief moment, my worries came to a halt.

Outside the schoolhouse, Charlene sat with Loretta, Wade's sister, on the splintered picnic table. I didn't blame Charlene for turning her back on me. I had thought only of myself at the carnival, and nothing about anyone else.

The school bell clanged and emptied the schoolyard of students. But not the straggler who appeared from around the corner.

"Well now," said Wade, a smirk on his face. "If it ain't the big tease with her new squeeze."

....

CHAPTER 12

FRANK

Same as the morning before, Frank rose early and waited for Irene to get out of bed. Apparently, greeting a new day wasn't on her to-do list.

"Ma, you should at least get up," he said. "Sit outside and get some sunshine."

"Hurts my eyes." She peeled her arm away from her face. "Did you get my aspirin?"

"Yeah. Tried to give it to you last night, but you pushed me away." Frank pulled the bottle from his pocket and tossed it on the mattress. "I'll get you some water."

"No need. I'm used to swallowing them dry. Did you learn anything yesterday?"

"I learned how backward this town is. No music halls, no speakeasies. Where'd you meet Bernice Crawford anyway? In a pothole?"

Irene ignored the wisecrack and got dreamy-eyed. "At the little boutique in town. Grace's Lace. Cute little place, although not much to choose from. I was looking through the blouses when the door opened. Bernice walked in with her daughter, arm in arm, both giggling. I remember looking at her beautiful burgundy hair, how it was pinned in a chignon as if she'd had it professionally done."

"Bernice or her daughter?"

"Bernice. Emma June wears her hair in a cute bob parted on the side."

Yeah. He remembered.

"Anyway, Bernice caught my eye and stared at my dress, the one I'd bought in New York. I prepared myself for the *tsk-tsk* for it being a bit short and low-cut for Holly Gap. Instead, she winked and said, 'absolutely darling.' After that, I let out my first relaxing Holly Gap breath."

Frank rolled his eyes, but his mother continued.

"Then she went straight to the counter to pick up an order. I was searching through a bin of hair accessories when a frumpy old bitch walked in. Took one look at me and shook her head. Pursed her lips like a duck. Then the bug-eyed biddy told me I looked sinful. Believe it or not, I wasn't the one who called her out. Bernice turned to her and said, 'Why Edith Johnson. I think you would look absolutely marvelous in her dress. Just imagine how you, too, could turn heads.'" Irene laughed at the memory.

"After that," she continued, "we went to Rosie's for Coca-Colas and chatted for two hours. Mostly we giggled like schoolgirls. It was the best time I'd had in a long while."

"That bitchy woman. Mrs. Johnson. Does her husband own Johnson's Variety?"

After Irene nodded, Frank told her how he'd gone there looking for aspirin. "I didn't meet her, though. Just the husband."

"What about Charlene? Did you meet her?"

"Who?"

"Charlene Johnson. Their daughter. She's Emma June's best friend."

"Nah. Didn't see her. But—"

"Charlene's nothing like her mother, thank God. You might like her. She's a chatty thing but fun."

Having a girl hadn't been at the top of Frank's to-do list. He had broken up with the last one a month before and needed a break from the pressure. But then Irene had shown up at his door. Now, compared to being his mother's errand boy, girlfriend drama seemed as easy as a stroll down Bourbon Street during Mardi Gras.

"I saw Bernice's daughter, though," he said. "Pretty brown hair and hazel eyes."

Irene bolted upright. "You saw Emma June? Why didn't you tell me?"

"Didn't talk to her. First, I happened by her at Johnson's. She was with some guy who smelled like college. You know, nice clothes, clean around the edges. Blond hair."

"Doesn't sound familiar."

"I saw her again at Rosie's. Heard her talking to the joint's owner."

Irene smiled. "Miss Atta. A strong, brave woman."

"Kind, too." Frank had watched the scene unfold. The girl had looked so vulnerable, so broken down. But the owner embraced Emma June and tried to patch her up with consoling words.

"So was Emma June all right?"

"I didn't want to tell you. I know how you care about her. But she was upset."

"What do you mean by upset?"

"Her mother hasn't been home since carnival night."

"What?" Irene gasped. "Where is she?"

Frank shrugged. "Apparently, Bernice dropped Emma June off at home that night, then left again. Hasn't come home yet."

"And you're just now telling me this?" Her eyes turned as hard and flinty as her tone.

"Some people blouse when they get mad, Ma." *Or when they have an itch for the big life*, Frank thought. "I didn't think it was such a big deal."

"Well, it is. It's a huge deal. You don't know Bernice Crawford like I do." Irene clutched the bedsheet, her eyes collecting moisture.

"Maybe she just needs time."

Irene shook her head. "No, no, no. Something's wrong. Bernice would never leave her family. Ever."

"Well, she did. Miss Atta told Emma June her mother would return any moment and for her to be patient. Maybe you should try the same."

"You don't understand. You couldn't possibly understand."

She was right. How could he possibly understand two dames he barely knew?

"No one knows who you are. But I'm stuck here, Frank. You're not."

Yeah, he thought. *If only that were true.* "What are you thinking, Ma?"

"Try to get a job at Rosie's. Miss Atta has a soft spot for the younger folks. Most of them around here either work their parents' farms or are too lazy to do anything."

He had to admit it wasn't a bad idea. The place was a hub for gossip. He'd enjoy the vibes of the joint, the comfortable feel of the place, while making enough dough to buy a train ticket back to New Orleans. Best of all, he'd get out from under Irene's thumb and the strings that went with it.

"But whatever you do," she said, "don't tell Emma June you know me."

Don't worry, Frank thought. That wouldn't be a problem.

CHAPTER 13

EMMA JUNE

A t the schoolhouse, with Wade smirking at me, I felt his foul grip on my breast all over again. "Go chase yourself," I said. "You don't even know my name."

Wade continued his saunter toward us. Samuel stood firm with a finger point. "Who's this?"

"None'a your business. Who the hell are you?"

"Ignore him, Samuel. Let's breeze." I pulled him away.

"You know that gal you're with?" Wade snarled. "Don't even know how to attend a pettin' party."

I wanted to slap him. But Samuel, about the same height as Wade, was doing a fine job staring him down. "Sounds like she has good taste then. Go home, pal."

Wade shoved Samuel's shoulder. "Who you think you're talking to?"

I expected Samuel to throw a punch. Instead, his jaw muscles clenched and his blue eyes narrowed at Wade.

"No one," he said, his eyes unflinching as he stared at Wade. "I'm talking to *absolutely* no one. Emma June, ready to go?"

"I'll be watching you, yellow-bellied frat boy," Wade hissed and walked away.

I shook off the slimy feeling and shouldered Samuel's arm. "Sorry about that."

"About what? You deserve much, much better."

The way Samuel said it, his eyes locked on mine, I almost believed him.

"Emma June, I'll go with you to visit the sheriff. If you'd like, that is. If you need some . . . reassuring."

Reassurance had always been Mama's job. Without the squeeze of her hand or her encouraging guidance, I felt my confidence, my backbone, slipping.

"I need to help Miss Atta with the breakfast crowd. Meet me there at ten?"

Rosie's served breakfast and lunch daily and supper on Friday nights. On Saturday nights, music was the only thing on the menu.

Wherever a customer sat, whether at the counter, a booth, or a table, we waited on everyone regardless of skin color or what they did for a living—standard protocol insisted upon by the owner, a woman who wasn't allowed to vote.

Miss Atta had made a name for herself. Not only did she have a fine establishment, customers remembered her fun-loving Tony. Although many couldn't see past her dark skin and wouldn't be caught dead in her restaurant, plenty more were like me and thought she hung the moon with a golden ladder.

I ignored the seated customers, did a quick wave toward Miss Atta, and hurried to the storage room to grab my apron.

"Tell me she's home, honey," Miss Atta said, startling me with her quick appearance in the doorway.

I shook my head. She wrapped me in her arms.

When I first met Miss Atta, my head barely came up to her waist. Before she owned Rosie's and doubled as a fry cook and janitor, I knew how hard she worked by looking up at the sweat-soaked red bandana wrapped around her head. Now she worked just as hard, but I was several inches taller, and her red bandana was long gone. Twice a month, she greased and pressed her hair into a bob that covered her ears in soft tufts of black hair. But the look of kindness in her eyes never changed.

"You don't have to be here, shortcake." *Shortcake.* The name she began calling me when I was six.

"I need to be here. At least get you covered for breakfast. Then I thought—"

"Then you take the rest of the day off. More if you need it. You got more important things on your plate right now and those things ain't bacon and eggs."

I returned to the dining area. Mayor Bo Gibbons, Sheriff Gunny's brother, sat at his regular table up front where he could greet his constituents as soon as they entered. Although round like his brother, the mayor was shorter, fuller in the face, and a couple of years younger. His Panama hat, which usually covered his few strands of remaining hair, sat next to the ashtray holding his gnawed cigar.

"Morning, Mr. Mayor. Have you ordered yet?"

He pulled the newspaper down from his face. "Why, morning, Miss Emma June. How's life treating you on this fine day?" Clearly his brother hadn't told him about Mama.

"Peachy. You?"

"Can't complain. Unless you've run out of biscuits and gravy."

"Two orders as usual then?"

"Now we're talking. And a buttermilk flapjack with plenty'a syrup. Only one, though. Trying to watch my figure." He guffawed, patting his belly. "Oh, and a coffee refill."

I turned away to take another order when he said, "Say, Emma June. You talk to Miss Helen today?"

"Briefly. Why?"

"I got a big to-do coming up. Just wondering if she's revving up her machine like she said."

I pictured the distillery hidden in Miss Helen's moonshine thicket. "Steaming and burping as usual, Mr. Mayor. Any louder and your brother would get a disturbance call."

His chuckle behind me, I headed toward the kitchen and spotted the short, barrel-chested man sitting on a counter stool. Two Foleys in one morning was like a bad hangover. Not to mention that Earl Foley coming to Rosie's meant he came for nefarious business. The Diner, cheaper and closer to his house, was more to his liking.

"Hey girl," Earl Foley said, his bushy eyebrows raised. "Can't I get a refill on this coffee, or'um I invisible?"

I wished the answer was yes, that I couldn't see the town thug taking up space at one of my tables. I gave him a quick nod.

Normally, during breakfast hours, Miss Atta stayed at the counter. She wasn't there.

In the kitchen, Rags Gunnison, our fry cook, flipped eggs while whistling an unfamiliar tune—his way of relaxing while hovering over a hot griddle. Miss Atta sat slumped in the corner.

"Miss Atta, what's wrong?"

"I'm fine. Just . . . Earl Foley. Every time I see him, my heart beats a little too fast. He's got the devil in his eyes, and they sting like scorpions."

"Yeah, and the apple doesn't fall far from the tree."

When I returned to the dining room, Earl Foley had joined Mayor Gibbons at his table. To our ambitious mayor, votes from scoundrels were as good as any.

....

After my shift, Samuel and I stood beside the sheriff's office window, its pane etched with a lone star inside the shape of Texas. "Ready?" he said, his smile unassuming.

Even if the sheriff had a bell attached to his door, he wouldn't have heard our entry. Percy Yates, Betty's prince of a boss, slept in one of the two cells inhaling nails. Gunny sat at his desk staring at papers, his chin resting on a supporting palm. I cleared my throat.

Gunny looked up. "Emma June?"

I sat in the chair across from his desk and introduced Samuel, who remained standing.

"No word on Mama?"

"I was about to ask you the same thing." No doubt he hoped Mama had returned so he could cross another burden off his to-do list.

I told him about Betty going with us to the carnival, my limited details on her argument with Mama, and about going into Betty's room and finding the note. "Betty left town the morning after the carnival."

"Betty Bedford." Gunny glanced upward and squinted. "You talking 'bout that citified woman all the fellas gawk at? The high-falutin dresser from New York City that I seen your mama with on occasion?"

"That's right." Mama had told me that when Betty's husband died, he left her enough cash to live the good life in New York. She might have had nice clothes, but she owned a jalopy and lived in a paltry room.

"Maybe your mama and her are together. Met up somewhere."

The thought had already occurred to me. I dismissed it. Mama would never have left without telling us.

"You got the note?" Gunny said.

"Yes, sir." Samuel reached in his sports coat pocket and handed it over.

Gunny slipped on his cheaters and peered down at the words I knew by heart. *Last chance. Bring the dough tomorrow or cat's outta the bag.*

"Well," he said, crimping his mouth to one side. "Sounds like she knows something and is being blackmailed to keep it."

"Impressive deduction," Samuel muttered under his breath.

I told him Betty didn't have money to spare.

"Percy!" Gunny hollered toward the cell. "Wake up!"

"Ain't done sleeping," Yates mumbled.

Gunny rolled his eyes. "Emma June, you think your mama knew 'bout this note?"

"Not unless Betty told her on carnival night."

Gunny, still sitting, rolled his chair closer to the cell. "Percy, I don't give a rat's ass about your hangover. Wake up."

Yates hoisted himself to a sitting position and squinted toward us. "Huh?"

"You know anything about your waitress being blackmailed?"

"Mabel? You crazy?"

"No, jackass, the young one. Betty."

"I ain't no blackmailer, Sheriff."

"Not what I asked. I asked if you knew anything. If this Betty gal ever gave you an indication she was being threatened. That something was amiss?"

"Amiss? Amiss is her taking off and leaving me shorthanded. Only fluster I saw her wearing was when her sister died. Took time off a couple'a weeks ago for the funeral."

So Betty had lied about meeting up with her ex-beau. I turned to Samuel, grateful for the sympathetic look in his eyes. "She never told us she had a sister."

"Emma June," Gunny said, "just how well did you know your mama's friend?"

Obviously, not well at all.

CHAPTER 14

....

EMMA JUNE

lthough I felt better telling the sheriff what we knew, the meeting was less than productive. We left his office after he said, "Let's wait for her to come home. But if it makes you feel any better, I can telephone New York City police, see if they got a file on Betty Bedford. Maybe she got involved in some shenanigans up there."

Instead of searching for truth, our sheriff tossed ideas in the air. And he had no problem waiting a long time for them to land.

Samuel pointed to the bench outside the sheriff's office. "Mind if we sit for a minute?"

I sat beside him but felt like the wood beneath me, worn and splintered.

"I'm afraid I wasn't much help," he said. "I don't like feeling useless."

He rested his elbows on his knees and stared at the ground. "I lost my father when I was fourteen. He died suddenly. A heart attack."

"I'm sorry."

"I remember walking around in a daze, part of me looking for him around every corner expecting him to show up. Like it had all been a bad joke."

I told myself that unlike Samuel, at least I had hope. I knew Mama wasn't dead, that she'd come home, and things would return to normal.

"Anyway, we lived in Austin back then. That's when I started spending more time alone. Walked a lot, sat by the Colorado River, chucked rocks. Anything to keep moving away from the thought of him being dead." He stopped and turned to me. "Your mother will come home, Emma June. I saw how much she cared for you, the look of fear in her eyes when I carried you to her. So relieved you were only drunk."

Only drunk, right. Too zozzled to be any good to anyone.

I appreciated Samuel's kindness, his desire to be helpful. Stupid or not, I wanted to return the favor. "Miss Atta told me not to come back to work today. So, I was thinking. You know that spot on the Brazos I told you about? The place by my house? I can grab Choppers and we could chuck a few rocks."

"Sounds good." He gave me a slight smile and the kind of wink that said *it's going to be okay.*

And for the first time, I thought it was true.

We returned to the Munsons' house where Miss Helen pressed me on the news. "Nothing," I told her as I stared toward my house. No breezer. Ol' Bess still gone.

A loud finger whistle and the one truth I could count on barreled toward me on three paws.

"Let's go to the river, Chops." After nuzzling my face into his fur, I led the way to the river.

"Impressive." Samuel laughed.

"What?"

"Your whistle. I don't know many girls who can do that. Shoot, *I* can't do that."

"You can't whistle?"

"Not like that." His grin lit up his blue eyes.

"Curl your tongue back with your thumb and middle finger, then blow." Feeling cheeky, I pranced my way down the steep path, then tripped over a bulging tree root. I fell smack dab on my vain butt. "I'm fine, I'm fine," I said, hiding my blush. I shook my head at his attempt to help me up. "And just think, I used to be a tomboy."

"You?" He chuckled. "Not sure I can picture that."

"Yep. A pea-shooting tree climber. Gave it up for reading."

My room was cluttered with a potpourri of books. Even the ones from my youth couldn't make it to the trash bin.

We wove our way down the cliffside through the greenbrier shrubs and Texas thistle, then settled on a gravel bar at the river's edge.

The gentle flow of dark green water curved around the bends and out of sight in both directions. *Rio de los Brazos de Dios*, the "River of the Arms of God." I wondered which direction Mama had gone and, if Daddy's prayers worked, if His arms would carry her home.

"It is a nice view, Emma June. The bluffs, trees, outcroppings of rocks. Plenty of water."

I stared across the wide river. "It varies, though. I've seen it both flooded and so low you could almost walk across it without getting wet."

Mama told me once that seeing the Brazos during a drought made her feel like the world was seeping through the cracks, but seeing it flow gave her hope.

"So you're a reader," he said. "What books do you like?"

"Everything. Books that get me thinking. Like the one I just finished, *The Bridge of San Luis Rey*. Have you read it?"

"Afraid I haven't."

"It makes us question how much of our lives are driven by free will, happenstance, or divine intervention."

"Ah, philosophy. Then I must read it," he said without sarcasm or disinterest.

"You like to read?" The boys I knew would rather use the pages of a book to build a fire or practice rolling tobacco.

"Of course. These days, though, I'm stuck with reading mostly textbooks."

"You like it? Going to college, I mean."

"I like learning. But I'll like it more when I graduate and become a doctor. Maybe someday I can prevent a father from dying too young. I really miss him."

His words carried a heavy sorrow. Like Mama and I, Samuel had been close to his father.

"What do you want to do, Emma June? After you find your mother, that is. Do you want to go to college?"

My future had been an imaginary framed photograph of me with a husband and two children. Yet women had started doing so much more than raising a family. But what could I do? I couldn't sing or dance like Josephine Baker. I couldn't paint like Georgia O'Keeffe. I never wanted to work in a factory or waitress a Miss Mabel-lifetime.

I'd once thought of becoming a teacher. Unlike Miss Primrose, I would encourage students for their efforts instead of pointing out their failures.

"Mama wants me to go to college," I said. "But I don't know what I'd study."

"Literature for starters. You'd have tons of books to devour."

Daddy was the one who instilled in me the love of reading. Although he mainly read true stories instead of novels, he said learning about all sides of the world gave you perspective and made you wise.

Mama preferred telling stories over the written word. She brought her stories to life; her words were as vivid as the pictures in *The Velveteen Rabbit*. You knew when she reached the end because the good guys always won.

"What are you reading now?" he asked.

"Right now, Anita Loos. *Gentlemen Prefer Blondes*. But I'm looking forward to my next book . . ." I let my words fall off an invisible cliff. How could I talk about books, about a future I couldn't count on without Mama?

Samuel put a hand on my shoulder. I didn't want to move, to give him the impression it made me uncomfortable. "What is it?" he said.

"Everything."

His hand moved to my far shoulder and gave it a one-armed squeeze.

He had a pleasant scent about him, strong, masculine, yet not dominating. Like the way his arm felt around me.

Squirrels scampered up trees. Choppers lapped river water. Birds called out to their family members. All familiar, yet different somehow.

I turned my head and found his blue eyes peering into mine. "How can a person be with someone almost every day for six months and not know them?"

"You mean Betty?"

I nodded. "We had so much fun together. Movies, picnics, swimming. She taught Mama and me all kinds of things about her life in the big world. I admired her, how she could take off on her own, be herself and not care what others thought."

I asked Betty once how she found her free spirit. She got dreamy-eyed and told me she'd caught that spirit like a good sneeze in the heart of Manhattan. It was the day she saw Zelda Fitzgerald swim in the Union Square Fountain.

"Go on," he said.

"Betty got us all excited about the possibilities being endless."

"I'm not sure there's anything wrong with that."

"No. But it was dishonest how she kept things from us. Where she lived, her money problems, the fact she had a sister she never told us about. And she never mentioned that threatening note."

"You think Betty told your mother those secrets on carnival night? Secrets that made your mother mad?"

"I'm sure of it." I just didn't know what they were.

Samuel picked up the stick Choppers dropped at his feet, then stood and chucked it into the water. Instead of sitting back down next to me, he stared across the river. I felt stupid for sharing so much and thought he'd become tired of consoling me.

"I'm sorry," I said. "I shouldn't have—"

"No, I was just thinking." He sat back down and, knee touching mine, he looked me in the eye. "You know how, when you work closely with someone, see them all the time, how you really get to know them?"

I nodded, thinking of Rags, Rosie's fry cook. I could tell when he had troubles by how he stopped whistling in the kitchen or stirred the chili with two hands instead of one. I thought I knew everything about Miss Atta until I started working for her. I learned her husband died before Toby learned to walk. That she held weekly lessons at her house to teach those interested how to read.

"Well," Samuel said, "I think you should go back and talk to Miss Mabel. Ask her the right questions, and maybe she'll tell you something more worth knowing."

Any idea was worth trying. "If Mama's not back tonight—"

"But I'm afraid I won't be able to go with you this time. I promised my uncle I'd do rounds with him tomorrow. Then I have to go back to school."

One blink of his company, then over and out. Samuel was leaving, and I had blabbed like I had known him for years.

"It's okay. I can go myself."

"How will you get there?" he said.

"What?"

"To The Diner. How will you get there?"

"Walk, get a ride from Miss Helen or her husband."

"I'm sorry. I wish—"

I turned away from him. "It doesn't matter. I mean, it's fine. I can manage. Right, Choppers?" I stood, brushed the dirt from my dress. It needed a good wash.

Samuel hopped up and grabbed my hand. "It's not true, you know."

"What?"

"Gentlemen preferring blondes." He touched the parted side of my hair and trailed his fingers down to the blunt ends. "I've never met someone quite like you, Emma June. Besides being kind and beautiful and smart, you're determined and courageous. You went to work even though you were worried sick about your mother."

"Miss Atta needed me—"

"That's what I mean about being kind. And how good you are to Scooter."

"I—"

"And the way you marched into the sheriff's office, the way you leaned forward in that chair to make him look at you. How you told him that if your mother wasn't back by tonight, you'd be back bright and early."

I didn't know how to respond to the compliments. I wasn't sure I deserved them.

He leaned down the four inches and gave me an eye-to-eye gaze. "I know I can't be a steady beau to you right now, but I'll be back before you know it. And I'd like to spend more time with you."

Is this what Mama had felt when she first met Daddy? A thrill and a calm all wrapped into one feeling?

"What about all those college girls?" I asked, feeling the heat in my cheeks.

"Truthfully, I'm not sure why some of them are there. Many seem more interested in their social lives than studying. Besides, they're not Emma June Crawford. If I write to you, will you write back?"

In a heartbeat. "I told you I could read. You're only assuming I can write."

He grinned, then planted a soft kiss on my cheek.

Samuel seemed to have all the right qualities. But one thing I'd learned since Mama left—people hid things.

....

CHAPTER 15

FRANK

First thing in the morning, Frank stood outside the door of Rosie's Café and waited for the sign to flip from closed to open. At seven on the dot, a tall, dark-skinned man opened the door.

"Morning, sir." Frank introduced himself.

"Rags Gunnison."

Frank stuck out his hand and got a firm but quick handshake.

"I don't have an appointment, but I'd appreciate a chat with Miss Atta."

"'Bout what?"

"Just blew into town and I'm strapped. I could use a job."

"We doing just fine here. Don't think—"

"Rags?" Miss Atta called. "Why you blocking the door? Let that fella in. Bet he could use some coffee."

While Gunnison headed for the kitchen, Miss Atta pointed to a counter stool. He sat and glanced over his shoulder. The joint had a good feel to it. A place where a fella could hang his hat and his troubles on the same hook and allow the ceiling fans to blow away the badness. Unlike The Diner where wooden tables were carved by brawlers wielding knives, he imagined Rosie's table scratches came from normal wear and tear, used by people enjoying a good meal over a civil conversation.

"You were in here yesterday," she said, her eyes brightening.

"Yes, ma'am. For coffee. I'm here for another reason today." Frank told her he needed a job. "Probably just for a month or two until I get settled further south." Back home to the real world of jazz and a city bursting with energy. "I'm a hard worker, ma'am. And," he said, spotting crates stacked by the back door, "I'm used to carrying heavy loads."

"I can tell." She grinned then looked up and tapped her fingers on the counter. "I don't have a job that would pay much."

Frank held his breath.

"Just a little grunge work, different things here and there."

"I'd be grateful, ma'am."

"Where you from, son?"

"New Orleans. I worked at the shipyards."

"Well, this here will be a change of pace." Miss Atta laughed. "We might not have the Mississippi, but we do have a river. Though the only thing we get from it is some fish and cooling off in hot weather. You seen it?"

"No, ma'am. Haven't had the chance yet."

"How 'bout you start tomorrow then? Take today to get the lay of the land."

He'd done it. He had landed the job. Now he wouldn't have to spend his days cooped up in a hovel. And he'd be working for a nice lady, instead of the tyrant shipyard boss he had in New Orleans.

Miss Atta reminded him of a darker-skinned version of his Aunt Patsy. Same kind eyes, easy nature, and a disposition that spilled integrity from bones to skin.

"Any places you suggest I check out?" he asked.

She looked up as if deep in thought, a state Frank believed she visited often.

"Younger folks like that big flat section on the Brazos for gathering. Just a stretch down the road behind Main Street you'll find the cliffs that lead down to the river. Keep your eye out for riffraff, though. Nice as this town can be, it's like all others. Has a dark side. And I ain't talking my side of town," she said, shaking her head.

He figured Moody and the Foley men sat on the top tier of that darkness.

Frank headed toward the river, following Miss Atta's directions. The closer he got, the thicker the scrubby trees and grasses. He followed the pathway down the cliff and spotted two guys sitting on the riverbank. Both looked disheveled, poor, and harmless.

"Morning," Frank said.

Both eyed him head to toe.

"I'm Frank. New to town. Thought I'd check out the river."

The skinny, pimple-faced boy nodded. "Louis," he said. "This here's Jeb."

Jeb wore a pair of overalls and a soft felt hat. A farm boy. "You ain't dressed fer the river in them clothes," he said, pointing to Frank's trousers and white shirt.

"Nah. Next time, though. Just scoping out the territory. Mind if I sit?"

After they shrugged, Frank settled on the pebbled ground. He pulled out his Lucky Strikes and held out the pack. Both Jeb and Louis accepted his offer and lit up.

"I've met a few folks," Frank said, breaking the silence. "Met Miss Atta and Rags at Rosie's."

"Good place. If you can afford it, that is," Louis said.

"I met a fella named Wade at The Diner."

Frank didn't miss the look Jeb and Louis shared at the mention of Wade Foley.

"Know him?" Frank asked.

"We know him all right," Louis said. "Don't see him much no more."

"Hell, you say," Jeb said. "Jest saw him at the carnival."

"That don't count. He got a free pass is all."

Sounded to Frank like Wade had been behind bars. "Free pass?"

Louis chucked a rock, then waited for the ripples to settle. "His pa and that new fella keep him busy, I reckon."

"What new fella?"

"Don't rightly know his name," Louis said. "Big guy. Works with Wade's pa. Chopping mesquite."

Moody.

"Must not be too good at their jobs." Jeb chuckled. "We got just as many mesquites now than before."

Deciding to play along, Frank laughed too. "Maybe the new hire plants more mesquites while they're not watching. You know, for job security."

Jeb squinted his confusion. Louis shook his head. Both boys seemed dumber than the rocks under their butts.

"Security sounds about right," Louis said. "Never woulda thought Earl Foley would need to pay fer muscle."

Even with Irene's blackmail money, Frank seriously doubted Earl Foley had the dough to hire anyone.

....

As the darkness settled, Frank ate a can of Van Camp's Pork and Beans, then sat on the mattress next to his mother.

"You can't keep on this way, Ma. You might not be able to go anywhere, but you have to get up. Move around. Go outside, for Christ's sake."

"I can't."

"Sure you can. One foot in front of the other. Come on. I'll help you."

She waved away his hand.

"Okay. Have it your way. But this place stinks. You haven't bathed since we got here. Barely eaten any food."

"I'm not hungry."

The woman was shriveling faster than a picked flower. "All you did was tell her whatever truth you were keeping from her. You can't help it Bernice took off."

"Earl or not, I never should have told her."

Curiosity finally got the best of him. "Told her what, Ma? What was this big secret?"

"That I knew her husband. Theo."

"So?"

"In my younger days, when I was barely a woman, I came to Holly Gap to visit my cousins."

"We have family here?"

Irene shook her head. "Not anymore. They moved. Anyway, we were at the Brazos Dance Hall when a drunk Earl Foley came up and started pawing me. I kept pushing him away, but he wouldn't listen. I was scared shitless. Especially after what happened. You know. When I was thirteen."

The rape. "Go on."

"I screamed and Theo came to my rescue. He punched Earl in the face and told him to scram. After that, Theo and I saw each other every day for two weeks. I was quite smitten at the time, and," she added, "Earl knew it."

Her cat was out of the bag, first to Bernice, now to him. Dame problems, not his. He stood and picked his jacket up off the floor.

"But I was a different person back then," she continued. "A young girl named Irene who wore long hair ringlets and no cosmetics. Who would recognize me now?"

"But Earl did. After all this time."

"Yeah. Me, the girl he wanted until Theo intervened."

"Must have hurt the goon's pride."

"Who cares? He's scum."

"Obviously. He made you pay to keep the secret from your best friend."

"She *is* my best friend, Frank. As least, she was. When I first met her, it never occurred to me she could be Theo's wife. The Theo I knew was much too . . . too old-fashioned to be married to such a freethinker. But I liked her so much I didn't admit to knowing him. I thought I'd let things unfold naturally. In the meantime, I'd just enjoy her friendship. But one day when in town, Emma June nudged me and pointed several storefronts down. She wanted me to meet her Daddy. I recognized Theo right away and feared he'd recognize me too. I dodged into Johnson's Variety."

Irene kept talking about how, after that, she managed to avoid Theo by contriving things for Bernice and her to do away from the town's center.

"All those times Bernice talked about Theo, I said nothing. I was afraid she'd misinterpret things. Afraid she wouldn't understand."

"Her husband never mentioned he knew you. That's not your problem." He stared at his reflection in Irene's small mirror mounted on the wall. The stubble on his chin itched.

"He doesn't know, Frank. Theo doesn't know Irene came back to town. To him, I'm some citified woman he hasn't met named Betty Bedford who befriended his wife."

"I still don't understand why you didn't tell her right away," he said, turning back toward her. "What would it have mattered?"

"I couldn't just blurt out, 'Oh, by the way, I knew your husband a long time ago. What? Did I forget to tell you?' I worried she'd see the truth as a betrayal, like I was covering up something. I didn't want to risk losing her."

Yet Irene didn't care about losing him. She had given him up long ago.

"We have to find her, Frank."

No doubt *we* meant *him*.

Frank grabbed his flat cap off the chair. "Guess you'll have to come up with something. I'm going out."

"Frank, wait," she said, reaching toward him.

He, for one, would never spend his days curled under a worn sheet of helplessness and secrets. He'd jump off a cliff first. "Gotta go," he said, and headed for the diner.

He didn't like to admit it, but Irene getting mixed up with the wrong guy *had* become his problem.

Fifty yards from the hash house, his eyes narrowed in at the shadows by the road.

"Hey, New Or-*leans*."

"That you, Wade?" Frank continued forward until he saw the scoundrel's eyes.

"Got somethin' for us to do."

Beneath the moonlight, the second shadow shifted like a lion ready to pounce.

Moody.

....

CHAPTER 16

EMMA JUNE

I flung Agatha Christie's *The Murder of Roger Ackroyd* to the floor. Not only did the book have more characters than Holly Gap had citizens, but the story revolved around a woman being black-mailed. The plot hit too close to home.

Over a week had passed without a word from Mama. Despair hit deeper in the evenings. The feeling of hopelessness, betrayal, how things could have been if only I hadn't been so stupid. The self-pity. I wondered if Daddy would become used to turning over in the middle of the night and finding the other side of the bed cold and empty.

I had yet to visit Miss Mabel at The Diner. Or, for that matter, gone to work or walked Scooter to school. With Mama missing and Samuel back at college, I spent most of my time on my bed of pins and needles while listening for her breezer.

I waited for Charlene to show up, to offer up brief words of sympathy, then commence with her nonsensical chitchat to take my mind off things. But she never came, which I thought unusual since the gossip mill had surely revved up. Everyone in town must have heard about Mama.

Daddy spent his time at work, visiting the sheriff, and driving around in hopes of finding his wife sitting on the hood of her breezer waiting for him. At home, he slumped and paced, and when his eyes watered, he hid under the hood of Ol' Bess in the pretense of repairing something he couldn't fix.

They had met at a church picnic. According to Daddy, he was eyeing Mama from afar when he spotted a man stagger toward her. Mama scowled when the man touched her elbow. She jerked away and slapped him across the face. When the man thrust an open palm toward her, Daddy chucked his lemonade and ran toward them. He shoved the man with enough force to knock him down. Daddy turned his back to check on the "beautiful lady with hair the color of God's wine," then felt the man's tug on his shoulder. Daddy turned to face the brute and, before the man could say anything, Daddy punched him in the nose.

Mama had a somewhat different version. She said she slapped the man because he made a crass comment about her bubs. But he wasn't going to hit her, she said. He was raising his hand, grinning, and calling over one of his buddies to meet her. And Daddy didn't just punch him in the nose. He hit it hard enough to make it pop and spew blood. "And," she said, laughing as she recounted the story, "your daddy's so-called lemonade on his shirt sure did smell like spilled beer." Either version had the same result. Daddy defended Mama.

I didn't move to pick up the hurled book. Instead, I stared out the window. Laundry hung haphazardly on the clothesline—Daddy's attempt at household chores. I could almost see Mama standing there, laughing as she reclipped the clothes to perfection. Her dress swaying in the May breeze. Fingers pushing stray strands of hair from her eyes while calling through the open window, "Turn up the volume on the phonograph, will you, doll baby?"

We did that many times together. Danced outside with the windows open to let the music out and our joy in. A joy so pure that even when our feet had stilled, our spirits continued doing the Charleston.

"*Emmy! Emmy!*"

Choppers barked, then whined. He knew the voice as well as I did.

I sat on the top step of the front porch, too tired to run and greet Scooter as usual. Miss Helen trailed behind him.

Scooter sat next to me and nuzzled under my arm like a baby bird under a broken wing.

"Sakes alive, Emma June Crawford," said Miss Helen. "You look like you've been sleeping under a porch."

"The spiders keep me company."

"Bless your heart, honey." She tsked. "Scoot over Scooter, give me some room."

"Scoot over *Scoot*er." He laughed as he hopped up, then chased Choppers around the yard.

Miss Helen patted my knee. "For supper, I'm making you a big dish of Munson's goulash," she said, referring proudly to her home-made recipe.

"Great. I'll just pretend the next five meals don't contain ketchup and noodles." The meals she'd already cooked for us still sat half-eaten in the icebox.

She ignored my snippety comment. "Scoot and I are going to town. You're coming with us."

"I don't—"

"I know you're down in the mouth with everything so cattywam-pus and all. But sitting at home all day in your pajamas won't do a thing to help. I hear that Mrs. Levine has stocked Grace's Lace with new dresses. Handmade to perfection, as usual. We don't wanna miss out on that, do we? Plus, I'm having a brief word with Mayor

Bo-peep about my next supply. Maybe we can stick a burr up his butt and get him to prod his brother to search harder for your mama. Our sheriff's about as good as an eyeless needle."

The thought of doing something, anything that might help, got me standing.

"And for Pete's sake," she added, "throw a cloche hat over that dirty hair."

During the five-minute drive to town, Miss Helen drove in her usual Roadrunner attire—red satin tam pulled down to her eyebrows, floral scarf around her neck. Her buxom bosoms leaned into the steering wheel while her elbows stuck out like chicken wings. And although unnecessary in a roofed motorcar, she wore thick goggles like the pilots from the Great War.

After she parked on Main Street, Scooter ran to the front of Johnson's Variety and stared in the window. "Yo-yo's *calling* for Scooter!" he hollered and clapped.

A dowdy woman, walking toward us holding the hand of a young girl, stopped. "Look away, Trudy," she said loud enough for us to hear. "That boy's an imbecile."

She must have been a visitor in town—though why someone would want to visit Holly Gap was anyone's guess. Townsfolk knew that insults directed at Miss Helen's son meant a slap to the face. Which is precisely what she got.

The woman held a hand to her cheek. "How dare you!"

"I dare just fine," Miss Helen said, smoothing her dress. "If you come near my boy again, you better whistle first."

Scooter paid no attention to the scuttle. He continued tapping on the window showcasing the yo-yo.

"I'm telling the sheriff!" the woman screamed, the child behind her staring wild-eyed.

"You do that," Miss Helen said, tapping each word into the

woman's chest. "And while you're at it, tell Sheriff Gunny Gibbons he left his Stetson on my kitchen table."

The woman huffed off.

If it wasn't for Miss Helen's moonshining abilities, I doubted she'd be quite so popular.

Miss Helen fluffed the back of her wavy hair. "First, a yo-yo for Scooter."

Charlene wouldn't be working during school hours, so I didn't bother going inside Johnson's Variety. I glanced down the street at Rosie's. The top portion of the glass window that once read ROSIE'S CAFÉ—THE BEST DINER IN TEXAS was covered by a piece of plywood.

I yelled to Miss Helen, telling her where I was headed.

Thank God, everything on the inside appeared the same. Including Gunny, who sat on his usual stool at the counter talking to Miss Atta. If the world was different, those two would have been married years ago.

"What happened to the window?" I asked.

Gunny nodded at my presence, and Miss Atta broke out a wide grin. "Hi, shortcake. I sure have missed your smiling face."

"I'll be back tomorrow," I told her, already dreading the thought of forcing happy when none existed. "So what happened?"

"Hoodlums, we 'spect," Gunny said. "Threw rocks through the window 'bout a week ago now."

The town had yet to reach its quota of stupid. "I'm sorry, Miss Atta. I'll keep my ears open. If I hear anything, I'll let you know."

"Miss Atta?" A young man appeared from the kitchen. The same new fella I'd seen at Johnson's Variety the morning after Mama disappeared.

"Frank," Miss Atta said, "meet our best waitress and right-hand gal. Emma June, this here is Frank Sanders. He just moved to town and needed a job."

"Pleasure," Frank said through a one-sided grin.

Since when did we need more help? Between me, Miss Atta, Rags, and on occasion Rags's cousin, Jacoby, we did just fine. But I had sulked too long under my covers and had left Miss Atta shorthanded.

I shook the hand he offered and added a quick and pissy, "You, too."

Frank turned away. "Miss Atta, Rags needs more ketchup. Where—"

"I'll show him." Miss Atta didn't need bothering with his trivial questions.

Frank followed me to the storage room. "Pretty nice nosebaggery you've got here."

"What?"

"This restaurant. And I hear you have a jazzy blues band on Saturday nights."

"If you consider Stinger Jones and Whiskey Malone a whole band, then yeah."

"Names like that, it's gotta be good. The most fun I've had since I've been here is throwing rocks at snakes."

I pointed to the high shelf. Frank reached up, the form of his muscular back showing through his white shirt.

He grabbed a bottle of Heinz. "Now, I've met the ketchup."

His smile, the way it crinkled the outer corners of his deep green eyes, added more sheik to his appearance. And he knew it.

Like Samuel, he stood about four inches taller than my five-six. Unlike Samuel, he had a mischievous look about him.

"Rocks, huh?" I asked. "You have something to do with Miss Atta's windows?"

His smile faded. "Girl, you're off your trolley." He headed back to the kitchen mumbling, "They were assholes."

I pushed open the back door and stood in the sunlight. Had Daddy seen me light up, he would have yapped on about my unladylike behavior. But I needed that sweet inhale to calm my nerves.

I kicked a cardboard box aside and leaned against the old brick building thinking of the new boy. If he wasn't a bad egg, he knew the hoodlums who were. For Miss Atta's sake, I planned to find out who had broken her window. First, I had to question the sheriff about Mama.

Back inside, Miss Helen had taken over Gunny's stool and sat jabbering to Miss Atta.

"Where's Gunny?" I asked. "And Scooter? Where's Scooter?"

"Calm your horses, Emma June," Miss Helen said. "Scooter's outside with the new boy, Frank. Miss Atta says he's a mighty fine worker."

"You left Scooter outside with *him*?"

"Give the young man a chance, Emma June," Miss Atta said. "You might just take a liking to him."

Miss Helen grinned. "A good liking. That boy's a real looker."

Never mind that Samuel had just left. Miss Helen was already trying to play matchmaker. Frank didn't hold a candle to Samuel.

I hustled to the front and peered out the bottom of the window, the unbroken part. Frank held a cigarette in one hand and blew a harmonica with the other. Scooter clapped, but not to the song's rhythm. He applauded as if he'd just witnessed Babe Ruth hit a home run.

Frank pulled the harp from his lips. "So, Scooter. That song's called 'Has Anybody Seen My Girl?' You ever heard it before?"

"Miss *Bernice*. Plays it on Victor *Victrola*."

"Well then, I'd say your Miss Bernice has good taste."

"She's *gone* now. Don't *know* where she is. Maybe you can *find* her. *Blow* her back home."

Frank cleared his throat and wiped the spit off his harp. "How about you take a blow on my harmonica. Practice, and maybe you can play her something when she gets back."

Scooter, saucer-eyed, took the harmonica and held it like a bird's egg.

"Go ahead, put it up to your lips and blow."

"Well, I'll swan," Miss Helen said, startling me with a hand on my shoulder. "Looks like my Scooter has a new friend."

Scooter blew into the harmonica, the sound of one note lighting up his eyes.

If Frank hurt Scooter in any way, shape, or form, he'd pay a steep price. That is, after I was done with him.

CHAPTER 17

FRANK

A s soon as he'd shown Scooter his blues harp, the kid's smile lit up like a night at Mardi Gras. And for a moment, Frank didn't think Holly Gap was such a bad place. Scooter, who appeared slow in mind at first, proffered a contagious enthusiasm like a gift. A happy outlook easy as a single note.

Most people built walls around themselves for protection. Not Scooter. He let others see his true self without fearing the consequences. Trusted, even.

Frank was first to admit he hid behind the wall he'd built around himself. Emotions and vulnerable spots were best tucked under a thick skin. Probably the reason he was in awe of Scooter doing just the opposite.

"Sounding good there, Scooter," he said.

Scooter stopped blowing long enough to grin, then stuck the harp back to his lips.

It seemed like Emma June built her own walls fairly tall—yet not so high as to hide her vulnerability from Miss Atta that day she sobbed in her arms. And by the way Emma June reacted to him, she wasn't too keen on him being hired. Maybe she had good instincts.

Keeping her in the dark about his mother didn't feel right. Neither did keeping mum about the café's broken window. He'd tell Emma June, but not yet. Building trust was a sticky wicket.

Scooter still beside him, Frank felt the peering eyes from inside Rosie's. He leaned back against the lamppost and cringed thinking of the night when rocks smashed through Miss Atta's window. It hadn't been his proudest moment. Especially since Miss Atta had kindly given him a job earlier that day. He didn't break the window, but he didn't stop it either.

Wade had been in his usual mischievous state. He had coaxed Frank to follow him and Moody into town. Not that Frank needed coaxing. What he needed was information about Wade's father and how Moody played a part in the Foleys' doings. So Frank had gone along for the ride.

The town closed down for the night, he had sat with Wade and Moody on the curb across from Rosie's drinking rotgut. While Wade fidgeted and rattled on about the Dumb Doras in town and how his pecker needed attention, the muscled ox sat quiet as a church mouse.

Wade had pointed to Rosie's. "Woman who owns that place, she's a colored."

"Yeah?" Frank said, wondering his point.

"Ever hear of such a thing? Them owning a business?"

Frank managed a "huh." He didn't mention he knew several such businesses in New Orleans. Or that his favorite people played their instruments with dark hands that lit up an entire club.

Moody spat off to the side. "Out of sight, out of mind," he said, breaking his silence.

"Not accordin' to our sheriff," Wade said with a snort. "You seen how he looks at that hashslinger?"

Wade insulting Miss Atta burrowed deep in Frank's craw. One day, he'd pound that punk's ass deep into a mesquite hole.

Wade left the curb and returned with rocks the size of his fists. He stood in the middle of the street and called Frank over. "First things first. Let's see who can throw the furthest. Straight line down Main Street."

Frank beat him in distance and accuracy.

"Well, guess you won," Wade said. He ran off to retrieve the thrown rocks. When he returned, he thrust one in Frank's palm. "Now you get to chuck this through that winder." He pointed to Rosie's.

Frank wanted, needed to be, in their circle. And not just because Irene wanted him to play sleuth. Earl, it seemed, was from the same kettle as Frank's old boss at the dock. The drunkard absconded with not only Frank's wages but also the earnings of fifteen other hard-working boys. They never caught him, never got to make him pay.

How could anyone get away with blackmailing Irene Sanders, anyway? According to Aunt Patsy, his mother once hit her landlord with a fist after he tried double-charging her in rent. The landlord's wife laughed at the gutsy move and discounted her a dollar.

"You hear what I said, boy?" Wade spat. "Break that colored's winder."

Frank made a fist but remained smart enough not to use it. He'd never damage the property of a woman he already respected. He exhaled just enough agitation to appear calm. "Nah. Remember, I just got thrown out of one town. Don't need another notch on that belt."

"Bet you'll do it for a quarter," said Moody. "Wade, give him one."

"A whole quarter?"

Moody gave him an evil squint. "That's what I said."

Wade hesitated, then pulled the coin from his pocket and handed it to Frank. "Better make it good."

Frank pocketed the quarter. "Easiest money I made in a long time."

Wade slapped his back. "Yeah, well, earn it. Throw the dang thing."

Frank wanted to elbow him in the nose. Instead, he stood, walked a good twenty feet away from Wade and Moody, and took aim. The rock hit just where he wanted, on the brick wall to the left of the café door. "Sorry, fellas. Aim's off. But thanks for the quarter." Frank backed away, ready to head home.

"Sonofabitch," Wade called. "Git back here."

Moody held on to Wade's arm and let out a deep chuckle.

Frank began his walk home listening to the sour notes of breaking glass.

But that was then. Now, while he sat outside Rosie's next to Scooter, he thought of Emma June. He knew what it felt like to look out the window and wonder when your mother would return. Maybe, as Scooter said, he could find a way to blow Bernice Crawford back to the family who missed her.

When Scooter's knee grazed his, Frank heard a different kind of music. The kind inhaled and exhaled by a kid who knew how to set the notes free. And he blew hard and loud enough that the passersby grimaced and kept going. Damn, he liked the kid.

....

CHAPTER 18

EMMA JUNE

Miss Helen said she had already grilled the sheriff—probably why he left Rosie's so quickly. It took no effort to leave the chipper Miss Helen and her harmonica player behind.

I expected to see Gunny but found the office empty. No jail-birds in the cells. No one to answer the ringing telephone. I hollered toward the back room, where Gunny lived, but heard no response.

I found no note informing the townsfolk of his whereabouts. On his desk sat a bottle of Dr. J. Collis Browne's Chlorodyne, the label claiming it could cure everything from diarrhea to gout. Next to that, a stack of papers.

The top paper was a crudely drawn map of directions to the old wedding pavilion on Route 90. Flipping through the papers, I stopped when I saw a photograph sent by Western Union. A brut-ish-looking man.

Homer "Buzz" Whitfield. 5/10, 190 lb., black hair, cleft chin, quarter-sized red port-wine birthmark on his right cheek. Scar on middle of forehead. Wanted for theft and racketeering. Last seen in Dallas.

Beneath the mugshot flyer, a notice offered a twenty-dollar reward for the finder of Mrs. Hutchings's missing dog.

It gave me an idea. If Gunny put out a missing person's flyer of Mama, the photograph of her standing next to the breezer, someone might recognize either her or the motorcar. I wrote a note to Gunny with a request to do so, then left.

Only four steps out the door, I heard a ruckus before I saw it. Miss Helen stood in the middle of the sidewalk quacking at Mayor Gibbons. I sat on the bed of a parked Runabout to enjoy the spectacle.

"There's no reason to get your dander up, *Mister* Mayor." Miss Helen thumped his chest. "You've got more money than you can shake a stick at. Just how many three-piece suits and Cuban cigars do you have anyhow? Hire someone to help me."

"And I don't understand why you can't tell Leonard to take Scooter to the rodeo another day."

"Because they planned it a month ago and I'm not taking that fun away from Scooter. It's not my fault Cliff can't pick up the order as usual."

"And it's not Cliff's fault his wife's about to pop out her first young'un at any moment."

"Then whose fault is it? The mailman's?"

The mayor removed his Panama and rubbed the top of his balding head. "Why can't *you* just bring the shine to the pavilion?"

"Like I told you, that's not my job. Besides, I need to get started on another batch."

Mayor Gibbons slapped his hat against his thick thigh. "Lord have mercy, Helen."

Mr. Baxter, owner of the hardware store, headed down the sidewalk toward them lugging a large toolbox. When he reached Mayor Gibbons, he gave him a nudge. "You need some reinforcements there, Mr. Mayor? Need me to call the sheriff fer ya?" He chuckled and kept going.

Mayor Gibbons sighed. Both he and Miss Helen stood silent. I waited for the next storm after the calm.

"There's gotta be someone in town that'll do it for cheap," Mayor Gibbons continued. "Someone with a motorcar, of course."

Miss Helen held up a finger. "Hold your horses." She stared down the street toward Rosie's.

Mayor Gibbons pulled the cigar from his mouth. "What? What are you thinking?"

"Miss Atta hired a new boy in town. He's strong, capable."

I hopped off the truck and faced Miss Helen. "You don't know anything about Frank. I wouldn't trust him any more than a coiled snake."

Miss Helen stared at me wide-eyed. "I know he's good with Scooter and that counts in my book. And Scooter's taken a big liking to him. Just look"—she pointed down the street—"They're still out front playing the harmonica."

The mayor turned and stared at the newcomer crouched down beside Scooter.

"Isn't he supposed to be working?" I asked.

Miss Helen ignored me and kept her eyes on the mayor. "I'll hire him, but you're gonna pay him."

"Fine," the mayor said. "As long as he's not a rat, I'll take him."

"Then I'm going with him on that delivery," I said. Not only could I size up this Frank guy, but I could also listen to the townsfolk rumble. Maybe get information that would help me find Mama.

"You lost your marbles?" Miss Helen sneered. "Your daddy—"

"He won't have to know. But I'm going. If Frank plans to be Scooter's friend, I need to judge his character." A deal clincher.

Miss Helen hugged me. "You're a good girl, Emma June Crawford."

"Fine. That's settled," Mayor Gibbons said. "And Helen, be ready for the next one." He pulled the gold chain attached to his vest and stared at his watch. "Oh, and Miss Emma June, sorry to hear about your mother. I'm sure she'll be back faster than green grass through a goose."

The mayor seemed to think Mama had left for some grand adventure. I didn't voice my frustration. Instead, I said, "I wonder if the grass is greener once he's shat it out." Then I made a sharp turn away from him.

As we headed back to Rosie's, Miss Helen let out an exasperated sigh. "Mayor *Bo*-peep is gonna pat himself on the back enough times to break his arm. I will *not* be intimidated by the likes of that baby kisser. Not ever. Emma June, you ever see this lady-legger tremble in her boots?"

"Maybe that one time when—"

"Hey, Frank!" she hollered from several storefronts away. "I have a job for you."

After Miss Helen told him the skinny and got a "hell yes" response, I asked her to drive me to The Diner. I needed to follow up on Samuel's suggestion.

"Didn't you just hear what I told Frank? That he needs to come over after he finishes work? I can spare thirty minutes but no longer. And don't look at me like that, Emma June. It means you can size Frank up sooner than later. Wait for me in Roadrunner." Miss Helen escorted Scooter inside Rosie's and returned without him.

"We're not taking Scooter?" I asked.

"Nah, he's happy staying with Miss Atta. She can help untangle his yo-yo."

At The Diner, the engine off, Miss Helen leaned her head back and twiddled her thumbs.

"I take it you're not coming in," I said.

"I've had both lice and crabs only once in my lifetime, and I don't plan on getting either a second. You go ahead, though."

I couldn't understand how the woman I'd known all my life, the woman who said my mother was like a daughter to her, could be so callous and self-absorbed. "Aren't you worried at all about Mama?"

Miss Helen stopped mid-twiddle and turned to me. Although she was too stubborn to admit it, the moisture in her eyes told me plenty. "Tell me if you learn something, honey," she said and looked away again.

The inside smelled worse than usual. A mixture of burnt food, stale cigarette smoke, and old man sweat.

Percy stood at the counter slamming flies with his flyswatter. He looked up when I approached. "Your mother still missing?" he asked.

I nodded, remembering he had been in the cell that day when Samuel and I talked to Gunny. Percy *hmphed* and retreated to the kitchen.

Miss Mabel, order pad in hand, stood over a man drooling snuff down the side of his chin. The charming side of Holly Gap. I side-stepped away and waited until she returned to the counter.

"You doin' all right, Emma June? You look a bit pasty. It's hard missing kinfolk, 'specially a mama."

"I'm okay, Miss Mabel. But I was thinking. You know the day Betty left?"

"Shor I do," she said, wiping a veined hand across her forehead. "Percy had a fit he had to work."

"I don't mean when she quit. Before. Percy said she left to attend her sister's funeral." Different from what she'd told Mama and me.

"Didn't seem too upset about it. Tired, though, like she needed two beds instead'a one."

"Did she say where the funeral was?" I hoped Betty mentioned a location, a place she might have gone.

"Didn't seem to wanna talk about it so I left her be."

It occurred to me then. Percy wasn't the same kind of boss as Miss Atta. Betty was better off telling Percy she needed two weeks off for a funeral than needing time off for a romantic rendezvous. So maybe she lied to Percy, not Mama and me, and really had met up with her former beau.

"I for one don't give a monkey's ass where she went." Percy huffed through the kitchen window. "I wouldn't let her work here now if she wore mops on her shoes. Good riddance, I say. Waking me up early just to quit." He wiped the angry spittle from his mouth with his sleeve.

"One more question. Did Betty say anything else when she quit, anything at all?"

Miss Mabel threw a thumb toward her boss. "You mean after she done told Percy to stick his spatula where the sun don't shine?"

Percy slammed a skillet on the stove and reached for lard.

Unlike me, at least he had something to grasp.

....

CHAPTER 19

EMMA JUNE

A s Miss Helen pulled up her drive, I glanced at my house. The painted cow on Ol' Bess stood visible in the shadows. Daddy was home.

Frank stood on the Munsons' front porch with Leonard towering over him a good three inches.

We'd barely made it out of Roadrunner when Scooter bolted toward Frank. "*Blow* the harmonica. *In*hale, *ex*hale."

"Hey, buddy," Frank said, and I wondered if his term of endearment was real or if he was merely licking Miss Helen's boots to gain favor. He kept his focus on Scooter, too busy to notice my skeptical eye.

"Okay, boys and girls," Miss Helen said, slamming the motorcar door. "I'm about to be busier than a one-eyed dog in a smokehouse. We've only got a few days to get ready so let's get started."

"*Can* I Frank? Can I *blow*?"

"Sure." Frank handed Scooter his blues harp, then put a hand on his shoulder. "Take good care of it, now. It's the best thing I own."

Scooter scurried off like a train at full steam.

"Honey," Miss Helen called after him, "don't bury it, now."

Frank turned to me, his eyes wide, his mouth open.

I shrugged. "Maybe you can use a toothpick to get the dirt out of those little holes." I gave him a rascally grin.

While we followed Miss Helen's arm-swinging determination toward the moonshine thicket, Frank stopped every few feet to turn a wary eye back to Scooter.

"Here she is." Miss Helen puffed out her ample bosoms and pointed to the still.

It dawned on me for the first time. The copper boiler and tubing coiling inside the oak barrel matched the color of her dyed hair.

Frank let out a slow whistle. "She's a beaut, all right."

"Scoot?" Leonard bellowed from somewhere out front. "Stop digging now."

Frank made another quick turn toward the house. "Uh—"

Miss Helen closed her eyes and inhaled. "Smell that?"

"Prunes and yeast," I said.

"Not just that." Miss Helen lifted her chin and patted the barrel. "Fermentation. This gal's ready for pouring."

That was enough to take Frank's mind off his harmonica. He wet his lips.

"Don't worry, son," she said. "I'll give you a sample."

Frank squeezed his eyebrows together. "This distillery might be under a bunch of post oaks, but it's right on your property. Not very well hidden."

"And why in tarnation would I hide it? Next you'll ask why I don't wear wooden blocks on my shoes."

"Huh?"

I explained how moonshiners in other parts of the country sometimes attached wooden blocks to their shoes, the bottoms carved like cow hooves. The tracks threw law enforcement off the trails leading to the distilleries.

"Okay," Frank said. "But last I heard, making booze to sell is against the law."

I rolled my eyes, this time making sure Frank noticed.

"The law? In Holly Gap?" Miss Helen guffawed. "You're making a delivery for Mayor Bo Gibbons. And the sheriff is Gunny Gibbons, the mayor's brother." She held up a finger. "Let me tell you about those two. Mayor Monkey Gibbons thinks he caught gout from his brother. And Gunny the Gutless can't find his butt with both hands in his back pocket. Those two might have been built in a stupid factory, but they know a good thing when they see it."

Frank let out another whistle. "I'm starting to like this town."

Miss Helen patted the wooden barrel. "I like it plenty."

Miss Helen's comment disturbed me. If our sheriff was stupid, how could he find Mama? And calling in the Feds would result in the shutdown of all the stills, including Miss Helen's. I didn't want to see her out of work and in jail.

Frank eyed the contraption. "Looks like you have a good business going."

Miss Helen broadened her smile. "Andrew Jackson smiling at me from crisp bills makes it easy. Lots of worries with it, though. Making sure the mash is right, worrying about leaks, blowing a cap, things like that. What's important is temperature, filtration, whether the beading's right, and making sure that when it goes down, it doesn't burn your gullet." Miss Helen glared at me. "This brewmaster does *not* make rotgut." Her unsubtle reminder not to drink any shine but hers.

Frank gave a lopsided smile and made a clicking sound with his cheek. "I gotta say, I've worked up quite a thirst."

Miss Helen led him toward her hooch house, the outdoor storage shed adjacent to the still. Inside, he would find Mason jars filled with a drunkard's treasure. I'd seen it many times before and had no need to see it again.

"I'm going home," I called out.

Frank, his back to me, merely raised his hand.

....

I walked the avenue home and stared at the illusion of a perfect house. Pale green clapboard, the wooden planks aligned perfectly with one another like a family was supposed to be.

I stopped at the top of the porch. Although the screen door was the same, a new white-paneled front door replaced our old one.

Inside, no hungering smells from the kitchen. No chime of our grandfather clock. No parental chatter. Only the crinkle of a newspaper.

"Daddy?"

"In here, Emma June."

In his bedroom, Daddy's legs stretched out on his side of the bed, his back against the headboard. Mama's side was wrinkle-free and depressing.

Daddy tossed the *Dallas Times Herald* aside. "Hey, Bug. What do you think of the new door? Just finished putting it up."

"But why—"

"Your mama's been wanting a new door for months now. I finally got it in. She'll be happy when she walks through it."

For a moment, I had high hopes Daddy had learned something. "When? Do you know something I don't?"

Daddy tilted his head back and closed his eyes. "I suspect when she gets her fill of gallivanting around with that Betty woman, she'll come home. Things will get back to normal then," he said, his words soft.

"You think she's with Betty?"

"Gunny seems to think so. And where else would she be? And yes, I know Betty went with y'all to the carnival."

"Mama didn't tell you, because she thought you'd be upset."

He pounded on his bedside table and stood. "Well, she was right. We all would have done just fine if that woman never moved here. A woman with the reputation of being loose as ashes in the wind."

"Who told you that?"

"Learned about her when she first came to town," he mumbled. "Heard she paraded around town in fancy short dresses. That she drinks like a sailor and smokes like a chimney. If she liked the big city so much, why'd she come to Holly Gap in the first place?"

Unless Gunny told Daddy about Betty's note, it wasn't the time to bring it up. Daddy's flushed cheeks and pulsing jaws told me he'd had enough.

He let out a heavy sigh. "Your mama said Betty always needed adventure. So one time, after your mama had known her about a month, she came home late, drunk. Your mama rarely drinks more than a glass. She'd been with Betty."

"Where had they been?"

"Your mama said they were in Mineral Wells, at a picture show. That they drank all the way home. Betty even gave her a shiny flask as a token of their new friendship."

I remembered that plain and simple flask. Nothing like Betty's ornate beauty with scrolled vines. But Mama had given it away to Mr. Finch, the old bench sitter, so Daddy would stop fussing over it. "She got rid of it, remember?"

"Not the point. I'm going outside." Daddy stormed out the new front door.

"And what if they're not together, Daddy?" I yelled after him. "What if she's in trouble and Gunny is too lazy to look for her?"

Daddy raged toward the Brazos.

Out of habit, I glanced at our grandfather clock—still 8:07. Neither Daddy nor I would wind it until Mama came home, the mutual but unspoken decision.

The phonograph sat mute, unattended since Mama left. I selected a song and set the needle on the spinning disc.

> *Pack up all my cares and woes*
> *Here I go, singing low*
> *Bye, bye, blackbird.*

I prayed Mama really had met up with Betty somewhere, and that she had a good reason for not leaving us a note telling us where she was going.

> *So make my bed and light the light,*
> *I'll arrive late tonight,*
> *Blackbird, bye, bye.*

Mama had never said goodbye.

I yanked the record off the phonograph and hurled it against the wall.

....

CHAPTER 20

FRANK

F rank couldn't blame his soreness on that piece of crap floor pallet. Not this time. The new ache in his muscles came from Irene's insistence to tear apart her jalopy to "cover her tracks." Yet she'd never driven it in town and the only people who knew about it were Percy and Mabel. But he'd busted it apart like he was told and either hauled off or buried the scraps. Only a sad-looking shell remained hidden in the brush. A shell, like his mother, hiding under the covers.

He stretched, the pop in his back giving him enough relief to face the day. Except for the notes he'd blow on his blues harp, another day without music.

He had to admit, nature in the country had its own rhythm, silent though it was. Valleys of wild grasses swayed with the wind. Shadows kept time of day as they moved across pink limestone bluffs and rugged sandstone cliffs. The silence wasn't as good as music, but definitely better than the sound of glass breaking.

He peeked in the bedroom and found only crumpled bedsheets. "Ma?"

"Out back."

Irene sat outside staring into the expansive field of trash brush, her back against the house.

"You got out," he said, surprised.

"Before it rains." She pointed to the dark clouds moving closer.

"If it does," he said, not trusting the hope for rain. "I have some news that might cheer you up."

Irene jerked her neck toward him. Her eyes brightened. "They found Bernice?"

"Sorry. Not that."

She continued her gaze out into the vastness.

"Besides Rosie's, I've got myself another gig. Hauling moonshine for the mayor and Helen Munson. I suppose you know her."

"I've never been to her house, but yes, I know her. And Scooter. Bernice and I often took him and Emma June on outings."

"That boy? He's a swell fella. Thinking I might teach him the harp."

Irene smiled, her first one in a while. "He'd like that. Scooter is curious about everything. People don't always understand that boy. He knows more than he lets on." Her pale face lifted toward him. "You see Wade again?"

"Nah. Can't wait for that to happen. He might just have a bone to pick with me."

"Because you didn't break the window?"

Frank shook his head. "Because I kept his quarter."

"Father and son. Apple doesn't fall from the tree."

Frank hoped he was a better man than Pete Sanders, the so-called father who up and left his wife with a young child.

"The other Gibbons, the mayor. He a family man?" Frank asked.

"Not married. I suppose he likes pecking all those women's cheeks without having a wife to contend with."

"I saw him and Miss Helen on Main Street. Looked like she was giving him a tongue lashing."

Irene nodded. "She's good at that. Helen's a tough cookie. Hard to see it, but Bernice told me her heart's made of gold. She'll do anything to defend the people she cares about."

"And the ones she doesn't?"

"You don't want to be one of those."

Frank thought about the people in town who had crossed his path more than once. "Anyone else I should be paying attention to?"

"Charlene Johnson," she said without missing a beat. "She's cute as a button, but don't say too much in front of her. Once her gab gets going, it won't stop until she's asleep. Emma June told me she learned the hard way not to trust her with anything important."

"Why? What did she say?"

"Ha. Never you mind. One thing your mother is not is a gabber."

Irene tried to hoist herself up from the ground but sat back down. Frank offered his hand and helped her stand on wobbly legs.

"Ma, when did you eat last?" He escorted her back inside.

"Fried me an egg this morning."

An improvement. Still, Irene didn't eat enough to keep a cat alive.

"So I met with Miss Helen and Emma June at the Munsons'. I learned this little town doesn't exactly follow the rules. Mayor buys bootlegged liquor and his brother, the sheriff, looks the other way."

Irene reached her bedroom at a snail's pace and laid back down. "It's true. You won't have any trouble. How is Emma June?"

"Acts okay. Not sure she likes me much."

"Give her time."

"She's coming with me to deliver the mayor's shine."

He thought about the girl he was getting to know. The girl with the long eyelashes she batted when irritated—which happened a lot when she looked at him. "Emma June. She look like her mother?"

"Maybe a bit. And don't get any ideas, Frank. I don't want her hurt more than she already is."

Emma June wasn't his type, anyway. Dames with brown hair reminded him too much of women who deserted you.

"Emma June says Bernice and me look like we could be related," she continued. "Similar body type, brown eyes. Her hair is dark like mine. But like I told you, hers is burgundy. She's prettier than me." Irene covered her eyes with her forearm. "Frank? Think you can find something to cover that window? It's awfully bright in here."

"It's not bright in here. What? You have another headache?"

"Everything's starting to ache."

He couldn't imagine being so heartsick about someone that you couldn't get out of bed. "We'll find her."

"Will we, Frank? Will we find her before it's too late?"

"What are you talking about?"

"I'm not just upset, Frank. I'm really sick." She turned toward him. "Doctor confirmed it in New Orleans."

CHAPTER 21

EMMA JUNE

My teeth had learned to grind at night. I woke with an aching jaw and memories of a dream about a wolf with large teeth wearing aviator goggles yelling, "Where is she?"

I spiced up the Cream of Wheat with brown sugar and butter. It still tasted like stale air.

Dressed and ready, I headed to the front door, hating the newness of it, and found a note from Daddy. Next to it, a letter from Waco. Samuel.

Daddy's note: *Sorry Emma June. Forgot to give this to you last night. I love you, honey.*

I tore open the letter.

Dear Emma June,

I hope this letter finds you well. Well enough, at least, since my uncle said he has not received word that your mother has returned. I am so sorry. I wish I could be there to help and support you.

Well, you're not the only one who drank too much. The boys had a bash at our dorm, and someone got ahold of enough liquor to serve us all. We had a poker game and the good news is, I was winning. The bad is, the more hands I won, the more I drank. Let's just say that I learned nothing in the next day's early morning class!

I miss your beautiful hazel eyes, the way you cock your head to the side when you are puzzled. I miss how your arched eyebrows give you a look of perpetual curiosity. And the way you try to cover up the cigarette smell on your clothes with lavender powder (some parts weren't fully rubbed in). I love the determination in your loud whistle (you'll have to give me more lessons) and the graceful way you stumble to the ground. (Smile.)

I was thinking that when I arrive this summer, I could teach you how to drive—if that is, you haven't already learned. I think the two of us would make a great team negotiating the curves in the road together, both the smooth and rough patches.

It would be really great to hear from you. I hope you feel like writing back.

Sincerely,
Samuel

I held his letter to my chest and dared myself not to feel a positive emotion. His metaphoric meaning of curves in the road did not escape me. I believed he saw me in his future, one longer than his summer break from Baylor Medical School.

Walking to Scooter's, I pictured Samuel and I laughing and carrying on in Miss Helen's roadster. This time, with me as the driver.

Daddy had taught Mama to drive a few years back. She was a jumble of nerves during that first lesson, but he remained calm, patient. Mama kept looking at the back seat. "You okay, baby? You okay?" she asked me. Daddy reminded her to keep focused on the road. But we didn't have to worry about crashing. Mama never went more than two or three miles an hour.

Daddy had turned to me and winked. "Hope you're not too hungry, Emma June. This might take a while." When we got home, Daddy told Mama how proud he was of her. Then Mama turned to me and said, "I'm proud of you, Emma June. You didn't throw up."

But I'd thrown up plenty on carnival night. I had to find Mama and apologize for being drunkenly sick when she needed me.

This time, as I trudged toward Scooter's, a different kind of nausea hit my gut. I felt like a trapped moth, dizzily circling in the light of a faded lampshade looking for answers that weren't there.

I found the Munson clan sitting at their kitchen table.

"Now wipe that syrup off your face, Scooter Bug," Miss Helen said. "You're sweet enough without all that goo on your face."

Leonard, his empty breakfast plate pushed aside, sat reading Miss Helen's newest copy of *Cosmopolitan*. I knew Leonard. He would have read anything to avoid unnecessary conversation.

"*Emmy*." Scooter grinned.

"Hey, Scoot Bucket. You ready for school?"

"Grab your *muskets*, boys."

"He's learning about the Alamo, aren't you, honey?" Miss Helen said.

"Davy Crockett. 'Be always *sure* you are right then go ahead.'"

"What he said, all right," Leonard drawled out.

Scooter's ears were fine-tuned like the strings on a good fiddle, his accented words, the force behind his inner music.

Miss Helen rubbed the top of Scooter's head. "And *you* need to go ahead and get to school. Your noggin's not done learning yet, and your mama has work to do."

While Leonard helped Scooter gather his things, Miss Helen stopped me before I reached the door.

"Emma June, you hear anything last night?"

"Hear anything?"

"Middle of the night, I heard some rustling out by the moonshine thicket. Went outside and gave my shotgun a good, loud cock but didn't see anything."

The roosters would have crowed long before Leonard had made it out of bed. Shot in the leg during the Great War, Leonard carried a limp that slowed him down. That left Miss Helen the primary defender of the Munson Alamo.

"Maybe just some night critters," I said.

"Heavy footed ones, then."

On the way to school, while Scooter sang his version of "Pack Up Your Troubles," I thought of Samuel and tried to think of how I would respond to his letter. I couldn't get past *Dear.*

"Say, Scooter?"

He held up a wait finger and finished singing, "So pack up your troubles in an old kit bag and smile, smile, *smile.*" He pressed his nose to mine.

"I'm trying, Scoot." I gave him a forced smile. "So, about Samuel. You like him, right?"

"He's funny."

"Funny? How?"

"At Doc's. He pulled a *nickel* out of my ear. Good as *Houdini.*"

Scooter loved Harry Houdini, the magician and escape artist who had died on Halloween two years before. When we heard the news Scooter had cried, dug holes, buried whatnots, and cried more. After he had buried his entire set of Tinker Toys, a separate plot for every two, he wiped the dirt off his hands and the tears from his face and said, "There. That ought'a do it." Then he went about the day in his typical, unique fashion.

"And *Samuel* gave me a *red* sucker. Made my lips *Betty*-red."

Betty.

"You like Betty?" I asked.

Scooter stopped and put his hands on his hips. "Emmy *June*. Silly as a cow wearing pajamas."

"What did you like about her?"

"Got naked as a *jail*bird and went swimming," he said, his grin wide and happy.

As always, he remembered correctly. On that hot day at the end of September, Mama, Betty, Scooter, and I had gone to the Brazos for a picnic. Betty, who was three sheets to the wind, stripped down and jumped in the river. Scooter had doubled over, his laughter sucking the air from his lungs.

"I miss . . . Miss *Bernice* more," he said, his face solemn.

"I know. Me, too, Scoot. Me, too."

Almost to the schoolhouse, Scooter sang Miss Helen's version of "Down in the River to Pray."

> *Oh, Scooter, let's go down*
> *Let's go down, come on down*
> *Oh, Scooter, let's go down*
> *Down in the river to pl-aaay.*

"You're the best, you know that, Scooter?"

"The *berries*," he said, using Charlene's expression.

I hugged him goodbye and whispered, "Scoot, do you think Betty's a good person?"

He squinted up at me, his face unusually serious. "Good as she knows how," he said, this time with no emphasis.

....

I was welcomed back to Rosie's with a "so good to have you back, shortcake," from Miss Atta, a kitchen length shuffle-off-to-Buffalo from a shoe-tapping Rags, and a "you're looking kippy today, Emma June" from Frank, whose hands were submerged in dishwater.

Except for having to contend with the new hire, being near Miss Atta comforted me.

She caught me staring at the photograph adhered to the icebox. Her son, Toby, a permanent grin stuck to his face, held his young cousin on his lap.

She put an arm around my waist. "Your mama, wherever she is, is just fine." She pulled a handkerchief from her pocket and wiped the corners of my eyes. "I understand, shortcake. Not knowing is darker than night. But light always comes."

Yet the sun continued its trail down the western sky.

CHAPTER 22

....

EMMA JUNE

Frank found me leaning against Rosie's brick wall, trying to puff away the day with a smoke.

"Butt me," he said.

I tossed him a Lucky Strike and the cheap lighter I had bought at Johnson's Variety when Charlene had worked the front counter.

"Hold on." He sauntered back inside.

My shift was over and I didn't want company. I was sick of mouths shutting when I passed, eyes that looked away when they saw me.

I thought about the workday, how Mr. Peterson had a conniption that we were out of chocolate cream pie. I suggested the lemon meringue, only to be told, "Ain't eatin' no calf slobber."

The banker's wife, Mrs. Mercer, had caught her long string of Chicago-bought pearls on the back of the chair. The disaster sent the beads bouncing around the floor and Mrs. Mercer into a tizzy.

I'd overheard the town seamstress and her husband talking about "the poor girl's missing mother." They'd left me a sizable tip.

On the good side, Rosie's had a new windowpane.

Frank returned with two small wooden crates. He set one beside me, settled on the other, and exhaled a big cloud of smoke. I stayed quiet, hoping he'd take the hint.

Frank cleared his throat. "You know where I can find myself a poker game?"

"Huh?"

"My hands are itching for a full house."

"Leonard, Scooter's daddy, plays occasionally. If you don't mind playing with old men who blow snot on the floor."

"You don't have to be old to do that."

"That's disgusting."

"Is what it is. Men can be pigs."

"Huh. Just when I thought you weren't enlightened."

Frank cracked a smile. "I have my moments."

Even from outside, I heard Rags's loud whistle. Not a tune this time. His beckoning trill.

"Rags needs something," I said. "You better go answer his call."

Alone again, I blew my cigarette smoke toward the neighborhood behind Rosie's. The line of modest yet neat houses seemed to come alive with sounds of children playing and smells of supper cooking. Normalcy.

"Not a bad place to work," Frank said when he returned.

"What?"

"I said this café seems like a good place to work."

I looked down at Frank sitting on the crate, his eyes concealed by the brim of his flat cap. "Surprised you like it here. I saw what you had to do. Crawl on your hands and knees to pick up precious pearls."

"Hey, she tipped me a clam."

I wondered how low he would stoop to make money. Was he a swindler? Petty thief? He was handsome enough to be a lady's escort—if one preferred the rough type to the more refined.

Frank pulled a small rectangular box from his trouser pocket and flipped open the lid. *Hohner*, the word printed on the inside in red letters.

He took the harp out of its box. "After it seemed destined for Scooter's burial, I thought it needed a little protection."

"A harmonica?" I asked, intrigued in spite of myself.

"I write songs." He placed it to his lips and, after a few notes, he sang.

> There's a song you can't be singing
> 'Cause your eardrums won't stop ringing
> So you keep the worst and best things deep inside.
> It's a story not worth telling
> 'Cause your throat, it keeps on swelling
> "Son," he says, "let's take a joyride."
> Then the devil moves you this way, and the Jesus moves
>   you that . . .

He stopped. With his bluesy pipes, Frank could have been a white Blind Lemon Jefferson singing "Black Snake Moan."

"Well, go on," I said and settled on the empty crate beside him.

"All I've written so far."

"Nice," I said, although it was better than I let on. "Where'd you learn—"

"New Orleans. That's where I moved from. I knew a bunch of musician cats. One taught me the harp, another the cornet."

"Cornet in your other pocket?"

"Ha. Very funny. One of these days I'll save up enough to buy one." He looked upward. "Crazy bunch of fools they were. Sure miss those blues boys."

"Then why'd you move here? Most of the younger folks want to move away."

"Ma told me to pack a suitcase. We landed here."

"You still live with your mother?" Strange, for a grown man.

"Temporarily. She doesn't get out much. I'm kinda . . . help-ing her," Frank mumbled. "Besides, a little change doesn't hurt," he said, perking up. "Ma says I might have better opportunities in Holly Gap."

"Here? Only if you compare Holly Gap to living in a gopher hole."

Frank chuckled, then reached behind him. He pulled out a dented flask and offered it up.

Although my head was empty of ideas of how to find Mama, it had become too heavy and muddled to hold up. I passed on the hooch.

Frank unscrewed the cap and took a swig then sang, "'Yes sir, that's my baby. No sir, don't mean maybe. Yes, sir, that's my baby now.'"

"You better be careful with that. One-eighty proof. And you should feel honored. Miss Helen only sells to the high-hats. You got yours for free."

"A whole Mason jar at that. It's because I'm saving her butt by making that delivery for her."

"Us. *We're* making that delivery."

"I know. I'm keen on that. You're a crackerjack, after all." He smirked.

I looked him in the eye. "Fair warning. I don't come with a little prize at the bottom of the box."

"Not expecting any."

I didn't tell Frank about Samuel. I wasn't sure how much there was to tell.

Frank arched his back and made a popping sound. "I'm not used to such a small town."

"Yeah. Holly Gap is at the edge of nothing. Big news is when someone gets sprayed by a polecat. Bigger news and the townsfolk gather like cattle in a rainstorm."

I knew what they were saying at that very moment: *Did you hear about the Crawfords? Horrible how a mother could up and leave her family like that. Such a shame. They seemed like such a close-knit family.*

For the next few moments, the only sound came from Rags banging pots inside the café.

"You like music?" Frank said and handed me one of his hand-rolled butts.

"Used to," I said, coughing out his potent tobacco.

"That's another thing this town doesn't have enough of. Music. Ever noticed how a single note can change everything?"

Yeah. A single whistle and Choppers would have been by my side instead of under the wheels of a truck. A single tick of our grandfather clock meant Mama was home.

"A single note means the beginning of something that can fill our soul from top to bottom," he said.

"Well, aren't you a positive pearl," I said sarcastically. Frank grinned.

"Not always. I guess it can also remind us of things we don't want to think about." He paused, glancing at me. "Hey, sorry about your mother."

I didn't want sympathy. I wanted to go back to worrying about what to wear, how I would fill up my calendar, and whether or not Mama liked the cloche hat I picked out from the Sears and Roebuck catalog.

"Filled me up when I heard Jelly Roll Morton play in New Orleans," he said after my silence.

I remembered Mama's elation when she purchased Jelly Roll's newest recording. "Baloney. You didn't really see him."

"Okay. I heard him, though. After I weaved through the beggars and thieves, the music was so loud you couldn't help but hear. Drowned out the sounds of slaughterhouses, the shipyard, even the whores calling out for customers."

Beggars and thieves. And mischief-making rock throwers. "Miss Atta's new window looks nice."

"Huh? Oh . . . yeah. You weren't here when they put in the new pane. I met the sheriff. He was overseeing the work."

"Gunny protects Miss Atta. But that's not why I brought it up."

"Figured," he said, without the chirpy tone. "I didn't break her window, Emma June."

"But you know who did."

"I'm not a rat."

"They need to pay for what they've done."

Frank threw his butt down and ground it with the toe of his work boot. "Oh, they'll pay all right."

"You better watch yourself. You don't want to throw away all this Holly Gap opportunity by landing in jail."

"Not worried."

"Don't do anything stupid before tomorrow night's delivery. You do, and you'll be dead center on Miss Helen's warpath."

"Why would I blow the chance to have heavy pockets?" Frank rose from his crate. "Gotta breeze. Ma needs me to stop by the drug store. Tomorrow then." He saluted a goodbye and swaggered off, his posture erect like a man on a mission.

I, on the other hand, sat slumped over on a splintered box with one motive: to hear the rumble of Mama's green breezer as it drove toward me.

....

CHAPTER 23

EMMA JUNE

On my walk home, I stopped several times to pick dandelions swaying by the roadside. With each blow, I made the same wish. When the feathery tufts disappeared into the air, I knew I was merely chasing shadows impossible to pin down.

I returned home, surprised to find Charlene on my front porch. I hadn't seen her for weeks, not since the morning after the carnival.

"Charlene?"

"Your daddy poured us water." She stopped rubbing Choppers's belly and handed me a glass. I sat next to her on the top step.

"Thanks."

"Say, Emma June. Don't be mad but I have to ask. Are you over Wade?"

I sat there, dumbfounded. Charlene was supposed to be my best friend, yet her first comment in weeks had nothing to do with Mama. Or me, for that matter.

"I'm just asking because Loretta says he's causing more ruckus than usual."

"What a surprise."

"No lie. She said Wade's been angrier than normal. Apparently, their wretched father is working with a new fella. Loretta says he's a creep show, and Wade is constantly fuming."

"Why are you telling me this, Charlene? You were right about Wade. I don't care about any of him anymore. He's a pig."

"What about Loretta? You still okay with her since she's Wade's sister?"

"I don't dislike her. We just don't seem to have anything in common."

"You mean because she's poor?"

I squeezed my glass to keep from throwing water in her face. "Oh, please, Charlene. You know me better than that. What do you have in common with Loretta?"

"Well, obviously, not as much as I have with you. But she's nice, and . . ." Charlene rubbed a finger around the rim of the glass. "Maybe I just feel sorry for her. Her family is dreadful. Her mother is such a little mouse, she won't even stand up for Loretta. Or for herself when Mr. Foley treats her like crap. Two people who fight that much should never be married." Charlene gasped and threw a hand over her mouth. "I'm sorry, Emmy. I know Bernice and your daddy had a fight."

"And why the hell would you think that?" I didn't want to admit she was right.

"One of the rumors," she muttered.

No doubt, there were many. "Charlene, why are you here?"

"You don't have to get snippy, Emma June. Miss Bernice is the real reason I came over. I wanted you to know I stuck up for her. I caught Lucy Hodges's mother in a huddle with Mrs. Mercer and Mrs. Levine. All three prattling on about your mama."

Who cared about a high-browed rancher's wife, the wife of the bank president, or for that matter, the town's dressmaker?

"I defended her! I told them your mother left town to buy you something special for your eighteenth birthday."

I wanted to wallop that satisfied smile right off her face. Clueless Charlene had fed the town another lie to chew on.

I unclenched my jaw. "Can we talk about something else?"

"Betty's not working at The Diner anymore."

"I know. What's your point?"

"Seems strange, is all. Both disappearing at the same time. Mama says the two are together in a big city."

It was the biggest rumor of all, apparently, and the one Daddy believed.

"What do you think, Charlene? You've never put any stock in anything your mother's said. Are you believing her now?"

"Just makes sense, is all. But I was thinking. Remember Madam Zola from the carnival? You know, the fortune teller? Maybe you could find her. Ask her where your mother is."

I knew I'd had enough when the thought of pounding my head against a wall sounded like relief. "She's a scammer, Charlene. A grifter, same as all the others at the carnival."

I realized it then. Since learning about Betty, I'd become a cynic. Skeptical about everything and everyone.

"Emma June," Daddy called. "Time for supper."

The excuse I needed to break away. "I gotta go."

"Not asking me in?"

Between Mama, Daddy, and me, one of us always asked Charlene to stay for supper. A ritual we never broke. But that was before. "Our house is different now, Charlene."

She nodded as if she understood. She didn't.

"Okay, but before you go in, I have a question." She stood and leaned toward me. "That new boy? The one who works with you at Rosie's?"

"Frank. What about him?"

"He's a real sheik, don't you think? Or do you have dibs on him, too?"

I turned away and flung open the screen door. "He's all yours." I slammed the ghastly new door behind me.

....

Not all the flour had gone into the making of chicken and dumplings. Plenty covered the apron Daddy had draped around his neck.

"Daddy?"

"Surprise," he said, with a slight grin. "Found your mother's recipe. Dumplings are a bit . . . hard." He handed me a bowl.

I wasn't surprised. I was mortified. Daddy visited pots and pans only when he made bacon and eggs on Sundays. Or when he sampled Mama's cooking. Too many things had changed already and Daddy taking over Mama's routine felt like another betrayal.

"But we have Miss Helen's food."

"Don't like relying on the kindness of strangers. A week or two is fine. After that—"

"After that, what? You'll start doing the laundry? Taking me to the picture show and the beauty shop?" I mustered the strength not to fling my bowl across the kitchen just to hear the porcelain break.

Daddy stared down into his untouched bowl. "It's my job to take care of you, Emma June," he said, his voice quiet. "And that's what I aim to do until your mother gets back. I . . . will never . . . I will always be here for you." He pushed away from the table and retreated to his bedroom. His door closed without a sound.

I wanted to go to him then, to ease his sorrow. But when I didn't move, I knew the reason. Whether he meant to or not, Daddy implied that Mama had left me. I retreated to my room.

....

Dear Samuel,

How can people resume their day-to-day lives when my world has become so unraveled that I can barely move? I'm in a nightmare carnival, and the only escape ride won't stop to let me on. Darkness comes and I'm waiting like a fool. But dawn after dawn, the ride never slows. If it did, I'd have a fair shot at grabbing the guardrail to pull myself up to safety. That is, if I were stronger.

The fear overwhelms me. The "what ifs" paralyze me before I sleep. The unanswered "whys," a constant and poisonous serum in my veins. Muscles quiver and fingers shake. I go through the daily routine but without thought. Without clarity. A dense fog where my brain used to be.

I keep thinking of how you looked at Wade without fear. Then your arm around me, strong and comforting. I wish you were here to drive me through the countryside with the gas pedal at full mash. I need you to remind me what it feels like to believe in something again.

I wadded up the letter of self-pity, chucked it in the trash can, and started over.

Dear Samuel,

I think I might take you up on the driving lesson! I've been walking Scooter to school in the mornings and back and forth from work. Driving would make life so much easier!

My mother has not yet returned. The questions I ask around town seem to only lead to more questions.

But Mayor Gibbons is holding a constituent party and Frank and I are delivering moonshine to the event. Frank is the new fella Miss Atta hired. And since he took a liking to Scooter, Miss Helen took a liking to Frank. You know how she is. Anyway, she gave him the delivery job and I'm going with him with my ears open. With so many townsfolk there, maybe I'll learn something about Mama's whereabouts. I'm keeping my fingers crossed and my chin up.

Hopefully, I'll have better news next time I write.

Thank you for thinking of me.

Sincerely,
Emma June

P.S. I really enjoyed your letter. Please write again.

Lame. Barely worth the two-cent postage I stuck to the envelope.

I heard Daddy's bedroom door open, then his heavy footsteps heading back to the kitchen. Pots banged. Glasses clinked. Sounds that made the hollowness of our house seem louder.

I found Daddy standing with his palms pressed on the kitchen counter, his head pointed down at the empty sink.

CHAPTER 24

FRANK

Raindrops pinged on Frank's shoulder as he headed down Main Street and back to the shanty he called home. He couldn't shake the feeling that the coming storm had little to do with the weather.

He thought about his talk with Emma June. Although a mother needing help was a legitimate excuse for missing work, he shouldn't have mentioned living with her. What grown, capable man still lived with a parent unless he was a bum? On the other hand, even if word got out, who would suspect Frank Sanders's mother was the person Holly Gap knew as Betty Bedford? And nobody knew where he lived. No one visited. Besides, who would recognize the skinny woman wearing a dingy housecoat and scraggly hair as the vivacious Betty?

"Yoo-hoo. Wait up."

He turned toward the voice. A cute blonde hip-wiggled toward him. Button nose, blue eyes. Unlike Emma June, she had a little meat on her hips that accentuated her thin waist.

"Hi. I'm a friend of Emma June's. And you must be Frank."

"That's me." He smiled and stared at her full lips.

"I'm Charlene Johnson. My daddy owns Johnson Variety."

The girl Irene had told him about.

"Well, I'd say it's my lucky day, Charlene Johnson."

"And I'd say since you are new to town and all, you might need someone to show you around. Emma June's busy trying to find her mother and besides, she's goofy over a boy named Samuel. He found her at the carnival after she puked. Even carried her to her mother's breezer."

Seemed like Emma June had as much fun at the carnival as Irene.

"Samuel, huh? Haven't met him." He'd seen him, though, at her father's store.

"He doesn't live here. He goes to college. My daddy saw them together at the Variety. He's a sheik, too. Like you." Leaning up against a storefront, she inched up her dress and showed a rouged knee.

The gal certainly wasn't shy about flirting, and Frank's bold wink and grin encouraged her further.

"So, what do you say?"

"About Emma June and Samuel?" he said, trying for coy.

"No, silly," she said, hands on her hips. "About me being your tour guide."

He had a feeling it would cost him in dough. Charlene seemed the type who needed tokens of affection. She'd be disappointed. "I'd say I'd be a lucky fella."

"Well, then—"

"About Emma June. I heard about her mother. Damn shame."

"Miss Bernice?" Charlene waved a hand. "She's fine. She's just off somewhere with her best friend trying to patch up their relationship."

"Why? Was it broken?"

"Just a falling out of some sort."

"And how do you know that?"

"I saw them argue. But Miss Bernice and Betty are like birds of a feather. They have too much fun together to let a silly argument get in their way."

He wanted Charlene to keep talking. To hear a different perspective of the mother he knew as a gadabout-turned-recluse. He didn't get the chance. A woman two stores down called out to Charlene.

"Rats. That's my mother. You think about where you'd like to go, and I'll come running." Charlene batted her eyelashes, then sashayed back to Johnson's. She'd be a fine diversion. Something to take his mind off Irene and her troubles.

He reached the end of Main Street and veered onto the country road. A half-mile to home, Frank took in his surroundings. Funny thing about the world: it could give you sprawling land for cattle ranching and rich soil for growing cotton and wheat. But it could also serve up a big helping of cancer.

No matter what Irene said, he wasn't sure he believed her. Maybe her "cancer" was losing her precious best friend, an excuse to stay in bed all day and barely give him the time of day.

Part of him knew the real reason he'd followed her to Holly Gap. He had held on to the hope Irene would redeem herself for deserting him. That she'd ask him to spend time with her doing things that didn't include playing detective and cleaning up her messes.

Why was Irene so scared of a country bumpkin anyway? She could just throw a punch to Earl's jaw like she had to her landlord, show him she wouldn't be messed with.

He'd barely noticed the rumbling behind him until the dented and scratched pickup passed then cut in front of him, blocking him off.

Wade got out of the driver's side. The man in the passenger seat, plump-faced and sweating, glared at Frank.

"Well, if it ain't the smart ass," Wade said, sauntering toward him.

"Evening, Wade," Frank said. "You mad I missed that window?"

"You done it on purpose, you chicken shit."

Frank nodded toward the truck. "You're not with Moody. Is that your old man?" He took a step toward the clunker, but Wade grabbed his arm, stopping him.

"Yeah, what's it to ya?"

Earl Foley. The man who had blackmailed his mother. "Just wanted to introduce myself."

"Wade," his father called out. "That boy stole yer quarter. Don't be no yeller-belly. You make him give it back."

Wade needed to prove to his father he could take on Frank. That much was clear. So was the fact that Earl Foley ruled his household, or at least his son, with an iron fist.

Wade held out his hand, palm up. "Plant it right here."

Frank wanted to plant it, all right. But not the quarter. A fist to the weak mustache Wade couldn't seem to grow. "Don't have it. If you'd caught me ten minutes ago it'd be in your pocket by now."

Wade reared back a fist. Frank could have popped him but held back. Mustering self-control, Frank took the punch. Not a bad hit, but he'd had much worse. He squinted as if his cheekbone hurt.

"Next time I see you," Wade said with a point, "you'd best have my quarter."

One day, after he whooped Wade, he'd knock that sneer off Earl Foley's smug face.

....

CHAPTER 25

EMMA JUNE

A s I got closer to Scooter's house, his happy squeal lifted my spirit.

"Emmy, *Emmy*."

"Hey, Scoot Bucket. Where is everybody?"

"Daddy's on the *pot*. Mama's in the *hooch* hut. DeFord *Bailey* is . . ." Scooter scoured the front acreage, ". . . *there*." He pointed to Frank, who strutted toward the house with broad, purposeful steps.

"Who's DeFord Bailey?" I asked, focusing my attention on Scooter.

"*Best* harmonica player in the *world*. He had *polio*. And Frank knows his *harp* like his *onions*. He's full of *smarts*."

"Yeah?" I said, but thought, *he's full of it, all right*. If Frank really knew so much, he wouldn't be walking toward me with a black eye.

Scooter pointed to Frank's face and giggled. "You're a puffy, *red-eyed raccoon*."

"Right-io," Frank said. "And this raccoon has a meeting with your mama."

Nice first impression. "Trying to make new friends?"

"Ran into a door." He turned away and poked the top of Scooter's head. "Hey, buddy. How's the noodle today?"

"Spit and *polished*."

"Attaboy. Just like I told you."

"*And* I'm going to a *rodeo*." Scooter galloped off holding imaginary reins.

Like Scooter said, Miss Helen was in the hooch hut, her head shoved in a cabinet of Mason jars.

"We're here," I called out.

She banged her head on the shelving. If she felt the impact through her thick skull, she didn't let on.

"And right on time." She held up a clear gallon jug of moonshine. "See this here? This will—"

"Take the iron off a chair?" I said, repeating the words I heard her say all too often.

"Well, aren't you bright as a new penny? And what in God's name happened to your eye?" she asked Frank.

"The door lost," he told her.

"Well, Mr. Sanders, you better not cause any ruckus tonight. You have to, do it on your own time, not mine."

"Yes, ma'am. My best foot forward."

"Best you do. Mayor's having another shindig soon, so you might just get yourself another job. Depends. You tip over the outhouse, you're a goner. Understand?"

"Got it. No outhouse tipping."

Frank was smooth, all right. But the black eye meant he kept his jagged edges close by.

"Okay," Miss Helen said, hand on her hips. "First things first. Mayor's delivery place is seven miles from here. It's a gin mill venue for his reelection campaign. A big to-do. They expect my finest, and I aim for them to get it without a hitch. Savvy?"

Miss Helen's business side. Straight and to the point. An about-face from her fits and starts.

Frank threw a thumbs up. "Without a hitch."

"Next," she continued. "Y'all probably heard God flinging barrels last night and plenty of rain came with it. Don't get stuck in any mud. Frank, you'll officially meet our mayor. Wears a three-piece suit, a Panama hat, and a fake smile. Usually holds a cigar in his fat fingers. It's four-thirty now. Win-dig starts at six-thirty. Delivery no later than five-thirty." She sighed her full bosoms back down to their hanging position and pointed to the side of the hooch house. "Crates are over there." She put a hand to the side of her mouth. "Leonard!" she hollered. "Pull up the truck!"

The truck. I had looked forward to taking Roadrunner and imagining Samuel sitting beside me. But the heavier load required the pickup.

"Emma June, you can help put the soap bags on top when they're done loading."

I remembered the advertisement: "Luxe soap, rich in fragrance."

"If you're stopped by an outsider," she continued, "say y'all are delivering soap to Common's Drug Store in Mineral Wells. And for heaven's sake, get there faster than Holly Gap gossip. But *without* breaking anything."

Overdressed in my matching skirt and sweater, we bumped down the road in hillbilly fashion. Frank had dressed casually in a green shirt and brown vest, no tie.

"You got the directions?" he asked.

"In my pocket." But I knew the way. I had already seen the map that day at the sheriff's office. *Old wedding pavilion—Route 90.* "Okay, now tell me why a door punched you in the face."

"What do most people want?"

"Answers," I said, thinking about Mama.

"Not answers. Dough, cabbage, scratch. Call it what you want, but it's still money most people are after. Either that or revenge."

"So which was it?"

"Both."

"Come on, Frank."

Frank flicked his lit cigarette out the window. "Rosie's Café. The window."

"You *were* there."

"Yeah, but I didn't break it." He admitted to being stopped on the side of the road by a fella with a beef.

"You didn't hit him back?"

"Nah. Wasn't worth the trouble. I just headed home."

"And where's that?"

"Not far from The Diner."

Shanty Town. Dilapidated clapboard houses, tumbleweeds for pets. Where the Foleys lived.

I'd been inside the Foleys' house. It was no wonder that when Loretta came to mine, she kept asking to listen to the radio or play music on the phonograph. She awed over the electric icebox and the ease of making chilled iced tea. It made me uncomfortable.

"You been there?" he asked.

"The Diner? Betty used to work there. She was Mama's best friend. Turn right at the next road."

"Used to be?"

I didn't want to talk about Betty. Didn't want to think about her hip-swaying her way into a bright future after leaving us without saying goodbye.

"I saw the flyers of your mother. Pretty lady."

"Yeah. She is." On my way to Rosie's that morning, I had spotted three missing person flyers of Mama standing next to her green breezer, a playful smile on her face. *Missing! Mrs. Theo (Bernice) Crawford. Contact Sheriff Gibbons with information.* One hung on the hardware store's door, one at Johnson's Variety. The last greeted me at Rosie's before I walked through the door.

I reminded myself that the more people who saw the flyers, the greater chance of finding her. I tried not to think about the ignorant townsfolk who looked at those posters and saw a woman who had left her family just to be with her best friend.

"So, the one who hit you," I said, changing the subject. "I bet he has a scar over one eyebrow. Veer right at the Y."

"Like I said before, Emma June. I'm no stool pigeon."

"You don't have to be. I already know it was Wade Foley."

Frank didn't correct me. We sat in silence as wheat and corn stalks waved at our passing. Cows looked up and mooed their greetings. Old barns stood vacant and abandoned. Bluebonnets and Indian paintbrushes gave me a glimpse of the beauty that still existed.

Frank slowed when he came to a large water-filled pothole. As he sped up, the truck backfired and scared the bejesus out of me.

"Damn, gal." He laughed. "You almost jumped out of this stutter bus. You remind me of those fellows back in New Orleans who served in the war. Plenty of them came back all whacked out crazy. Hid every time they heard a backfire. Your daddy serve in the war?"

Daddy. He didn't know I was running a delivery. He thought I was going to Charlene's. "Daddy never served. Between him breaking his leg and getting a farm furlough, he didn't have to go. Leonard served, though. Except for putting up with Miss Helen, he's not crazy. You noticed his limp?"

"Hard not to."

"He got that in the war. Daddy said he was a sharpshooter." I'd always found that hard to believe. If Leonard so much as found a bug in his house, he'd carry it outside to safety. "What about your father? He serve?"

"He ankled when I was one. Nice of him, huh? No skin off my back since I don't remember him."

That familiar sinking feeling took a chair in the pit of my stomach and settled in.

After pointing out the last turn, Frank threaded the truck between the branches on the skinny road until it opened up to the lit pavilion. Of the few motorcars parked out front, the mayor's new Cadillac stood out—a midnight blue six-passenger sedan, its silver wheel fenders partially covered in mud.

The mayor also had a strongman named Jacoby Pines, a big, meaty man. I'd always liked Jacoby. He often pitched in at Rosie's when we needed a hand.

Jacoby hustled over to the truck. "Ready for me, Miss Emma June?"

I introduced him to Frank, who took stock of the muscles bulging through the big man's suit. "Unloading shouldn't take long," Frank said, smiling as he shook Jacoby's hand.

More motorcars pulled up, their headlights bouncing off the trees that surrounded the covered pavilion.

As they unloaded the hooch, I spotted the mayor already handing out shoulder pats, handshakes, and kisses as if they were blue ribbons. I recognized no one as a Holly Gap citizen.

But I recognized the voices behind me.

"Wade, tell him . . . you tell him everythin's right as rain."

"I know what to do, Pa," Wade said, followed by the slam of a motorcar's door.

....

CHAPTER 26

EMMA JUNE

arl talking to the mayor at Rosie's was one thing. But some-thing had to be amiss if Wade and his father had shown up at an uppity political event.

While Earl backed his clunker into a hidden canopy of trees, I headed to the pavilion before Wade spotted me standing alone.

Frank, eager to get started, already stood next to Jacoby and the mayor. I joined them just as Mayor Gibbons puffed out enough cigar smoke to make Frank squint.

"Okay, boys," the mayor said. "We'll drink Helen's first. The other moonshine we'll use for backup. And what we don't drink, I'll return to its owner."

"Like hell you will. The owner doesn't take returns." A mid-dle-aged man appeared from nowhere. Like most men, he towered over Mayor Gibbons a good three or four inches. He stood out, and not just because he was dapper-dressed in a dark suit with a match-ing vest and waistcoat. His black fedora, pulled low to his eyebrows, didn't hide his eerily imposing presence or the tight squint in the one eye I could see from his profile.

Mayor Gibbons cleared his throat. "That'll be all, boys. No need to mingle. Just make sure everyone has a filled glass. And Emma

June, since you're here, you keep to the washtub and rinse out the glasses as needed."

Frank and Jacoby wove through the now-crowded pavilion toward the crates of hooch.

Lucky Strike in hand, I backed away and pretended to scour my purse for a light while I listened.

"Whitt," Mayor Gibbons said. "Didn't mean to insinuate yours wasn't any good. Just that Helen's—"

"Is damn good. *And*, I don't like it. Get rid of it. You're using my moonshine, no one else's. Like I told you, this market, this territory, is mine."

Mayor Gibbons leaned on one hip, then the other. "Now, Whitt, I've done you fair the past few months. Getting my brother to allow your passage through town ought'a count for something."

"A good start. Yet prosperity grows, does it not? It's growing for me. Just thought you felt the same way. And if this Helen woman wants in, she has to pay me a percentage for the honor."

"Helen's been bootlegging since long before—"

Whitt poked the mayor's suit lapel and leaned in. "We're pulling your Podunk ass upward. And you've got a Cadillac to prove it. I'm your supplier now. Easy little town you're running. You want to keep it that way."

"Need a light, doll?" I didn't recognize the woman's voice, high-pitched and squeaky.

I turned away from the mayor's flushing cheeks. The blonde woman next to me, a towering presence in silver pumps with rhinestone heels, obviously didn't shop in Holly Gap. Or Mineral Wells, for that matter. She appeared to be in her twenties, and wore a rhinestone-beaded headband and a gorgeous coral beaded dress with a handkerchief hem. Every girl's dream dress. Pearl drop earrings hung down to her sharp jawline, and her necklace, also of pearls, hung in long, layered strands.

She lifted an arm to light my cigarette, her green, turquoise, and silver arm bangles jingling. The fur stole draped over one arm was either authentic fox fur or dyed rabbit. I had a feeling it was the real deal.

"Thanks," I said, inhaling the smoke.

She lifted a shot glass from the nearby table and took a dainty sip of moonshine. Then another. "Where's the jazz? I thought for sure they would cough up the dough for a real party."

Our cheapskate mayor would never spend money on a band. "Looks like it's not that kind of party."

She placed a hand on a thrusted hip. "Well, it should be, considering."

"Considering? You mean our mayor?"

"Mayor?"

I pointed to Mayor Gibbons.

"Him? He's the mayor of what? Pancakes?" She laughed. "No, silly. I mean, if this is a fundraiser to build a speakeasy and casino in the Baker Hotel, they should at least have a few craps tables set up."

"Yeah, right," I said, hiding my surprise.

"Who are you here with, doll?"

"My date," I lied. "He's helping with the alcohol."

"A worthy date, then." She smiled and took another sip. "My name's Kitty."

"Emma June. What about you, Kitty? Are you here with your husband?" The woman had so many rings on her fingers, I thought one of them had to be a wedding band.

"Me? A husband?" She nearly spat out her drink. "In this day and age? Doll, life's much too short. Who wants to be chained to some dumb cluck who yells your name whenever he wants something? No, thank you. I'm here with . . ." She held up a perfectly manicured fingernail and glanced around at the crowd. "He was just here." She shrugged.

"Excuse me. Emma June?" Frank grabbed my elbow. "Can I have a word?"

"Why, this must be your date." The woman eyed him top to bottom. "Lucky girl."

Frank gawked at her backside as she sauntered off. "Who was that?"

"Kitty somebody. Frank, this isn't a political party for the mayor. It's a fundraiser to build an illegal drinking and gambling hall at the Baker Hotel."

"Okay," he said, drawing out the word. "Now my tidbit of information. Wade is here. He's standing under those trees, away from the lights." Frank nodded behind him.

"I know. I saw him. Stay away from him. No ruckus, remember?"

"I remember. The shit's gotta stay in the bucket. But it won't stay there long once Miss Helen finds out we had to put her hooch back in their crates."

"Yeah, that Whitt fella we saw talking to the mayor? He wants to force Miss Helen out of business. You think he can?"

"He's part of a mob, I'll bet."

"Mobsters? Here? In Holly Gap?" I knew we had a few Ku Klux Klan members in town. But mobsters seemed a stretch.

"Looks that way. I say we hit the booze."

I followed Frank to the makeshift bar. Perched proudly atop a wooden table covered in a white cloth sat dozens of Dandy glass bottles with short necks and corked tops. Next to them were rows of clear shot glasses.

Frank poured two glasses and handed one to me.

I took a swig. Not bad, but not nearly as smooth as Miss Helen's.

We stood at the far edge of the pavilion, eyeing the crowd. A mixed gathering of young and old, but primarily boisterous men who clucked and postured. The few women I saw, including Kitty, looked bored and ready to leave.

The voices behind us in the dark got our attention.

"What do you mean? Pa said it was taken care of." Wade.

"Because I'm surrounded by stupid palookas, we're back to square one."

"I can't see," I whispered to Frank. "Is that Whitt?"

Frank nodded.

"I don't catch your meanin'." Wade again.

"Doesn't surprise me. Just do as you're told."

"Guess we ain't putting up a missing person sign. You know, like they did for that ma who's missing."

"Clam up, you little smart ass," Whitt hissed. "Which reminds me, Moody taking good care of your mother and that little sister of yours?"

"Yeah," Wade said, his voice muffled but audible.

"Good. And just think. If your old man wasn't such a dumbass, Moody wouldn't have the pleasure of their company."

Moody. The man Loretta didn't like. The man who worked with Earl Foley.

"Stay here," Frank told me, then walked toward the voices.

I turned toward the crowd but focused on the voices behind me in the dark.

"Wade? Is that you out there?" Frank said.

"You need something, boy?"

"No, sir. Just need to pay Wade what he's due. Just wanted to make things right. Here you go."

I stopped listening to Frank and Wade when Whitt reemerged under the pavilion and headed toward Kitty.

"There you are, Daddy," she said, her voice honeyed as she stroked her stole like petting a cat. Authentic fox, all right, just like the sly one standing before her.

The phony pretentiousness of the event gave me the heebie-jeebies, so when Frank returned from the darkness, I told him I wanted to leave.

"You said you wanted to find more clues about your mother, right?"

"Yeah. And her friend, Betty. But what could these people know? They're not from Holly Gap."

"Give us another hour to keep our ears open. Just in case."

As time went on, the crowd got more ossified, spilling their hooch, stumbling over each other, and jawing about making fortunes. We learned nothing more and we both had enough.

Frank headed for the truck, his stride brisk and purposeful.

"So what was that all about?" I said, hurrying to catch up. "Why were you snuggling up to Wade like that? He broke Miss Atta's window and punched you in the face."

"I'll learn more if I keep my enemies close. I gave him back his quarter."

"What in God's name can you learn from Wade Foley?"

"For one, I can steer him away from Miss Atta."

A good point. "For another?"

"Unlike Whitt, Wade's easy pickings. Maybe I can rub elbows with him, find out what's going on. And when I'm done getting answers, I'll punch his lights out."

On our drive back to Miss Helen's, Frank and I talked about all the pieces of information that didn't fit.

We agreed that Mayor Gibbons was on the take. His shiny Cadillac, a gift from Whitt, was a dead giveaway. The mayor had also lied to Miss Helen. It was not a party for his constituents.

"I wonder what the mayor will tell Miss Helen," I said. "You think he'll buy her moonshine for the next event?"

"Shady dealings with mobsters. The big cheese always has the upper hand. You give them something, they give you a payback. Like a new Cadillac. The cycle continues until they own you."

"You really think Whitt's part of the mob?"

"Sure looks that way. Involved with illegal bootlegging and

gambling. Threatening the mayor. Even the way he's dressed. And from the sound of it, Whitt has Moody keeping tabs on the Foleys."

Whitt and Moody worked together. And Whitt had solicited Earl and Wade for some dirty deeds, including locating a person of interest. Whoever that someone was, they didn't want the public to know. I thought of Betty and her threatening note.

"I think we should tell the sheriff," I said.

"That his brother's on the take by a mobster in town? How would that go over?"

I didn't know if the mayor and the sheriff were tight-knitted brothers or of the Cain and Abel variety. I *did* know that Sheriff Gunny Gibbons didn't like being bothered with big problems. And this was a doozy.

A mobster in Holly Gap. Although I never saw him up close, Whitt gave me the creeps.

"Why so quiet, Emma June? What are you thinking?"

"None of this will help me find Mama. It has nothing to do with her."

Frank took his eyes off the road and stared at me. "How can you be so sure?"

I didn't like the serious tone or the grave look in his eyes. At that moment, I wasn't sure of anything. I did know one thing. I needed Daddy, the sheriff, and even Charlene to be right: that Mama was with Betty and far away from mobsters.

....

CHAPTER 27

FRANK

Jazz night at Rosie's wouldn't compare to the New Orleans music scene. Still, any scenery was better than watching his mother shrink further into an illness he couldn't fix. An hour to go, then no worrying for a couple of more.

"You'll be great, Frank," Irene coughed out.

What did she know? All she'd heard was backyard practice.

"Where'd you get the harp?"

Frank pulled the Hohner from its case. "Remember Aunt Patsy's friend, Tyrone? The fella who taught me to play?"

"Vaguely."

"He got me a deal at his music store. I saved up for three months to get this beauty. Best thing I own."

"You look real nice, too."

"Bought the tie and jacket with the money from last night." A three-piece tan suit with a blue tie. Not too bad for a second-hand suit from Johnson's Variety.

"I'm sure Helen appreciated you filling in. And Emma June? How was she?"

"Fine, I guess. Distracted."

Irene gave a slow nod. "And did Mayor Gibbons drool on about how important he is?"

"Turns out, he's not as important as he thought. He's on the take from some gangster named Whitt."

Irene's eyes widened. She pushed herself up to a sitting position. "What?"

Frank told her the real reason for the gathering, the so-called fundraiser for a speakeasy and casino in the Baker Hotel. And how Whitt was on the hunt for someone.

"A gangster? What did he look like?"

"A bit shorter than me. Dark hair under his fedora. Looked to be a birthmark on his face. But maybe it was lipstick."

"Oh, Lord. God, no." Irene's face dropped into her hands. "Bernice is in real trouble."

"Ma, I think it's time you spit it out. What really happened?"

"It's all my fault," she said through her fingers. "That man you described. He *is* a gangster. Just before I picked you up in New Orleans, I saw him at The Diner with Earl. That's when the real trouble began, *after* Earl had started blackmailing me." Her tears kept coming.

Irene had never been around to ease his growing pains. Aunt Patsy had taken on that job, consoled him when he needed it. And when she lay dying of tuberculosis, consoling Aunt Patsy had felt normal, natural.

Frank sat on the mattress and draped an uncomfortable arm around his mother.

Through stops and starts, tears and breaths, she told him.

Irene had been sitting on a low stool behind the counter, wiping out glasses. Earl had already bled her dry, so she stayed hidden to avoid another confrontation. But she could hear them.

Whitt wanted control of the bootlegging business in Mineral Wells and the surrounding counties. And if all the competing distilleries were destroyed, the Baker Hotel had no choice but to buy solely from him.

Frank didn't like his next thought. "Ma, surely they don't think Miss Helen's still is competition, do they?"

"Helen's? Her mom-and-pop operation is nothing like the ones down river. Those distilleries deliver to small towns along the Brazos. Helen only sells locally."

Although not really an answer, her words eased Frank's worry. For now, he wouldn't mention Whitt's plans to Miss Helen or Emma June. Plus he wouldn't have to lie about how he got the information. Instead, he'd just keep another damn secret.

"Anyway," she continued, "Earl asked if he would get a bonus for destroying the stills. Whitt laughed and said, 'You get to do it for free. Remember, I know what you did.'"

"What did Earl do?" Frank asked.

"No idea. But whatever it was, Whitt's holding it over Earl's head and using him to get what he wants. Then Whitt said, 'Politician or not, I have no problem getting rid of a nuisance. Any nuisance.'"

Whitt's nuisance was most likely Mayor Gibbons. Then again, Whitt clearly knew many politicians, some crooked and others who wanted to put a stop to his corruption.

"So Whitt was planning on killing someone," Frank said more to himself than to Irene.

Irene trembled. "Sounds that way. What if, for some reason, they thought Bernice was a nuisance?"

Irene always said Bernice was on the up and up. So unless she had left something out, how could Emma June's mother be of any concern to the likes of Whitt? He brought her a glass of water and told her to take a few breaths.

Whitt had both the mayor and Earl Foley in his pocket. Mayor Gibbons, it seemed, had put himself in that spot out of greed. But it looked as if Earl didn't have a choice. Whatever that old shyster had done, it was bad enough that Whitt could use it against him. And no doubt Wade had to pay for the sins of his father.

"Finish the story, Ma. Did they find you out? Learn you'd been listening?"

Irene closed her eyes and gave a slow nod. "Mabel came back out and refilled their coffee. Before she returned to the kitchen, she stopped and looked down at me. I put a finger to my lips at the same time she told me to get up and take a break. That's when they knew."

"And?"

"Percy and Mabel were in the back when Whitt pulled me outside. He choked me until I thought I would pass out. Then I heard Earl tell him I wouldn't talk. That he had goods on me if I did. Whitt let me go and said, 'Remember, I have a knack for eliminating problems.' That's when I left for New Orleans to get you. But when he saw me at the carnival spilling the beans to Bernice, the gig was over for Earl and he knew it. I can only hope they think I've run off and left for good. If they find me, they'll kill me."

Irene, his mother, who knew too much and got away. And Bernice Crawford, the woman who knew nothing and was missing.

Frank left for the kitchen and guzzled a glass of water. He wiped the sweat from his forehead and returned to her side.

"Ma, I understand why you wanted to get away. So why did you come back here? You could have gone anywhere." He handed her a handkerchief to mop up her face.

"I didn't want to die with a bad conscience. I wanted to come clean with Bernice. I hoped for forgiveness."

"But you didn't get it?" A rhetorical question.

"No," she said, choking the life from the handkerchief. "I just wanted things to be right between us again."

The person his mother wanted to make amends to, to spend her last days with, wasn't him but Bernice Crawford. She didn't care about making things right with him, the boy she had left behind. He was nothing to her but a free gumshoe detective.

If he didn't leave now, he'd be late. "I gotta go." He tore out the front door.

"Hold on, Frank," Irene called out to him. "There's something else."

With her, there was always something else. Whatever it was, Irene could hold it between her knees for all he cared. Now was the time for music. The only thing to relieve the burn. He didn't turn back.

....

CHAPTER 28

EMMA JUNE

jazzed up my drop-waist lavender dress with a pearl necklace and added a matching bandeau to my forehead. It was small potatoes compared to Kitty's glamorous attire. In reverence to Daddy, I settled for pink lipstick instead of red but doubled the kohl smudges on my eyes.

Mama loved Saturday nights at Rosie's, pulling Daddy to the dance floor, clapping and swaying to the music. And I loved watching them. The way they stared at each other when they slow-danced as if the world belonged only to them. Daddy even drank Rags's home-brewed beer, the yeast and barley malt syrup legal and easy to buy.

Daddy said he had no intention of going to Rosie's for music night. Although he didn't explain, I knew how he would hate the pitiful looks and questions from the townsfolk. Nevertheless, Miss Helen insisted he needed a diversion from his worries and promised to drag him by the ears if necessary.

I entered Rosie's and out of habit, scanned the hat rack by the front door. Before, when I had foolishly mooned over Wade, I started my workday by looking to see if the creep's gray flat cap hung on one of the pegs. If it did, I revved up my hip sway and tried to think of ways to flirt.

I shook away that disgusting memory and focused on my favorite night of the week. Saturday night, when Rosie's served only music and we all set aside our differences and celebrated our common interest. Regardless of how rich or poor, folks wore their best bib and tucker, including their finest hat.

With a room full of people standing and milling about, hats were easy to spot. I scanned the room looking for the mayor. He never missed a Saturday night at Rosie's, his chance to keep constituents stitched firmly in his pocket. The only Panama hat I spotted belonged to the banker.

Whiskey Malone and Stinger Jones were already on the raised platform Leonard had built as their stage years before. Whiskey sat on a stool shining his trumpet, a broad grin on his middle-aged face. Old Stinger had settled on the platform's edge, his straw hat pulled down to his eyes. With skin like fine dark leather, his narrow cheeks sunk in with each draw of his cigarette.

Stinger kept most words to himself. When I was younger, I used to think the reason he stayed so quiet was because his lips were too tired from playing the saxophone to carry on a conversation. As I got older, I realized he communicated best through his music.

"Emma June!" Charlene caught me at the entrance.

Obviously, Charlene's mother had caught her before she ran out the door. She looked almost matronly, her attire whittled down to a simple skirt and cardigan. Except for pink lipstick, she wore no other cosmetics.

"Any news on your mother?" she asked.

I shook my head.

She pulled me in for a hug. "I'm sorry."

Grateful for Charlene's surprising thoughtfulness, I still didn't want to talk about Mama. Charlene's own mother was a stodgy old bitch, but at least she didn't leave her family.

We moved away from the door, making room for more patrons.

"How are things with you?" I asked.

"Peachy keen, I suppose. Not counting my mother telling me to stay away from bad influences."

"Like me?"

"Or Betty if she comes back. And school is awful. Loretta hasn't been there for days. I finally went by her house today. Her mother opened the door a crack, told me Loretta was sick, then shut the door in my face."

"Was anyone else there? Wade or Mr. Foley?"

"Didn't see them. Why?"

"Just wondering if they were sick, too." I knew better, of course. "What about that man you said Mr. Foley was working with. You see him?"

"Moody, you mean. And nope. He was probably chopping down mesquite trees with Loretta's father."

I couldn't tell her what I had learned at the mayor's shindig. She didn't need more fodder to add to the town's gossip.

"Where's Frank?" Charlene asked, surveying the room.

"Probably getting himself spiffy. He's performing tonight."

"Performing? Berries!" She pulled red lipstick from her purse.

I left her swooning over thoughts of romance and found the Munsons sitting at the big table in front of the stage, the one Miss Helen always claimed the rights to.

"Where's Daddy?" I asked her.

"Sorry, Emma June. You know your daddy. Flexible as a two-by-four."

"And Frank's going to *blow* the harmonica like a *hurricane*," Scooter said, grinning.

I sat next to Scooter and received the hug I could count on.

"Helen," Leonard said, "tell Emma June—"

"Oh my, I almost forgot," Miss Helen said. "Your handsome Samuel telephoned. He's calling back tomorrow at ten. You be there, now. He wants to talk to you."

"Probably to tell me he's found a girlfriend."

Miss Helen gave me a scowl. "If you think that, you've got a big hole in your screen door."

I needed a change of subject. "Where's the mayor?"

"Hell if I know." She scowled. "Tried getting ahold of him about the next delivery, but the nitwit hasn't returned my call. I reckon he's too busy shining that new Caddy I heard about."

Gunny sat on his usual stool at the counter talking to Miss Atta and Rags.

Like always on Saturday nights, Miss Atta had gussied up in her rose-colored tiered dress with a matching side waistband. She sashayed to the stage just as Frank ran through the front door. He wove through the crowd and downed the water Rags handed him at the counter.

"Welcome, blues fools." Miss Atta's voice boomed to the audience. "As always, Stinger Jones and Whiskey Malone are here." The crowd whooped and hollered. "Tonight, another musical guest is joining them." She turned to Stinger and Whiskey. "Light us up, boys."

The trumpet and saxophone showered the room with joy. Folks swayed in their seats. Shoes, ranging from heeled Mary Janes to old work boots, tapped to the rhythm. Customers wore genuine smiles as if *hardship* was a word in an obsolete dictionary.

After three songs, the trumpet and saxophone quieted. Stinger held up a finger to silence the crowd and motioned Frank to the platform.

"Met this here foundlin' the other day. From N'awling," he

mumbled, his voice deep and raspy. "Liked him, even. Fella's got a set of pipes. Gots some words, too. Listen up now."

If Frank was nervous, it didn't show. He stood erect on the stage and grinned at the crowd. He tapped his harp on his palm three times then started playing. Soon after, Stinger and Whiskey joined in with their horns. He pulled the harp from his mouth. "A little something I wrote called 'Gopher Hole Blues,'" he said and started to sing.

> There's a song you can't be singing
> 'Cause your eardrums won't stop ringing
> So you keep the worst and best things deep inside.
> It's a story not worth telling
> 'Cause your throat, it keeps on swelling
> "Son," he says, "let's take a joyride."
> Then the devil moves you this way, and the Jesus moves
>   you that
> But there's nothing you can settle on for long
> Just a pair of empty shoes
> As they tighten up your screws
> Till you're back inside the gopher hole of blues.

So Frank had finished writing the song. I remembered telling him that living in Holly Gap was merely a level above living in a gopher hole. I'd been useful for something.

After he played the last note, Frank nodded. The crowd cheered.

One man stood up and slapped his giant palms together, his white teeth flashing. "That boy can strut and sit at the same time."

"Frank hit on *all* sixes!" Scooter yelled.

The crash came first.

Or was it the fire? I can't remember.

When Miss Helen grabbed Scooter's arm and yelled for me to hurry out, the reality set in.

People screamed, shouted. Some ran out the back door. Others rushed toward a screaming woman, her dress on fire.

Gunny and Rags ran out the front door looking for the culprit.

"Out! Out! Out!" Miss Atta yelled to the customers, pointing to the back door.

Frank, Jacoby, Leonard, and a few others doused the flaming table and chairs with water-filled containers. I backed away.

Mr. Baxter from the hardware store pulled out a pistol, aimed it upward, then stood clueless about what to shoot.

A woman I didn't recognize lay rigid on the floor, her eyes in a dead-open, a hand clutched to her chest.

"Call Doc Ferguson!" someone shouted.

....

CHAPTER 29

EMMA JUNE

The next morning, Gunny sat on our sofa giving us the limited details.

Mrs. Peterson, who had a heart condition, didn't survive. Multiple people suffered minor cuts from broken glass. The only person burned was Mrs. Porter, whose dress caught on fire. Luckily, the burns were not severe.

I pictured Charlene holding a hand to her forehead and prattling on to some poor, rapt listener about how she'd escaped near death. In truth, when the bottle bomb crashed through the window, she'd been in the bathroom out of harm's way.

"Found a note, too," Sheriff Gibbons said. "Out front held down by a rock. Said, 'Let the Heathen be judged in Thy sight.'"

"Any ideas, Gunny?" Daddy asked, handing him a cup of coffee.

"Still asking around. A Prohibitionist, a leftover KKK member. Miss Atta doesn't deserve this kind of bullshit. Oh, excuse me, Emma June. But this chaps my ass. All our folks wanted was a little music to wash their troubles clean."

"I'm going over this morning," I said, "to help get things back to normal."

Daddy gave a firm shake of his head. "No, Emma June."

Gunny flicked his eyes toward Daddy. "'Preciate that, Emma June. Bunch'a folks were there bright and early this morning. 'Cept for the windowpane, it's probably all taken care of."

Daddy leaned forward in the rocker and glared at me. "Don't go back to work until they catch the attacker." He had seen me when I arrived home smelling like a burnt woodpile.

"Thing is," Gunny continued, "this ain't the only problem in town."

Yeah, a mobster's in cahoots with your brother, I thought. "My mother is missing," I spat out, my words harsher than intended.

Gunny cleared his throat. "That's right. And we got hooligans on the prowl. Girl was assaulted a few days back. Tallulah Cobern, best friend of Miss Atta's niece. Could be the same ones who did this to Miss Atta's place."

"Remember Tallulah, Emma June? Friend of Berta's?" Daddy said.

Of course I remembered. I was twelve when I first met Tallulah. Mama and Daddy had sat at Rosie's counter while Scooter and I sat in a booth with her and Berta. They taught me how to play checkers while Scooter tried to buff out the scratches on the table with a piece of his daddy's sandpaper.

"JT Sampson turned on his porch light," Gunny said. "Scared them away before something worse happened. Gal's clothes were ripped up. Bruised her up pretty good, too."

"Nobody got a good look at them?" Daddy asked.

"Nah, just shadows in the dark."

"Not even Tallulah?" I asked.

The sheriff shook his head. "She might'a got a better look had the other boy not shined a flashlight in her face the whole time. White boys, though. That much she could tell."

Although Louis did most things Wade told him, I couldn't see him being part of this. Moody and Wade, on the other hand . . .

I couldn't risk ratting out Wade for throwing a rock through Miss

Atta's window. Wade's ties to a big-time thug seemed firmly knotted. Although I wanted to know what Whitt and Moody were up to, I didn't want them looking in my direction.

But I did give Gunny something. "Did you know Earl Foley is working with a new fella? A young man in his twenties, I think."

Gunny squinted. "Can't say I do. What about him?"

"Loretta doesn't like him. Says he's full of mischief. And he and Wade are together a lot. His name is Moody."

"Loretta tell you this?"

"No. Charlene."

Gunny said he'd look into it, but the doubt in his eyes didn't match his words.

I reached the Munsons' house fifteen minutes early, hoping Samuel wouldn't renege on his promise to call. Scooter sat next to me on the front porch, his face buried in Choppers's fur.

"Scooter, your mother doesn't like it when you lick dogs."

"*Doesn't* like it when I lick dirt, *too*."

"You know why?"

"Because *she's* stuck in the *mud*."

I laughed. "A real killjoy sometimes, huh?"

"Right-io, buffalo." He looked away. "And *fire* can kill."

For the most part, Scooter had remained calm during the attack at Rosie's. Once we made it out the back door, Miss Helen paced and repeated, "Oh Lord, oh Lord." Scooter followed her around, saying "bless your heart" and "easy does it."

"Emma June?" Miss Helen's voice flitted out to the porch. "You'll never guess who had the gall to show up at my door yesterday." She didn't wait for a response. "Earl Foley. Not only did he want me to sell him moonshine, he had the nerve to ask if 'that poor little gal's mama' was still galivanting. Playacting like a concerned citizen just because you used to go to school with his daughter."

Miss Helen was right. The man cared only for himself, which included drinking Miss Helen's better moonshine. And nobody seemed to care about Mama anymore.

The whole town seemed like they'd forgotten Mama's character. I wondered if her friends at Widow Larson's beauty shop missed their gab sessions with Mama. Or if her Methodist church members hoped she would return before the upcoming bake sale so she could turn the Judas volunteers back into team players. Was Mama now merely the subject of crude gossip by all of Holly Gap?

The telephone rang.

I bolted through the door. The chair next to the candlestick telephone had been cleared of magazines. I lifted the earpiece and sat.

"Hello?"

"There you are." Hearing Samuel's voice, I almost forgot about everything else.

....

As Leonard drove Scooter and me to Rosie's Café, I sat a bit taller in the truck.

Samuel said he thought of me all the time. Not just about my worries, but about me. How he missed my mischievous grin, the tilt of my head, my hazel eyes looking back at him.

When I told him how hard the days had become, he said, "There is a land of the living and a land of the dead and the bridge is love, the only survival, the only meaning." A quote from Thornton Wilder's *The Bridge of San Luis Rey*. He had taken the time to read the book I loved.

Toward the end of our conversation, Samuel quoted another line: "Henceforth, letter-writing had to take the place of all the affection that could not be lived." He finished by saying, "That is, until I return for summer."

I couldn't think that far ahead.

Books in my bedroom that had once lain open begging for attention now remained closed like answers behind a locked door. Each time I tried to read, questions interrupted the written words. *Where is she? How can I find her? Will she ever come home? What will I do if she doesn't?* The only characters I wished to visit were the ones in Mama's storytelling who lived happily ever after.

Samuel had asked about Frank. I heard his hesitant pauses, the suspicion in his voice. "No," I had told him. "I don't think of Frank in that way."

Frank did have a way about him. He had nothing but dust in his pockets, had grown up without a father, but still managed to remain positive and determined, cocksure of himself. Talented and street smart, he was easy to be around.

Samuel was less easy to be around, but for a different reason. He made my palms sweat and my heart skip rope. I had only known him a short time, yet he weakened my knees and quivered my belly. When I thought of him, his comforting arm around me, his kiss on my cheek, the lonely nights became less terrifying.

And unlike me, both Frank and Samuel were moving forward with dreams—free, untethered, not stuck to wooden posts and storefront windows with the word MISSING written in capital letters.

CHAPTER 30

EMMA JUNE

Leonard unloaded lumber from his truck while Scooter and I entered the bleakness of a restaurant assaulted by hatred.

Frank and Charlene sat together wiping soot off the wooden floor. After a slight wave, I headed for the kitchen.

"It ain't the worst thing that's ever happened, Rags," Miss Atta said, standing next to him.

"Bad 'nough. Bastards." Rags spotted me and apologized for his language.

"Nothing for you to be sorry about, Rags. But I sure am sorry about last night." I hugged Miss Atta and welcomed her strength, the anchor I needed.

She pulled away and looked at me straight on. "Rain might beat the leopard's skin, but it don't wash out the spots. We fix it up and keep going."

"And I heard about Tallulah."

"Uh-huh, a string of badness. Poor thing. Scared out of her mind. She was lucky nothing more happened."

Lucky. Right.

"Shortcake, you can help Frank wipe down the floors. We need to get Rosie's back to normal."

A lesser person than Miss Atta would have said "enough is enough" and thrown in the towel. Rosie's needed to stay open to keep me sane. And after so much loss, Miss Atta needed the place for her heart's survival.

I grabbed a rag, ready to scour the floor anew, and returned to the dining room.

"Oh, I knew Betty, all right," Charlene told Frank as I sat beside them.

"What about Betty?" I said.

"Frank asked about her," Charlene said, brushing ash from her hands.

Frank tossed a filthy rag aside and reached for a new one. "Just thinking about what you told me, Emma June. About your mother leaving around the same time as Betty."

"Betty was *fun*." Scooter plunked a two-by-four on the floor and sat cross-legged next to Frank.

"Remember, Emma June?" Charlene said. "When she took us to Mineral Wells that time? She paid for all our tickets to see *Love* with Greta Garbo. We sat in the back row and drank Coca-Colas and ate popcorn. And Scooter, you ate so much cotton candy, it turned your whole face pink."

Actually, his face had turned from pink to green. When he leaned over, Charlene and I thought he would throw up on our new shoes.

"Anna left her *son* for a *man*," Scooter said.

"Typical," Frank muttered.

"Right, Scooter." Charlene poked the top of my head. "Remember when we were walking out of the theater, Emma June? How we teased your mama and Betty for crying at the sad parts?"

"Yeah, after our own eyes had already dried, we teased them for being saps."

Frank smiled. "Sounds like they were great friends."

"Until they weren't," I said.

"Says you, Emma June," Charlene said. "Best friends always stick together." She didn't bother looking at me.

For the first time, I hated Betty. Daddy was right. None of this would have happened if the wolf in sheep's clothing hadn't moved to town.

"So did Betty have any other friends here?" Frank asked. Charlene and I looked at each other.

"She—"

"Not everyone thought she was the bee's knees," Charlene said, interrupting me. "I think the women were just jealous."

"Her *dance* card was always *full*."

"Well, not here, Scooter. In New York City," I reminded him.

"Buildings so tall they *scraped* the sky."

"That's right," Charlene said, dreamy-eyed. "And a city square with lights so bright you'd think it was daytime. And don't forget the revolving doors. Can you just imagine?"

Betty had spoken of speakeasies like Chumley's, where writers gathered. How people hung their clothes out to dry on the balconies of high buildings, and how the sun's rays shone through Grand Central Station.

"And Harlem," Frank said, a glow in his eyes. "Best musicians in the world are there. 'Least that's what I've heard. Man, what I wouldn't give to visit the Cotton Club. See Duke Ellington and his band."

Scooter nodded like a cowboy bucking on a bull. "Emmy, Charlene, and *Scooter* in the Cotton *Candy* Club."

Thanks to Scooter, the smell of smoke and the evil that came with it momentarily disappeared, replaced by laughter.

"You were so brave last night, Frank." Charlene batted her eyelashes.

"Me? I didn't do anything. Just like the last time I was in this sort of situation."

"Last time?" I asked.

"Yep. I was in a nightclub in New Orleans when the Feds raided the place. Before I hoofed it out the back door, one of the officers saw a man reach in his pocket. Thought he was pulling a gun instead of a cigarette. Shot him dead. Dumb cluck should have kept his hands up like he was supposed to."

I had a feeling Frank's past experiences included many close shaves.

Charlene pulled Frank's flat cap down to his eyes. "Now, don't do anything without me. I have to wash up. I'm not keen on the hobo look." She giggled.

While Charlene sashayed off to the toilet, Scooter headed to the lunch counter to build the Missouri Pacific railroad with dinner knives.

I turned to Frank. "Why are you so interested in Betty?"

"Because . . . she was your mother's friend."

"Yeah? So?"

"Because I'm your friend, Emma June. And all that business at the mayor's shindig got me noodling." He paused. "Never mind."

Part of me wanted to tell him to butt out. But truthfully, having him in my corner could prove useful.

"Damnit!" Leonard said, looking away from his lumber and staring at his thumb.

"And Frank? Speaking of the shindig. You didn't say anything to Charlene about our moonshine run, did you? She's, you know, chatty."

"A looker, though." Frank grinned. "But, nah, I kept my mouth shut."

"Problem is, Miss Helen's still firing on all cylinders. I leave my window open, I get drunk from the fumes."

"A smell worth inhaling." Frank chuckled.

"Miss Helen said she hasn't spoken to the mayor. I have a feeling Whitt's threat melted his spine."

Frank nodded. "Yeah, she probably won't be the supplier. I can't see Miss Helen taking that sitting down."

"Nope." And I didn't want to be around when she got the news.

Frank nudged me. "So I hear you're goofy for a fella named Samuel, the one who rescued you on carnival night. That true?"

Charlene wasn't just chatty. She was a blabbermouth. I wanted Samuel to remain secretly tucked away like a good present.

"You carrying a torch for Charlene?"

"Maybe." He cocked his head. "Always have been partial to blondes."

"And hers is natural. Not bleached like her mother's." It reminded me. "Speaking of, did your mother come hear you play last night?"

He looked away. "Wasn't up to it. She's been feeling poorly."

Frank rarely spoke of his mother, and I had a feeling they didn't get on. But if she was the sickly type, he had to take care of her.

Frank went back to scrubbing the floor. "What about your old man? I thought I'd meet him last night."

"Couldn't face the crowd asking questions, I guess. Frank?"

"Yeah?"

"You did yourself proud last night."

He smiled, looking pleased. "Yeah, I really heated up the place."

Too close to the truth, neither one of us could suppress our nervous laughter.

After the silence, I asked if he had heard about Tallulah.

"Yeah," he said through gritted teeth. "Wade and Moody."

....

CHAPTER 31

EMMA JUNE

Choppers sighed, satisfied that his midday meal had filled his belly. But I had forgotten what hunger felt like. Instead of grabbing something from the icebox, I sat in an empty house staring straight ahead. I was quickly becoming that old woman from the legend of Crazy Water, the one who slowly lost her mind. Except, unlike her, I had yet to find the healing spring to drink away my madness.

More time had passed without a word. I feared unspeakable news would blow in and crumble what was left in my hollow bones. I couldn't find Mama any more than I could find a whisper in a whirlwind.

Before she disappeared, my idea of despair and melancholy meant missing a party or being unable to go to the river because of rain. But those were mere disappointments, a small black weevil in a massive barrel of shiny white rice. I hadn't known how lucky and easy my life had been.

When Daddy was home, he spent his time staring out the window, fidgeting under the hood of Ol' Bess, taking Choppers for long walks. Sometimes he swept the front porch or flicked a dust cloth across the furniture. On rare occasions, I would come home to find him listening to the High-Jinkers on the radio. His scowl would loosen enough to set free a dimpled grin.

The sound of Choppers's gentle snoring was the only sign of life in our dormant house. Daddy and I had become two sapless bodies trying to survive, as listless as two pinwheels without a breeze.

The repeated blast of Roadrunner's horn broke the silence.

"Emmy June! Emma June!" Miss Helen's frantic shriek.

She bolted through the door, her orange hair poking up like cactus needles.

I lurched from the chair. "What is it? What happened? Is it Mama?"

"It's Scooter. We . . . we don't know where he is." She held a hand to her chest, unable to catch her breath. "Miss Primrose . . . She said . . . Oh God, just hurry. Come with me to the sheriff's office."

"Where's Leonard?" I asked as we scrambled inside Roadrunner.

"Out searching. Talking to neighbors," she said, her hands trembling on the steering wheel.

Scooter never strayed far by himself. If he took a walk alone, he always stopped at the perimeter's edge and hollered, "property *line!*" My stomach clenched thinking of the day Samuel and I had run into Wade at the school. Wade alone was bad enough. I had a feeling Moody was worse.

"What did Miss Primrose say?"

"That he didn't come in from recess. Nobody saw him wander off."

Tears rolled down Miss Helen's face as she drove. "If anything happens to him . . ."

Miss Primrose knew she had to keep a watchful eye on Scooter. Her lack of attention was probably due to her need to powder her nose and apply lipstick every thirty minutes, or because she was constantly turning her back and spritzing perfume to mask the smell of our poverty-stricken students.

The motorcar screeched to a halt. I followed as Miss Helen burst through the sheriff's door.

"Gibbons!" she panted.

Gunny sat behind his desk with his gout foot elevated on an upside-down mop bucket.

"Helen. What—"

She stood over him, her words bursting out in torrents.

"Now, Helen. Scooter couldn't have gone far."

Unless he'd been hurt and dumped in the woods. I thought of Moody, the man I had yet to encounter, and Whitt, the man I had.

"He's been gone almost two hours now. Get your lazy ass up and do something!" she hollered.

I stopped pacing when Gunny stood. "You start searching east. I'll go west."

Miss Helen was in no condition to drive. Neither was I. My hands shook too much to pick a small flower, let alone manage a steering wheel.

Miss Helen, a quivering mess, drove toward Shanty Town and The Diner.

"Worst day of my life," she said, swerving around a large fallen branch in the middle of the road.

"I know," I said. Because I did.

I imagined Scooter talking his way out of a dangerous encounter. Years back, a bully at school had pinned his shoulders up against the wall. He called Scooter names and threatened to steal his pocketknife.

"*Silly* noodlehead. My name is Scooter." Then he smiled and tickled the boy's ribs. The boy, not getting the attention he wanted, shoved Scooter to the ground. Scooter leaned up on an elbow and said, "A worm is the *only* animal that *can't* fall down."

Scooter worried more about others than himself. If he learned someone was sick or injured, he was the first to show up. Usually, he would bring something he had plucked from nature—a flower, a curiously shaped stick, or a rock. But if someone threatened his friends or family, his eyes narrowed, his fists clenched. Like that day Miss Primrose had smacked little Janey's fingers with a ruler for stealing a pencil and Scooter had yelled, "Leave. Her. Alone."

As we drove east of town, the land lay flat and desolate, the same way we felt. Prickly pear cactus wickedly called for us to take a seat. Wildflowers, booby-trapped by Texas thistle, taunted to be picked.

"What—" Miss Helen pointed through the windshield.

Squinting, I saw two figures walking in our direction. One tall. One short.

"Scooter!" Miss Helen screamed. She braked and leaped out of Roadrunner, forgetting to cut the engine. The motorcar coasted toward a ditch. I leaned sideways, found the gear, and reined her to a stop. My big contribution for the day.

Miss Helen smothered Scooter against her chest.

"Mama. *Can't* breathe," Scooter said, his words music to my ears.

Miss Helen released her hold on Scooter and turned to Frank. "How dare you take Scooter without telling me." Then she slapped him across the face.

CHAPTER 32

FRANK

Frank remembered the last time a dame slapped him. Ten years ago Betsy Randell had flung her little palm across his face for not asking before he kissed her.

This one stung.

"What?" Frank tried but couldn't match Miss Helen's glare.

"I need to know where he is at all times!" Miss Helen cuffed the back of his head. "I was worried sick."

"I didn't take him. I was bringing him back. And geez, stop with the hitting."

"Bringing him back from where?"

"I was walking home from work and saw Scooter leaving the Foley place." Miss Helen didn't need to know the rest.

Scooter tugged on Miss Helen's apron. "Mama, *Mama*. I didn't *get* to see her."

"What? Who?"

"*Loretta.*"

Miss Helen's eyebrows lifted halfway up her forehead. "You walked all the way to the Foleys? By yourself?"

"I know the *way*." Scooter picked up a sharp stick and pierced holes in the forgiving ground.

"How did you know, honeypot?"

Emma June cleared her throat. "He went with me, Miss Helen. We've walked there together a couple of times. Remember when Loretta busted her leg and we had to drop off her home-work package?"

Miss Helen smirked. "Yeah, so Miss Primrose wouldn't have to plop her lazy rear-end in her motorcar and deliver it herself." She bent down and tapped Scooter's back, interrupting his ant inspec-tions. "Let's go, precious pea. Your mama's busy as a pigpen fly."

Miss Helen walked toward Frank. He backed up and held up his hands in surrender. She stopped and grinned wryly. "You can put your hands down now. I didn't bring my pistol. How about I give you a ride back to your house?"

Not on your life. "No. I'm good."

While Miss Helen and Scooter headed back to the motorcar, Frank grabbed Emma June's arm. "Listen—" he started.

"What?"

"Scooter wasn't just leaving the Foley place. He was running away from it."

Miss Helen beeped the horn. "Hurry up, Emma June."

He spoke faster. "He told me a mean tall man answered the door, told him Loretta wasn't home, and yelled at him to scram."

"Moody, you think?"

"Yeah, fits his description. Thing is, I was thinking about going there myself to talk to Wade. See if I could get any information from him. Before I got to the Foleys, I ran into Wade on the road. He told me not to come to his house. Ever."

"One thing's for sure. They don't want company."

Another blast of the roadster's horn and Emma June left him with his thoughts.

Frank hated the fear he'd seen on Scooter's face. When he'd found him running from the Foleys' house, the kid's eyes were the size of tractor tires. For good reason. Moody was as gentle as a feral cat.

He thought of Charlene, his spicy diversion from all the messy business. She had something up her sleeve and said to meet her at the Variety. First, he'd check in on Irene.

After the short walk, he approached the shanty's front door with a double take. An open door wasn't good. Sweat beaded on his forehead. Bad mother or not, if they took her, he'd hunt them down. Like Aunt Patsy had taught him, if somebody does you wrong, you have two choices: forgive them or make them pay. He'd chose the latter.

He entered quietly, wishing he had a gun. He got his fist ready.

When the sound of humming came from the kitchen, his shoulders unhitched.

"Ma?"

"In here, Frank."

Washing dishes? "You're up."

"And at 'em." Her smile didn't exactly curl up at the corners, but it was there. And her cheeks held a touch of pink life.

"You're better?"

"Some days are worse than others, I guess. I'll take the good ones when I can."

"Well then, get on your dancing shoes. We'll go back to New Orleans and hit the nightclubs," he said, knowing it wasn't possible.

"Ha. Very funny. It's a nice thought, though." She got quiet. Stared out the window. "I should have been the one to teach you to dance. Not Patsy."

His mother should have done a lot of things. And *not* done some others.

Irene peered out back at the desolate field. "Join me outside for a butt."

He had time. Charlene wasn't expecting him for another hour.

Smoke from two Chesterfields drifted away from the house and into the clear afternoon. Irene coughed out her second puff and leaned against the wood siding.

"Want me to bring out a chair?" Without the support of the house, Frank doubted she could stand on her own.

She shook her head. "I'm fine." Another cough, smokeless this time. "You know, I sat outside for a bit today. It was nice. The cardinals called my name."

"Huh?"

"You've never heard them? Geez Louise, Frank. They say it plain as day. I-*rene*, I-*rene*, I-*rene*, I-*rene*." She grinned.

His mother had a nice smile. A shame she didn't do it more often.

"Wow, Ma. You're a bird translator. Your skills run deep. And all this time I thought they were saying *chirp*."

She gave a friendly shove to his shoulder.

Both silent, he realized the quiet was comfortable, not strained as it had been. He liked the moment, standing beside her, the ease. Maybe Irene was finally showing her good side. Or maybe it had always been there, but he'd been too heated to see it.

"Things better at Rosie's?" she said.

"Yep. Fixed up good as new." Except for his lingering outrage at the senselessness of it all.

"Did you meet Theo?"

"Nope. Emma June wanted him to come. She said he wasn't up for it."

"Theo's a good father to Emma June. She's lucky to have him." Her face turned somber.

"What is it?"

She shook her head. "I know how much Theo misses Bernice. They might have squabbled at small things, but their love was strong."

"Was? Not anymore?"

Irene gazed far into the horizon. "I don't know." She paused and turned to him. "I'm scared, Frank. Thinking the worst." Her familiar melancholy had returned.

"You know what Aunt Patsy always said? Fear is just Future Events Aren't Real."

"I hadn't thought of that in a long time," she said, a faraway look in her eyes. "Yeah, she used to say that to me when we were younger. It helped, sometimes. It's not helping now." Irene coughed through another puff then crushed the butt with a heel. "Frank, how was I to know that a fleeting, ugly encounter with Earl so long ago would come back to haunt me? Two short weeks with Theo, then I moved back to New Orleans where I met Pete."

"Yeah. Pete Sanders, father of the year. He left you alone with a young kid."

Her face paled more than usual. "Well—he had good reason." She tried to light another cigarette but gave up on her shaking hands. "He found out I lied to him."

He had the feeling Irene was about to give him another tidbit of dirt he didn't want to hear. But secretly, he already knew. Irene had always struck him as a floozy, a woman who would cheat on her husband.

Her face turned grave.

"I lied about you."

The seriousness behind her eyes left him cold. "What are you talking about, Ma?"

She held a tight fist to her chest. "Theo and I had been lovers."

Lovers. Not just a youthful crush. His mind raced.

Frank thrust himself away from the clapboard house. He plodded toward what he once thought of as an open field with possibilities. Now, it was nothing more than a wasteland. He turned on a heel and faced her.

"You're not telling me this was . . . was twenty-one years ago?"

Irene gave him a sorrowful nod.

He felt it then. The gut punch, the tightening in his chest.

Now he understood. He understood too well. He'd been a fool. Stupid he hadn't put it together before.

From the beginning, Irene had spoon-fed him bits of information. Now he had the whole ugly bucket of truth. If that bucket held rocks, he'd break every window in town.

"I gotta go."

"Frank, wait."

He headed inside the house, stopping only to collect the box of *Scoot's Booty.*

"Frank, please," she called after him.

"No more!" he screamed and slammed the door on his way out.

He could have turned around and confronted her. But why bother? She was a liar, a con artist, a sorry excuse of a mother. What did he care if she was sick? Maybe she'd lied about that too. Betty and Irene, two liars in one body. To hell with both of them. The one person he'd ever really trusted lay six feet under in a New Orleans cemetery.

He had a life to live and living it would be easier without her. He'd leave tomorrow. Let her drown in her own mess of secrets and lies.

But first, he'd meet up with Charlene and throw back some *Scooter's Revenge.* Or whatever the hell it was called.

CHAPTER 33

....

EMMA JUNE

I sat at the counter savoring an end-of-the-day grape Nehi when the bells pinged on Rosie's door. Charlene entered arm in arm with Frank, who wore the same tie he'd performed in on firebomb night.

While Frank stomped toward the kitchen with a scowl on his face, Charlene flitted toward me in a new yellow drop-waist dress, her lips a bright red.

"What's up with him?" I asked.

"Just a little grummy, I guess. I've tried everything to get him to take me to Crazy Theater in Mineral Wells to see *The Circus*. Charlie Chaplin plays a tramp who finds the girl of his dreams at a circus. Guess I've kept him too busy," she said with a giggle.

"Too busy with what? Or should I ask?"

Charlene turned away from me. I followed her gaze to where Frank stood behind the counter. She wiggled her fingers toward him in a flirtatious wave.

"Charlene? Too busy with what?"

"My party at the Brazos Dance Hall," she mumbled.

"But it's not open anymore." No thanks to the Holy Baptist Church, the place had been closed down and boarded up. Although some of our elders had overlooked the liquor, they weren't keen on young couples using the hall for petting parties.

Charlene grinned. "We opened it. I told Frank about the place and voilà! We spread the word. Like a real speakeasy except without a password. The best part? The town forgot to shut off the electricity. Since the windows are boarded, no one will see when we turn the lights on. And I nicked our old phonograph from the attic. We've got records and everything. It's tonight. Wanna come?"

"Tonight? You never told me, Charlene. Neither did Frank."

"I told him not to. I wanted it to be a surprise."

No—she hadn't told me because she was jealous of my friendship with Frank. Or she didn't want a killjoy at her party. "A surprise, all right. What time?"

"About an hour."

I gave a perturbed squint to the person who had once been my best friend. Who used to include me in everything. Insisted, even.

"But you can come late if you want," she added, knowing perfectly well I wouldn't walk there alone at night.

It didn't matter. I wanted nothing to do with a party that included dancing and gaiety. Especially one where I had been invited as an afterthought.

Frank sidled up to Charlene and handed her a Coca-Cola.

"You ready to go, Emma June?" he asked.

"I didn't know about it. I don't have time to get ready."

"Ready? You're dressed better than most will be."

"Who's invited?"

"Different folks. Some even from my upscale side of town." He smirked. "Berta and her friend Tallulah are coming."

"Will Loretta be there?"

"No," Charlene said. "Her mother sent a letter to Miss Primrose saying they were taking a little trip and not to expect her back for a few weeks."

I leaned toward Frank and raised an eyebrow. "A trip, huh? And this close to the end of school. Imagine that."

"Come with us," Frank said, ignoring my skepticism. "Might just be fun."

Fun. I had forgotten what that felt like.

Charlene stood beside Frank, waiting for my answer.

I gave her a scowl. "Think I'll pass."

"I completely understand, Emma June. I'm sure your daddy needs you." She laid a phony sympathetic hand on my arm. One I wanted to fling off. "Well, I need to freshen up before we go. Be back in a dash." She smiled, pecked Frank on the cheek, and headed to the toilet.

Before my ire had a chance to settle, Frank nudged me. "You really should come. No need to look forward to it. Just fact-gather while you get drunk. That's what I plan to do. Especially the drunk part."

There was something different about him, the way his eyes pleaded for me to come. Perhaps he felt bad for not telling me about the party. Justifiably so.

Regardless, if I went at least it would piss off Charlene. It seemed worth the effort. "I'll grab my purse."

When I returned from the storage room, Frank was speaking to Rags at the counter. I telephoned Miss Helen from Rosie's and told her to let Daddy know I'd be home late. After what happened with Tallulah, he'd become more protective, almost to the point of hovering.

Charlene leaned against the door, her arms folded, an icy grimace on her face.

"What?" I asked.

"Nothing. I just don't like that Frank pressured you. You know, with so many things on your mind and all."

"How considerate of you, Charlene. And, you know, Daddy's a grown man and Frank's right. I might just have fun."

The old Brazos Dance Hall sat alone a good quarter mile off Main Street. The pitiful old building looked as if it had given up, as if its worn, tattered boards wanted to collapse from boredom and loneliness. Around back, someone had torn off a few rotten planks, making an entry space.

Inside, the hall was bare. The buckled floor had been newly swept. Charlene used the built-in stage as a table for her phonograph. Beside it were a stack of records that Charlene stood busily sorting.

Frank left the hall but hustled back with a box of moonshine. "Let's open this baby up." He pulled out a Mason jar and held it high. The newest label, *Scoot's Booty*, replaced last month's *Scoot's Loot*.

"She sold it to you?"

"Gave it to me. I bought Scooter his own harp from Johnson's Variety the other day. Guess she was grateful."

"Yeah, a little Scooter tenderness goes a long way in her book."

He funneled the hooch into a flask and handed it to me. "Swig?"

After a few swallows of the smooth shine, I handed it back and let the warmth settle. Charlene flounced to Frank's side as Bessie Smith's "Downhearted Blues" played on the phonograph. "Okay, my sheik. Let's slow dance before everyone gets here."

Frank gave Charlene a kiss on her cheek and a sip from the flask. "Let's do it," he said with a wink.

Watching them, I yearned for Samuel to hold me close and sway me to the soft melody. I needed to forget, if only for a night, that the cracks in my armor were growing wider.

Within thirty minutes, a gathering of young folks turned up and licked their lips before filling their flasks.

The crowd, like Choppers, was a mixed breed. Lucy Hodges, the rich girl whose father owned an oil rig, came with Peter Mercer, the banker's son. A couple of girls I'd known from school, both a few years younger than me, steered away from the hooch but danced like cats on fire.

A farm boy named Jeb showed up with a cousin. Both stayed in the corner getting fried. Young cowboy ranch hands arrived with their dates. Louis, Wade's friend from carnival night, came with a Mexican migrant farm girl, the two looking quite smitten with one another. Louis would know something about the Foleys.

Berta and Tallulah brought Sawyer, their friend built like a barn. Good thinking on their part.

My list of people to talk to was growing. I planned to wait for the group to settle in with their booze before bombarding them with questions.

I had to admit, Charlene had picked out a swell selection of records. Louis Armstrong, Jelly Roll Morton, Bessie Smith. And to satisfy those who had yet to learn the beauty of jazz, Charlene played a little Gene Austin, too.

I stood alone, fearing sympathetic stares and judgmental finger-pointing. As it turned out, they all seemed more focused on having a good time than on the woes of Emma June Crawford.

Lucy and Peter took the spotlight dancing the Charleston in perfect unison. A few couples sat knee to knee, smooching. The smoky room filled with laughter and sweat.

But it was Tallulah and Berta who stole the show. They taught everyone how to dance the black bottom. Stomping and hopping, backside slapping, pelvises gyrating. Daddy would have had a hissy fit. Mama would have hidden a grin behind her hand.

And Betty, I thought—she would have kept up without breaking a sweat.

Louis sat in the corner with his gal, whose dress looked only a tad nicer than a flour sack. "Excuse me, Louis. Can I have a word?"

"Shoot." He stayed on the floor, his arm around the girl.

"Loretta hasn't been in school. Are the Foleys out of town or something?"

"Ain't seen Wade. Not since a week or so. Went by his house but didn't stay. That muscle fella was yelling at him by their fire pit."

"You hear what happened to Tallulah?" I pointed to her dancing.

"Naw. What?"

Louis might have been a palooka, but he didn't shy away from the question. He showed no sign of guilt.

"What about Rosie's? Surely you heard about the fire."

"Yeah, I heard. His old man prob'ly made him do it. The mister hates Miss Atta. And Wade does pert'near everything his pa tells him."

Louis's date kept staring down at her lap.

I bent down. "Hi. I'm Emma June Crawford."

"Isabela," she said. "Mucho gusto."

Louis gave her a squeeze. "She don't talk much English."

They had that in common.

Half-seas over from hooch, Charlene swayed toward me, stumbling in her high-heeled Mary Janes. "Having fun?"

"Oodles. You?"

"And how! Frank is a dreamboat. And I'm floating out to sea." She giggled like a twelve-year-old. "I just need time alone with him."

What Charlene needed was a life preserver to keep her above ground and conscious.

"This party taking your mind off your mama?"

"Nothing takes my mind off Mama, Charlene."

"I don't know why you're so grummy. Just think of all the stories she'll tell when she gets back."

"After all these years, you don't know Mama at all. Or me." I stormed off, hoping she would topple over on her smug face.

Standing close to the back entry, Frank pulled out his harmonica.

He played along with Gid Tanner singing "Dance All Night with a Bottle in Your Hand," which had a few pairs of cowboy boots scooting across the floor.

"He's really good, huh?"

I turned to the familiar voice. Berta. I pulled her in and felt her goodness.

When I was younger, I saw Berta a lot. Miss Atta used to watch over her at Rosie's during the summers. Mama would drop me off, and Berta and I would spend mornings or afternoons playing cards and checkers.

"Emma June, I'm sure sorry to hear 'bout your mama," she said. "Aunt Atta prays for her and your family every night. Me, too. Miss Bernice always been real good to me. No word yet?"

"Nothing."

Berta looked down and shook her head. "Not like her one bit. And your daddy? How's he fairing?"

"As you'd expect. Gloomy. Confused."

"Well, you need anything, you come tell me now."

Her words soothed me as if she'd taken a small piece of my burden and planned to carry it a while. "Thanks, Berta. And Tallulah. Besides being a dancing fiend, how's she really doing?"

"Like you, she's tough."

Tough. I felt anything but. "Do you think she'd mind speaking to me? About what happened to her?"

One eyebrow lifted, one eye squinted. "She'll sure to Jesus tell you if she ain't. Stay put. I'll grab her."

I scanned the room while I waited. Jeb, the farm boy, sat on the floor with his legs stretched out, head against the wall. Then he leaned over, upchucked, and laid a kerchief over the mess he'd made.

The banker's son and his rich girlfriend stood off to the side pointing at Louis and his girl.

The place, hot and stuffy from all the dancing bodies and smoke, had some folks slipping out back for fresh air.

Berta and Tallulah strutted toward me arm in arm. Tallulah came to my side and squeezed my hand. We talked light for a minute or two, and then I moved on to the hard stuff.

"Tallulah, Sheriff Gibbons said you couldn't tell who it was. That someone held a flashlight in your eyes."

"Uh-huh. And a kettle ain't black."

"What do you mean? You know who it was?"

"A'course I knew. You think I was gonna tell the sheriff? I aim to live a good long life."

"Can you tell me?"

Tallulah gave my arm a gentle squeeze. "Swear not to tell the sheriff?"

"I swear."

"Tall fella. Wade called him Moody. First, I thought Wade was talking 'bout his temper. Then I learned it was his name. Wade held the flashlight. Kept telling Moody it was time to go. But Moody, he told him to shut up. He let go'a me when Mr. Sampson's light come on. Sure did give me a scare."

"I'm sorry, Tallulah," I said and wondered if Mama was out there somewhere, scared and waiting for someone to turn on the light.

....

CHAPTER 34

FRANK

D oozy hangover or not, who cared? After a couple of aspirin with a coffee wash-down, Frank would hitch a ride to Mineral Wells and take the train back to New Orleans. Put all this crap behind him. No more sleeping on the half-ripped army cot he'd found on the side of the road. No more hauling café leftovers back to a shack that smelled of deception. No more spilled secrets.

He grabbed his worn duffle bag from the corner and started stuffing.

Irene sat up, her nightgown drenched with sweat. "Fine. Leave if you have to. But not before you hear me out."

He already knew what was coming. He'd done the math. Frank turned and glared daggers at the frail woman who looked as sick as he felt. "I don't need to hear—"

"When I came to get you in New Orleans, I knew I couldn't tell you the whole truth. It was too much at one time. You never would have come."

"How long is this gonna take? I have better things to do with my time."

She held up a hand. "I was young and frivolous. Eager for kindness, for someone who cared about me. So when Theo defended me, I was drawn to him. He was kind, respectful. Asked permission before he kissed me. But as much as I liked him, I couldn't stay in Holly Gap to see where the relationship took us. I had to go home. Later, when I found out I was pregnant—"

The blood pumped from his chest to his fists. His headache worsened. "My whole life has been a lie. Don't you get that?"

"Let me finish, then judge me all you want." She took a breath. "I pictured myself going back to Holly Gap and telling him. An honorable man, he would have married me. I know that. Then I pictured a life stuck in the middle of nowhere catering to a husband I barely knew, raising a child in a place with no pulse. I couldn't do it. And Theo never would have moved from Holly Gap. He was satisfied inhaling the smell of farmland after a rain.

"So I looked for a husband in New Orleans, found Pete, and wooed him in my direction. We married quickly without him knowing I was pregnant. When it became obvious, he thought the baby was his. That is, until our big fight and I told him. That's why he walked out."

"You blame him? That's what lies do. They force people to leave. Like I'm about to." Frank threw his last undershirt into the bag.

"You wait just a minute and let me finish," she said, her voice straining to force a louder pitch. "I couldn't raise you by myself. I didn't know how and definitely wasn't good at it."

"No shit."

"I tried though. For a year. Neither of us was happy, Frank. I wasn't fit to be a mother. I felt trapped, and you needed more attention than I could give. And Patsy adored you. I saw how happy the two of you were together."

Finally, Irene had said something true. Aunt Patsy, the best mother anyone could wish for.

"So I kissed you goodbye and left for New York. Patsy told me it wasn't necessary, but I sent money when I could."

Frank remembered the number of times Aunt Patsy had opened a letter and pulled money from the envelope. "Look, Frankie," she'd said. "Your mommy sent you money. Time for a trip to the toy store."

"I spent every dime I made in New York. And with Patsy gone, I felt I had to do something to help you make ends meet. I came to Holly Gap to find out if Theo was still alive. If he still lived here. If he did, I was going to tell him the truth. See if he could help with your finances. But before I found him, I met Bernice. I adored her. I know, if I had just told her from the beginning, none of this would have happened. No blackmail from Earl Foley, no hidden secrets. I can't tell you the number of times I started to tell her. But I always stopped. I could never muster up the courage. And I certainly didn't plan on Earl Foley forcing my hand." Irene twisted her wrist like she was unscrewing a lightbulb. "I'm sorry, Frank. The truth is all I have left to give you. That, and a father and sister."

"What? Am I supposed to hop over to the Crawfords' house and say, 'Hey Pop, what's for supper?'"

She ignored his sarcasm. "No. Not yet anyway. I . . . *we* need to find out what happened to Bernice. And at this point, Emma June's not ready to hear she has a brother she never knew about. Or rather, that her father has a son, especially by a woman she trusted." Irene looked away. "I love that girl," she murmured.

Emma June, his sister. "So you told Bernice about me—"

"Yes. Then I ran for my life."

Which is what Frank should have done when his mother showed up on his doorstep in New Orleans. Now he understood what she meant when she said his life was about to change. It had nothing to do with money.

Yet he had a sister, one who deserved more help than his so-far lame attempts. And Theo Crawford, his father, a man he'd never laid eyes on. What would it hurt to meet him? To find out what he looked like and see if he was a better person than Irene Sanders.

Frank threw his duffle bag back in the corner, but left it packed.

....

CHAPTER 35

EMMA JUNE

A few days after Charlene's party, I walked home from Rosie's thinking of Samuel's surprise telephone call at work.

He said he missed me, and I finally admitted out loud that I missed him. I told him how events in Holly Gap weren't adding up. But with so many nosy parkers on the telephone lines, I omitted the details. Yet he heard the strain in my voice. He talked of catching the train from Waco to Mineral Wells and coming in for a long weekend. I plugged my enthusiasm. Hopes too often collapsed like old bridges.

Surprised to see Ol' Bess parked at home earlier than usual, I ran inside to find Daddy lying in bed under the covers.

"Daddy? What's wrong?"

"Hi, honey. Just a little fever is all. Some of the fellas at work have come down with it too. It'll pass."

If Mama were home, he wouldn't have been so stoic. He'd whimper and complain, reveling in Mama's nurturing care.

"Can I get you anything?"

"Nah. I'm fine. Now, tell me about your day. How's Atta Girl?"

"She's good. Daddy? I got a call today."

Daddy leaned up on his elbows. "Who from?"

"Samuel."

"A fine young man, that Samuel."

Having a beau without Mama around felt like a jar only half full. I couldn't tell her how hearing Samuel's voice comforted me and made me swoon at the same time. Or how I felt when he put his arm around me and kissed my cheek.

"He might come for a visit some weekend before his school's out," I said.

"That's nice."

Mama would have asked me what I would wear when he showed up at our door. She would offer to fix my hair and paint my nails so my shaking hands wouldn't do a shoddy job.

"I gather Gunny doesn't know anything?" I asked.

He laid his head back on the pillow. Tears formed in the corners of his eyes.

"Daddy?"

"I'm worried, Emma June."

The crack in his voice, the droop of his eyes. I couldn't speak.

He wiped his eyes with a sleeve. "I wanted to believe she was out gallivanting with Betty. But deep down, I know she'd never leave you. Especially without telling you. Something's wrong."

I laid my head on his chest. When Daddy squeezed my shoulder, I let the flood gates open.

I heard the triple knock on the front door and hoisted myself up.

"Anybody home?" Frank's voice.

I wiped the tears from my face and opened the door. Frank stood before me holding out a bouquet of flowers. "Bad time?" he asked.

"No. It's okay." I let him in and nodded to the sofa.

"From Tallulah and Berta." He handed me the flowers. "They wanted me to tell you they're thinking of you."

"Nice of them." I placed them in the crystal vase, the one Daddy bought Mama for Christmas. "You came all the way over here for that?"

"Not exactly. Uh, Charlene told me there's a nice river spot down your cliffside."

The place Charlene and I had spent millions of times together. The place I took Samuel.

"What do you say? Can you show me where it is?"

I wasn't sure I had enough pluck left in me for the five-minute walk.

Frank nodded toward Ol' Bess. "Unless you're getting a milk delivery, that must be your father's truck."

"Yeah, he has a fever. He came home early."

"That's too bad," he said as if he meant it.

"Theo! Theo!" Miss Helen yelled from outside. Her panicked voice threw Frank and me to our feet.

"Scooter?" I said, letting her inside.

"My crates of *Scoot's Booty*. Gone. Stolen!" she yelled, her cheeks a reddish-orange like her newly coiffed hair.

"Helen?" Daddy staggered into the sitting room and leaned against the wall for support.

"Theo, thank God."

"Sit down, Helen."

She shook her head. "No time. It's gone, Theo. Twenty crates. Gone."

"How—"

"I rushed out the door this morning without going to the hooch house. I went to Mineral Wells to get my hair done, gone all day. Came home and discovered it missing." She sat on the rocker and buried her face in her hands.

"You call Gunny?" Daddy asked.

When she looked up, her eyebrows lowered and pinched together. She shook her head back and forth and continued yelling. "That hooch was for the mayor and would have brought in a pretty penny."

"Your distillery okay?" asked Frank. "They didn't hurt that, did they?"

"My still? If the Feds were in town, I would have heard."

I knew what Frank was thinking, and it had nothing to do with Prohibition Feds. Whitt intended to sell his own booze and get the whole kit and caboodle of profits from the mayor's shindig.

"Mama, *Mama*," Scooter called from outside.

Miss Helen neared the door. "He's worried sick about me. He's not used to seeing me carry on like this."

Yeah, right, I thought. *And chickens don't cluck.*

Scooter followed behind his mother as she stormed out, leaving the three of us alone in a quiet house.

Daddy cleared his throat. "I'm Theo Crawford, son. I'd shake your hand, but I'm feeling poorly at the moment."

"Frank Sanders, sir. A pleasure."

Frank looked at Daddy with a kind of awe. I couldn't imagine growing up without a father, especially mine. Daddy was honest to a fault, and I trusted him with every inch of my being. Samuel had lost his father too early, but at least he'd had him long enough to build good memories. Unlike Frank, who had no memories at all.

"Well, if you'll excuse me, I need to put my legs up."

Frank watched Daddy cough his way down the hall, then turned to the front door. I followed Frank outside.

"You think they took it last night?" he said.

"Who knows. I didn't hear anything. Could have been this morning when nobody was around. We were all gone, including Leonard. He left early to deliver furniture."

"Pretty ballsy of them either way." Frank took off his flat cap and ran fingers through his thick dark hair. "This whole thing's got me worried. Not just because Miss Helen lost a good portion of dough, but because of the ruckus she might cause if she stirs things up."

"What do you mean *if*?"

"Well, she needs to control herself. Mobsters tend to get rid of troublemakers."

"Emma June!" Miss Helen hollered as she stomped toward us, Scooter on her heels.

"Speaking of," Frank muttered.

As annoying as Miss Helen tended to be, I couldn't picture a world without her in it. Then again, I never pictured a world without Mama. It wasn't just me who was breaking. The whole world was coming apart. We were the fluffy seeds of a dandelion, and God had let out a mighty blow.

I thought of *The Bridge of San Luis Rey*. Was this all God's plan, or just a bad hand from an unlucky draw?

"Emma June, I need your help." Miss Helen had tugged her hair into a twisted mess. No one would have guessed she'd spent hours at the Chicken Coop beauty shop. "Occupy Scooter for me while I sort out this foul business."

"Miss Helen?" Frank said. "What are you planning to do?"

"I'm gonna try to put socks on a rooster," she yelled back, heading toward her house. Her feet pounded the ground hard enough to scare me.

Scooter put a hand on the side of my face and turned it toward his. "It's a *conniption* fit."

"That it is, Scoot Bucket."

Frank patted Scooter's shoulder. "Hey, buddy. How about you show me that spot of yours down at the river? I feel like skimming some rocks."

"Not through a *window*."

"Of course not, pal. Across the river."

Choppers led the pack as we made it down the cliff. After settling on the gravel bar, Frank gathered flat stones and began skimming, counting the skips. He showed Scooter how to hold the rock and wrist-flick it across the water's surface. After several tries, Scooter made a one-jumper, enough to encourage him further. I knew Scooter. He would stay by the creek's edge flicking rocks until he had a good dose of accomplishment.

Frank sat beside me and rolled up his sleeves. "Getting hot."

"Yep. Almost time for swimming." If things were different, I would have hiked my skirt above my knees and allowed the cool, gentle current to swirl around my legs. But removing my shoes seemed like too much effort.

"Your three-legged dog says it's already time." He pointed to Choppers, who swam and lapped water at the same time.

"Frank, do you think we should tell someone what we know?"

He muttered something under his breath, but I didn't catch it.

"What?"

Frank shook his head and let out a deep breath. "That a certain person doesn't want Miss Helen's hooch at the mayor's next party." He stared across the wide river. "I'm noodling over what to do next."

"You mean, how you're going to help me find Mama?"

He removed his cap and ran fingers through his hair. "Among other things."

I didn't care about what else he was noodling. Who else could help me if not Frank? "Daddy believes me now. He knows Mama's in real danger, but his only solution is to put more faith in God. There's got to be something we can do."

"Your daddy's a devoted family man. That's obvious."

"Devoted, yes. But maybe too trusting."

He turned to me, squinting. "You say trust like it's a bad thing."

It didn't used to be. Then an impostor had showed up with her fancy flask and drenched me with misdoubt. "Well, he's trusting Gunny to find Mama," I said. "What a joke."

We sat silent for a while, listening. The breeze rustled through the trees. Squirrels chattered. Birds chirped their late afternoon springtime glee. And each time Scooter made a successful rock skip, he clapped.

"Doing good, buddy," Frank said. "A three-ripple humdinger."

"Like Loretta's *curtains*. She made them *ripple*." Scooter frowned and threw down the rock he was holding. He squatted on the ground.

"What's the matter, Scoot?" I asked.

"She wouldn't come *out* of the house."

"That day you went over there alone, you mean?"

Scooter nodded.

I had seen Scooter's disappointment in the slump of his shoulders, the sag in his face.

"Because she wasn't home, Scooter," Frank said. "That's why you couldn't see her."

"She *was* home. Curtains *rippled* when she *waved*."

Frank looked at me, then at Scooter. "Buddy, that man you told me about. The one who told you to scram . . ."

"He *lied*," Scooter said.

"Yoo-hoo. I can hear you." Charlene's voice traveled down from the top of the cliff. "Mr. Crawford told me y'all might be down there."

Scooter's familiar smile returned with a snicker. "*Frank*. Charlene's gonna *smooch you to pieces*."

"Yeah, that girl sure does like to kiss." Frank grinned. "After a session with her, I have to check the mirror for lipstick."

Not something I needed or wanted to hear about.

"Reminds me of Whitt," Frank said, his face pinched in thought.

"He had that red mark on his face. First, I thought it was a smooch mark from that swanky dame of his."

Kitty, the woman who had no intention of being tied down to a man. "I didn't notice any kiss mark. Every time I saw him, his hat was pulled down. Or he was in the dark."

"I got a decent look at him. He pulled his fedora off for a sec to scratch his head. It was a birthmark. Pavilion light hit his face good enough to see."

"Lucky you."

"Believe it or not, he looked nicer with his hat on. Looked like someone got ahold of Scooter's pocketknife and used it to slice Whitt's forehead."

A birthmark and a scar. Whitfield. The man on the sheriff's wanted poster. "Oh, God, Frank."

"What?" Frank flicked a butt into the river. It bobbed on the water's surface, then disappeared downstream like a floating dead man.

"Brought a flask!" Charlene hollered from the river cliff, then made her way down. "What'd I miss?"

....

CHAPTER 36

EMMA JUNE

Chicken and vegetables boiled on the stovetop. I opened the cupboard to retrieve the macaroni. Half a sack of pecans stared me in the face. Carnival night, when everything crumbled. I couldn't decide whether to eat every last nut or throw them to the ground like Mama had her prized pie. Whatever Betty revealed had turned Mama into an anomaly of herself.

I left the pecans on the shelf and slammed the cabinet door.

"Emma June, honey?" Daddy stood slumped in the kitchen doorway. He cleared the hoarseness from his voice. "Everything all right?"

"Just peachy," I said, regretting my edgy tone.

The strong, confident man I had always counted on for stability now seemed brittle and helpless. Every time I caught him crying, a piece of me faded like my once-pleasant dreams.

The hard truth of what I believed happened to Mama hit me in the gut and turned my fears into daytime nightmares. I dreaded telling Daddy.

Frank hadn't been surprised to learn that Whitt was a wanted man. He also didn't hesitate when I told him my plan.

Daddy sat at the kitchen table, hunched over his cup of coffee. "Feeling better?" I asked.

"Maybe a bit. One more day off work ought'a do it. You mind going to Helen's and calling the dairy? Let them know?"

"Sure," I said, knowing I'd have to deal with Miss Helen's rantings about her stolen moonshine. I dumped the macaroni into the soup.

"Emma June? I know I haven't been much help. I'm sorry about that."

"Chicken soup is easy to make."

"No. I mean, supporting you. Comforting you."

"Oh, Daddy." I wrapped my arms around his shoulders. I understood. It was impossible to support anyone if your own bones were weak.

He stood and kissed the top of my head. "I sure am lucky to have you, honey. Don't know what I'd do without you." He gave me another squeeze and shuffled back to his bedroom.

"Don't forget to check the soup," I called after him, sounding too much like Mama.

Leonard sat motionless in the rocking chair on his front porch. "Emma June," he said with a nod and a grimace.

"Hi, Mr. Leonard. Scooter at school?"

"Yup."

"I need to use your telephone."

"Go 'head on."

"How's Miss Helen?"

"Balled up."

"She inside?"

"*Empty* hooch house."

It was midmorning and Leonard had already closed up for the day. The fact he talked at all was a rarity. When agitated, he stayed silent as a fence post.

The inside of their house looked worse than usual. Tiny cars, marbles, spinning tops—toys Scooter had yet to bury—lay strewn around the floor. Vacuum attachments and radio parts added to the clutter. I made the call to Klinger's Dairy and headed toward the hooch house, leaving the clutter behind.

I followed the familiar hums and thumps coming from the moonshine thicket and found Miss Helen. She sat on a wooden stump in front of her still, staring downward. Rarely had I seen her so motionless.

"Your ole girl's still working," I said.

Her head popped up. "Of course she is. She's getting tired, though. Competition doesn't suit her."

"Competition?"

Miss Helen stretched out her legs and, palms together, dented the fabric of her dress between her knees. "Remember that small potatoes lady-legger who lives an hour south of town?"

"No. Why would I?"

Miss Helen rolled her eyes. "Yes, you do. She came over that time. The fat bleached blonde who got her dander up."

"Oh, right." I remembered that day. Mama had to get in between the woman and Miss Helen to keep them from brawling. "You told her that her hooch could help folks forgo trips to the gas station."

"Well, it was true. That swill was terrible."

"So what about her?"

"Telephoned me. Someone took an ax to her still."

I stayed silent, waiting for her next words.

"They come near mine, I'll have Leonard pull out his sharpshooter."

"I'll keep an ear out, Miss Helen. So will Choppers."

"Like he did when they stole my hooch? Uh-huh."

"I'm sure he barked. Just, no one was around to hear him."

"And you know what else? Little *Bo*-peep Gibbons wasn't even mad when I told him about the thieving. Just told me he had a backup plan for his hooch and not to worry." She smacked her thigh hard enough to hurt. "The man who pinned me down like a cat on a mouse whenever his delivery date was coming up. Now he doesn't give two hoots and a holler that I can't make the next one. Sounded almost relieved."

The mayor had appeased Whitt, his puppet master.

"Clear as a bell to me now," she continued. "Big-time bootleggers have entered my territory. I can't compete with them."

She didn't know the half of it. "You can still keep Rosie's supplied. And the townsfolk."

"Small potatoes hardly worth boiling."

"I'm sorry, Miss Helen. What are you going to do?"

Palms to knees, she pushed herself up. "Make meatloaf." She stomped toward the house, her arms barely swinging.

....

Rags stirred pancake batter while whistling "Little Old Cabin in the Lane."

"Morning, shortcake." Miss Atta had entered behind me holding a box of new glassware.

"Morning it is," I said, trying to sound chipper as I helped unload the box.

"Frank's gonna be a bit late today. Doesn't matter, though. Not many customers. Seems like that firebomb scared a few from coming back."

"The slump won't last," I said, hoping I was right. "Did you hear about Miss Helen's moonshine?"

Rags raised a curious eye.

Miss Atta turned to me. "Problem?"

I told them about the theft.

Miss Atta shook her head. "I had a sour-gut feeling when that man came by."

"What man?"

"Fella wanted me to buy his hooch. Said he worked for a supplier who had plenty of good stuff on hand. Even offered me a discount. A'course, I turned him down. Can't be doing that to friends."

"They was twisting her arm real tight," Rags said.

"They stole Miss Helen's hooch so you'd have to buy from him," I said, without explanation.

Rags slapped down a pancake harder than necessary. "Don't like it one iota. People have the right to run their own business the way they see fit. I done tol' Miss Atta. That firebomb was 'cause she said no to his offer."

"Who was this man, Miss Atta?" I asked.

"If he said his name, I didn't catch it. Tall fella with muscles big enough to pop your eyes. Black hair."

I wondered why Moody's mugshot hadn't made it to the sheriff's desk.

....

CHAPTER 37

FRANK

Frank folded the army cot and chucked it back inside the contaminated shack. And he didn't mean contaminated with a deadly disease. He hadn't spoken to Irene since the day she diffused the entire bomb.

He headed down Main Street toward Rosie's and couldn't help overhearing the two women huddled in his pathway.

"Bernice's daughter might be a little smarty-pants, but can you imagine her mother leaving a man as good as Theo Crawford?"

He reached Rosie's, unhitched his shoulders, and relaxed. Good folks worked inside, honest, caring folks, including Emma June, who forced a smile as he walked past her, clueless they were related. Clueless, like he had been.

"Forget the apron," she said, following him to the storage room. "We have an errand to run, remember? It's past time."

On her heels, he almost bumped into her when she abruptly stopped. "What?" he said.

"What if Gunny is so distracted with his brother that he forgets to focus on Mama? What if telling him louses everything up?"

"All facts lead somewhere, Emma June."

"What's that supposed to mean?"

"Just saying. You told me Betty wasn't herself at the carnival. That she argued with your mother. That in itself ain't nothing. But getting a note beforehand saying to keep her trap shut, lamming off right after, and then your ma goes missing? That is something."

"I just want her home," Emma June choked out. "She should be here, taking care of my sick father so I don't have to worry about him, too."

"He find out what's wrong with him?"

"Nothing serious. A cold, I think. But he looks beat up. And his Bible's been thumbed to death. Guess God hasn't supplied any answers."

Maybe he could finally have a real conversation with his father. See what he was about. "Tell you what. I'll cover your shift so you can go on home and be with him. I'll get Rags to pack me up some food. I'll bring it over after work."

"You don't have to—"

"Besides, maybe I can calm Miss Helen's tail feathers so she won't stir up trouble. Whitt, Moody, and the Foleys can't know we're on to them. Too dangerous."

Almost to the sheriff's office, Emma June grabbed his arm. "Frank. One thing. I kinda . . . well, I did something dishonest. Sheriff doesn't know I snuck a peek at his file. I really want to keep it that way."

"What does it matter at this point?"

Cheeks flushed, she looked down. "It doesn't, I guess."

Emma June had scruples—a noble trait Frank liked. Maybe she'd inherited it from Theo.

"Don't worry," he said. "I'll cover for you."

Sheriff Gibbons stood in an open cell pushing a mop, probably thinking about his bum foot instead of a missing citizen.

"Hi, Sheriff." Emma June got his attention.

Gibbons leaned the mop against the cell door and hobbled to his desk chair. "What can I do you for?"

"I wanted to thank you for putting up the flyers of Mama."

"Hasn't helped, I'm afraid. Your daddy comes by here pert'near every day to check. I hate having nothing to tell you folks."

"And poor Miss Helen," Emma June continued. "All that moonshine for your brother is gone."

"Sorry for Miss Helen. And I'll look into the thieving. As far as my brother goes, he shouldn't be spending money on constituent parties anyhow. Folks around here are used to him. They'd reelect him without all the hoopla."

Constituent party. If the sheriff didn't know about the casino and speakeasy plans, he did a fine job hiding it.

"Thing is, Sheriff," Frank said. "I think I know who stole the hooch. I saw a peculiar-looking man at the hardware store the other day."

The sheriff chuckled. "You haven't been here long, son. We got plenty of peculiar men."

"No, I mean, shady-like. Didn't fit in. Sharp dresser."

Gunny Gibbons held on to his grin. "Probably the banker, Mr. Mercer."

"I've seen Mr. Mercer before," Frank lied. "Wasn't him. This man looked like a wise guy, a mobster."

"Truth is, Sheriff," Emma June said, "I was in here the other day and saw a flyer of a wanted man. You still have it?"

Frank had to smile. Unlike his mother, Emma June wasn't good at hiding her own secrets.

The sheriff squinted at her and slid open a desk drawer. He slapped down a single sheet of paper.

Homer "Buzz" Whitfield. 5/10, 190 lb., black hair, cleft chin, quarter-sized red port-wine birthmark on his right cheek. Scar on middle of forehead. Wanted for theft and racketeering. Last seen in Dallas.

Whitt looked like the old photographs Frank had seen of Butch Cassidy, except meaner. Squinty eyes, narrow lips, birthmark, and the scar across his forehead. No doubt about it. Same man from the pavilion. Same man who tried to squeeze the life out of his mother.

"Sheriff?" Frank said. "You might want to put this one up."

Sheriff Gibbons rolled his chair back, stared at the photograph, then at Frank. "What? You think it's the guy from the hardware store?"

"I made that part up. Buzz Whitfield was at your brother's event."

There it was, out in the open.

Gunny clenched his jaw. "At the old pavilion?"

"That's right."

"Sure it was the same man?"

"Sure as a clear day."

Gunny stared off and drummed his fingers on the desk. Like Emma June, Frank stayed quiet, waiting. He wasn't sure how much more to tell him.

"Homer *Buzz* Whitfield is a big-time bootlegger," Emma June said. "His muscle man, Moody somebody, hangs around Earl and Wade Foley. Your brother was seen talking to Earl at Rosie's."

The sheriff squinted and leaned back. "So? Foley's a constituent. Albeit one without scruples."

Emma June leaned forward. "Whitfield was most likely responsible for stealing Miss Helen's hooch. And Moody muscled Miss Atta, tried to get her to buy his hooch. After she turned him down, someone hurled a firebomb through her window. Curious, don't you think?"

It was news to Frank, but smart thinking on Emma June's part.

The mention of Miss Atta got the sheriff's attention. Jaw pulsing, his eyes turned dark. "Why didn't she tell me?" he asked, the question directed to himself.

Now that Gunny was finally showing his ire, Frank needed to keep the momentum going. "Something else. In case you're wondering why a wanted man, an out-of-towner, was at your brother's event. It wasn't a political fundraiser. It was an affair to drum up interest and cash for a gambling room and speakeasy at the Baker Hotel. And if you wondered how your brother got his new Cadillac . . ." Frank raised his eyebrows and let his voice trail off.

Gunny pounded his fist on the desk. "Damnit!" He stared off to the side and took a few breaths. "I'll talk to my brother. Y'all do absolutely nothing. Say nothing. To *nobody*. Hear me? This is way over your head. And Emma June, you got enough worries with your mama gone and all. This ain't child's play."

"I'm not a child, Gunny."

Gunny pushed away from his desk and stood. "Y'all need to run along now. Let me do my job." He hobbled toward the door, shoved his Stetson on his head, and turned back toward them. "Like I said. Keep quiet about this." He reached for the doorknob.

"Hold up, Sheriff," Frank said, stopping him. "This whole mess could be tied to Mrs. Crawford's disappearance."

"And Betty's," Emma June added.

Frank said nothing. He knew exactly what had happened to *Betty*. Each day it became harder to look into Emma June's trusting eyes. The guilt felt like the tuning pegs on a guitar, tightening his strings to the breaking point.

"Now, Emma June," Gunny said, "I can't see how a hard bootlegger would have anything to do with your mama. Betty, maybe. With that blackmail note and all. Maybe Betty knew something. For all we know, this Whitfield fella nabbed Betty when she didn't pay up."

Frank felt it then: that sinking feeling where your thoughts take you to a bleak and dark place. He hoped Emma June wasn't thinking the same thing.

CHAPTER 38

....

EMMA JUNE

I reached the front of my house just as Reverend Thompson bounced down the porch steps.

"Good day to you, Emma June." He tipped a hat and continued toward his Model T.

"And to you, Reverend."

For an old man, the head of Holy Baptist Church always carried a spring in his step and a Bible in his front pocket. I liked him well enough. Unlike many of his flock, I never heard him judge a person's character or preach to anyone who didn't want to listen. Maybe he'd made that mistake early on and learned it wasn't the best way to steer folks to God. But when the reverend preached? He shot sparks straight into the souls of his listeners.

The young pastor of Mama's Methodist church was different. He walked in uppity shoes and held his nose a little too high. His congregation didn't care. They stayed busy planning the next dance or picnic while keeping track of whose turn it was to spike the punch. At every turn, the parishioners reminded the collared newcomer how things were supposed to be done *by God*.

I saw no point in conversing with either man of the cloth. God clearly wasn't listening.

I'd heard folks prattle on about the importance of following the Word of God, yet they judged their neighbor without thought. They preached kindness while beating their children and prayed for more money to put food on their table after they'd spent it all on moonshine.

Like Daddy and most folks in town, Miss Atta believed in the pearly gates of heaven. I wanted to. I liked thinking heaven was a place without fear, where all prayers were answered. Where souls continued to evolve even after death.

It was Miss Helen who told me about Charles Darwin's theory of evolution. She had a cousin, Albert, who lived in Tennessee, the same man who taught her how to make moonshine when she was a young girl. During the Scopes monkey trial three years before, Albert had sat in the court for each of the eight days.

I remember Miss Helen scoffing when she first read Albert's letters about the trial. Then she thought of the former pastor who told her to ship Scooter off to the loony bin. She decided then and there that if those strict religious sorts were wrong about Scooter, they were probably wrong not to believe in Darwin.

A few days after her insight, Scooter got in trouble at school for telling the class we all had great-great-great-grandfathers and grandmothers who were apes. The day after Scooter mentioned Miss Primrose's scolding, Miss Helen marched into the classroom and spoke her mind. "There's nothing wrong with evolution talk, *Miss* Primrose," she said. "God knows how to plan far ahead. Starting out like a hairy ape's not so bad. Unless you're Will Baxter at the hardware store. He could speed up his own evolution if he bought himself a new razor." The class died laughing until Miss Primrose picked up the glass flower vase from her desk and nonchalantly dropped it on the floor.

I believed in Charles Darwin's theory. I believed it even more so on carnival night when the caged gorilla stared at me with such sadness in his eyes. Darwin said it's not the strongest or the smartest who survived but the ones who could adapt to change. If that was true, I was failing.

Daddy lay stretched out on the sofa, a glass of iced tea in his hand. "Feeling better?" I asked.

"Honey, you're home early. Anything wrong?"

He didn't know the half of it. "Let me get a glass of that." I headed to the kitchen.

Looking through the back window, Choppers sat on his haunches staring up at a post oak. He barked until satisfied the hounded critter was no longer a threat, then sprinted back to his water bowl, happily lapping up his success. Choppers had not only survived, he had adapted.

I sat in the rocker and faced Daddy. "Frank and I went to see Gunny today."

He bolted upright. "Anything?"

"No. Different news."

"Go ahead, then," he said, attentive as always.

"Before Betty took off, someone left her a blackmail note."

"To pay up or her secret would be out. Gunny told me. What did I tell you—"

"I bet Gunny didn't tell you our mayor is in cahoots with a wanted gangster."

Daddy squinted and leaned forward. "How do you know that?"

"Frank recognized him from a wanted poster at the sheriff's office. Saw the mayor talking to him at a fundraiser to build a gambling room and speakeasy in the Baker Hotel. This gangster is a big-time bootlegger."

I told him how the Foleys were somehow involved with Whitfield and his goon, Moody.

Daddy let out a deep exhale, followed by a cough. "You know those tarp-covered trucks that come through Holly Gap once a week?"

I knew where the conversation was headed. Yes, I'd seen them numerous times, always curious as to why the trucks never stopped so we could sample Snyder's Peanut Butter and Nuts, as advertised on the canvas tarps.

After my nod, Daddy explained the details. The trucks carried liquor, not peanuts. Some anonymous bootlegger sent cash to the sheriff for the privilege of using our country road to bypass the Feds. Gunny may have pocketed a few clams from the deal. But most of the money he put back into the community, and the townsfolk didn't complain about filled potholes, newly painted signs, and donations to the churches. Those who pretended to take offense at the lawlessness shook their heads in mock outrage. Then, when they took a seat on one of the new storefront benches, they smiled at the town's good fortune.

"Daddy, those are Whitfield's trucks and they're stockpiling hooch for the Baker Hotel's speakeasy."

"Could be."

"No. They are." I remembered Whitt saying as much at the fundraiser.

"As long as they keep passing through," Daddy continued, "I'm not going to worry about what happens in Mineral Wells."

"But they're not just passing through anymore. Whitfield has infiltrated Holly Gap. The firebomb through Rosie's. Miss Helen's stolen hooch. If Mama isn't with Betty, maybe she got caught up in Betty's blackmail."

Daddy bolted from the chair.

"You can't go to Gunny. He told us not to tell anyone until he talks to his brother."

Daddy pulled the lace curtains from the front window and peered outside. The porch light shone through the glass pane and poked at the moisture in his left eye. "I'll give him till tonight. No longer." He headed toward his bedroom.

"Do you trust him, Daddy? Do you think he'll do the right thing?"

Daddy pivoted in place. "Gunny Gibbons is a decent fella. Problem is, Holly Gap has always been an easy town to run. Never required a go-getter."

Daddy finally admitted, in kinder words, that his friend, our town sheriff, was an incompetent fool.

"That being said," he continued, "Mayor Bo is an all-for-himself kind of fella. Always wants something bigger and better. Gunny's nothing like his brother. He cares about folks. So yeah, I think Gunny will do the right thing."

Daddy walked slump-shouldered into his bedroom and closed the door.

I had managed to doze for a while until Choppers's *gotta-go* whine roused me off the sofa.

Outside, the late afternoon breeze carried a nip of cool freshness. If things had been different, I would have run to Scooter's for a two-person game of kickball. Or sat on the porch with Charlene gossiping and painting each other's nails. Better yet, gone for an evening drive with Mama, the two of us laughing as we belted out "Baby Face." Instead, I kept spinning around and around in an endless loop of nothing.

Choppers barked and ran toward Frank, who traipsed across the avenue carrying a box.

He shoved the box toward me. "Food from Rosie's."

"I told Daddy about Whitfield. And about the mayor."

"Okay." He raised an eyebrow. "What'd he say?"

"He's even more worried about Mama. But he thinks the sheriff will do the right thing and look into it. How far is anybody's guess. You think he'll show up at the next venue? The sheriff, I mean."

"That would be the smart thing. So again, anybody's guess."

"Emma June?" Daddy called from inside. "Who are you talking to?"

"Frank's here, Daddy," I hollered back. "He brought us food from Rosie's."

Frank turned toward the screen door. "Fried chicken, Mr. Crawford. Mashed potatoes and green beans. Miss Atta said it was your favorite."

Daddy appeared on the porch in a fresh white shirt and combed hair. He looked like the father I was used to seeing, and it felt a bit like home again.

He nodded to the box. "Thanks for that, son."

"A pleasure, sir."

"Well, I don't think I have a fever anymore. Might as well come in. You eaten, Frank?"

"Yes, sir. Full as a tick."

The three of us at the kitchen table, I picked at my food while Daddy told Frank about the dairy business. How last week the electricity shorted out and put a hitch in their whole operation. I stopped listening when Daddy told him about the big deliveries he made to creameries.

Daddy's question to Frank got my attention. "I understand you live with your mother. Does she work?"

Frank looked away, his expression sitting somewhere between anger and gloom. "Not now. She's sick."

"She seen Doc Ferguson?" Daddy asked.

"Afraid he can't do much for her." Frank cleared his throat. "She's got cancer."

Cancer? Frank had never told me his mother was gravely ill. I suddenly felt extremely selfish.

"Sorry to hear that, son. Anything we can do for you?"

"No, sir. But thanks. I'm taking care of her the best I can. Right now, she just coughs and rests a lot."

"I'll have our congregation pray for Mrs. Sanders then. I can have the church women bring y'all some meals. They have a group—"

"Oh no, sir. Not necessary. Miss Atta provides plenty for both of us."

"So you told Miss Atta but not me?" I asked.

"I wanted her to know in case I had to miss work. Now, only three people know. Don't really like talking about it."

I understood. Good intentions or not, questions and sympathy felt more like interrogations and pity. I was sick of both.

At the sound of tires crunching up the distance to our house, I was first to reach the door to find Gunny's Packard. He peeled himself from the motorcar, his expression grave.

....

CHAPTER 39

FRANK

Gunny fumbled with his Stetson in the Crawfords' doorway. Frank had seen the sheriff complacent many times, even angry. But he'd never seen him so jittery. "Emma June, I need to speak to your father," he said, all business.

Theo greeted him at the door. "Gunny? Come in, come in. What is it?"

"Mind if I sit, Theo? You might as well, too. I've got some news. It's not great, but it's not terrible either," he said.

Standing in the kitchen doorway, Emma June cringed. She sat next to her father and folded her hands in a white-knuckle squeeze. Theo covered her hands with his own. Comfort from a father. Frank didn't put any stock that he'd ever feel that kind of warmth from Theo. Not when he found out the truth.

"Spit it out, Gunny."

"Someone spotted Miss Bernice's motorcar."

Emma June gasped. "Where? Was she—"

"Let him finish, Emma June. Go ahead, Gunny."

"About a mile east of The Diner, parked under some trees in the cross timbers. It was abandoned. Montgomery's boy and his girl-friend found it."

Montgomery's boy. Louis. Frank remembered him from that day at the river, and then again at the Brazos Dance Hall.

Theo leaned forward. "The breezer? Secluded?"

"Yeah. Looked like it had been driven over the grasses and hid there."

"Oh, God." Emma June paled.

Theo started to stand but sat back down.

"I'm sorry it's not better news, Theo. But I wanted to tell you right away."

Theo shook his head and stared at the floor.

Emma June looked up, her eyes wide and hopeful. "Maybe Mama left it there on purpose."

"Why in God's name would she do that?" Theo said, squeezing his eyebrows together.

"Maybe she left it there when she took off with Betty. It makes sense, Daddy. If she didn't want to be spotted, they would have taken Betty's jalopy. The green breezer sticks out like a sore thumb," she said, her words running together in one long breath.

Theo said nothing. For good reason. Emma June was reaching for straws. False hope as a last resort.

"I want to see the motorcar," Theo said to Gunny. "Take me there."

Gunny shook his head. "Not now. One, it's dark. Second, I tried turning the switch on the coil box. Wouldn't start. How about I take you out there first thing in the morning? You can work your mechanical magic and drive it home. Say I pick you up at seven?"

Theo opened his mouth and then closed it. If he wanted to bring up the mayor's ties to a gangster, he'd changed his mind. He let Gunny see himself out.

The three-legged dog stopped nibbling his fur. He stood, spun in a couple of lopsided circles, and settled to the floor. Frank wanted to curl up, too, sleep and wake up with answers on his pillow.

"So many questions and not any answers," Theo muttered.

Emma June wiped at her eyes. "I'm going to lay down." She left Frank alone with their father.

Frank tried to see himself in the man before him. Physically, he didn't see much resemblance, maybe something around the eyes. He tried to picture Theo twenty-one years earlier when he had first met Irene. The kindness he'd shown her, the gallantry at defending her against Earl Foley.

"It's a hard thing, a child not having a mother," Theo said, breaking the silence.

"Yes sir, I can't imagine." Although he could. "You don't know me well, Mr. Crawford, but I'd like to help. What can I do?" Frank meant what he said. Seeing his real father before him, the stress wrinkles around his eyes, Frank wanted to see things through. Find out if his hunch was right about Emma June's mother. And if she was alive, find her.

"I appreciate the offer, son. Not sure what that would be at this point. You have any ideas?"

Frank had ideas, all right. In the perfect scenario, he'd walk right up to Whitt and Moody and threaten to shoot them dead if they didn't tell what they knew.

"Maybe I'll sniff around. See if I can collect more information on the Foleys and this Whitfield character."

"Sounds dangerous, son. I'm thinking you just keep an eye out for Emma June. Once she gets a burr in her side about something, she won't stop till it's gone. Worries me."

"Yes, sir. That I can do."

Frank left after shaking the hand of his father. Something he had never thought possible.

He trudged toward home. Just a house, really, where the only thing waiting for him was a liar and a troublemaker.

When the truth came out, and sooner or later it would, Frank wasn't sure how Theo Crawford would take the news. From what Emma June told him and from what he'd witnessed, Theo was a good man of high morals. Maybe he wouldn't blame Frank.

Emma June would hate him. She wouldn't understand that keeping Irene-Betty a secret was the only thing keeping his mother alive. Which was better, anyway? Dying by violence or from cancer?

Who did he owe his allegiance to? The mother who'd left him and put him in this situation? Or the Crawfords, who had done nothing wrong except befriend a woman they shouldn't have trusted?

He passed by Rosie's. Like most businesses in town, the lights were off, the doors locked for the night. Maybe Charlene was still at the Variety sweeping up or counting receipts. He tapped on the door. A moment later, the blinds peeled down. Blue eyes stared back at him.

"Frankie!" Charlene pulled him inside the store.

"Hey, doll. On my way home. Just wanted a smooch before bedtime."

He got what he wanted.

"Where've you been anyway?" she asked, drawing a finger down his cheek.

He told her about dropping food off at the Crawfords'. He didn't tell her the breezer had been found. She'd find out soon enough.

Charlene squeezed her eyes together. "Did you use food as your excuse to see Emma June?"

Frank didn't care for possessive women, but Charlene's demeanor struck him as more playful than jealous. "Doing what the boss tells me keeps change in my pocket." He kissed her again, then asked about her day.

"School was god-awful as usual," she said, playing with his hair. "Oh, but if the Foleys took a vacation, it was a mighty quick one.

Loretta came back to school today. Quiet as a mouse. Wouldn't even talk to me. Can you believe that? I think I'm the only friend she's got."

"Did she say where she'd been?"

"Nope. Buttoned up like a tight corset. Which, by the way," she said with a mischievous grin and a tilt of her head, "we women don't have to wear anymore."

"And a fine thing it is." And, thinking of Loretta, so was his idea.

When he arrived back in Shanty Town, darkness had settled in. It didn't matter. Dark or not, he knew exactly which path to take.

He inched nearer to the house and kept to the shadows. Earl's old pickup sat off to the side, a rusted icebox next to it. Front door closed, a light shone through the house's center window, curtains drawn. Eerily quiet.

Frank started to sneak around back but stopped when shadows moved from inside. Then voices from the opened door.

"It's just a smoke." Wade.

"Smoke it in the house." Moody.

"Need some fresh air. I ain't going nowhere but the porch."

Moody followed Wade out front. Wade sat on the step and lit up. Moody stood like a sentry at the door. Neither spoke. The surroundings too quiet for Frank to move. He waited.

Dogs barked on the next property over, faint in the distance. Then the sound of water and pots and pans came from an open window in the back. He'd take the chance. He felt out each spot with his boot before stepping down. He couldn't afford to snap a stick or trip over a rock. Slowly, he crept toward the back of the house.

"You hear something?" Moody, his voice muffled from the distance.

Frank flattened up against the side of the house and tried not to breathe.

When Moody and Wade continued mumbling, Frank made it to

the back and found the open window. A careful corner-peek revealed a girl Emma June's age with reddish hair standing at the sink, her eyes focused downward. Loretta.

He couldn't just pop his head up. If she screamed, all bets were off. He removed his flat cap, inched it upward, and waved it slowly like a white flag. He put a finger to his lips and showed his face.

Loretta hitched in a breath and leaned back, her eyes wide.

"It's okay, Loretta," he whispered. "Charlene sent me." A lie, but an advantageous one. "I'm Frank. I know you need help."

Loretta glanced behind her at the front door, then faced him again.

Frank motioned her closer. The kitchen sink kept her from leaning more than an inch closer.

"Still going to school?" Frank whispered.

She gave a slow nod.

"I'll get in touch. Don't tell anyone I came by. Not even Charlene."

She nodded again. This time, without reservation.

....

CHAPTER 40

EMMA JUNE

When I was seven, my favorite doll Sally, with the cracked face and worn dress, went with me everywhere. Then I lost her.

Mama and I had been to the town bake sale. With so many tables set up and so many treats to salivate over, I became distracted. I set Sally down and forgot to pick her up again.

Mama didn't tell me I had been irresponsible, or not to worry because she would get me a new doll. Instead she said, "Oh, no! Let's keep looking."

We searched under tables, under the arms of other young girls who might have taken her, thinking finders-keepers. We backtracked all our steps. Sally was nowhere.

While I worried about Sally being alone, Mama held me and wiped my tears. She said it was hard to lose good friends. Then she told me about a friend she had when she was little. "We were inseparable, Vivi and me. And because folks in town never saw us apart, they called us Pea and Pod." That put a smile on my face.

"Which one were you, Mama? Pea or Pod?"

"Why, I don't even know. I guess it never really mattered."

Mama told me how sad she'd been when Vivi moved away. That it took a while before she felt back to normal again.

That night, as I nuzzled against Mama, she stroked the side of my face and said, "Emma June, baby, hard as it is, you might just have to be sad for a while. In the meantime, look into the eyes of people you love. It will make you feel better."

The last time I saw Mama I'd been too drunk to remember.

The morning after we learned about the breezer, the sun rose in deceptive brightness. I hated the thought of Mama's motorcar sitting deserted, alone and hidden.

"Daddy?"

I found him staring out the front window. His shoulders pumped up and down, his tears silent. I placed a hand on his shoulder. He turned to me, his olive skin stained with tears. Daddy's hands on my cheeks, he tried to speak but no words came. I sobbed when the fear took over, and my legs threatened to give way.

A few minutes later, after I assured Daddy I'd be all right, he left the house and approached Ol' Bess with slow, reluctant steps.

The truth was, I didn't know if I would be all right. The fear strangled me and took me back to another memory. To a place where the limbs of dead oaks hung down like skeleton arms, each one reaching to grab me. My eight-year-old body darted over fallen tree logs and briar patches. Brambles scratched my legs. The dusk played tricks on my eyes. But the noise had been real. "We're coming for you, little girl," the deep voices growled.

Somehow, I made it home to Mama's arms. She held me, wiped the dirt and tears from my face, and said, "Shh, shh, doll baby. Everything is all right now. Running away from danger is a good thing. And you did it well. They were stupid, mean boys who've been playing tricks on the girls in town."

"But what if, what if next time I can't get away?" I had asked.

"Then you put on your brave face, look them in the eye, and scream for them to back off. Loud as you can."

With Gunny's news, I wanted to run again, away from the paralyzing fear and into the arms of comfort.

The fifty yards a blur, I made it to Miss Helen's in plenty of time to call Samuel before walking Scooter to school.

Miss Helen sat alone in her front room. "Leonard's getting Scoot ready," she said, pulling the tuffs on her ugly housecoat.

I moved the papers and toy car from the chair to the floor and sat by the telephone. "Can I use it? I need to call Samuel."

Miss Helen flipped a hand my way. "Be my guest." She didn't move. Just stared at me.

I pulled the dorm number from my dress pocket.

"Saw your father with Gunny this morning. He told me about the breezer."

My nod forced more tears down my face. She handed me a tissue.

"Messy business, all this. I'm sorry, honey."

"Have you talked to the mayor?" I asked, no longer caring what Gunny did or didn't want me to say.

"Quiet as a mailbox on Sunday. Won't talk to me since he doesn't need my moonshine anymore." She let out a heavy sigh.

"That's because he's getting it from a big-time bootlegger. A gangster."

"Bo Gibbons?" She guffawed. "Shoot, if he was working with a real gangster, they would have eaten him for lunch by now."

"Well, he is. I've seen them both. Together."

Miss Helen pressed her lips together.

"What?" I asked, knowing that look.

"You know those moonshine trucks that come through here once a week?"

Another adult letting out the town secret. "I know. The sheriff accepts payment to let them through."

"Gunny didn't wanna do it at first. Our mayor talked him into it."

"And the mayor got a shiny new Cadillac in the deal," I said.

"Seems about right."

"I remember how mad the mayor got that time when you laughed at him."

She squinted. "Which time?"

"When he told you he aimed to become a state senator."

"Oh, yeah," she said with a slow nod. "When I couldn't stop my side-splitting, he reminded me how President Coolidge had once been a mayor himself. I told him if he wanted to be like Coolidge, he'd better graduate from a college, that is if he could get into one. He didn't speak to me for a week. When he did, he told me the next mayor might not want my hooch so I should appreciate him while I could." She shooed away an invisible fly. "Nobody takes him seriously. Our townsfolk just brush his pompous talk away like salt off a shoulder."

I decided to tell her an edited version of the truth.

"Here's what I think. I saw Mayor Gibbons schmoozing with a mobster by the name of Buzz Whitfield. The night we made your delivery. It was a fundraiser to build a speakeasy in the Baker Hotel. I think Whitfield promised to boost his political future a while ago."

"In exchange for what?"

"Talking his brother into allowing the moonshine trucks to cut through town. And helping him fundraise for the casino."

"Okay, maybe I was wrong. They'll snack on him for lunch and eat him alive for supper."

"And Miss Helen? I think Betty and Mama are connected to this in some way."

"I don't see—"

"Helen," Leonard called from Scooter's bedroom. "What are you two talking about in there?"

"About you, Leonard," she hollered back. "You need to take Scooter to school. Emma June has other things on her mind right now."

I told Miss Helen more of what I knew but left out who I thought was responsible for stealing her hooch. If she ran after Wade and Moody with a few choice words, she'd tip our hand.

I lifted the mouthpiece. Miss Helen sat there, staring at me.

"How can I connect your call?" said the gruff-toned switchboard operator.

"Okay, Scooter," Leonard said, entering the room. "Let's save your Emmy hug for later. Let her talk on the telly. And Helen?"

"What?"

"Leave the girl be."

....

Miss Atta stood beside me folding napkins. I went back to filling saltshakers.

Daddy said he would call when he knew something. Each time the telephone rang, my skin prickled with cold sweat.

I had caught Samuel before he left his dorm. Surprised, yet thrilled to hear from me, he didn't care I was making him late for class. I told him what I knew while trying not to sound hysterical through the crackling telephone line. He listened until my words ran out.

So far, I had witnessed no change to his original character. Kind, patient, generous.

At the end of the conversation, without a smidgen of sap, he said, "Every part of me misses you, Emma June."

He didn't know every part of me. He didn't know my snippy, sarcastic side or the other side, the girl filled with self-pity.

I grew up hearing Daddy tell me time and again, "If you can't say something nice about someone, don't say anything at all." Even when I didn't voice my rude comments aloud, I increasingly thought them. The sheriff was inept, the mayor crooked. Betty was a liar, Charlene a self-absorbed twit.

Then I thought of Samuel. I told Miss Atta how much I liked him.

"Well, honeypot, he sure sounds like a keeper to me. And he comes from good stock. Doc Ferguson is a fine man."

"Where's Frank?" I asked. "Isn't he supposed to be here by now?"

"Family matters, maybe."

"He told me about his mother. I know how sick she is."

"Well, then, I guess it's fine we talk about it. Such a shame. And Frank said he's only got a mother. No one else."

Miss Atta read through my silence. "Oh, shortcake. You just remember, however far a stream flows, it doesn't forget its origin. We're gonna keep hoping and praying. You understand? Nothing's been said or done. And when it is, we'll handle whatever comes, good or bad, with a strong arm."

Good or bad. The first time anyone had hinted the outcome could be the worst possible.

Charlene barreled through Rosie's door, panting. "Emma June! Emma June! I saw your mama's motorcar pass by the Variety. She came back, Emma June. Your mama is back."

But I knew the truth.

"Emma June? Did you hear what I said?"

I hated Charlene's joy, her sham of excitement. "I heard you, Charlene. But you didn't see Mama driving, did you?"

Charlene's head tilted. "Well, no. I couldn't see the driver. Only the back of the breezer."

"Daddy was driving then. They found her car. That's all."

"Oh," she said, then paused. "I, uh, just assumed—"

I gave in to her look of disappointment, the slump of her shoulders. "It's okay, Charlene. I would have thought the same thing."

"If she wasn't in her breezer, then where is she?"

A rhetorical question, one she surely didn't expect me to answer. If I knew where Mama was, I wouldn't be standing next to Charlene with a scowl on my face.

"Charlene," Miss Atta said, "how about an ice-cold Coca-Cola? You done worked up a sweat running over here."

Charlene looked under her armpits. "Rats. And I have to go back to work like this."

"Why aren't you in school?" I asked.

"I was until Miss Primrose got sick and had to leave. Geez, too bad about that." She smirked. "Hey, where's Frank?"

Frank had only told three people about his mother. Charlene wasn't one of them. Sweet on her or not, he knew Charlene couldn't keep her mouth shut. And if he was anything like me, he didn't want the pity.

"He'll be here directly," Miss Atta said. "I'm sure he'll pay you a visit at the Variety when he's done working."

"Tell him I can't wait to smooch his face." She giggled, then turned serious. "And Emma June? About Miss Bernice . . ."

"We'll find her. And tell *your* mama I said hello," I said, regretting my sarcasm.

When the call finally came, Daddy said they had discovered no clues and nothing of interest inside the breezer.

Sitting on the crate behind Rosie's, each exhaled smoke of my Lucky Strike swirled aimlessly into a future I couldn't grasp. One that seemed barren and empty of promise. Hope drifted out of reach, replaced by a foreboding intuition.

....

CHAPTER 41

FRANK

Irene roused from her sleep with a moan of either pain or despair. Although Frank tried for indifference, seeing his mother wither wasn't easy. Sympathy was slowly replacing the anger he had accumulated over the years.

What was it like for a thirteen-year-old girl to be raped, then three years later, get pregnant and be forced to become responsible when she wasn't capable? Once on her own, she spent years trying to find her place in the world and finally met the best friend she ever had only to lose her from a past mistake.

Well, everyone made mistakes. And everyone had to live with them. The problem was dying before you made things right.

Frank brought Irene a glass of water.

"Thank you." She sipped the water with a shaky hand. "Frank, inside my bag is a bottle of laudanum. Would you hand it to me?"

"Laudanum? How long have you been taking that?"

"I haven't. A doctor in New Orleans gave it to me for when I needed it. I need it now."

"I'm sorry you're sick, Ma. Really."

Irene looked at him, tears welling. "I . . . I wish things were different."

"Me too. But we've gotta play this hand for better or worse. And," he added, feeling the swell in his own eyes, "I'll help you hold the cards." Frank didn't know if his words were formed out of pity or forgiveness. Maybe he was trying on nice to see how it felt.

Irene reached for Frank's hand. He held it. Squeezed it. Irene closed her eyes and let out a deep breath. He had to tell her.

"Ma, Emma June said the night of the carnival Bernice left to finish a conversation. She would have gone to The Diner to find you."

"Yes?"

"You'd never met Moody. And he didn't know what you or Bernice looked like. Just a general description. Except for differ-ent colored hair, you said you two looked alike. Earl must have told Moody he saw you spill the beans at the carnival. Then Moody kid-napped Bernice thinking it was you."

"I know." Irene sobbed. "I've thought of that. It's the . . . the only thing that makes sense."

"They found her breezer, Ma. Hidden and abandoned."

Tears flooded her cheeks. "No, no . . ."

He waited for her breath to calm and her tears to slow. "Ma, Whitt and Moody know they messed up, took the wrong woman."

Irene covered her face with her hands and shook her head back and forth, back and forth. "Do you . . . do you think they would let her go?"

He sat beside her, his arm around her shoulder. "No, Ma. They wouldn't just let her go."

Frank could no longer console her. The best thing he could do was see that justice was done. Whitt, Moody, and Earl Foley needed to pay. And Emma June and Theo needed to move on with their lives.

....

Behind Rosie's, Emma June sat slumped on a crate, a rag doll without the bones to hold up her head. Frank cleared his throat, trying not to startle her. "Mind if I sit?"

She motioned to the crate next to her.

"Your father feeling better?"

She nodded. "Back at work."

"Ran into Charlene. She told me about your father driving the breezer."

"Yeah. Won't take long before the whole town knows they found it. Without Mama inside."

"Because Charlene will spread the word?"

"Charlene likes the attention she gets from perching her butt up on a flagpole."

Frank recognized Emma June's anger. It had nothing to do with him or Charlene. The anger came from her lack of control, her inability to change the facts around her. He knew the feeling all too well. He said nothing.

"I miss the old Charlene," she said. "The one I used to count on for fun and laughs. But you learn a lot about friendships when times get hard."

"I get it."

"How could you possibly?" She snorted.

He felt his hand form into an involuntary fist. "Emma June? You think I've lived twenty-one years in a bed of roses?"

She looked up at him then.

He couldn't help it. He glared back. "Well, I haven't."

"Sorry." She took her time tapping the ashes from her Lucky Strike. "Your mother. How is she?"

"The same. Either can't or won't get out of bed. We're not close, Emma June. Not like you and your mother. When I was growing up? She never gave me the time of day, discarded me like flicked ashes. She didn't even raise me. My aunt did."

"Oh. I . . . I didn't know. I'm sorry."

Frank bit his tongue. He didn't want sympathy. He changed course. "I have news."

"Go on."

He told her about going to the Foleys the night before and speaking to Loretta. And how, that morning, he'd stopped Leonard and Scooter before they reached school. "So I gave Scooter the note. He promised to give it to Loretta and to keep it a secret. Will he?"

"As long as he believes the note won't hurt her, he will. What did you write?"

"Asked if she was okay and why Moody was controlling her family. I told her I would help her and to write back through Scooter."

Her eyes narrowed. "You didn't ask about Mama?"

"Not yet. She doesn't know me. I want her to trust me. We'll see if the note system works."

She shrugged what little life she had left in her shoulders. "Worth a shot, I guess."

He couldn't tell her the truth, but he needed Emma June to understand. "Speaking of notes, the one Ir . . . Betty got? Mobsters don't leave threatening notes. They do it in person."

"Who wrote it then?"

He exhaled a big puff of smoke knowing his next words would be a half-truth. "I'm betting it was either Earl or Wade Foley."

"Why can't you corner one of them? Make them tell you what they know?"

Frank shook his head. "Wade's always with Moody. Probably busy cutting down mom-and-pop distilleries instead of mesquite trees."

"Earl then? He'd probably know more than anyone."

"Yeah, but he won't talk. He knows Whitt or Moody would kill him. I think we go straight to the mayor."

Emma June stood and crushed her cigarette with the toe of her shoe. "Let's go now."

....

In New Orleans the city hall with its giant concrete columns stood tall and proud. Holly Gap's was a one-story brick building at the corner of Main Street and Possum Road.

Inside the small front room, a middle-aged woman sat behind a desk. She peered above the rim of her peepers.

"Do you for?" she asked, simply.

"I need to see Mayor Gibbons," Emma June said, her words forceful and determined.

"Have an appointment?"

Emma June leaned forward. "Mrs. Shutterfield? Is he here or not?"

"Hold on a minute, Emma June." She pivoted her chair in a half-circle. "Bo!" she hollered to one of the closed doors behind her. "Folks here to see you."

"Well, send them in," he yelled back.

Mrs. Shutterfield pointed to her right. "Go ahead."

Frank followed Emma June inside a room thick with cigar smoke. Books, papers, and framed photographs filled the tall shelf behind him. A large photograph of President Coolidge hung on the adjacent wall. Coolidge, the president who kept trying to clean up the scandals left by Harding, his predecessor. If a new mayor happened to win Holly Gap's next election, he'd probably have to clean up the messes left by Bo Gibbons.

"Emma June?" The mayor stood and gave her a sheepish nod.

"We know about Whitfield and the Baker Hotel," she said, refusing to sit in the proffered chair.

"Shh. Keep your voice down." The mayor waddled to the door and pushed it shut. "Now before you start in—"

"I should have come here right after that event of yours. Maybe I was stupidly thinking your brother would handle your shenanigans."

"Now wait just a minute, little lady. You don't know—"

"Oh, I know, all right. You are in cahoots with a wanted gangster, a man who most likely kidnapped my mother."

Relieved Emma June had come to this conclusion herself, Frank hated she had to face such a hard awareness.

The mayor's cheeks reddened. "First of all, I just learned his mug's on a wanted poster. And what in tarnation do you mean kidnapped? I thought your mama's with that other gal." He eased into his chair.

Emma June slapped his desk. The mayor flinched. "That other gal you're referring to is Betty Bedford," she said. "Before she left town, she received a threatening note not to talk. Whitt or his crony, Moody, stole Miss Helen's hooch and are destroying all the distilleries in the county. But that's nothing compared to what they're capable of. Somehow Mama got mixed up in this and they took her. I just know it."

The mayor took a quick peek out the window. "It's dangerous for y'all to be here. For all three of us." He dabbed a handkerchief across his sweating forehead then swiped it down his flushed cheeks.

Frank leaned in. "Moody is also keeping close tabs on the Foleys at Whitfield's direction. Both Earl and Wade Foley are somehow involved with Whitfield. We saw them at your fundraiser."

"The Foleys?" Bo Gibbons crinkled his bulbous nose. "Those two are always up to no good."

"Then why were you talking to Earl at Rosie's?" Emma June said.

The mayor squinted, looked around. "Oh. Earl asked if he could help at my shindig. I told him no."

"Well, they were there," Frank said. "Earl stayed parked under some trees. I caught Wade talking to Whitfield in the shadows. Apparently, Whitfield has dirt on Earl Foley."

Emma June turned to him. "He does? How do you know that?"

Frank had said too much.

Mayor Gibbons stood. "First of all, it's no secret folks are taking advantage of Prohibition and making a little money. So what and don't mind if I do. However, working with a gangster ain't something I planned or wanted. Whitfield's more trouble than he's worth."

"Even with a new shiny Cadillac?"

The mayor grimaced at Emma June's dig and took another peek outside. He turned back to Emma June. "If either one is responsible for your missing mama, I'll do my best to get to the bottom of it. Now, y'all best be going. I'm gonna holler y'all out."

The man was true to his word, at least about the hollering part. He opened the main door, looked around the street, and shouted after them, "And don't be causing any more trouble!" He slammed the door behind them.

CHAPTER 42

EMMA JUNE

Choppers sat on his haunches barking at me as I paced the sitting room floor. I needed to tell Daddy about my talk with the mayor. And my thoughts about Mama being kidnapped.

He'd been right not to trust Betty. Still, I wanted to believe Betty cared for us, that she didn't mean the trouble she'd caused. I didn't want to think of myself as the greater fool.

"Emma June?" Miss Helen squawked.

My head already throbbed. Letting her in meant more pounding.

While many folks in town found Miss Helen irritating, I'd become accustomed to and even liked her obstinate, strong-willed ways. But recently my skin had started to feel raw from her rubbing me the wrong way.

She came through the door, leaving me no time to hide in my room.

"Emma June? You seen those Gibbons brothers? Gunny and little *Bo*-peep?"

"Why?"

"Because I can't get ahold of either of them is why."

I pictured the two round men heading out of town in the mayor's Cadillac, happily leaving their duties behind as they discussed the horrors of gout.

"How should I know?" I asked.

"Well, you don't have to get snippy."

I didn't apologize. Didn't ask why she wanted to speak to them. At the moment, I didn't care.

"You okay, honey?"

"Just a headache. Everything else is right as rain."

"Yeah, any better and we'd be dead," she said and sighed. "I'll leave you be. You holler if you hear from either of those dimwits so I can give them a piece of my mind." She let herself out.

I curled up on the floor next to Choppers and rubbed the stump of his missing leg. The leg he no longer remembered.

An hour later, the creak of the front door sat me upright and out of my doze.

"Honey?" Daddy said, weariness hanging from the bags under his eyes. "Everything okay?"

"I have to talk to you."

I told him about the conversation with the mayor, and what I thought had happened to Mama.

"Kidnapped? You think a kidnapper thought she was Betty? Jesus Christ." He stood and paced until a knock at the door stopped his movement. "Who is it?" he said, his voice gruff.

"Frank Sanders, sir."

After Daddy let him in, I cast aside any worries Frank had brought bad news. Unless he was good at hiding it, his expression remained casual.

Frank shook Daddy's hand, then looked at me. "I stopped by the Munsons' to give Scooter a harmonica lesson. Nobody was home, so I thought—"

"I told Daddy my theory."

Frank blew out a breath. "I'm sorry, Mr. Crawford. It's the only thing that makes sense."

"I suppose," Daddy said, his voice barely above a whisper. "No motorcar accident. And even for a good friend, Bernice would never up and leave us like that."

I tried to erase the image in my mind, but it kept coming back. Mama, tied up to a chair, her wrists raw from the chafing rope. Her lips dry from the kidnapper depriving her of water. That was bad enough. I wouldn't allow myself to think of the darker scenario.

Daddy rubbed the nape of his neck, then stretched it side to side. "Sure wish we knew where Betty took off to. That woman has answers. For all we know, she's working for those mobsters."

Frank took a seat beside me. "You think that too, Emma June? That Betty is the type to associate with mobsters? Purposely do something to hurt her best friend?"

"You don't know her, Frank. Yes, she was our good friend. But she lied and kept secrets. Like where she lived, about her being blackmailed, not to mention whatever she told Mama. I gave her the benefit of the doubt for too long. Now I'm tired of protecting her."

"And nobody's seen her," Daddy said. "She disappeared into thin air. Believe it or not, Gunny tried to find her. Contacted New York City police, talked to Percy and Mabel to get a description of her motorcar, put feelers out in neighboring counties. Nothing."

Frank stood from the rocker, pivoted to the window, and stared out. His expression reminded me of Daddy's pondering pose. "What is it, Frank? What are you thinking?"

"Nothing," he mumbled. "I just . . . I'm just wondering if the mayor's gonna cut his ties with Whitfield." He turned and faced us. "And maybe I'm thinking about Betty a little. She could have run away because she was scared of that blackmail note. Maybe scared of Foley because she found out he worked for Whitfield and learned what they were up to."

"And you think that's what she told Mama?"

Frank sat again, ankle perched on a knee, his foot a constant jiggle. "I don't know. Maybe."

"Then Mama would have tried to help Betty. Offered to hide her or something. She certainly wouldn't have been mad."

Frank shrugged. "Maybe their fight didn't have anything to do with Whitfield."

"Okay," Daddy said. "What was it about then? All Bernice told me was that I had lied to her about Betty." He stared down at his scuffed work boots. "Made no sense."

I told Daddy and Frank how, just before the carnival, Betty had returned from a two-week trip with an old boyfriend. I didn't mention she had lied to Percy, telling him she'd gone to her sister's funeral. "They were fine before that night. But driving to the carnival, Betty wasn't her usual chipper self. She seemed distracted. Sad even. Almost like she knew whatever she was going to tell Mama wouldn't sit well." I gasped at my next thought. "What if it had something to do with her old boyfriend? What if Betty's old boyfriend is a mobster like Whitt? Or even Whitt himself?"

Frank shook his head.

"And Betty didn't say anything else on carnival night?" Daddy said. "Give any hints at all why she was distracted?"

I pictured that night in the breezer, the four of us driving to the carnival. As Betty sipped from her flask she'd made every effort to act cheerful, but she spent most of the ride fidgeting or staring into the dark. "She was mostly quiet."

Daddy sighed. "I need to talk to Gunny again."

"If he's around." I told Daddy about Miss Helen trying to track down both the sheriff and the mayor.

Familiar voices spilled in from the darkness and through our open window.

"Scoot, baby. You see me walking in those trees? Aim that flash-light on the ground so I can see where I'm stepping."

"Helen?" Daddy said.

Scooter entered first and gave me a tight squeeze. The hug he gave Frank was less enthusiastic and secretly made me feel better.

Miss Helen plopped next to me on the sofa and shoved an enve-lope in my hand.

"What's this?"

"It's a rectangle pouch made out of paper," she said, rolling her eyes. "One that's been licked and sealed tight." She puffed air from her cheeks. "Finally found Gunny. He'd locked himself in his office like a gutless jellyfish. I had to pound on the door till he let me in. Why can't he live in a regular house instead of the back room of a jailhouse?"

Miss Helen stopped. I gave her a moment to catch her breath, then asked if she'd learned anything.

"He said he has a hunch who stole my hooch but wouldn't say more. Probably embarrassed I know his brother is butt-cheek to butt-cheek with a gangster. Gunny had the nerve to make me wait until he wrote you his letter, so I could hand deliver it. Then licked it up tight like he couldn't trust me."

Which meant I wouldn't open it until she left.

Scooter took off his flat cap and pulled out an envelope tucked in its rim. "And *special* delivery for *you*, Frank. From a secret admirer."

"Thanks, buddy." A note from Loretta. Frank gave me a know-ing glance.

Daddy cleared his throat. "Appreciate it, Helen. Need me to walk you back over?"

Miss Helen rolled her eyes. "Oh, I think we can manage. Come on, Scooter. Let's leave them to letter reading."

After she made her exit down the porch steps and toward the avenue, we heard, "I still don't understand why I couldn't deliver that school note for you, Scooter. Do you know how many secrets I've kept in my lifetime?"

"Did you *bury* them?"

After their voices faded away, Daddy pointed to the letter. "Go ahead, honey. What did Gunny say?"

I read aloud.

> *Miss Emma June, I talked to my brother. We decided it best for him to keep working with Whitfield so he can keep an eye out for the goings-on. He'll let me know when I can make a move and catch them in the act of something illegal. Meanwhile, it's best you and Sanders keep your distance. Messy business, this is. Also, Jacoby Pines will be watching over Miss Atta instead of helping my brother.*
>
> *Sheriff Gibbons*

I threw the note off to the side.

"Look at it this way, Emma June," Frank said. "At least he talked to his brother."

"Maybe he's finally acknowledged the danger Bernice might be in." Daddy bolted upright. "Emma June, you've put yourself smack dab in the middle of all this business. Talking to the mayor, the sheriff. I don't like it. I know you're trying to figure out what happened to your mother, but you need to stay out of it. It's too dangerous. Do you understand me?"

For the most part, Daddy had kept his worries bottled up and sealed tight for my sake. But I could tell by his clenched jaw and furrowed brows that his bottle held a gasoline-soaked rag like the one thrown through the window at Rosie's. Telling him more of what I knew would only light the match.

"Nothing to be done tonight," he said. "I'll be staring at the ceiling if you need me."

I waited for the click of Daddy's bedroom door and turned to Frank. "What's it say?"

Frank tore open the note and read.

Wade and Pa gotta do what Moody tells them or says he'll hurt Ma and me. Heard him tell Pa that a noose could kill two fellas good as one. Pa and Wade try to act brave but they're scared too. Moody cleared out all Pa's guns and knives. Nailed shut the back door. Don't know why he's here. Shooting him dead would solve the problem.

"It wouldn't solve anything," I said. "Somehow, we need to catch Moody off guard and make him tell us where Mama is. Write another note, Frank. Ask Loretta if she knows anything about Mama."

"I will." Frank sat there, unmoving.

I ran to my bedroom and returned with a fountain pen and piece of paper. "Well, do it now."

"Torn from a Big Chief tablet? You twelve again?" Frank smirked.

Although I wasn't in the mood for playful banter, I appreciated him trying to ease the tension in the room. I smirked back.

As he sat at the kitchen table, nib pointed to the paper, a knock on the door made us both jump. I flicked off the sitting room light and peeked out the window. "Doc Ferguson's motorcar. What could he want at this hour?" My heart pounded.

I opened the door and suddenly wondered: How could moonshine be illegal but not the dangerously comforting smile of Samuel Ferguson?

CHAPTER 43

....

FRANK

Frank tipped his chair back from the Crawfords' kitchen table to get a better view of the two lovebirds.

Samuel, the fella who had rescued his drunk sister at the carnival and set her back on her feet in more ways than one, was tall and handsome. At least for gals who liked that college look. Blue eyes, blond hair. Dapper-dressed.

"I'm sorry it's so late, Emma June. My train just got in, and I couldn't wait till morning to see you."

"I can't believe you came." Her words muffled against Samuel's chest. "You really came."

Samuel pulled away from the hug but held on to her hands. "How are you holding up? Any news?"

"Some. Oh, God. I'm sorry. Come in, come in." She pulled him to the sofa. "I wasn't expecting you. I must look a mess."

Why did gals always say that anyway? Always apologizing for not stepping fresh out of a fashion magazine.

Samuel removed his spiffy tweed flat cap. "As beautiful as I remembered, Emma June. Maybe just a bit tired around the edges."

Frank cleared his throat and got Emma June's attention.

"Oh, sorry. Samuel, that's Frank. I've told you about him."

"You have." Samuel gave him a distrusting glare, then a quick nod.

Frank put down his pencil and moseyed over to Samuel. Shook his hand. A firm grip for a textbook reader. And not as soft as he'd imagined. "Good to meet you. Heard a lot about you." Not that he had, but it wouldn't hurt to say so.

Emma June brushed past Frank on the way to the kitchen.

"I understand you've been helping Emma June," Samuel said. "I appreciate that. New to town, and you're Johnny on the spot."

Although he heard no sarcasm in Samuel's voice, Frank felt his suspicion. "Miss Atta wouldn't have it any other way. She thinks of Emma June as kin. Miss Atta, you met her?"

"Of course. A fine woman. But you've done more than help out at Rosie's."

"Just doing what I can," Frank said, trying not to sound smug.

Emma June handed Samuel a glass of water and nuzzled up against him again. "Frank? Are you finished with Loretta's note?"

Frank took the hint. She wanted to be alone with Samuel. "I think so. Want me to read it to you?"

"Of course I do. Read it aloud."

Opening the circle of trust usually spelled danger. Frank felt uneasy. "Okay, here goes. 'Sorry this is happening to you, Loretta, and thanks for trusting me. Emma June is having a hard time, too. We think Moody and the man he works for, Whitt, a.k.a. Homer Whitfield, have something to do with her mother's disappearance. Have you heard them say anything about her?' That work?"

"Yeah. It's fine."

Samuel rubbed his chin and looked at Frank. "Can I make a suggestion?"

Emma June grabbed his arm. "Please do."

"If you want Loretta to trust you, she needs to know that you plan to help her. Also, this Moody fella has to sleep sometime. Ask her where he sleeps and what time."

Frank liked Samuel's thinking. He just didn't like the fact that Samuel thought of it first.

"I'll finish it at home. We can't get it to her until Monday anyway."

He left Emma June in Samuel's hands. The college boy seemed like a good enough fella. But even if he wasn't, what right did he have to butt in? He wasn't a real brother with his name written in the family Bible. Frank Sanders was only written in the margins with invisible ink.

Now, after ten o'clock, only dates at petting parties were awake. He'd take the risk again and stroll past the Foleys' place.

Getting closer, he knew things were bad when he wished a gun sat in his pocket instead of a harmonica. Encountering random thugs was one thing. He'd done it plenty of times in New Orleans. But if he had to face Moody and Whitt, he needed protection.

He changed course and headed for the shanty.

Irene sat up in bed, pen and paper in hand. Writing seemed to be everyone's pastime tonight. In a different world, he'd be sitting in a New Orleans club listening to fine jazz and writing song lyrics.

She put a hand to her chest. "Frank! You scared me."

"Sorry. I'll knock next time," he said flippantly.

"It's late. Where've you been?"

"The Crawfords'."

"Well, tell me. What happened?"

Frank told her everything he knew, including note-passing with Loretta.

"A good idea. And your father? How is he?"

Frank thought about the evening. How the truth sat on his tongue, begging for release. "*My father?* You mean the man I continue lying to?"

The once-glamorous woman from New York City fidgeted with the hem of her old house dress.

The Crawfords thought his mother was a villain, a partner in some crime. They were wrong about her. She might have been guilty of many things, but purposely hurting Bernice wasn't one of them.

"When are we going to tell them, Ma? I can't do this much longer." The secrets were eating a hole in his belly.

"As soon as it's safe."

"And when's that? After we bury his wife?"

Irene stared down at her writing, her hands trembling.

"I'm sorry, Ma." He cleared his throat and started over. "What are you writing?"

"A letter to Bernice and Emma June. So many things I didn't get to tell her. Just in case you find her alive and I'm not around. You'll see she gets it, won't you?"

Frank felt like Scooter's yo-yo. Up and down with his feelings, his stomach tangled in knots. "If that happens, I'll see to it. I won't leave till we see this through." He didn't say he'd stay until her last breath. But he would. He knew too well what it felt like to be left. Maybe staying by her side, doing the honorable thing, would scrape away some of the rubble of his guilt.

"Thank you."

"So, how you feeling?"

"Tired. Sick. Everything hurts."

Frank needed to focus on his task, not stare at her pale and gaunt face. "Ma? I need a gun."

She set her letter aside and looked at him with worry. She said nothing.

"For protection. Emma June's. Mine."

Irene gave a subtle nod. "Look in my carpet bag."

She had a piece? He headed toward the worn suitcase sitting in the corner.

"Not that." She pointed to the other side of the mattress. "The bag under those clothes."

He grabbed what looked like an Oriental rug with handles and plopped it beside her. She pulled out cosmetics, a cloche hat, and the keenest silver flask he'd ever seen. Frank whistled. "Where'd you get that?"

"Pete. When we first got married. You can have it if you want."

He rubbed his fingers over the fine etching of vines. "Geez, don't mind if I do." Her initials, I. S., were engraved near the bottom. "Might have to be like you, change my name. Something that starts with an *I*. How about Igor, as in Stravinsky?" he said, although his first thought had been *Illegitimate*.

"How about Ike, as in Ike-can't stand this town?" She grinned.

"Well, what do you know? My mother's shown her sense of humor."

"Found it." Irene pulled out the weapon.

Frank didn't know much about guns, but the small pistol had to be better than none at all. Plus, he could easily tuck it in his pocket.

"I guess I could have used this on carnival night," she said. "I never thought to take it. You ever shot a gun before?"

Frank shook his head. He didn't grow up with a father to take him hunting. He grew up with men whose power came through the instruments they played.

"Leonard Munson was a sharpshooter in the war. Ask him to teach you."

Frank thought of the quiet man who took his time drawling out his words. "Good idea. Might have to ask and answer my own questions though."

Limp in her bed, Irene managed a chuckle.

CHAPTER 44

EMMA JUNE

Samuel had stayed for an hour after Frank left. In between snuggling and smooching, we chatted more about Mama, about his school, and about how we would spend the summer together. He made it clear he would have to do rounds with his uncle, but other than that, he said he was all mine. We never ran out of things to say.

Midmorning, we sat on a blanket by the riverbank enjoying the sandwiches, apples, and oatmeal cookies he not only brought but had baked himself. I'd never met a man who made anything in the kitchen except bacon and eggs.

"Frank seems like a nice fella," he said with a casual air. "You are . . . comfortable around him."

He was right, of course. Not that I didn't feel comfortable around Samuel, because I did. But being around Frank took no effort, no prepping for my appearance. I simply didn't care what I looked like around Frank. Or how the tone of my voice sounded. With Frank, it was all about finding answers. Finding Mama.

"I guess I've gotten used to having him around. He's not so bad unless Charlene's attached to his arm. Then he acts like a puffed rooster."

"They're still an item?"

"You should see how Charlene swoons around him. It's almost embarrassing to watch. You'll see tonight when we go to Rosie's to hear Stinger Jones."

Since the firebomb weeks before, Miss Atta was finally ready for another Saturday night run. She said Gunny wasn't keen on her opening up for another music night, but she shushed him with a finger to his mouth.

"Can men swoon?" he asked.

I stared into Samuel's blue eyes and felt their waves.

"Because if they can," he continued, "it explains the dizziness I feel when I'm with you. I guess I better lay back until it passes."

I laughed and slapped a palm to his chest. Lying beside him, I allowed his gentle touch to become my armor.

The gunshot bolted Samuel upright.

"It's just Frank," I said. "He bought a pistol. Leonard is giving him shooting lessons." Frank had stopped by earlier, grinning when he showed me. I didn't know much about guns but the small weapon looked like something Scooter would have buried and gladly forgotten.

"It would make me feel better to check," Samuel said. "Mind if we go up?"

We found Daddy outside. He liked the peace and quiet of the country and didn't much care for the racket next door. Especially since it came from a gun.

"How long you reckon this is gonna last?" Daddy asked as we joined him on the front porch.

"Apparently that little pistol Frank bought draws to the right," I said. "Leonard has to teach him to compensate and make adjustments. Why don't you go inside, Daddy?"

Daddy lit a cigarette, a rare occurrence. I wanted to grab it, scold him, and smoke it myself.

"I'd rather watch," he said. "Dangerous business for a young man. Though if he really thinks he needs a gun, Leonard's the one to teach him."

"Leonard doesn't hunt anymore, does he?" I asked.

"Naw. He said there's plenty of meat at the grocer's so why bother. I think he'd seen enough damage in the war. You know how to shoot, Samuel?"

"Yes, sir. Hunted rabbits with my father when I was younger. Don't have time for hunting these days."

Across the field, Frank and Leonard stood with their backs to us. About ten yards in front of them, a row of tin cans sat atop an old workbench. I had yet to see any metal take flight.

"Samuel, I hear you're taking Emma June to Rosie's tonight. You need to keep a good eye on my girl."

"Yes, sir. I certainly will."

"If you came, Daddy, I'd have two handsome fellas watching over me. Please come."

Daddy sighed. "I don't know, honey. I'll ponder on it."

Another bang from across the field.

"Okay. I've had enough," Daddy said. "Think I'll go inside to . . ."

A different kind of racket stopped his words and got our attention. Gunny's Packard pulled up the Munsons' drive. Curiosity egged the three of us forward.

Halfway across the brown ribbon avenue, I spotted Miss Helen running out her door.

Before Gunny managed to free himself from the motorcar, Daddy, Samuel, and I were already standing next to Frank, Miss Helen, and Leonard.

"Morning, folks," Gunny said, his voice taut.

Miss Helen, hands to hips, poked out her ample bosoms. "You find my hooch?"

Gunny shook his head. "I'm on my way over to the Foleys'. Thought it best to let folks know where I was headed."

Scooter came running from the side of his house, Choppers chasing him. "*Samuel* came *back*."

"Just like he said he would, Scooter." In my head, I counted the people I knew I could trust. Daddy, Scooter, Miss Atta, Frank, and Samuel.

"Earl stole it, didn't he?" Miss Helen huffed. "I bet he's guzzled every drop by now."

Scooter pointed to Gunny's Stetson. He placed his hat on Scooter's head and gave it a pat. "It's a good bet, Helen."

Frank stepped forward. "I'll go with you, Sheriff."

Gunny shook his head. "Now, son—"

"I live nearby anyway. You can give me a ride home."

Relief swelled on Gunny's red face. "Well, in that case."

"No pistol," Leonard drawled out, staring at Frank. "You ain't ready."

"Pistol?" Gunny said.

Leonard nodded to the gun resting on Frank's palm. "Twenty-five caliber."

"Right," Gunny said with a snicker. "No need to stir the hornet's nest."

Miss Helen scoffed. "Hornets all right. Fitting description for that Foley clan."

Scooter tugged off the Stetson and slapped it across his thigh. "Mama! *Loretta* is *not* a hornet. She's my *sad* friend."

Miss Helen drew a finger across Scooter's cheek. "I'm not talking about her, sugar pot. I'm talking about her daddy. I'm gonna bring Earl Foley a poo pie when he's sitting in jail."

Frank, who had barely acknowledged our presence, shifted from one foot to the other. "Ready, Sheriff?" He headed for the Packard, Gunny puffing to keep up behind him.

"And Gunny," Miss Helen called out. "Don't you be cowing down to that piece of dog shit. Fill out those breeches you're wearing and bring Earl to justice."

When the dust settled from the Packard's exit, Samuel turned to me. "What do you think will happen at the Foleys'?"

"Hopefully Frank won't draw that pistol," I said, trying to keep the worry out of my voice. "He's a terrible shot."

CHAPTER 45

·······································

FRANK

According to Leonard, the gun in Frank's pocket "could work good enough as a threatening tool." Some sense of security. He had the feeling a knuckle knife, up close and personal, could do more damage.

Bouncing down the country road, Frank turned to the sheriff. "You know Miss Helen's only half right about Wade Foley. He's just doing what Moody tells him. But the orders come from Whitfield."

"Whitfield got wind the Feds are looking for him."

"Got wind? You mean your brother told him?"

"Now, look here, Frank," Gunny said, white knuckles squeezing the steering wheel. "Bo wants him caught more than anyone. Bootlegging and making money is one thing. Kidnapping and whatever else he's done is a different kind of kettle. Like I said, Feds are on his tail."

"Well, I hope he's not hiding out at the Foleys'."

Gunny swiped a handkerchief across his forehead, but the sweat kept coming.

"When we get there, let me off at the road," Frank said. "I'll stay hidden off to the side and keep an eye out." Not because he was scared, which he was. He didn't want Wade to see him with the sheriff.

Close to the Foleys', Gunny pulled off to the side and reached under his seat. A revolver. Unlike Frank's, the sheriff's gun was a nice, sturdy-looking piece. When Gunny tucked the revolver inside his usually empty holster, Frank considered chucking his out the window.

"You done much shooting on the job?" Frank asked.

"Fair enough." Gunny cleared his throat. "Mostly clearing out wild riffraff, the four-legged kind."

Frank didn't say good luck. The man was jumpy enough as it was. "I'll be over there." Frank pointed to the covering of trees near the entrance of their short drive.

The sheriff dropped him off where Frank still had a view of the front porch. Hopefully, he wouldn't have to save Gunny's ass.

The Packard rolled up to the house. Gunny maneuvered out of the car, the engine still running. He'd barely made it five feet when the front door opened. Earl Foley closed it behind him.

Earl held up a palm. "And that's fer 'nough, Sheriff. What brings ya out?"

Earl Foley was shorter than his son but stockier, thick around the shoulders. Random strands of dark hair, combed over, unsuccessfully covered his balding head.

Gunny stopped. "Need to have a word, Earl. Come on down here so we can talk proper."

Earl looked behind him at the house, then took a few steps forward. "What's this about?"

"Helen Munson."

"What?" He laughed. "She's got you runnin' errands fer her now? Needs me to chop her trees?"

"Someone stole her moonshine. Every last crate."

Earl stuck his hands in his overall pockets and rocked on his toes. "Well, ain't that a shame. Hers is the best in town."

"And I hear there's a new bootlegger in town who doesn't like the competition." Gunny stopped and rubbed his chin. "Earl, you went to see Helen just days before it was stolen. Scope things out, did ya?"

"Paying my respects is all."

"Uh-huh. Mind if I look around?"

"Got yourself a search warrant?"

"Think I need one?"

"Seems right."

"How's the family, Earl? Millie and the kids doing all right?"

"Fair to middlin'. Like everybody else around here."

"I haven't seen Millie in a coon's age. Loretta neither, for that matter. Time to pay my respects."

Earl stared at the sheriff, then at his house. "Hold on."

Earl took his time walking inside. Gunny shifted one foot to the other.

Frank could have smoked a whole butt in the time it took Earl to come back out. When he did, Loretta and an older dowdy-looking woman stood behind him, both wide-eyed with mouths struggling to lift at the corners.

Gunny removed his hat. "Morning, ladies. Just making my rounds. Everything all right out here?"

"Je'st fine, Sheriff," the woman said.

Loretta nodded and mumbled something Frank couldn't hear.

Physically, both appeared well. Unbeaten, at least.

Gunny took a step closer. "Say, y'all hear anything about Emma June's mother? She's still missing."

Loretta and her mother shook their heads and remained silent.

Earl spat in the dirt. "Shame fer a woman to leave her family like that."

"Yeah, well as it turns out, Miss Bernice didn't leave her family. We think she was kidnapped."

"You don't say." Earl scratched his temple. "Didn't think the Crawfords had that kinda dough." He turned to his daughter and wife. "You gals kin go inside now. Too hot out."

The heat was on Earl, and he knew it.

"It's not about money, Earl."

"Anything else, Sheriff? I got chores that ain't gettin' done."

"Where's Wade?"

"Inside. Wanna pay more respects?"

"If you don't mind."

"Wade? Get on out here," Earl boomed.

As if Wade's ear had been glued to the door, not a second passed when he emerged. "What happened to you?" Gunny asked.

Wade didn't answer. Just stood there, slumped, a pissed look on his face. Hard to tell, but from where Frank stood, Wade's eye looked discolored.

Earl shrugged. "Sometimes a boy needs discipline. Family business. None'a yours."

"Fine then, Earl. And I'll be back with that search warrant."

Earl didn't move, just stood there watching Gunny climb back in the Packard and drive off.

Frank couldn't let Gunny know where he lived. He told the sheriff to take him to The Diner. On the way there, Frank asked what he thought.

"I think all them holes in Earl's teeth come from years of lying."

Frank opened the passenger door but stayed in the seat. "So what's next? You really gonna get a search warrant?"

"Depends on who owns the judge."

After the Packard drove off, Frank pounded the dirt toward home. He had to clean up, get ready for music, and get rid of the corruption and lies in his head.

Inside the shanty Irene's cough sounded worse, raspy. Her breathing almost as loud. Something he hadn't thought of before—if his mother died, all secrets died with her. He didn't have to tell Theo he had a son. Or Emma June that she had a brother. How hard would it be to live the rest of his life without family? At least then he wouldn't have to admit to being an impostor.

Irene lifted her head and just as quickly let it fall back to the pillow. "You . . . shoot?"

"Yeah. You rest, Ma. I'm going to Rosie's for some tunes. Need anything?"

"Water."

He filled a glass and held it to her dry lips. She swallowed and closed her eyes. The woman who had drunk and danced her way through New York City and into the hearts of strangers, now survived on a liquid diet of water and laudanum and barely moved.

He'd hated her for so long. Even though he'd had Aunt Patsy, he never shook the feeling of abandonment. If someone left you, it meant they didn't care enough to stay. Plain and simple.

Irene was dying. Was she paying the price for leaving him?

But she had returned. With shame. With regret. The things she had broken she wanted to fix. Now it was too late. And she was about to abandon him all over again. He hated her for that.

Frank hurried to shave and wondered if his clean shirt smelled of disease like the rest of the house. He rushed out the door hoping the night breeze would blow away the sickness sticking to his skin.

He wanted to shoot something. Watch that something explode. See it come apart in front of him instead of having to feel it in his gut.

He'd settle for getting drunk.

······································

CHAPTER 46

EMMA JUNE

Sheriff Gunny Gibbons stood at Rosie's door greeting the folks he knew and sizing up the ones he didn't. Frank told me he had acted like a real sheriff during the Foley visit. He had asked the right questions and stood firm without a wobble.

As expected, Earl didn't give anything up. But Frank told me about the fear he'd seen on Loretta's and her mother's faces. And he knew Moody was inside the house tightly pulling the strings to keep them in place.

Samuel and I joined the Munsons in front of the stage. Considering what happened last time, a nice size crowd had showed up.

Whiskey sat on the platform, buffing his shoes. Stinger, next to him, nodded his thanks to Miss Atta for bringing him a glass of brew.

"Your father?" Samuel said, leaning into me. "Is he coming?"

"Still pondering, I suppose." But I wanted him there. I needed the safety and comfort of the two men I loved most in the world.

I spotted Frank and Charlene by the back door and nudged Samuel.

Samuel smiled. Perhaps seeing the two kissing would convince him Frank and I were nothing more than friends.

"This seat taken?" said a familiar voice.

I barely recognized him. Instead of his usual work shirt and trousers, Daddy wore his handsome attire, a light-gray suit and a straw hat. "You came!"

He gave me a squeeze. "A little music shouldn't hurt too bad."

Miss Atta strutted toward us all aglitter. "Well, if it ain't Theo Crawford."

Daddy stood and wrapped his arms around his old friend. "How's my Atta Girl?"

"Right as rain, sugar. And so glad to see you."

Samuel leaned to my ear. "Wonder what's going on over there?" He nodded toward Frank and Charlene.

Charlene had Frank pinned against the wall with an index finger to his chest, her other hand on her hip. As her mouth ran amuck, Frank narrowed his eyes and removed her hand. He said something to Charlene and headed out the back door.

Charlene's shoulders slumped, then quivered. She ran to me, her kohl eye shadow smudging.

"I hate him," she cried. "He doesn't care for me at . . . at all. He said everything's a disaster. I think he wants to go back to New Orleans."

It felt strange, placing my hand on her shoulder. How long had it been since she needed me for anything?

"Had he been drinking?" Samuel asked, handing her a handkerchief.

Charlene nodded.

"I'll bet he'll be begging your forgiveness before the night's over."

"And," I added, "maybe Frank's just nervous. He's performing tonight."

Scooter backed out of his chair and came around to Charlene's side. "I got an *extra* sucker, Charlene. It's for *you*." He presented the red lollipop like a bouquet of roses.

I wanted to follow Frank outside to our break area, sit on a crate, and ask if he needed anything. I decided it wouldn't sit well with

Samuel. Whatever it was, Frank would figure it out. He was smart and capable, not to mention resourceful and talented.

"Why, what a pleasure to see you, Mr. Crawford." A woman's voice crawled up my neck and sent shivers down my spine. Miss Primrose.

Daddy stood and offered his hand. "Good evening, Miss Primrose. Nice to see you." As he started to turn away Miss Primrose grabbed his arm.

"How is everything, Mr. Crawford?" She smoothed a hand down her shimmery dress. "I hope well, considering."

I'd never liked Miss Primrose. Seeing her flirty side set my teeth on edge.

"He's doing fine, aren't you, Theo?" Miss Helen said. "He has plenty of help from his neighbors. Not that he needs any. No slack in that man's rope. Right, Emma June?"

It was one of the few times I appreciated her butting in, and I couldn't hide my grin. Miss Helen tossed me a wink like Mama often did.

"No need to concern yourself, Miss Primrose," I said. "Daddy's got a firm grip on his saddle. Considering," I added sarcastically.

Samuel squeezed my hand and smiled.

There would be no firebomb tonight. Surrounded by Daddy and good friends, I was untouchable.

Charlene settled in beside me, even managed to sway along to Whiskey and Stinger's first few songs. Daddy tapped his fingers on the table, matching the music's rhythm. If Mama had been there, it would have been the perfect evening.

Miss Atta introduced Frank to the stage. The crowd waited, scanning the room for his appearance. "Frank Sanders? Where you at? Your girlfriend's right here," Miss Atta said, making the patrons laugh.

Frank emerged through the back door. He stumbled up the raised platform, catching himself from falling at the last minute.

"Sor . . . sorry for the delay, folks," he slurred through his chuckle. "Needed a refreshment."

"Oh, brother," Charlene mumbled.

Frank prided himself on performing in front of an audience. I wondered why he would jeopardize the moment by getting drunk.

Stinger stepped forward. "A'fore we hear this youngster, I got a little something for him." Stinger opened a shabby case and pulled out a horn. Frank's eyes widened.

"Cornet borrowed from a kin," Stinger said.

Frank stared at his favorite instrument. "Haven't played one of these in a while," he mumbled, soft enough only the patrons in front could hear.

"I . . . I, um, will give it a try."

He blew into the horn, no melody, no song, only notes. "This'll do," he said and cleared his throat.

An introduction, jazzy and soulful. Frank nodded for Stinger and Whiskey to keep playing, then pulled the horn down to his side, and sang.

> *There's a place I can't get into*
> *'Less I jump the hole and fall through*
> *'Cause the door that's locked, not swaying*
> *Won't let me in.*
> *Perhaps a drifter's way'a paying*
> *For the games that he's been playing*
> *Always cheatin'*
> *Yet still never seems to win.*

"See," Charlene said, sniffling. "He's not happy here. He doesn't even like me." She dabbed her eyes with Samuel's handkerchief.

I gave her a brief pat on the back and shushed her. "Let's hear him finish."

So where's that silver linin' then?
A little four-leaf clover?
It's an organized crime when
You think the game is over.

Another cornet solo, not one wrong note.

So if you think you hear me comin'
Wait to hit the road a thumbin'
And float me down an oar before you go
'Cause, I'm tired of this running
Empty songs ain't worth the humming
Life is shorter than this paddle that I row.

The crowd applauded and I breathed a sigh of relief. Drunk or not, Frank pulled it off. I was proud for him yet saddened by the song's depressing words. I thought of what it must have been like for Frank to grow up without either parent. And now, although his mother had returned, he had to care for her.

One by one, I looked at the people around me. Daddy, Samuel, the Munsons, and my friends, including Frank, were my bedrock, my strength. They kept me rooted and watered, refusing to let me wither. For the first time since Mama disappeared, I felt, well, lucky.

Scooter waited for Frank to step off the platform, then rushed to his side. Frank whispered something to Scooter, then staggered out the back door.

Miss Helen smiled and leaned across the table. "Didn't I tell you, Theo? When it comes to music, that boy knows his onions. And just look how much Scooter loves him. If I'm not a good judge of character, nobody is. And that's the God's honest truth."

Samuel and I faced each other and snickered. "How about you and me go for a walk?" he said, his blue eyes sparkling.

Charlene tugged my arm. "Did you see, Emma June? He didn't even look at me. That whole time he sang, not one wink in my direction. Please, Emma June. Go talk to him. Find out why he's ignoring me."

"I, um—"

"Go ahead, babe. I'll be here when you get back."

I kissed Samuel's cheek and promised a quick return.

Frank sat slumped on his crate at our usual spot. Even in the darkness, I noticed his look of defeat.

"Another grand performance, Frank."

"Yeah." He spat off to the side.

"What's wrong? You did great out there. Is this about Charlene?"

"Charlene? What's she got to do with anything?" he mumbled and took a swig from the flask he pulled from his pocket.

"She said y'all had a tiff. Plus, I saw you stumble on the stage. You're drunk."

He belched. "Not enough."

Samuel had traveled all the way to Holly Gap just to spend two short days with me. He was inside, waiting. But the person slouching on the crate before me, the person who had helped me the most, wasn't the light-hearted Frank I knew.

"Mind if I have a swig?"

"Suit yourself." He tossed it up to me.

The hooch went down smooth and warmed my throat.

The back door opened, the light from inside spotlighting where I stood.

Charlene stood with her hip against the doorframe. "Well? What's going on out here?"

Again, I lifted the flask to my lips, then stopped. I studied the etching on the shiny silver surface, the scrolling of vines. I wasn't sure at first, not until I saw the initials at the bottom. No matter how watery my eyes had become, I couldn't make the *I. S.* disappear.

CHAPTER 47

....

FRANK

hit, shit, shit.

S He'd forgotten about Irene's flask. Didn't even consider Emma June had seen it before. Frank reached for the flask, but Emma June pulled it away, holding it with both hands. Charlene smirked. "Emma June, you didn't even drink tonight. What's wrong with you?"

Emma June's cold dark eyes glared at him. He could feel her anger, the awful sense of betrayal. The flask trembled in her hands. "Where did you get this?" she said through gritted teeth. He couldn't undo what she'd seen. Couldn't make up a lie to fit. He stood, mouth agape and wordless.

Emma June held up the flask but kept her eyes on Frank. "Recognize this, Charlene?"

Charlene squinted and touched the flask's surface. "Betty's?"

"I said," she yelled, "where did you get this?"

"Emma June?" Samuel appeared next to Charlene. "What's happened?"

"He knows something about Betty. Oh, God, this . . . this is Betty's flask."

Maybe, just maybe, had he been alone with Emma June, he would have stayed, talked it through. Instead, he bolted.

"Stop him, Samuel!" Emma June roared.

The liquor made him slow, clumsy. He had almost made it to the end of Main Street when Samuel grabbed his shoulder and threw him to the ground. Frank didn't feel the impact.

He lay on the road, panting, not wanting to get up. Why bother? He could easily stay there. Let a motorcar run him over. Offer up his body to the buzzards so they could pick his bones until he disappeared.

Samuel stared down at him. "You've got some explaining to do."

Frank deserved to be yelled at. Instead, Samuel's voice was steady, too calm. He heaved himself up to a sitting position and took a few breaths.

"What's this about, Frank?"

There was a time when he had risen each morning knowing what to expect. Then Irene had barged into his town.

Frank lit a cigarette and inhaled deep. "You ever have someone show up unexpectedly and rewrite your lyrics?" The hard thump against his chest didn't stop.

"Just tell me how you got Betty's flask."

"It's a long story." Endless, it seemed.

"If this involves Emma June, I've got all the time in the world. Get up."

Frank slowly maneuvered his way up and followed Samuel to the side of the road. He sat where Samuel pointed, next to him against a pile of bricks.

Frank readied himself. He needed a good cleansing, something to wash away his lying, betraying soul. "First, you have to under-stand something. I didn't want anything to do with this mess. It was dumped in my lap." *And created by a two-week love tryst.* "I'd never do anything to hurt Emma June or her family. Ever. You have to believe that."

"Go on."

Frank's hooch buzz was ending. He needed another drink. Only half an inch remained in his mother's flask, the flask he left in Emma June's hands.

"I've known Betty all my life."

"What? How—"

Frank held up a finger. "My story. My telling."

Samuel waited.

"Let's just say I didn't know Betty Bedford. I knew her as the mother who never stuck around." He wouldn't give up her real name. Not now.

"Betty's your mother." Samuel's voice stayed level, no octave-change of surprise.

"You could say that."

"Why isn't she helping us find Emma June's mother?" Again, Samuel kept his voice steady, nonaccusatory.

"She wants to, bad as everyone else. Mrs. Crawford is Ma's best friend. But she can't leave the house. And not just because she's so sick with cancer. If Whitt or Moody find her, they'll kill her."

"I know about your mother's cancer. And about Whitt and Moody."

Frank's shoulders relaxed. Unnecessary, but Frank told Samuel how his mother took off when he was young and how Aunt Patsy raised him. Then he skipped forward to the day in New Orleans when she showed up at his door, begging for help. But none of that was important. What mattered was making Emma June understand his motives and finding her mother.

"Okay, I get that you didn't exactly sign up for this," Samuel said. "But why do they want to kill her? The blackmail note said to bring money or the cat's out of the bag. What does that mean?"

"Ma overheard a conversation between Whitt and Earl Foley. Whitt didn't trust her to keep quiet. We think Moody kidnapped Mrs. Crawford thinking she was my mother." Although true, the note had nothing to do with mobster business.

"A few things don't add up. First of all, why were they arguing? What did your mother say that made Mrs. Crawford so mad she had to storm off in the middle of the night to finish the conversation?"

"Ma told Mrs. Crawford about her lies and past mistakes. Her husband didn't die, he took off when I was one." More truth. Just not all of it.

Samuel nodded and didn't press the point. But the boy was smart. No doubt he was seeing through the holes in Frank's story.

"Okay. But why would your mother lie about that?"

"Embarrassed, I guess." He'd wait to spit out the whole sordid story. First, he had to prove he was worthy of trust. One way or another, Frank was going to set things right. Ironically, that's what his mother had been trying to do.

Samuel stood and brushed off his trousers. "I better go check on Emma June. And you need to come with me. Tell her what you told me."

"She's too mad to listen. It'll set better coming from you." Besides, he couldn't face Emma June. Not yet.

Samuel gave a slow nod, agreeing to do the dirty work. Even that small sense of relief had Frank breathing again.

"Tell Emma June I'm sorry. Explain how I couldn't tell her Betty was my mother. That Ma's been in hiding so Whitt couldn't find her. I might not have grown up with my mother, but I didn't want her dead because of me either."

Both walked away in opposite directions, Samuel toward the lights of town, Frank back into the dark.

"Hey, Frank?" Samuel called out.

Frank turned but continued walking backward.

"Just wondering. Your mother's past mistakes. Was her leaving you one of them?"

Hearing the question aloud stopped Frank in his tracks. The woman who raised him had given him everything. "Nope. Aunt Patsy and me did just fine."

Irene Sanders had only cared about herself. A quality he didn't like, a character flaw he didn't want. Not anymore.

Sure, Holly Gap was a small, Podunk town with old-fashioned ways. But many of its citizens had hearts big enough to learn from. He thought of Miss Atta, who handed out kindness with unlimited supply even though she didn't always receive it. And Miss Helen, rough around the edges but reliable to a fault. And Scooter, the best kid he'd ever met, who focused on the good inside of folks.

Emma June and Theo might not ever forgive his lies and deception. But maybe it wasn't too late to boost the chance they might.

Frank made a slight detour on his way home. He stayed hidden among the trees in the periphery of the Foleys' house.

The shack was dark, buttoned down for the night. But the movement on the floor of the Foleys' front porch got his attention.

Now he knew where Moody slept at night.

He trudged on and tried to feel that cornet against his lips. If nothing else, the audience at Rosie's liked him.

CHAPTER 48

EMMA JUNE

loathed Frank Sanders with a devil's passion. Like his mother, Frank was a master of deceit, a fraud. All that time and he never said one word. And not telling was the same as lying. Betrayal at its worst. I never wanted to set eyes on him again. I wanted Miss Atta to fire him.

Daddy joined me on the front porch the next morning and handed me a cup of coffee.

"Doing okay, honey?"

"He'll be back in three weeks. Then I get him for the whole summer."

After the long night of Samuel having to spill Frank's lies, he had left to catch the morning train back to college.

"That's not what I meant." He sat next to me on the porch step. "How are you feeling about learning the truth?"

"Frank should have told me."

"Yeah. I know."

In the distance, a deer and her fawn stared ahead, motionless through Daddy's pause. "But you understand why he didn't, right?" he said.

"Are you really going to defend him right now?"

"It's not about defending. It's about seeing the big picture."

"Well, it's not a pretty one. Frank double-crossed me." *And played me for a fool,* I thought. I had proved on carnival night I could do that on my own.

"Honey, sounds to me like Frank didn't create the mess."

"Maybe not. But don't you see, Daddy? Because of his lies we've wasted precious time."

"What could we have done different?"

"Anything. Everything. Frank withheld facts that could have led us to Mama. If we'd known the truth, Mama could be home by now."

"We can't foresee the future any more than we can undo the past. He'd been thrown into the situation by a mother who didn't care enough to raise him. Still, he protected her."

"Yeah, I know. He didn't want to be responsible for his . . . his mother's death." My chest tightened. My throat threatened to close.

Daddy wrapped his arm around me. "You didn't do anything wrong, Emma June."

"If I hadn't gotten so drunk, I could have stopped her. We have to find her, Daddy. I have to . . . have to tell her how sorry I am." And then they came. Tears of lost hope you couldn't hold in anymore because the levee had broken and you're scared of drowning.

Daddy pulled me closer, squeezing in his indisputable love.

"You have nothing to be sorry for, honey. This wasn't your mess. And feeling guilty doesn't do any good. Guilt's a big old noose around our neck that we gotta learn to untie. I should know. I keep thinking if I'd forced myself to stay awake and listen, I could have stopped her."

I knew he was right about the guilt. Beating ourselves up kept us from moving forward. When Choppers lost his leg, my guilt stung so much I could barely look at him. Then I realized his sadness had nothing to do with losing a limb but was from my lack of attention. He wanted me to love him regardless of how many legs he had.

According to Frank, Betty was being blackmailed by Earl and Whitt for overhearing some nefarious plan. She also admitted to having a son. Either way, Mama would have worried about Betty's safety and probably felt disappointed her friend had kept such a secret. But not so angry as to storm out of the house in the dead of night to discuss it further.

Frank wouldn't tell us what Mama and Betty had fought about. Either he was keeping it to himself or he truly didn't know.

"Maybe Betty can give us some ideas of where Earl or Whitt might have taken her. Sick or not, Daddy, I need to talk to her."

"Me, too. And I'll go with you. Wait till I get back. I just need to run to the dairy for a bit. Two hours at most, then we'll find her. Deal?"

Ol' Bess out of view, I didn't have the energy to hoist myself from the porch. I threw the ball for Choppers while thinking of Betty. How glamorous she was in her shimmering dresses and perfectly applied cosmetics. How she brightened a room with her unconventional ways and easy laughter. Had it all been a sham? Window dressing to cover up a past she preferred to keep hidden? Surely some parts of Betty's character had been authentic.

Choppers's ears perked. He dropped his ball and aimed his bark toward the Munsons'.

I spotted him then. Frank, tearing through the air like an arrow shot from a bow.

I followed Choppers's charge and found Frank talking through a pant beside Miss Helen.

"Leonard's running errands with Scooter. I'll take you." She threw the hoe aside and headed for Roadrunner.

I stood beside Miss Helen. "What's going on?"

"Ma, she needs a hospital, a doctor. Something," he panted out.

"I'd like to go with you, Frank."

"She's not up to answering questions."

"No questions. I just want to see her again." That part was true. I wanted to find out how I felt when I looked at her.

Frank nodded. "We gotta hurry."

Miss Helen started the engine and headed down the drive. "Theo already told me the skinny but don't you worry about me judging her, Frank Sanders. Who wouldn't hide if a gangster was on their tail? And you can bet the farm I'd protect my family the same way you did. If someone was after Scooter, I'd hide him away too and die with the secret. And Leonard? Hitch in his gitalong or not, Leonard can take care of himself just fine."

Sitting in the back, I thought of the lengths people go to to protect the ones they love. How Gunny protected Miss Atta and presumably his brother, who was rumored to have gone to Austin for a mayor's conference. I thought of how Daddy had rescued Mama at the church picnic years ago. And Scooter. He protected everyone.

Frank had sacrificed his music and well-being to move to Holly Gap just to help the mother he barely knew.

"So, Frank, what happened to . . . your mother?"

"I found her on the floor too weak to get up. She's having trouble breathing."

Miss Helen hit the gas.

Outside, the rotting house creaked in the wind. Inside, the house smelled of a subtle decay, the gradual seeping of a life.

I stepped over a broken radio, a screwdriver next to it. A chair with only three legs lay on the small sitting room floor alongside a jar of liquid paste. Papers torn from a Big Chief tablet marked with music notes dotted the scratched floor along with a couple of *Etude* music magazines. On top of a thin pallet lying across a weather-beaten army cot, a worn and tattered copy of a book. *An American Tragedy* by Theodore Dreiser. The irony didn't escape me.

I followed Frank and Miss Helen into the small bedroom, ignoring the stench of sweat and disease. Betty lay curled on a floor mattress.

Seeing her, the urge to scream in her face drained away. The woman looked nothing like the Betty I knew. No Max-Factored eyelashes. No bowed red lips or styled bob. I recoiled at the sight of her sunken cheeks and eyes, a pale skin mask over a skull. Her eyes remained closed, but her eyeballs *tick-tocked* beneath her eyelids.

Miss Helen frowned and shook her head. "Let's not stand here gawking. We gotta get her in Roadrunner."

I stood aside while Frank and Miss Helen maneuvered Betty out the door like litter bearers in the Great War hauling wounded soldiers. Except instead of a stretcher, they carried her in a sheet.

After Miss Helen snapped for me to open the roadster's back doors, they threaded Betty like a fleshy yarn through the eye of a needle into the back seat.

Once on the road, I looked back. Betty was curled on her side, her head on Frank's lap.

"How's she doing?" I asked.

"Same. She's squeezing my hand, though."

She wasn't squeezing his hand. He was squeezing hers.

"Em . . . Emma?" Betty mumbled, her eyes fluttering.

"It's me, Betty. Everything will be okay." But I knew better.

CHAPTER 49

·······································

FRANK

Frank got out of the roadster and eyed Main Street. Folks carting groceries, a pram with a crying baby, friends greeting each other with handshakes and shoulder pats. People going about their business as if his mother wasn't dying.

He ran inside and gave Doc Ferguson the short version of the need for secrecy.

The coast clear, the two of them carried his mother inside the doctor's office. They laid her on an examining table in a small room smelling of antiseptic. His mother blinked up at Frank but didn't speak.

Emma June leaned in the doorway, her arms folded across her body as if closing herself off. "She never said anything to us about being sick. Only acted her happy-go-lucky self."

Those *happy* times when his mother showed up on Aunt Patsy's doorstep seemed so long ago. She'd give him a chirpy "Hi'ya Frankie!" only to stay a day or two before skipping back to the train station with a bigger smile.

"Didn't want to worry you, I guess," he said.

"Betty Bedford," Doc Ferguson said, his tone sorrowful as he looked at Frank. "I remember telling her to go to a big city hospital months ago."

"She went," Frank mumbled. "She just didn't stay." He dared a glance at Emma June, who gave him a sorrowful nod. Maybe, just maybe, she could forgive him.

Doc dipped his head. "Not much I can do at this point, son. I'll carry her to the nice bed we have in the back. Between myself, Nurse Louise, and my wife, we can make sure she's comfortable. Sarah's in Graham with her sister. I'll call, tell her to come home."

It didn't seem right, pulling someone away from their family. "I could stay with Ma," he said, but wasn't sure he meant it. "Your wife shouldn't change her plans."

"No need, son. With my busy schedule, Sarah goes to Graham just to have something to do. She loves being helpful."

Frank nodded and thought about the big question. The one he didn't want to ask but had to know. "How long's she got?"

Doc Ferguson frowned, then fixed his eyes on Frank. "Wish I could tell you more. That one's up to God. Right now, we need to get her started on fluids. And son, might wanna go bring some of her things over. Fresh clothes and such. It'll make her feel better."

Frank thought of Samuel. In a few years, like his uncle, he'd be a good doctor. He pictured Samuel standing over some poor soul, listening with rapt attention, collecting information. After all, he had practiced on Frank last night.

Frank patted Irene's hand. "Ma, you hold on. I'll be back with some good news."

Irene, doped up on laudanum, managed a brief curve of her lips.

He'd find out what happened to Emma June's mother. But would Irene live long enough to hear the news?

He backed up to the doorway, refusing to turn away from his mother.

"She really does love Mama, doesn't she?"

Frank spun around to meet Emma June's eyes. "More than you know."

Her chin dropped as she peered downward. "So maybe I'm not such a bad judge of character."

Frank wanted to say something, keep the conversation going. But since he couldn't tell the whole truth, he said nothing.

"Of course I'll pay her bill, Louise," Miss Helen huffed from the front. "What? You think I'm a tightwad? Don't you believe everything you hear. The only reason I didn't pay Hank was because he cheated me on sugar for the last time. I saw his fat finger on the scale."

Frank relaxed when Emma June lifted the corners of her mouth into a slight grin. "I'm having a smoke outside," she said. "Wanna join me?"

They sat on the wooden bench outside the doctor's office. Inhaling, blowing out smoke, inhaling, blowing out smoke. "We're moving up in the world, Emma June," he said, breaking the silence. "A bench under our butts instead of a crate."

"Yeah. And all is right with the world." She reached in her purse and pulled out his mother's flask. "I believe this is yours."

Frank took it, stared at the scrolling, and thought about how something so fetching had transformed into a grimy piece of metal. "Ma didn't want it anymore. Guess her drinking days are over."

"I'm sorry she's so sick, Frank. Truly."

"And I'm sorry she created such a mess."

"She didn't mean to overhear a mob conversation. And I understand that she had to stay hidden. But why couldn't she send word through you? Why all the lying? I could have had answers. What did she say that made Mama so mad?"

He had to change the subject. "You know, you're lucky to have grown up with your mother. You did things together. She took care of you, sheltered you even. Most of my life, I never really knew where mine was."

"You think knowing Mama cared for me makes losing her easier?"

No bitterness in her tone. Still, that one stung.

Frank hesitated and rubbed the whiskers he didn't have time to shave. "Your father. Does he hate me now?"

Emma June let out an agitated breath. "No. Believe it or not, he understands your motives."

"But you don't?"

"Not yet. Not until you answer my questions. I know you're worried about your mother. But at least you know where yours is." She threw her smoke down and crushed it into dust.

"Frank?" Miss Helen flounced out the door toward them. "No bones about it. You're staying at our house till your mother gets . . . well, better. Makes no sense you staying in that shack by yourself."

"Don't like my fancy abode, Miss Helen?"

Honking got their attention. Inside the familiar truck coming toward them, the one he'd driven on delivery night, Scooter leaned into Leonard and continued pumping the horn.

"What in tarnation?" Miss Helen said.

Scooter hopped out first. "Where is *Betty*?"

"Scoot, baby?"

Scooter ignored his mother and ran inside the doctor's office.

Leonard limped out from behind the wheel. "Boy's upset. Wouldn't take no for an answer."

Unlike most folks who had an unfavorable impression of his mother, Scooter liked the woman he knew as Betty. Even cared enough to want to see her.

"Well, he won't be any less upset when he takes a look at her," Miss Helen muttered.

A shot rang out, and Frank ducked. He did a quick scan of Main Street. Left, right, no Moody or Whitt. The shot rang out again.

Miss Helen pointed to a backfiring vehicle and Frank's breath returned. The weather-beaten rickety truck rumbled to a stop in front of them.

Jacoby Pines, the man who now watched over Miss Atta instead of muscling for the mayor, hopped out and hustled to the passenger door.

"Good Lord," Miss Helen said. "He's pulling out Wade Foley."

"Motherfucker," Wade wailed, pressing the blood-soaked bandage on his left arm. If Frank hadn't known better, he'd have thought the wetness on Wade's face wasn't sweat, but tears.

Jacoby supported Wade as they headed for the doctor's office door. "Fella's been shot. Ain't near bad as he's carryin' on."

"Hell it ain't," Wade panted out. He shrugged off Jacoby's hold and entered the office.

"What?" Miss Helen asked Jacoby. "You finally had enough of the Foleys too? Decided to pick them off one at a time before I had the chance?"

"Naw. Folks like the Foleys do themselves in all on their own. Found the boy running on the road 'way from his house."

"Did he say who did it?" Frank asked, thinking the possibilities were endless.

"Mumbled somethin' 'bout killing Moody. Wanted me to swear not to tell Sheriff."

"Probably doesn't trust our Texas Wyatt Earp," Miss Helen mumbled. "Leonard, let's get us a bite at Rosie's. All this ruckus has worked up my appetite. And Emma June? You mind grabbing Scooter when he's done whispering sweet nothings in Betty's ear?"

Wade Foley without a guardian. Finally, their chance for answers. And Frank had the urge to squeeze out each one through that bloody hole in Wade's arm.

CHAPTER 50

....

EMMA JUNE

didn't care how much Wade hurt. Catching him without Moody meant making him talk.

Frank stood in the doorway of the room Betty had occupied moments before. Wade had taken her spot on the examining table.

As Doc Ferguson examined the wound, Wade's cussing and moaning couldn't drown out the random harmonica notes coming from down the short hall. In all the madness, Scooter kept being Scooter.

"Was it Moody who did this to you or that upstanding father of yours?" Frank asked.

"Leave me alone." Wade covered his eyes with his good arm.

Frank laughed. "You think they meant to miss, or you just got lucky?"

"*Ouch*, dammit!" Wade shrieked. "That burns!"

I wanted to tell Doc Ferguson to press harder, to throw more stinging disinfectant on his wound.

Wade grimaced. "I gotta get back to Loretta."

"Loretta?" Frank asked. "What happened?"

Wade's jaw pulsed. His fist clenched. "Hurry up, Doc."

"Moody? He deserves what's coming to him," Frank said. "I can help with that."

Wade stared at Frank. "Might be you can."

"Just a graze," Doc said. "After I stitch you up, you'll be good to go." He wrapped a clean bandage loosely around the wound. "I'll be right back."

Ordinarily, Doc protected his patients and wouldn't allow anyone in the room. I doubted Samuel had confided in his uncle but for whatever reason, Doc didn't ask us to leave.

I pushed past Frank and stood at Wade's side. "What about Loretta? What happened to her?"

Wade looked down and shook his head.

Frank moved in. "We know Moody is muscling you and your family. We also know your father's taking orders from Whitfield."

Tears filled Wade's eyes. "We're prisoners in our own house. Prisoners because of that sonofabitch who calls hisself a father. Paying for a crime—"

"Hear that?" Doc entered the room smiling and placed the sutures and gauze on the table. "Not sure Betty's awake enough to notice, but Scooter's playing the harmonica for her. Even laid a lollipop on her pillow."

Wade's eyes grew wide. "Betty?" He swallowed.

"That's right, Wade," I said. "Betty Bedford. Remember her?"

"Nope. Nope." He shook his head back and forth, back and forth. "Betty ain't around no more. I heard them say she'd run off. They're not huntin' for her no more. Someone else," he muttered.

"I don't care who they're looking for now," Frank said, his voice rising. "My mother, Betty to you, is lying in a room down the hall. Moody took the wrong woman."

"Huh?"

Doc backed up to the wall and stood with his arms crossed.

Disgusting as it was, I leaned closer to Wade's face. "My mother, Wade. They took *my* mother. My *mother!*"

"What? But your ma—"

"Was an innocent bystander. She had nothing to do with your mobster friends. Your father wrote that blackmail note to Betty, didn't he?" I remembered the words. *Last chance. Bring the dough tomorrow or cat's outta the bag.* Frank had merely suggested Earl wrote that note. But he knew. He knew because Betty had told him. "Why was he blackmailing her, Wade?"

"Hell if I know. All's I know is Pa counted on her for a regular payment. That coulda been for, well you know, 'bout anything."

Frank glared at Wade then placed a hand on my shoulder. "Emma June, we need to back up a second."

I jerked his hand away. "I'm done backing up. I want answers."

Silence. Even the harmonica down the hall had quieted.

Frank turned to Wade. "Why'd you get shot? What happened to Loretta? And what crime is your father paying for?"

"Where is my mother?" I screamed in his face.

Wade, always so arrogant and cocksure of himself, curled on the table and wiped at his eyes. A baby in a mother's womb.

Doc moved toward him. "Son," he said, his words gentle. "These folks are suffering as much as you are right now. And by helping them, you'll free up that boil that's been growing inside you too long now. First, I'd like to know how you got yourself shot."

Wade struggled to sit up. His eyes stayed on his dirty work boots as he recounted the event.

He told us how he heard the muffled struggle coming from Loretta in her bedroom. He ran in and found Moody standing over his sister, tearing at her clothes with one hand and covering her mouth with the other. His mother saw what was happening and had retreated to her bedroom. Wade yelled for Moody to stop, to leave Loretta alone. But Moody only laughed and told him he was a worthless piece of shit. When Wade rushed him, Moody let go of Loretta long enough to pull his pistol.

Still aiming, Moody backed Wade into the kitchen and said, "Have yourself some breakfast till I'm done."

Wade looked up from his telling long enough to shoot me a sorrowful glance. "I might like girls, but I'd never do . . . never do nothing like that. You gotta believe me, Emma June. I tried talking Moody outta grabbing Tallulah, but his mind was set on what he called 'dark meat.' If Sampson hadn't turned on his light, no tellin' what woulda happened."

"Where's your father? Why isn't he protecting his daughter?" Frank asked.

"Good question. It's always me doing the protectin'. Couldn't do it today." Wade bit into his cheek and looked away.

"Go on, son," said Doc. "What happened next?"

Wade rubbed a palm back and forth, back and forth, atop his thigh. "Moody went back to Loretta's room. He'd nailed the back door shut weeks ago, so I climbed out the window. To run fer help. Next thing I know, Moody's yelling, 'run, rabbit, run!' I heard the shot before I felt it. Thought I was gonna die."

I leaned in so close I smelled his stench. "You know why you didn't die, Wade? You didn't die because you're going to help make things right."

"How? It'll take the Texas Rangers to take down Moody. He's a mean sonofabitch. Stronger than anyone I know."

"You think Moody's still at your house?" Frank said.

"If he ain't, Whitt'll kill him. Moody's job's to keep us pinned down, treat us like bootlickers. If Whitt don't kill Pa, I'm gonna. Soon as I find him. Pa's the one who put us in this perdicament in the first place."

"By sending Betty a blackmail note?"

"Had nothing to do with that," Wade stared down again. "Pa met Whitt years ago at a KKK meeting. Whitt called himself Buzz back then."

I remembered the wanted poster. Homer "Buzz" Whitfield.

"Then what was it?" Frank said. "What was Whitt holding over your old man?"

"He . . . he saw Pa kill someone." Wade's voice shook as much as his hands. "Then Whitt moved outta state. Came back about six, eight months ago. Threatened to rat out Pa unless he worked for him. Bashing stills, finding out where the competition was, had Pa set up a meeting between Whitt and the mayor to use our roads for transporting shine."

"When did this murder take place?" Doc asked.

"Seven . . . God." Then Wade, the crass, arrogant bully who never cared about anyone but himself, hid his face in his hands and sobbed.

Doc put a gentle hand on Wade's shoulder. "Go ahead, son. Get it out."

"Seven . . . seven years ago. He . . . he made me watch." Snot and tears ran down Wade's face. "I was only a kid. An eleven-year-old kid. I couldn't do nothing. Other men were there, helping Pa. Stringing that boy up on that tree . . ."

Toby. The boy whose smiling face greeted me each time I entered Rosie's kitchen and stared at his photograph. My gut wrenched. I tried to block the image, but the bile kept inching up my throat.

Wade wiped his sleeve across his face. "Whitt held my head so I couldn't look away." Silence lingered between his breaths, followed by wails of grief. "That boy screamed and cried . . . begged . . . and there wasn't a goddamn thing I could do but watch."

·······································

CHAPTER 51

FRANK

Doc telephoned the sheriff's office and let it ring long enough for Frank's patience to erode. He took off down the street to find the sheriff's door locked. No surprise. He thought of breaking in and finding a real gun, one that actually worked. Instead, he ran to Rosie's, the second place Sheriff Gibbons spent most of his time.

"Good God, Frank. Something on fire?" Miss Helen's voice.

A quick glance. Gunny wasn't there.

Loretta needed saving. If it wasn't already too late.

Nobody had saved his mother. After Irene was raped, she admitted to never being the same. Like the men who had come back from the war, something snapped inside of her. Like Wade having to live with what he'd seen. A deep cut that never healed.

Frank returned to Doc's office. It dawned on him then. While Wade told his story, not once had he thought of his dying mother just down the hall. Some son he was.

Emma June appeared by his side, worry written all over her face. "Did Scooter follow you out the door?"

"What? No."

"I can't find him."

"Scooter?" Doc said. "Last I saw him he was peeking in at Wade."

Emma June threw a hand to her chest. "While Wade talked about Loretta?"

Doc nodded, then whispered something to the panicked boy slumped on the table.

"Oh, God. Shit, shit, shit. This isn't good."

"Settle down, Emma June," Frank said. "He's probably at Rosie's with his folks. Lining up spoons or something. I ran in so fast, I didn't notice anything." He hated the worry on her face. Hated how much she'd been through already. "You go check. I have to get to Loretta."

"No. I need you to come with me. I don't want to face Miss Helen alone if Scooter's not there."

Frank turned back to Wade. "You stay put. When I get back, we're gonna help Loretta."

But all his ideas amounted to a bullet in his own head.

They searched Rosie's, including the kitchen and storage room. No Scooter.

"Emma June?" Miss Helen asked.

"We can't find Scooter," Emma June said, the words catching in her throat. Miss Helen's face turned slack. Leonard leaned back in his chair. In a burst, Frank told the Munsons about Scooter listening to Wade's story, how he talked about the events surrounding Whit and Moody, including Loretta's assault. Frank didn't mention Toby's murder. He and Emma June agreed beforehand that bringing that up wouldn't help the current situation.

Leonard's bum leg didn't hinder him from shooting out of his chair. "Gotta get something from home first," he muttered, heading for the front door.

Miss Helen bolted after him. "Not without me, you're not. And Emma June? You go back to Doc's place in case Scooter shows up."

If he ran, he might get to the Foleys' faster than Leonard in his truck. But once he got there, then what? He picked up his stride not caring he had left Wade behind. He'd only slow him down.

Jacoby. He could have helped. Then again, Frank didn't recall seeing either Miss Atta or Jacoby at the café. Better that way anyhow. Jacoby had no business being anywhere near the likes of Whitt and Foley.

Main Street behind him, Frank's legs burned as much as his lungs. He stopped on the side of the country road. Bent over, hands on his knees, he tried to catch his breath. He'd never signed up for this. Too late now. He just wanted the whole thing over.

He ran until he reached the Foleys' place, then stayed hidden, watching. No sign of Scooter or Loretta. Only Moody, who paced in front of the house, rubbing his hands through his hair like his scalp was on fire. The agitated muscleman stopped every few paces to peer down the drive that led to the country road. Either he was expecting someone or worried the wrong person would show up. Maybe one and the same.

Frank waited. When Moody tromped to the far side of the house, Frank edged forward. Moody came to a stop next to a black Model T, one Frank had never seen there before. Perhaps Whitt had finally paid him for his services. Or Whitt was also holding something over Moody's head and didn't have to pay him a dime.

When Moody peered under the motorcar's open hood, Frank hunched down and ran. He reached the back of the house and tried to calm the thunder in his chest.

He made it to the kitchen window and peeked in. Loretta sat in a chair, her hands tied behind her back. Scooter, crouching behind her, was sawing through the rope with his pocketknife while whispering in her ear.

Frank recognized the sound of Leonard's truck, its rumble getting louder as it neared the house.

He leaned toward the open window. "Scooter, Loretta, come on," he said, keeping his voice to a loud whisper. After he pulled Loretta out the window, she took off running across the back field. Scooter, still inside, froze in place when Moody burst in.

Frank ducked.

"Where is she, boy?" he screamed.

"That's my *daddy's* truck out there."

"Your daddy, huh?"

"Scoot?" Leonard shouted from out front. "You in there?"

Frank risked another peek through the window. Moody was pulling Scooter by his shirt collar toward the front door. Scooter's pocketknife remained on the floor beside the cut rope.

Frank edged his way along the side of the house until he reached the front corner.

Moody had his back to the house, one arm wrapped around Scooter's neck. His other hand held a pistol to Scooter's temple. Fifteen yards away, Leonard faced them, his eye staring down the muzzle of his rifle, his finger on the trigger.

"Let my boy go!" Leonard hollered, his mouth level with the rifle's stock.

Scooter looked up at Moody. "Uh-oh. My daddy is a *deadeye*," he said, his voice flat but audible.

Shit. Don't kill him, Leonard. A dead Moody couldn't tell them where he'd taken Emma June's mother.

"Let my boy go or I'll shoot you 'tween your eyes."

"Yeah?" Moody laughed. "What if I shoot him first?"

A split second. That's all it took. Moody's body didn't have a chance to bend. It launched backward and landed flat, a hole in the middle of his blank stare.

....

CHAPTER 52

EMMA JUNE

Doc Ferguson looked up from his desk. "Pacing's not going to help, Emma June. I'm sure Scooter will be back any time now."

But Doc didn't know Scooter like I did. I knew in my bones that after Scooter heard Wade's story, he had run off to check on Loretta. Frank knew it, too. Which meant they'd both entered the lion's den.

I couldn't leave on the off-chance Scooter returned to Doc's office. Which left me two choices, two doors to distract me from worrying.

I found Wade still sitting on the examining table, his head down.

"I hate your father. For what he did to Toby."

"No more'n me," he said without glancing up.

"But you had no problem throwing a soaked rag in a bottle through Miss Atta's window."

"Most times I did what I was told. Didn't throw that fire, though. Moody didn't trust my aim. And where's Frank? He shoulda found Scooter by now, and we need to get Loretta outta the house. Ma, too, if she'll come. These days, she ain't nothing but a turtle in a shell."

I didn't tell Wade that Frank had gone there without him. "You told us the truth, Wade? Everything you know?"

"If I knew more, I'd be tellin' you. I don't want nothing to do with them no more."

Foolish or not, I believed him. "Frank should be here any minute now."

I left him pacified and opened door number two. Years ago, Doc Ferguson's wife had spruced up the room for patients who needed to stay over. It looked more like a guest bedroom than a room in a doctor's office. Old photographs of the Brazos hung on light green wallpaper. A six-drawer dresser and a rocking chair sat next to the bed.

Betty lay under a pink and red-flowered coverlet. If she had to die, the room was a big step up from her place at The Diner or that shack she and Frank called home.

Her face sheet-white, Betty looked awful. Instead of her signature finger waves, her stringy hair pressed flat against the pillow.

"Betty?"

Her eyes blinked open into slits.

"Betty," she said, her smile as thin as her voice. "She had . . . she had the best friends."

"What did you tell Mama?"

She shook her head against the pillow. "Stupid. Selfish."

"I need to find her." My tears trickled.

"Yes. Find her," she muttered and closed her eyes again.

One thing was clear. She really did care for Mama.

I pulled the cosmetic kit from my purse. Oddly, my hands remained steady as I pressed the red color to her slack lips. Her eyes still closed, I added a touch of blush to her cheeks and saw Betty form an almost imperceptible smile.

"Emma June. Come quick," Miss Atta called out, surprising me. "You gotta see it to believe it."

I stood and turned away from Betty, the woman I once thought I knew well.

"Emma June," Betty wheezed out. "Your daddy . . ."

I waited for her cough to settle.

"Your daddy's a good man," she muttered.

An odd thing for her to say. I knew that already. Although Daddy never squeezed my hand exactly when I needed it, he was my shelter in the storm.

I left Betty then and went with Miss Atta out the office door.

"Now haven't I told you that at the bottom of patience lies heaven?" she said.

"Okay, but—"

"Rags was smoking out front and called me in so I could believe it with my own eyes. Sheriff pulled Earl Foley out of the Packard and walked him in. Handcuffs and all."

I doubted Gunny had already learned what Earl had done to Toby. But at least it explained his whereabouts when Frank went looking for him. "What did he bring him in for?"

"No telling. But we're about to find out. I need four eyes. It'll lessen the burn when I look at him."

On the way to the sheriff's office, I told Miss Atta the short version of what happened. She already knew about Wade being shot. Jacoby told her before she shooed him out of the café with a reminder she didn't need a babysitter. I told her about Wade's connection to gangsters, about Frank being Betty's son. And finally, about Scooter having run off again. I didn't tell her about Earl killing her son. Yet I had a hunch she already knew, had somehow felt it in her core.

With Earl Foley locked behind cell doors, Gunny sat with his gout foot perched on his desk and a puffed-toad grin on his face.

I decided not to mention Scooter or the events unfolding at the Foleys'. I had more faith in Frank and Leonard.

"Miss Atta. Emma June. Caught me a snake," Gunny said.

"You cain't keep me here, Sheriff," Earl said. "Cain't a person walk on someone's property jest to git to their door?"

Gunny folded his hands behind his neck and yawned. "You weren't aiming for the door, Earl. You were aiming for their still with an ax in your hand."

"Hmph. Feds would give me a job. Making moonshine's against the law."

"Made by two little old ladies for their personal use? And as you well know, destroying personal property is a higher crime in these parts."

"But you stopped me a'fore I could. So you gotta let me go."

"Probably. But it sure makes the day brighter looking at you through bars. I got you under lock and key. I can ask you questions, and you can't slam the door in my face."

I couldn't stomach the thought of Earl Foley spending only a couple of hours in a cell, then sauntering home with an arrogant smile. But I also couldn't tell the sheriff what I knew about Toby. Not with Miss Atta standing beside me.

"Oh, and guess what, Earl?" I said. "Betty didn't leave town. She's been here the whole time. And Frank's her son. He's not too happy about you blackmailing his mother."

Gunny looked at me and squinted at the news.

Before I could say more, Charlene burst through the door.

"Sheriff, Sheriff!" she said, then looked behind her. "It's okay, Loretta. Come in."

After a tentative step, Loretta stepped forward, her head bowed low. She wore a clean dress I recognized as Charlene's but other than that, dirt smeared down her tear-stained face, her freckles more prominent on her pale skin. She looked broken.

"Loretta?" Earl called from his cell. "What in the hell are you doin' here? Git on back home."

Loretta looked up for the first time. "Pa?"

"Ignore him, Loretta," Charlene said. "We have to tell the sheriff."

"Loretta. I said git! You mind me now."

Gunny stood and faced the cell. "Shut up, Earl. This is my jail. My rules," he said, worthy of the title Sheriff. He turned his back to Earl and approached Loretta. "Honey, wanna tell me what's going on?" he said, his voice low.

She shook her head. "No," she whispered.

"It's okay, Loretta," I told her, reaching for her hand. "I already know about Moody." I turned to Gunny. "We were looking for you earlier. Scooter's missing, and Frank ran off looking for him. And Moody shot Wade."

"What the hell?" Earl squawked.

Charlene stepped forward. "But Sheriff—"

"I heard the shot," Loretta mumbled through her tears.

Miss Atta enveloped Loretta and whispered in her ear.

"It's okay," I said. "Wade's fine now. He made it to Doc Ferguson's."

Charlene pounded her fist on Gunny's desk. "Sheriff, listen! Scooter's in real trouble. Moody had Loretta tied up to a chair. Somehow Scooter got inside without being seen and cut through her ropes. Then Frank helped Loretta escape out the window. But Scooter—"

Loretta inched away from Miss Atta's hug. "I ran till I thought I was safe then stopped to see if Scooter and Frank were behind me but they weren't and I think . . . I think—"

Fear gushed through my veins.

"Loretta, don't you say another word," Earl boomed. "You keep your mouth shut like you been told."

Loretta inched backward to the door. I thought she'd run. Instead, she stood there, frozen in place.

"Good God." Gunny grabbed his Stetson and opened the door.

Earl pounded the cell bars. "Loretta, do as I say. Get home."

Miss Atta jerked her head toward the cell and pointed an angry finger. "You shut your evil mouth, Earl Foley. God's sick to death of listening to you."

....

CHAPTER 53

FRANK

Rattling over the dry dirt road back toward town, Frank didn't mind one bit sharing the back of Leonard's truck with a dead Moody. He could kick the scum with his boot if he wanted. It seemed fitting. Scooter, on the other hand, curled away from the sheet-wrapped body and held tight to the cargo guards. "We gotta *bury* him, *gotta* bury him. And *not* unbury him."

Miss Helen sat in the front cab between Leonard and Mrs. Foley. She turned and aimed her words out the back. "Not everything needs to be buried, Scoot, baby. The turkey vultures have to eat, too, you know."

If anyone was a good candidate for buzzard bait, it was Moody.

Frank nudged Scooter. "You're a real hero, you know that, Scooter? The way you cut through the rope and rescued Loretta."

While Frank and Leonard had loaded Moody in the truck, Scooter had retrieved his prized possession. Scooter pulled the knife from his pocket. "It does *more* than whittle."

"Sure does. And buddy, you sure were brave when Moody grabbed you."

"He stunk like *cabbage*."

"Yeah. And he's about to smell worse," Frank mumbled.

"I *told* him. He *didn't* listen. Daddy's a *crack* shot."

"Guess he was as stupid as he was mean."

Scooter's face dropped. "Loretta's *gone*."

"We'll find her, buddy. You set her free and she ran to be safe. Lots of good folks in Holly Gap." It was true. Frank thought of the Munsons, the folks at Rosie's. And the Crawfords, his family, even if they didn't know it yet.

Frank perked up when he heard Miss Helen talking to Mrs. Foley.

"Mildred, you hear me? You're jumpy as a toad in a thunderstorm. I said your boy is fine. And Moody's dead. You don't have to hide away anymore. You got free rein of your own horse now."

Frank hitched himself up for a better view inside the cab.

Mrs. Foley stared out the window and held the truck's door handle like she wanted to jump out. "Earl," she said and added nothing more.

"Well," Miss Helen said, then paused. "You know what Will Rogers said. 'Even if you're on the right track, you'll get run over if you just sit there.' You gotta pick yourself up."

Leonard's truck bumped its way to a stop in front of the sheriff's office. Frank hopped out the back and hot-footed toward the entrance, almost colliding with Sheriff Gibbons on his way out.

"Frank, good God. I was on my way—"

"No need, Sheriff. We've got Moody in the back."

Gunny pulled his pistol.

"No need for that, either. Moody's dead."

Scooter pulled on the sheriff's sleeve. "*Loretta.* Loretta needs *help*."

"She's inside, Scoot," Gunny said. "She's okay."

Relief coursed through Frank's veins. At least he had helped one person escape danger.

After Scooter bolted inside, only Frank and Miss Helen followed the sheriff into the office. Leonard stood guard next to the body. Mrs. Foley stayed curled inside the cab.

Inside, Emma June and Charlene rushed toward Frank, hugging him from both sides.

Scooter kept his arms around Loretta, squeezing her and bouncing her up and down. "You're *safe* now," he told her. "Moody is *dead*."

"What's that you say?"

Frank turned toward the voice in the cell and smiled. Earl Foley. Sheriff Gunny Gibbons had done something right.

Miss Helen poked the sheriff's arm. "Well, Gunny, just when I thought you couldn't bite a biscuit, you're next in line for a ticker-tape parade." She sauntered toward Earl's cell. "As for you, looks to me like I can bring you that shit pie after all."

"Ain't staying that long."

"No? Then you're as sharp as a mashed potato. I'll swallow those keys whole if it keeps you locked up."

After a few broad steps, Miss Helen stared down at the sheriff, who had already plunked himself in his chair. "Don't you dare let him out, Gunny. You do, and I'll see to it the next time you look for your badge it'll be pinned to your butt."

Frank stopped listening when Emma June tugged his arm. "Dead? Moody's dead?"

Frank told her how Leonard shot Moody between the eyes.

Miss Atta placed a palm to Loretta's face. "Honey, you, Scooter, and Charlene follow me back to Rosie's. Let's get y'all something cold to drink. You coming, Helen?"

"I'm coming. Long as you have something stronger than soda pop. Leonard's waiting on the coroner but, Loretta, we gotta peel your mama out of the truck. This heat's going to give Moody a quick lift to hell, and we don't want her breathing in his stink. She's done it too long as it is."

After they left, Emma June looked up at him, her eyes pleading. "But what about Mama? Did Leonard ask Moody about Mama?"

"I'm sorry, Emma June. Moody's time run out."

Emma June stormed to Earl's cell. "You bastard. This is all your fault. Your sidekick, Moody, kidnapped my mother. Where'd he take her?" she screamed, her voice bouncing off the wall.

"I'd tell you to ask him yerself, but . . ." Earl shrugged. "So let me outta this can. I done had enough of this shit."

Frank wanted to kill him. "Yeah, let him out, Sheriff. He won't make it far."

Gunny leaned back in his chair, his arms crossed over his belly, his eyes stern. "Oh, he ain't going anywhere. I aim to learn plenty without lifting a muscle."

Emma June white-knuckle gripped the bars. "Where's your good pal, Whitt? Hmm? Or should we call him Buzz?"

Earl looked up. A moment of fear passed over his face. He spat on the floor.

"That's right," Frank said. "Where's Buzz?" Frank wanted him riled up. Since Wade was too scared to cross his father, he hoped Earl would slip and say something to incriminate himself.

"Don't know who yer talking 'bout."

"No?" Emma June yelled. "Don't remember him from your old Klan meetings? Or maybe he didn't have that scar seven years ago."

"Sheriff! Open this goddamn door. You got no cause to keep me in this stink hole."

"Except one."

Frank turned to the voice.

Wade Foley stood in the doorway. Face flushed, eyes ablaze with anger, he stared at his father. "Time's up, you sonofabitch."

CHAPTER 54

....

EMMA JUNE

I t wasn't easy for Wade to get through his story.

He had just started sharing his horrible memory of Toby's death when Earl started yelling obscenities and denials. Gunny unlocked the cell door long enough for Frank to punch Earl in the face and gag him. Frank slammed the cell door shut with a shit-eating grin of satisfaction.

As Wade talked, he changed before my eyes. He wept. He apologized for not trying to stop the lynching. He apologized for being Earl's son. All his bravado was replaced by a sincerity I never thought possible.

Wade wasn't the only one I didn't recognize. The further along he got in the telling, the more the steam rose off Gunny. Frank had to hold him back and talk him down from pulling his gun. Had there not been bars between them, Gunny would have killed Earl on the spot. Wade, on the other hand, wouldn't have minded. He glared at his father with hate-filled eyes.

Wade's story over, Frank reached through the bars and removed Earl's gag.

"Boy," Earl yelled, "you tell that mouse of a mother'a yours she raised a yellow-bellied, good-fer-nothin' Nancy."

"Shut up, Pa. You're a sorry excuse of a man. Nobody in town thinks no different."

Gunny sat with his elbows on his knees and took a couple of deep breaths. "You, all three of you, head on now. Earl and me need to have a one-on-one. I don't want any interruptions."

Just before Frank closed the jailhouse door behind us, Gunny's voice rang clear. "I could string you up right now and it wouldn't bother me one iota. But if you wanna save your own neck, start talking."

I glanced up and down Main Street with no idea where to go. But I knew one thing. I needed quiet. A place without angry voices. A place without tears. Somewhere I could think and piece together everything that had happened.

"Wade, Emma June?" Frank said. "Let's sit for a minute." He pointed to the bench in front of Hank's Market, two storefronts down.

I wanted to sit beside the Brazos, take my shoes off and plunge my feet into the cooling water.

"Cain't," Wade said. "I need to—"

"Just for a bit."

Another bench, five total in the last four months, all made possible from Whitt's contribution to the town, the trade for his safe passage. Wherever he was, he was going to need it.

I settled my restlessness on the wooden slats. Frank and Wade remained standing.

"You did a good thing back there, Wade," Frank said and offered us both a cigarette.

"Yeah. First good thing. Probably ever." Wade grimaced as he lifted his injured arm to strike a match.

"How's it feel?" I asked.

"Not bad, considering. Coulda been a bull's-eye."

"Nope," Frank said. "Moody took that one. Never seen anything like it. Leonard didn't even blink when he took the shot. Like it never occurred to him he could miss and hit Scooter instead."

I had never seen Leonard fire his weapon. In fact, I'd thought he'd either sold his rifle or given it away.

I asked Wade if he'd spoken to Loretta.

"Yeah. Talked to her at Rosie's long enough to know Pa was in jail. Done told me how you helped her though," he said, nodding at Frank. "Appreciate that. Now, I gotta head back over there. Apologize for not protecting her better." Wade shifted from one foot to the other. "Then . . . then I gotta talk to Miss Atta."

"You had nothing to do with Toby's death," Frank said. "Nothing you could have done to stop it."

"Maybe. But the scene plays over and over again in my head like a bad picture show. Reckon it always will."

Although ninety-something degrees outside, my skin chilled imagining that horror.

"Best get to it." Wade headed down to Rosie's Café without looking back.

Frank sat beside me, crossing then uncrossing his leg. "Took a lot of guts. Him being that honest."

"We still don't know where Whitt is. Wade needs to watch himself."

"No. Whitt does. Earl's gonna sing like a canary."

"And Moody can't tell us where Mama is. One shot from a rifle, and we've lost the chance for answers."

"You could look at it another way. Like poker."

"Huh?"

"You're always behind before you hit the big hand. Then you win."

"That's a terrible analogy."

Frank shrugged. "Just trying to lighten the air, Emma June."

"Well, it's not working." The lump grew in my throat. My eyes blurred. "I just wish I knew what happened. What did they do to her, Frank? Mama wasn't deserving of any of this."

"I'm sorry, Emma June."

Although the arm around me wasn't Samuel's, Frank's seemed natural, comfortable even.

Frank poked my shoulder. "Look who's coming."

Daddy. His footsteps walking toward me, fast and determined.

I ran into his arms. "Oh, Daddy."

"I heard, honey. I stopped by Rosie's looking for you. I got the gist of what's happened."

"Did you see Wade?"

"I passed him on my way out. Saw his bandaged arm."

"Then you don't know everything. Wade was on his way to see Miss Atta. To tell her. Earl did it, Daddy. Earl killed Toby."

Daddy released his hug, his anger needing space. "You telling me Wade knew all along?"

"He couldn't tell anyone. Earl would have killed him. You think we should go to Rosie's? Be there for Miss Atta?"

Daddy shook his head. "Let's give Wade and her some time. It's going to hurt, but at least she'll know the truth. Wade's doing the honorable thing."

"Is that always the case?" Frank spoke up.

I had forgotten Frank was still behind me on the bench.

"What's that, Frank?" Daddy said.

"Doing the honorable thing even if you know it might make things . . . hard?"

Daddy rubbed the stubble on his face. "That's a tough call, son. Depends on the circumstances, I suppose."

Betty. I felt sure Frank felt torn about not taking care of her, not being by her side. Instead, he'd been busy rescuing Loretta and Scooter.

"Daddy, we had to take Betty to Doc Ferguson's this morning. She'll be staying there . . ." I let the words drift away.

"It's okay, Emma June," Frank said. "You can say it. She'll be staying there till she dies."

Frank's look of sorrow felt all too familiar. I had no words to offer.

Daddy sat on the bench next to him. "I'm sorry, Frank. Anything I can do for you?"

"I guess Ma did the best she could. You know, handing me off to my aunt when I was young. I guess none of us can help who we are. Who our parents are."

"That's right, son. We play the hands best we can."

"I'm not mad at her," Frank said. "Just disappointed we didn't have more time together."

My silent tears spilling over, I worried that my time with Mama had ended on carnival night. That I would never again see her smiling face, the reassurance behind her wink, the feeling of comfort in the squeeze of her hand.

Only then did I think of Frank. The memories he had of his mother were bits and pieces scattered over time. Which of those could he hold on to?

"Frank," Daddy said, "you can take that time now. Go be with her. Talk to her even if you don't think she can hear you. I think it might help both of you."

Frank nodded and slowly turned to Daddy. "I, um . . . Mr. Crawford?" He pulled his shirt collar away from his neck. "Would you like to meet my mother? Before she's gone?"

....

CHAPTER 55

FRANK

Frank wiped sweaty palms on his trousers. Emma June and her father—*his* father—were mere steps behind him as they approached the doctor's office. He felt the sagging in his shoulders, then did what Aunt Patsy had taught him. He straightened up and lifted his head high as he walked.

In moments, they would know the truth. And when they discovered he was a son and a brother, he'd either be thrown out of town on his ear or accepted for who he was. He wondered if there was anything in-between.

"Frank? Frank?" He felt the tug on his arm.

"Did you hear me?" Emma June asked.

"Sorry. What?"

"I said I'll take turns with you. You know, keeping Betty company. Remember, you need to collect your things and take them to the Munsons'. They're expecting you to stay with them."

Right. Miss Helen offered their house to him. If, that is, the Crawfords could stomach being a stone's throw away from the bastard son.

"Thanks." All he could say. The moment of truth just steps away, his nerves took a tighter hold. Nothing he could do now but suffer the consequences of his lies.

He finally understood how hard it was for Irene to come clean with Bernice. The fear of knowing they might never speak again. A relationship severed. Well, at least he'd met them, his sister and father. But had it been worth the pain he caused?

Nurse Louise greeted them at the front reception area. "She's resting, of course. Mumbles at times. But go on in."

He'd put Theo in a tough spot. Was it right for Emma June to be in the room when Theo saw his mother? But his father had the choice. He could either deny knowing Irene or come clean. That is, if he even recognized her after twenty-one years and shriveling from cancer.

Frank went in first and stood on the far side of the bed. Irene lay on her back, a floral bedspread covering her. He touched her hand and her eyes fluttered open enough to show the whites of her eyes.

"Ma, you have some visitors." Frank shifted his gaze to his father. His gut pleaded for the man not to storm out of the room at the moment of truth. "Mr. Crawford, this is my mother."

Theo stepped forward wearing a solemn smile, the kind reserved for family members at a funeral. He looked down at Irene, his face twisting with uncertainty. He turned to Emma June.

"Daddy? What is it?"

"She looks so much like, well, someone I knew a long time ago."

Irene stirred. "Th . . . Theo?"

"Irene?"

Frank's heart beat hard enough to shorten his breath. He had never corrected anyone when they called her Betty. But he, too, had a choice. He could still claim he didn't know Theo was his father, that Irene never told him.

"I'm . . . sorry, Theo," Irene whispered through her cough.

"Daddy? Betty? What's going on?"

Theo took hold of Emma June's hand. "Honey, your mother was right." Tears filled Theo's eyes. "I know her. I met her before I met your mother. But I knew her as Irene."

"What? Daddy?"

Frank felt Emma June's confusion, the questions bubbling under her skin.

"She changed her name, Emma June," Frank said. "When she came back to town."

"Wh . . . Why?"

Theo took Irene's hand. "Irene?" His voice cracked. "Can you hear me? Do you feel up to talking?"

"If . . . I," she whispered. Her eyes closed. "No, no. Not that dress, Bernice," she mumbled, her head moving side to side.

"It's the laudanum." Nurse Louise stood in the doorway. "She's been muttering nonsense for the last hour. Earlier, she told me, or someone, not to get stuck in the revolving door. And something about Emma June finding Choppers's leg."

"Be good to him." His mother grimaced and squeezed her fists. "Didn't do . . . right by him."

Frank may have felt like a three-legged dog, but he knew his mother wasn't talking about Choppers.

Emma June pulled a tissue from her purse and dabbed her eyes. "Choppers is fine, Betty. Irene."

"No . . . no . . ." she coughed out.

Nurse Louise positioned her upright until her cough settled.

"Such a . . . fine . . . a good father."

Theo turned to Frank, back to Irene, then Frank again. Awareness struck Theo's face.

"Can I have a moment with her?" Theo said. "If you don't mind, Frank? And, honey," he turned to Emma June, "I'll explain later."

His mother's glazed eyes turned to Theo. "You protected . . ."

Frank took a gentle hold of Emma June's arm. "Let's go have a smoke."

He hated the confusion on Emma June's face, her look of sorrow.

Outside, he lit two cigarettes. One he handed to his sister.

She slumped on the bench. "I'm so tired of these secrets," she whispered, almost as if to herself.

He could provide her with the clarity she needed, the truth she deserved. All he had to do was find the right words. For Christ's sake, he was twenty-one years old. A man. He could do this.

"Daddy didn't lie to Mama," she said. "He never met Betty Bedford. He met an Irene. But why didn't your mother tell us she knew Daddy? Why did she work so hard to avoid him? Why did she change her name?" Her voice calm, Emma June seemed resigned to the fact that her questions would never be answered, the secrets never revealed.

"She was afraid, at first. She wasn't sure if she was doing the right thing. Emma June?" Frank swallowed. "Emma June, Betty told you her husband died, right?"

"Yes. But you said your father left when you were one. So Betty lied. Unless you did."

"I told you the truth as I knew it. Pete Sanders left. But when Ma pulled me to Holly Gap, I found out she lied to me, too."

"About?"

He inhaled and blew out slowly. "I've always thought it was Ma's place to tell you, not me. But she can't."

Emma June turned to him. "Go ahead," she said, her voice cracking.

"Your father met Irene here in Holly Gap twenty-one years ago at a dance when she came to visit her cousins."

Relieved at the release, he kept the flow going. He told Emma June about the confrontation with Earl, about them forming a two-week relationship. About returning to New Orleans to marry Pete Sanders, the man who left her because of the big lie.

"The big lie?"

Frank held his breath, then forced the air back into his lungs. "Me."

She stayed quiet as he continued, her head staring down at her clenched hands.

"What?" she whispered.

He swallowed. He just wanted it over, even if it meant losing both Emma June and his father forever.

"Your father. He's also mine."

....

CHAPTER 56

EMMA JUNE

"Emma June, wait!"

But I didn't. I ran on pure instinct, my arms pumping.

Daddy had another life before he met Mama and a son he never knew about. And I had a brother. One who lied to me.

I landed hard on the ground. Leaves and twigs scratched my hands and face. I wiped the grit from my eyes, hoisted myself up, and propelled my legs faster, away from the truth, until I reached my house.

Nothing made sense. I pictured the fortune teller standing next to me, pointing and laughing. I spat the foulness from my mouth. How had I skipped across the bridge of an easy childhood and expected a predictable, safe landing on the other side? It had been foolish of me to think the taut ropes would hold.

"Emma June?"

Frank caught up to me, his breath heaving like my own.

I glared up at him. "Everything I've known has been a lie. Don't you get that?"

"As a matter of fact," he said, his voice soft, "I do."

The tears on his face matched my own.

....

For three weeks, since the news, Daddy's apologies fell hard and frequent until I finally told him to save them for when Mama came home. As he continued to ponder his moral aptitude, I realized Daddy was like the rest of us, imperfect.

The humid midsummer night made my clothes cling to me like a wet second skin. I sat on the front porch and drew the smoke deep into my lungs. I inhaled and exhaled freely, not caring that Daddy was only a few feet away inside the house, the windows open. He knew better than to comment on my habits.

The cicadas chirped so loud, the hard-of-hearing would have cringed. I stared into the noisy dark of night. Ironic, though, how I could finally see through the darkness. The lights had turned on, all my questions answered. Except one. Where was she?

Poor Mama had had her feet knocked out from under her.

Frank ended up telling Daddy and me the whole story, all the pieces Betty confessed to him over time.

Although twenty-one years had passed, it was Earl Foley who had recognized Betty as Irene. He saw through to the once-young girl with ringlet hair and knew she was Irene, the girl who had taken Daddy's arm instead of his. With this discovery, Earl pounced on the opportunity and blackmailed Betty to keep her big secret.

On carnival night, Betty spewed out the worst part first. She had a son and Daddy was the father. That was not the kind of news Mama could let roll off her back. No wonder she had stormed off that night to confront Betty.

Before Betty told Mama her real name, she spotted Earl and ran. Which meant that Mama, wherever she was, still lived with a painful half-truth. She believed Daddy had lied to her. But Daddy hadn't lied. He knew Irene, not Betty.

I stared down at the smokes beside me. Chesterfields. Frank had given me Betty's pack. Or rather, my *brother* had given me Irene's pack.

It wasn't just me who had been cut to the bone with the truth. Until recently, Frank had lived a lie. All his twenty-one years he had thought Pete Sanders, the man who deserted him, was his father.

Samuel, who returned six days before, reminded me of something on a daily basis. Although mistakes were made, neither Betty, Frank, nor Daddy had set out to purposely hurt anyone. That reality gave air to the wound. I was starting to heal.

Daddy wanted to add on a room to our house. But Frank, who remained next door rooming with an all-too-happy Scooter, said he hadn't decided what to do or where he would land after his mother passed. I wouldn't say it out loud, but I didn't want him to leave. I'd become used to having him around.

Frank spent most of his days at Betty's side. When possible, Daddy and I also kept vigil beside her, carrying on conversations we doubted she could hear. And Scooter, when not visiting Loretta, stood over Betty blowing notes from his harmonica that each day sounded more and more like a song.

The headlights blinding, I stood at the familiar sound. Gunny's Packard.

Once inside, he settled on the sofa and leaned forward. "Guess being transferred to a Mineral Wells jail got Earl thinking a little more seriously. He finally got to talking. Told us what happened that night."

Daddy and I sat motionless while Gunny told us the news.

On carnival night, Moody went to The Diner and nabbed Mama thinking she was Betty. He drove her back to the Foleys' place where Whitfield had waited. Whitfield, furious after opening the trunk to find the wrong woman inside, slapped Moody into kingdom come. He complained about having to drive an hour north to drop her off until he decided what to do with her.

"I didn't wanna get your hopes up," Gunny said. "But for the past week, the Feds and the Texas Rangers have been hunting down leads, scouring their map grid. But today, I got a call. The Feds learned Whitfield had stopped for gas and asked the attendant if the bridge at Bear Hollow had been fixed. The poor ole fella they questioned said he remembered that night clearly, saying Whitt scared the tar out of him just by his looks and rough manner. Anyhow, they've narrowed down the search area."

I remembered Miss Atta telling me, "When spider webs unite, they can tie up a lion." We were waiting for that last thread, for Homer Buzz Whitfield to be caught and Mama found.

Hope had been invisible for so long, I dared to reach for it again. But I did. I gripped it with tentative fingers, afraid it would blow away like dandelion tufts.

Two days after my birthday, Frank was supposed to escort me to the University of Texas to meet with counselors and view the campus.

"I can't go to Austin now," I told Daddy.

"Yes, you can, Emma June," he said. "Your mama always wanted you to go to college. The least you can do is visit, see if it appeals to you. Your appointment is set and the train tickets bought. Besides, you'll only be gone for two nights. And it's your birthday present."

Gunny shuffled his feet and cleared his throat. I'd forgotten he was there.

"Just wanted to give you the update, folks. I'll let you know when I learn more."

After he left, I stayed put on the sofa, seething.

"Emma June?"

"I told you, Daddy. I don't feel like celebrating my birthday."

"Eighteen is an important birthday."

"I used to think so." I remembered thinking how turning eighteen would be the happiest day of my life.

"Honey, it will be good for you to think of something else for a while. And good for you and Frank to spend time together."

"We're together plenty. How can I possibly go to Austin when all I'd be thinking about is Mama?"

"You'll do the best you can. Besides . . ."

Headlights shone through the curtains. Daddy turned to the window and stared out.

"Gunny's back?"

"Roadrunner. Scooter's getting out."

Nine-fifteen. Scooter was usually in bed.

"Mr. Theo. Emma *June.* You gotta come." Scooter stood at the door, panting. He pointed to the roadster. "Mama and Frank are *waiting.*"

"It's Betty-Irene," Miss Helen hollered out the motorcar window. "Hurry up and get in."

"I shouldn't have left her," Frank said from the front seat.

"You had to eat, Frank." Miss Helen didn't turn to look at him when she spoke. She leaned forward, her chin near the top of the steering wheel as she peered through the windshield into the passing darkness.

Daddy leaned forward from the back seat and squeezed Frank's shoulder. "Can't beat yourself up about it, son. You stayed with her most of the day."

"I should have known," Frank muttered.

I thought about the pine casket Leonard had already made for Betty. How it would soon be filled with her lifeless body. I was used to seeing Scooter bury his inanimate objects and accustomed to small mounds of dirt piled up to cover miniature graves. I wasn't prepared to see a hole dug six feet down and eight feet long. Especially knowing it would be filled with someone I knew. The thought of who could be next terrified me.

When we arrived at Doc's office, Samuel met me at the door and pulled me in for a hug, then gave Frank a quick pat on the shoulder. After Doc Ferguson led us into Betty's room, Frank, Daddy, Scooter, and I gathered around her bed.

Her breaths were slow, uneven. Each shallow inhale sounded like clicking marbles.

"It's called the death rattle," Doc said as if reading my mind. "That's why I called."

Frank squeezed his mother's hand. "It's okay, Ma," he said, his eyes glistening. "You put up a good fight."

Daddy patted her other hand. "And I'll take care of him, Irene. Just like I said."

Of all the fun Mama, Betty, and I had together during the good times, I couldn't think of one thing to say.

Scooter sang the chorus.

> *Swing low, sweet chariot*
> *coming for to carry me home.*
> *Swing low, sweet chariot . . .*

And when he inhaled a deep breath to finish, Betty Irene Sanders let out her last.

....

CHAPTER 57

FRANK

Frank stared down at his mother's body and wondered where she had gone. Unlike his true father, Frank wasn't raised to be a godly man. But he liked to think Irene was in a nice place. A place with dancing. A place where she wouldn't be judged.

He felt the hand on his shoulder and turned to find Theo's somber eyes staring into his own.

"You okay, son?" he said.

Frank wasn't sure. He nodded anyway and sleeve-dried the tears on his face.

For three weeks his mother had hung on in Doc's guest room. Not once, since they brought her in, had she stepped foot outside again. No fresh air. No red birds to hear calling her name—I-*rene*, I-*rene*, I-*rene*, I-*rene*.

Emma June and Scooter stood entwined on the other side of the bed, heads low, quiet tears on their faces. They had good memories of his mother. Somehow, the thought made things a little better. And a little worse.

"You're not alone, Frank. I want you to know that."

"Thanks, Mr. Crawford." Although Theo said it was fine to call him Dad, it didn't feel right. Maybe someday.

"When would you like to have the funeral?" Theo asked, his words soft.

Frank dreaded the funeral—what he would say, how he would handle it. And unlike Aunt Patsy's funeral, where half the town's musicians showed up, Irene would be lucky to get a handful of people. Holly Gap had never truly accepted the citified woman who called herself Betty. And half the town still blamed her for escorting Bernice Crawford to the wild side of life.

"Frank," Theo continued, "there's no time to schedule the funeral for tomorrow. And the day after that is Emma June's birthday. So maybe the next—"

"No," Emma June said. "Frank, the day after tomorrow is fine. I already told Daddy I'm not in the mood for celebrating anyway."

Theo puffed out a deep breath.

Emma June nodded to Frank. "Really. It's fine. Please." She grabbed Scooter's hand, gently peeling him away from the hold he had on Betty's arm. "Let's go tell your mama."

Frank looked at Theo. "Day after tomorrow, then." The sooner it was over, the better. "But only if you promise we will celebrate Emma June's birthday right after the funeral. Ma would want that."

"Not sure Emma June will."

"Let's do it anyway. Turning eighteen deserves a celebration."

"About the funeral then," Theo said. "Any thoughts on—"

"I've never planned a funeral before. And Ma, she wasn't the religious sort."

"Mind if I ask the pastor of my church? Reverend Thompson is a good man."

"That's fine." Again, Frank stared down at his lifeless mother.

"Mind if we step out of the room for a moment?" Theo said.

He followed his father into the empty examining room.

"Son, I can't fix the past. But I can make changes for our future.

I'm your father, and I plan to act like one. But you have to tell me how you see things. I'll respect your wishes either way."

He could go back to New Orleans where the streets bustled with more activity than gossip. Where the evenings were kept alive with music. And back to a job at a shipyard sweating his ass off for pennies.

"I never expected to live in a small town."

Theo gave a slow nod, disappointment etched on his face. "I understand Austin has a couple of jazz venues. Maybe you could take a few courses at the university. See how life unfolds."

"And so I can watch over Emma June?" Not that he minded. Family was family.

"Selfish thinking on my part. Not selfish thinking of you. You're talented, smart. You might really enjoy it."

He'd never considered college. Never thought it was a possibility.

"I gotta tell you," Theo continued. "We heard some news today. Now, Emma June's hesitant about going on that school visit."

Theo told him about the trail leading to Whitfield.

"I don't blame her," Frank said.

"I don't either. But it's an opportunity she shouldn't pass up."

"She's never given up hope that her mother will come home." *A positive pearl*—the words Emma June once used to describe him.

"I know." Theo stared down at his boots. "Wish I had as much faith as she does."

They both turned at the sound of throat-clearing. Emma June stood in the doorway.

"Frank," she said, her eyes glistening, "I'm so sorry about your mother." She stepped forward and hugged him.

Although his mother hadn't made it, Frank stood in an office where Doc Ferguson patched up most patients. With all the family he had left beside him, it felt like a healing place.

Back in the roadster, Scooter told Theo to sit up front. He wanted to sit in the back with Frank and Emma June.

Scooter nestled against him and grabbed his hand. He stayed silent, no words to emphasize, but his fingers, interwoven with Frank's, spoke just fine. Scooter's squeeze to Frank's palm didn't stop until the motorcar parked and the engine shut off.

CHAPTER 58

....

EMMA JUNE

Leonard's handmade casket held its dweller, its one and only occupant for eternity.

Frank, Daddy, Leonard, and of all people Wade Foley had carried and then lowered Betty into her final resting place. I believed Wade's volunteering to be a pallbearer was his way of making some kind of amends for his father's sins.

Although the hole was only six feet deep, it seemed like an abyss. The more I stared, the more the casket seemed to sink deeper and farther away.

Frank, who had worried no one would show up, stood at the head of the casket, a look of astonishment on his face. On one side of the hole stood Charlene, Loretta, Berta, Tallulah, and Samuel. On the other, Miss Atta, Rags, Jacoby, Miss Mabel, Doc Ferguson and his wife, and Louis and Isabell. Off to the side Stinger Jones lingered with Whiskey, and, strangely enough, Percy Yates. Mayor Gibbons remained in the background scanning the terrain, his eyes peeled. Surprisingly, I saw no sign of Sheriff Gibbons.

Reverend Thompson cleared his throat and ran a hand through his gray beard. "We have gathered here to release Irene Sanders—"

"Betty *Bedford*," Scooter cried out. "Her *name* is Betty *Bedford*."

The reverend stopped talking and squinted his confusion.

"Go ahead on, Reverend," Miss Helen said. "We're all ears."

"We have gathered here to release this woman into God's hands. Although she was taken at a young age . . ."

Frank's head hung low, his hands buried deep in his trouser pockets.

"The Lord is my Shepherd . . ."

Six feet separated the living from the dead. Above, the people still breathed, worked, told stories. Most of them hid some kind of secret.

"He leadeth me beside the still waters . . ."

Mama was still out there. I felt it like a calm day on the Brazos, like Daddy's arm now pressed around my shoulder.

"Thy rod and thy staff they comfort me . . ."

The squeeze of Mama's hand, always saying the right things when I needed to hear them.

"Emma June," Daddy whispered. "The Reverend's talking to you."

I looked up and found Reverend Thompson's patient eyes.

"I understand you'd like to say a few words?"

I fumbled with the notes in my pocket but decided I didn't need them.

I cleared my throat. "Betty was Mama's best friend. Even though we only knew her for six months, Mama took an instant liking to her. So did I. She filled us with new ways of thinking."

I glanced at Daddy. Ever since he had been reunited with Irene, his old-fashioned ways were dwindling, moving a bit closer to the modern age.

"Betty traveled to grand places and experienced more life and adventure than all of us put together. She reminded me that loosening our corsets and having fun was not a bad thing. In fact it was—is—a necessary thing."

Daddy grinned and shook his head.

"She taught me about cosmetics and dancing and 'for Pete's sake' to kick my legs higher when I danced the Charleston."

"Amen," said Berta, making me smile.

"Like Mama, she taught me to reach out for my dreams and try new things. I know Betty, Irene Sanders, had a life before I met her. One filled with hard choices, some right, some wrong. None of us are perfect. I know she struggled to make a life for herself. I think she did the best she could. I'm just sorry Mama didn't get to tell her goodbye." *I'll tell her for you, Betty, when I see her.*

My eulogy over, Daddy patted my shoulder. Frank nodded a thin smile in my direction. "My turn," Scooter said, a bit too loud for the occasion.

"Sure, Scoot. Go ahead," Frank said.

Scooter approached the casket. He stared down. "*Grow*, Betty! Grow to the sky and see God. Play him a tune." He reached in his pocket and tossed his harmonica on top of the casket.

Shocked, I caught Miss Helen's eye. "He has another," she mouthed out.

"And don't forget," he continued, "tell God *Scooter* says to show Miss Bernice the way *home*."

Like me, Scooter believed in Mama's return.

The sheriff's Packard crept up the dirt road. He parked but didn't get out. Instead, he motioned Daddy over, I assumed to make his apologies while blaming his gout for the delay.

Frank cleared his throat. "Ma left this earth finally knowing what it was like to have a best friend. Bernice Crawford made her smile again. In Theo Crawford, she learned what protection felt like. In Emma June, she was rekindled with her youthful spirit. I will no longer judge the woman who didn't raise me. She did what she thought was right. Ma knew she was dying so she led me back here to unite me with the family I didn't know I had." Frank pulled the harmonica from his jacket pocket and put it to his lips.

The notes from "Amazing Grace" wove through the air and into our hearts. I knew the mourners' sniffles and moistened eyes were not for Betty. They were for Frank, who had wooed the town with the same charisma as his father. Our father.

The service over, I caught Frank's eye and pointed to the sheriff's Packard driving away. I shook my head, disgusted he didn't have the decency to stay.

....

CHAPTER 59

FRANK

Frank appreciated the kindness, but he wanted to break away from the well-wishers. Find out why the sheriff had left, and why Theo's posture had turned stiff, his expression somber.

"Frankie?"

He shifted his gaze to Charlene.

"Such a beautiful send-off for Betty. Irene, I mean. You doing okay?"

He could almost see the reflection of his smile in Charlene's big blue eyes. "I'm fine, doll." She was a real pip, this girl wrapped in his arms. Chatty, yes, but something about her positive attitude and her desire for fun kept him coming back for more. At least for the time being.

He broke his hold on Charlene when Wade and Loretta strolled to his side. Both paid their respects.

"Say, Frank?" Wade said. "Hope you don't mind. Miss Atta done asked me to fill in for you. You know, just them two days when you go to Austin. I ain't planning on taking your job or nothing. Just that my family could use a little extra dough."

Frank smiled thinking of Miss Atta, the brave woman who drank acceptance and forgiveness like morning coffee. "No problem, Wade. Appreciate it."

"Listen up, everybody," Miss Helen boomed. "No one's seen that Whitt-less fella in a good while. So I cranked her up, boys and girls. This lady-legger's back in business. Let's all head up to my house and have us a good snort."

The best townsfolk in Holly Gap, previously still and somber, bustled away from the gravesite with a new spring in their step. A celebration was in order.

Just as Frank was about to approach Emma June, the mayor put a hand on his sleeve.

"You'll be staying on, Frank? Seeing as you have kinfolk here now?"

"Haven't decided, Mayor. We'll see."

"Well, aside from the occasional gangster, we got a real fine town here. Can't get much better than Holly Gap," he said, almost believably.

Once, Frank thought living in a gopher hole would have suited him better than this Podunk town in Texas. Then he'd met the folks who ended up coming to his mother's funeral.

"It's got its perks, Mr. Mayor."

"Well, then. We hope you'll become another official citizen."

And another voter, no doubt. The mayor's grin was all teeth with nothing behind it. A politician's smile.

Frank glanced back to where Emma June had been standing. He found her climbing in the driver's seat of her mother's breezer, Samuel beside her. Theo motioned him forward. For the first time since Aunt Patsy died, he felt connected. He had a family. He remembered Irene's words that seemed so long ago now: "Your life will change for the better, like it's meant to be." She'd been right after all.

"You coming, sugar?" Miss Atta said, her face a portrait of kindness. She pointed to Rags's old pickup. "Your friends are waiting for you."

Frank made his way over. Charlene, Tallulah, Berta, and Wade sat in the back of Jacoby's truck. They had all waited for him.

Choices. It felt good to have them.

"Thanks, guys. Meet you at the Munsons'?" he said without regret.

"Aw, Frankie." Charlene stuck out her bottom lip.

"Ten minutes, and we'll throw back a couple." He patted the truck's hard metal.

Frank sat in the back of the breezer beside Samuel and asked Theo if he should hold on to something before Emma June started driving.

"Very funny, Frank," she said and pulled the breezer forward.

Frank tapped his jacket's inside pocket. Still there.

As they began their bump down the cemetery road, he turned back and gave the mound of dirt a final look. That was enough of looking back.

Barely a minute had gone by when we heard the roadster honk as it passed the breezer like it was standing still. Frank caught a flash of copper-colored hair leaning forward, a nose to the steering wheel. Emma June turned to the back seat and laughed aloud.

For the first time in a while, he felt his shoulders relax.

"Daddy? Why didn't Gunny stay? Because of his gout?"

"No." Theo turned away from her and stared out the window. "He had business to take care of."

"So he had to go put his foot up on his desk then." She laughed.

"Could be."

He wanted to think Emma June was secretly happy she turned eighteen. Or maybe proud of her driving skills. Whatever the reason, she didn't seem to notice the worry on Theo's face.

Emma June dropped Frank and Theo off at the Munsons' with the promise to return after freshening up.

While Theo darted inside the Munsons' house, Frank headed for the moonshine thicket. Leveled wood stumps and crates served as chairs and surrounded Miss Helen's prized possession.

Standing under the cluster of trees protecting Miss Helen's distillery, the temperature felt a few degrees cooler. Which wasn't saying much, considering it was nearing a hundred.

Percy had kept his nose aimed at Miss Helen as she poured hooch into small glasses. Now, he sat off to the side, his toothless grin wide enough for pouring moonshine down his gullet.

But what got Frank's attention most were the pinwheels. Dozens of sticks were planted around the thicket. Although struggling to spin in the still Texas air, the twirly birds were Scooter's offering to Emma June.

"Leonard! Wade!" yelled Miss Helen. "Stop standing there gawking and help me move this table. Miss Atta's ready to put out the food."

As planned, Miss Atta had made fried chicken, potato salad, and beans. Whenever the mayor showed up, he was supposed to bring the cake. Miss Helen had told him, "If you can afford fine cigars and a gold watch, you sure the blazes can buy the cake. It's the least you can do for associating with feral cats."

Thinking again about what the sheriff might have told Theo, Frank's shoulders hitched back up to his ears. He needed to know.

Looking for his father, he scanned the large group that had gathered. Whether they had shown up for his mother's wake or for Emma June's birthday, it didn't matter. They had come.

Frank spotted him standing next to the reverend, who had a hand on Theo's shoulder.

About to walk toward him, Frank felt a familiar nuzzle. "Hey, doll."

Charlene kissed his cheek. "So we're surprising Emma June. Seems sort of insensitive to me. This should be a wake for your mother."

"My idea."

Charlene tried to hide her surprise. "Of course it was, my sheik. You always think of everyone else first."

Not always. Charlene hadn't been on his mind until she'd interrupted his thoughts.

She wrinkled her button nose. "I've known Emma June for forever, and she made it clear she didn't want a celebration. Still, I have a gift for her in my purse."

"That's nice of you," Frank said, trying to sound genuine.

"So where is the birthday girl?"

"Hasn't walked over yet."

"Maybe she's getting in a smooch session with Samuel before heading over." Charlene winked and leaned closer. "Doesn't sound like such a bad idea, does it?"

Frank ran a hand over his mouth. "Charlene, I doubt that's on her mind right now." Not to mention he'd just buried his mother. "Excuse me." He turned his back to Charlene and started walking.

"Frank! Wait!"

No, she could wait. The bad feeling in his gut couldn't.

"Excuse me," he said, interrupting the conversation between Theo and the reverend. "Can I have a word?"

The reverend shook Frank's hand for the fifth time in two hours, then left him with Theo.

"What did the sheriff really tell you?"

Theo cleared his throat. "I'll tell you what Gunny said, but I don't want Emma June to know until after her birthday celebration. And promise me you'll do your best to get her on that train to Austin."

After Frank's nod, Theo told him.

....

CHAPTER 60

EMMA JUNE

From my bedroom window, even from the distance, the wake looked more like a party. Stinger and Whiskey were carrying their instruments to the moonshine thicket. I thought it a nice touch for my brother to have music on his mournful day.

"You about ready in there?" Samuel called from the sitting room.

"Just a sec." I finished reapplying my lipstick, bright red, without guilt. Turning eighteen had some perks.

I turned when the door pushed open. "Choppers, you silly dog. What have you got there?" I pulled the fabric from his mouth. A floral head bandeau. "I can't wear that, Chops. It wouldn't match my dress." And it belonged to Mama.

"Ready?" Samuel stood in my doorway, a sly grin on his face.

I had just stepped off the porch steps when I saw Scooter peering around the post oaks in the path's center. He spotted me and then bolted back to his house, not toward me as usual.

Then I learned why. I reached the Munsons' yard to a chorus of "happy birthday." This wasn't supposed to be about me. It was about Frank. And Betty. Still, I couldn't hide my flutter of surprise and appreciation.

Scooter reached me first and threw his arms around my waist. He bounced me up and down. "You're a *grown-up* now, Emmy."

He was right. Still, I yo-yoed between feeling like an adult and being Mama's little girl. Turning eighteen without Mama felt . . . wrong.

Scooter's blue eyes widened. "You can drive us to the *picture* show."

How had I not realized Scooter had grown? Barely an inch shorter than me, I could no longer look down to see the top of his blond burr.

"I can drive you anywhere, Scooter. You and me are going places."

In the midst of friends, I received hugs and congratulations as Stinger and Whiskey played "I'm Sitting on Top of the World."

"Anyone seen little *Bo*-peep?" Miss Helen hollered. "He's late with the cake. My Emma June deserves better. And where is that numbskull brother of his?"

How I loved that woman. Complainer or not, she stood tall both within and outside of herself. There was no second-guessing a woman who told you exactly what was on her mind. Something to be said for that.

"Mama, *Mama*," Scooter said running toward her. "Look what I made." Scooter had dug up five of the many pinwheels he had planted for me and rubber-banded them together in the shape of a star.

Miss Helen hugged him. "Well, aren't you as handy as a skirt pocket?"

I studied the townsfolk around me. Percy, Miss Mabel, Doc Ferguson and his wife, all dug into the food I recognized as Miss Atta's cooking. Sweet Miss Atta. Earlier at the cemetery, she told me that forgiveness and hope were worth the effort.

Loretta and Tallulah sat by Miss Helen's still, talking. The survivors of abuse and trauma chatted and giggled like young schoolgirls. And Wade, the boy I once thought I loved, then loved to hate, crouched on the porch throwing dice with Frank and Samuel. On Wade's face was a bona fide smile without any hint of venom behind it.

I glanced at Miss Mabel. Stooped with age and still doing the same thing for forty years. That wouldn't be me.

"And then you know what Miss Primrose did?" Charlene said to Louis and Isabell, her dramatic voice carrying.

I didn't care about Miss Primrose. In fact, I wondered how much I cared for Charlene. Charlene needed fun. When I could no longer provide her the entertainment she craved, I saw through to her shallowness. As far as I was concerned, she had failed me. I wasn't sure our friendship would survive.

"Honey?"

"Daddy," I said, squinting up to him. "Did you know about this?"

"I did. But it was Frank's idea."

"Figures. But it's nice, seeing our friends gathered together."

"It is indeed. Emma June, I need to tell you . . ." Daddy stopped talking as Gunny rolled up in his Packard.

"The mayor's with him," I said, noticing the passenger. "Guess my cake is here."

Before the Packard's dust barely had the chance to settle, Miss Helen stormed toward them. "Well, finally. What? You had to wait till almost closing time so you'd get the cake half off?"

I left Miss Helen to her antics and turned back to Daddy. "You were going to tell me something?"

Frank sauntered over and stood by my side. "I have something for you." He reached in his coat pocket and pulled out a sealed letter addressed to *Bernice and Emma June*. "Ma wanted me to give this to you after she was gone. She wrote me one, too."

"What did yours say?" I asked.

"That she loved me the best she could. How proud she was that I turned out to be one of the good ones." Frank stared at his feet.

"Irene was right, son. You are one of the good ones. And I'm proud to have you as my son."

Frank wiped at his eyes and pointed to the letter in my hand. "You gonna read it?"

"I'll read it. I'll also save it for Mama for when she returns." I tore open the envelope and read aloud:

My dear Bernice and Emma June,

If you are reading this it means I've gone to that tall sky-scraper in the sky, the one with golden windows but no revolving doors.

Bernice, you were the best friend I ever had and I regret not being up-front with you. Not only about Frank and Theo, but about my real name. I changed it to Betty before I came back to Holly Gap. I wanted to lessen the chances I would be recognized before I confronted Theo with the truth. But I met you first and both my plan and my honesty went up in a puff of smoke. I didn't want to risk losing you.

Now that the truth has no doubt come out, I have faith that my lies and my soul have been purified, distilled like Miss Helen's moonshine. I hope you will both find it in your hearts to forgive me.

Bernice, I know Frank's full-grown now. But if you have it in you, please consider being his mother. He's such a fine and talented young man. And you and Theo are the perfect parents. Frank deserves much better than what I could give him.

Emma June, I am so proud to know you are consid-ering going to college. Your mother is keeping her fingers crossed it works out. She and I never had the chance to get a higher education. But you have that chance. Please show the world what a woman can do when she sets her mind to it.

I will always be grateful for the precious days I got to spend with both of you. I only wish I could have seen you one last time.

With love and apologies,
your forever friend, 'Betty'

Daddy handed me a handkerchief.

"It's a nice letter," Daddy said.

And one I would process later when I was alone.

A brief look at the front of the Munsons' house and my chin dropped. Miss Helen had given Gunny a peck on his cheek, then tapped the top of his Stetson as if to seal it in. Surprises all around.

"Honey?" Daddy said.

I didn't turn toward Daddy. Instead, I kept my gaze on the handsome young man walking toward me, a small wrapped box in his hand.

"Happy Birthday, Emma June," Samuel said, and kissed my cheek.

I didn't wait to open the box. Inside I found a set of red bangles, all three decorated with inset gems. They reminded me of Kitty, the glamorous woman I had met at the mayor's fundraiser. I threw my arms around Samuel's neck.

"Emma June?"

I pulled my gaze back to Daddy, his face somber.

"Mind if we take a walk? I need to tell you something."

He had that serious look on his face, the same expression Miss Helen had worn the morning she told me Mama had left.

I followed Daddy away from the Munsons' house, my legs wobbling with each step. Blood rushed to my head.

When Daddy stopped, he grabbed my hands. "Emma June, Gunny had some news today."

"Mama?" I said, tears already forming. "Is she . . ." I couldn't say the next word.

"We don't know, honey. But law enforcement agents looking for Whitfield discovered a cabin thirty miles away. Inside, they found one of his suits, his razor, and shaving mug. Women's stuff, too. A silver pump, no twin. A couple of colored arm bangles. Lipstick tube bright red, fancy beads under the bed."

I remembered the shoe and the bangles from the mayor's fundraiser. Kitty, Whitt's playmate.

"But that wasn't all," Daddy continued. "In a tiny room, they identified various sizes of ropes and a handkerchief shaped like a gag. Hostage paraphernalia. Next to the cot was an empty bottle of laudanum."

"So our hunch was right." My heart caved inward. "They kidnapped Mama thinking she was Betty."

"Looks like it."

"And they drugged her. Oh, Daddy." I fell into his chest and let my tears fall.

"Whitfield is dead. That's the good news."

I looked up at him. "How do they know?"

"Behind the house, they uncovered two shallow graves. Whitt was in one of them. They said he'd been dead less than a week. Shot at close range in the chest."

"And the other?"

Daddy shrugged. "An unidentified man. They said he'd been dead for a while."

"So where is she, Daddy? Where's Mama?"

EMMA JUNE

Scooter tiptoed back into my bedroom. "Are you asleep?" he whispered and poked a finger to the middle of my forehead.

"Just resting, Scoot Bug."

"Your daddy says it's time to *go*. And Samuel just got here. He wants to *smooch* your face," Scooter said, giggling.

Samuel. I didn't know what direction our relationship would take. As of now, we were still connected by the Brazos River. I hoisted myself up from the bed and threw the last of my things into the suitcase.

"That's not yours, *silly* dog," Scooter said, pulling Mama's bandeau once again from Choppers's mouth. "It belongs to Miss Bernice."

Mama. It had been so long since I'd heard the *click-clack* of her shoes on the wooden floor, or seen her vibrantly colored garments swaying from the clothesline. Even her lavender scent had faded into the woodwork.

"Daddy shot him a *rattler* today," said Scooter, interrupting my thoughts.

"Ugh. Scoot, you know I hate snakes."

"Not *all* snakes are poisonous, *silly* Emma June." Scooter slithered out the door, making me laugh.

Scooter was right, though. Not all snakes were poisonous. I'd once thought Wade was the worst kind of snake. Now I understood that his meanness, his venomous anger, had always been directed at his brutal father. And Betty—she may have had a slithery deceptive side, but her love for us was as real as Kitty's fox stole.

The malignancy, the poison, lived inside Moody, Homer Whitfield, and Earl Foley. Their fangs were as long as their greed and as deep as their need to render their victims helpless. But Earl Foley was behind bars. And we no longer had to worry about the likes of Moody. Leonard had seen to that.

As it turned out, Homer "Buzz" Whitfield was a mere peon in the mob hierarchy. The real guys in Chicago had sent him to do a job in Texas to test his worthiness, and he'd failed.

"What are you doing, Scoot?" I heard Frank say from outside my window.

"I'm *burying* one of Choppers's bones to see if he'll *find* it."

I thought about a day last fall when I walked Scooter to school. He made me stop halfway so he could bury a whole bag of Tootsie Rolls. Not the entire bag at once, which would have taken much less than an hour. He buried a few pieces at a time. On the way home from school he uncovered each hole, one by one, like the unveiling of secrets.

Scooter buried his whatnots, including my birthday pinwheels, as a way of germinating hope.

Outside, I found the people I counted on to brighten my days. Daddy, Frank, Scooter, Miss Helen, Leonard—who stood quietly off to the side—and Samuel. At that moment, seeing their faces, I was starting to remember what hope felt like. As Moody and Whitt lay rotting beneath our Texas soil, I believed Mama could very well be on her way home.

Choppers stopped barking long enough for me to hear it: the single note, one chime from our grandfather clock. Even if Daddy had given up on Mama, I hadn't.

Frank picked up my suitcase and nudged me. "Let's go shake up Austin, sis," he said with a grin.

I followed him to Ol' Bess, Choppers on my heels.

Miss Helen rushed to my side. "Oh honey," she said, tearing up. "I'm so proud of you. I always wanted to go to college."

"You did?"

She nodded. "For a minute. Until they told me I had to send them letters of recommendation." Then she let out her loud, buxom laugh, the kind I remembered hearing before Mama left.

I laughed with her and gave her a long, tight squeeze.

Choppers sniffed the air and cocked his head. Then he bolted. Not toward me, but away. I called him back with a loud whistle and smiled when Frank cringed. But Choppers didn't stop. He kept running, a dog on a mission.

"Come on, honey," Daddy said. "Don't wanna miss your train."

I turned to Mama's breezer, the hot Texas sun reflecting off its green hood, then faced the bluff leading down to the water.

It wasn't just a river. It was the Brazos, the arms of God, persistently stretching over one thousand miles with hope.

10 WEEKS AND TWO DAYS AFTER THE CARNIVAL

The bone had healed enough to make the trek home. She wouldn't accept a ride from a stranger. Not now. Not yet. It would take a while to work up that kind of courage. She stayed off the main road, cautious of the snakes who thrived in the Texas heat.

At the break of dawn, Kitty had dropped her off by the side of the road and continued west, eager to slip the wrath of mobsters tied to Whitfield. She had wanted to drive Bernice closer to Holly Gap, but was afraid someone would recognize Whitt's motorcar.

Seven miles of limping her way south, her ankle swelled and throbbed as much as the fear once had.

Keep going, Bernice Crawford. Your family is waiting.

The Brazos, although drying up from the summer heat, guided her way. Like the river, she was bone thirsty. Not just for water but to have her life back, her family.

A flash of confidence straightened her backbone. The rain would come again, and with it, the flow of promise. She had suffered through the worst of it and had survived.

That dreadful carnival night.

Gagged, her wrists tied, she had ridden in a trunk for over an hour. When Whitt finally let her out, he demanded to know Betty's whereabouts. When she said nothing, Whitt hurled her against the base of a large oak, snapping her ankle.

Kitty heard the screaming and ran out of the cabin. When she saw Bernice, she gasped. Whitt told her to "let the broad die."

One thing about Kitty, she knew how to use her feminine wiles to full advantage. With batting eyelashes and a sing-song voice, she told Whitt she wouldn't leave a woman to die out in the woods like a scared rabbit. Then she added, "Besides, Daddy, I'm bored. Tying her up will be oodles of fun."

Kitty's acting was so convincing that at first Bernice thought she was going to die in agony. But Kitty had a plan. Knowing Whitt was due to leave early the following day for yet another trip, she made sure he drank enough to pass out. During the night, Kitty took his motorcar and drove ten miles to find a doctor. She paid him two clams to show up the next day. When he did, he wrapped Bernice's ankle, told her to stay off of it, and gave her plenty of laudanum.

If it hadn't been for Kitty and Dr. Brunson, Bernice wouldn't be making the slow journey home now.

At first, Kitty kept Bernice fed but said little. As the days passed, they spoke more and more. Most nights Whitt wasn't there, and they stayed up talking.

"You say your daughter's name is Emma June?" Kitty had asked. "A thin little doll? Brown bob parted on the side?"

After Bernice drilled her on details and learned Kitty had met Emma June at the fundraiser for Baker Hotel's speakeasy, the two formed a bond.

Then, just a week ago, an agitated Whitt arrived at the small wooded cabin to find her still alive.

"I told you to get rid of her," he boomed at Kitty.

"You sure did, Daddy. But what's a girl to do? Hit her over the head with a fry pan? You forgot to give me a gun." She held out her palm.

Whitfield grinned and handed over his pistol. "Atta girl."

Atta Girl. At the time, Bernice didn't pay attention to his words. She just wanted the plan to work. Now, as she lumbered on, the thought of seeing Miss Atta again lightened the load on her bad leg.

Kitty, gun in hand, had played her part well: she aimed it straight at Bernice. Then she pivoted toward Whitfield. A single shot to the chest, and it was over.

Bernice shook the image from her head. She had to rest, if only for a few moments. Mindful of snakes, she sat on a large rock beside the dry riverbed and relieved the pressure on her bad leg.

All that blood. With Whitt dead, Kitty and Bernice spent the next few days scouring the floor, burying Whitt, and gathering supplies. Together, they had endured.

One foot in front of the other. Isn't that what she had taught Emma June? The thought of her daughter got her standing again.

She deviated a few steps to her right and picked up a sturdy branch for use as a walking stick. Everyone deserved the support of one kind or another. She continued onward.

So what if Betty and Theo shared a son? It wasn't important anymore. What happened between those two was long before she entered the picture. She was alive. That's what mattered now.

As soon as she reached home she would forgive Betty for keeping secrets. She'd forgive Theo for lying about not knowing Betty. But he'd sure have to make it up to her. And without question, he would. Theo Crawford was a good, decent man.

And she would introduce herself to Frank. If he was a good sort, she'd welcome him to her home.

Don't you dare give up, Bernice Crawford.

Slow, steady steps.

Not much further now.

It was thoughts of Emma June that had pulled her through the worst of the days. Sometimes, lying on that awful rusted cot, she thought she heard her daughter's loud whistle. Emma June, her doll baby. The girl with determination and grit.

She could almost smell Emma June's hair as she pulled her tight, could almost feel the strength of her fingers as she squeezed her hand.

Up ahead, something moved through the bushes. She came to a halt and tried to breathe.

And then he emerged.

She didn't need to call his name. He shot toward her as if propelled by arrows instead of determined paws—each glorious three.

ABOUT THE AUTHOR

Author photograph by Katie Lee

CAROLYN DENNIS-WILLINGHAM is the author of two previous novels, *No Hill for a Stepper* and *The Last Bordello*, and numerous children's books. She is currently a member of the Writers' League of Texas and the Society of Children's Book Writers and Illustrators (SCBWI).

A former early childhood specialist, she taught bias-free education to teachers at the local, state, and national levels and applies this fundamental principle in her writing.

Whether writing for adults or children, her stories revolve around empowering the readers (and listeners) to believe in their potential, to appreciate diversity, and to believe in the power of imagination.

When not on her laptop, she willingly serves as the lap-top for her five young grandchildren. In addition to writing, she enjoys boxing, hiking, dancing, strength training, and traveling. Occasionally, she pulls out the oil paints to see what emerges on a blank canvas.

Dennis-Willingham lives in her hometown of Austin, Texas.

www.ingramcontent.com/pod-product-compliance
Lightning Source LLC
Chambersburg PA
CBHW030235120726
47903CB00005B/1495